A SARA STEELE NOVEL

SHATTERED TRUTH

GARRY J. PETERSON

BOOK ONE OF THE *STARGATE EARTH* SERIES

Robert D. Reed Publishers • Bandon, OR

Robert D. Reed Publishers
P.O. Box 1992
Bandon, OR 97411
Phone: 541-347-9882; Fax: -9883
E-mail: 4bobreed@msn.com
Website: www.rdrpublishers.com

Editor: Cleone Reed
Cover Designer: Pam Cresswell
Book Designer: Amy Cole

Soft Cover: 978-1-944297-52-7
EBook: 978-1-944297-53-4

Library of Congress Control Number: 2019951686

Designed and Formatted in the United States of America

DEDICATION

This book is dedicated to three people who have had a great impact on me and my writing…

To my dad, Pete, for sharing his views on extraterrestrials, weather phenomenon, and the fourth dimension—time. He also inspired me to become a more curious and observant person.

To my daughter, Sarah, in a reverse mentoring role, for encouraging me to seek the answers that are often beyond our typical reach.

To my wife, Vaune, who supported me throughout my rather intense Type A behavior, always making sure that I had one foot firmly planted on the ground.

ACKNOWLEDGMENTS

My interest and passion for all things known about the speculative truth concerning humanity's past, and also launched my curiosity into post-humanity, was grounded in many movies, TV shows and science fiction-oriented specials on cable channels.

Having read many books on ancient alien theory that added so much substance to my storyline and plot points, the following journalists and authors had a significant impact on my writing:

- Eric von Daniken, author of *Chariot of the Gods* and *Twilight of the Gods.*

- Giorgio A. Tsoukalos, author of *Gods or Ancient Aliens?*

- Philip Coppens, investigative journalist and author of *The Ancient Alien Question.*

- David Hatcher Childress, author of *Technology of the Gods.*

Many thanks to Mark Terry, writer and author, for his guidance and support as my ad hoc writing coach that gave me the tools and self-confidence to take my novel from concept to completion.

Heartfelt thanks to my wonderful publishers, Cleone and Bob Reed, for believing in my story and vision and providing the encouragement to stay focused.

To my wonderful book cover designer, Pam Cresswell, my sincere gratitude for taking my initial cover idea and transforming it into a truly breathtaking visual.

For the tremendous formatting and book design provided by Amy Cole, you made my book beautiful to see and read.

And to transform the written character **Sara Steele** into a real heroine, with amazing attire and images to match her strength, I am truly thankful for the support of the following artists:

Design by Kate Knuvelder

Photography by Christopher Alberto, Dancing Lonewolf Photography

INTRODUCTION

The existence of alien life on planet Earth has been discussed and argued for centuries. The ancient alien theory phenomenon is now well established as one of the fiercest debates known today, joining politics and religion, with both sides enjoying their "sell" from classrooms to family barbeques.

The complex issue of "are there or aren't there… were there or weren't there" cannot be answered in simple yes or no. Rather, the only recourse left is to gather the facts and evidence, whatever that may be, and draw your own conclusion. As more documentation, artifacts, research technology and global structural similarities turn up, the number of believers grows. Alien theorist conventions and their attendance are growing as well.

The importance of this journey is to gain a hold on the facts and data that makes the most sense and that we can mostly agree is what has happened in the past, for it will be a precursor of what will happen in the future. For the time being, much of our opinions and thoughts are purely subjective, based on an analysis of what data is available versus our perceptions and beliefs.

Therefore, it makes sense to gather and analyze as many facts and data as we can, and using the remarkable technology of today, gain a more accurate view of what alien involvement there has been and from whence that involvement came. Because, history tends to repeat itself, whether it is a fact of humankind or a fact of extraterrestrial phenomenon.

This hard science fiction novel is the first of a five-book series that will provide a journey into the unknown cosmos and to a mental and physical labor of debating or debunking truth versus myth. It involves three generations of one family that begins an adventure that none could have imagined with results that defied accepted logic and belief. It is not just about the presence of aliens on Earth, but what would be their intention if and when they were here…

It is also laced with a fabric of humor, family history, actual incidents and wonderful stories. Scholars, historians and politicians over time, even with significant disagreements regarding politics, community, people and worldviews, will all agree that stories are remembered much longer than facts. It's just the way people are wired and what makes information 'recall' stick in the minds of people and will have an effect on their behavior.

Shattered Truth, as will the other four books in the *Stargate Earth* series, will deal strongly with unity. That is family unity, team unity, country unity and the unity of conviction and hope. It will also demonstrate the frail nature of leadership. As strong as a leader might be, mistakes and failure will most certainly occur. This is human nature and will indicate why we must press on regardless of the obstacles and setbacks in our way. If humanity doesn't take control of the issues we now face, the answers we seek will always be outside of our reach.

EVERY GENERATION HAS A LEGEND...

Sara didn't start out expecting to change the world. She inherited it from her dad and grandad, but she didn't expect it. For much of her early years, Sara thought her family was pretty weird, and there seemed to be plenty of evidence to prove it.

Her late grandfather Pete Stevenson, maybe the weirdest of all, was an automotive engineer whose hobby was trying to chase down proof of aliens and time travel all over the world.

Incidents throughout the years also showed that Grandad didn't do his artifact gathering by the book or entirely lawful. He was determined to take what scientists called informed speculation regarding alien presence to replace it with irrefutable evidence.

For the longest time Sara didn't think she had inherited the family weirdness gene, but boy, was she wrong.

1

ALIEN ENCOUNTER
OF THE THIRD KIND

It is February, 2018, and ancient alien artifact hunter Pete Stevenson was following a celestial premonition time slip from a month earlier and was driving his Opel Meriva rental car from Trelleborg to a pre-determined meeting place in Gislov, a very rural area in Sweden.

Pete headed east on E22 from Trelleborg toward Gislov per the map and instructions on the itinerary. His mind was over-thinking what might lie ahead and his beating heart belied his attempt at calm and relaxed. Pete looked down at his phone as if he needed to make an important call. He looked up… he looked down. Pete was anxious.

So, he did what any tourist in a rental car would do. He turned on the radio and surfed the FM bands for something, anything, recognizable.

From one Danish station to another Norwegian station, and not speaking the language, an in-car companion would be nice, he thought. Fingers tapping on the steering wheel, the tension was building in his shoulders.

After nearly 80 kilometers of driving, he came to the only road that departed from E22, and per the map, he turned onto the road. He thought to himself, this is just like the Sierra Nevada experience, only different… so different. He hadn't seen anyone in the last two hours this far from town.

As Pete was beginning to second-guess himself for seeking some unknown pot of gold at the end of an alien rainbow, he saw a bright light. A bright light in the middle of the day was very odd.

Clutching the steering wheel tightly, he continued for a short time and then stopped the car. His heart rate ratcheted up even further, making him wonder if he was going to have a heart attack. Blood roared in his ears, his breathing thick and hot in his chest.

He got out of the car and slowly walked in the direction of the bright, bluish light. That bright, bluish light was eerily similar to the episode in his cabin a month ago. What and who he saw as he approached the light's point of origin were absolutely heart-stopping.

A large, slowly rotating triangular-shaped craft now became visible. As it stopped rotating, Pete knew that it was unmistakably a spacecraft.

Walking slowly in that direction, Pete noticed physical movement near the craft. Several human-like forms appeared, as if waiting for Pete. Joy and terror were pulling at Pete's very being and at that moment, terror was winning!

Pete got out of his car and slowly closed the car door. He was looking at an alien spacecraft. As he approached the large triangular-shaped vehicle, reminding him of the old Mercury capsule but significantly larger, a door opened from this spacecraft.

Pete had an undeniable feeling of déjà vu and could almost foresee the next sequence. Several aliens, all human-like forms but with very small ears, exited the craft and moved slowly toward Pete. There was a sense of purpose, not fear or apprehension for Pete as well as these alien visitors.

Pete tried to remain calm, but his shaking hands and elevated blood pressure said otherwise.

Pete was now facing ten aliens in a triangle or pyramid formation, with one in front, and the remainder in formation. The alien in front spoke slowly.

"I am called Echo, Pete, and you have nothing to fear. I am the Commander of this ship, our Magellan in your recollection of history, and on my right is Pulse, my Lieutenant. I am the elder statesman and will be your guide. Please come inside."

Now the anxiety was somewhat lifted. Pete was feeling both apprehensive and excited as he entered the spacecraft.

Pete's first observation was a massive control room and bridge. He was directed to be seated near a large panoramic window. As Pete was seated, Echo spoke.

"We are here to provide you with the hard evidence you need to complete your work. We will circumnavigate your solar system and then on to infinity, as you know it to be. Nothing more. You are in no danger, Pete." Pete thought that Echo's attempt to simplify an enormously complex remark was as reassuring as it was implausible. "Please buckle into your chair."

At this point, Pete was anxious to start… however to whatever by whomever…

As the spacecraft effortlessly ascended, Pete was seeing the sight lines and navigation grid from space and their linear relationship to Earth's pyramids and how actual landings would be made by extraterrestrials. As they rapidly lifted off and moved into an Earth orbit, they circumvented the globe in what seemed to be minutes.

Pulse pointed out the grid from this elevation, and Pete saw how flight patterns, navigation and landings are all in identical coordinates. Then, almost immediately, they flew at nearly ground level to demonstrate landings. Pete had a sense of absolute time travel that was being accomplished in milliseconds.

Then, as Pulse used his arms and hands to signal the commander's intent, the ship began an almost instantaneous speed increase and nearly vertical trajectory. Mach One and then some!

Then the spaceship moved effortlessly out of Earth's orbit and into an orbit around Mars, literally in minutes. Laser-like pictures from this Martian orbit revealed the replication of Earth's ancient monuments and their existence on the surface of Mars. Pete was stunned.

Pulse spoke: "The sandstorms that have plagued the Martian landscape obscure the view that you now have, Pete. As you can see, a perfect replica of the Egyptian Pyramids and Sphinx can now be seen on the surface of Mars."

Pulse overlaid coordinates to show their identical dimensions. Pulse nodded to Pete; Pete nodded back in an understanding manner.

Now Pete was extremely comfortable with his hosts and their willingness to show and tell all that Pete had believed since he was a little boy.

Echo gave Pete a directive. "Pete, please be calm. We will now move at a speed that you have never felt."

Pete immediately had a sense of incredible speed and was almost rendered unconscious. He felt like he was both awake and asleep at the same time. His mind was alert; his body was limp.

Pete gained his senses to see what appeared to be a trip through a spinning black hole or wormhole. He had no sense of time but felt as if many hours had passed.

Pulse said, "We are now 444 light years from Earth, looking at a star cluster called Pleiades, known on Earth as the Seven Sisters. It houses many civilizations, including the Mayans, on several planets. It is 17.5 light years across. We have bases here."

Waiting for Pete to look from his vantage point in the bridge back to himself, Pulse went on: "We will leave you with evidence photos of this. We realize that verification alone will cause problems."

Pete replied. "I remember being able to see this Seven Sisters star cluster as a child even to the naked eye in the dark sky. Yes, incredible claims will require incredible proof."

The conclusion of the alien journey resulted in a startling observation and remarkable final words. Pete had a very vivid recollection of docking with, and then disembarking from, a massive space station in space.

He observed a floating city that was so big that he couldn't see end-to-end. What was even more remarkable was that he could see Earth from his vantage point, but, obviously, no one on earth could see this cloaked, massive structure. The return trip home then began.

Within a few minutes, he was back on the ground where the journey began and felt an incredible surge of knowledge and humility.

Echo looked directly at Pete, almost as a parent would, and said. "Pete, you now have an enormous responsibility. We want you to continue your work and, with the new facts and data that you have, we hope you are able to convince that small but critical core of the scientific community that alien theory is alien fact. There are many reasons why we do not want to reveal ourselves to the world right now, as only panic, fear, and hysteria would occur. Pete, you need to be mankind's finder of the truth."

When Pete regained his senses, he was back in his rental car, alone, and with no one in sight. He felt exhausted and mentally drained, but at the same time absolutely energized with the events that has just occurred. In his lap were new notes taken during his "journey," amazing photos and his diary, covering the entire time he was gone, and Pulse had written the word **ARAS**, in all caps, on his hotel itinerary.

Pete thought he had been gone for a couple hours…
He had been gone for three days!

2

SARA'S SEEDS
PLANTED

Sara Stevenson's dad, Mike, the logical and fact-based decision maker that she respected and loved, turned her recent life into a series of incidents, encounters, calamities, and life-changing experiences, all in pursuit of alien existence.

Mike gathered the irrefutable evidence that existed in plain sight and bundled it with the wild and weird artifacts of Sara's Grandad Pete to put the most logical spin on the collection of fact versus myth of alien existence.

Sara was wired similarly to her dad and grandad but was more of an entrepreneur. She was intelligent, curious, and creative, and she had an insatiable desire to prove and/or disprove what was known.

She found an irresistible challenge in any debate of science fiction and what was now described as informed speculation. From conventional thinking regarding issues of authority, she enjoyed challenging the status quo. Her mantra was always, "Don't assume; verify."

Once, when only four years old, as the family was moving from a home in Michigan to a new home in Toronto, a realtor asked Sara's mom, "Does your daughter have any friends in Toronto?"

Sara's Mom Christine replied, "Ask her."

"Okay. Sara, do you have any friends in Toronto?"

Looking up from a graphic middle-grade book she was intently reading, Sara quickly replied. "Yes, I do. I just haven't met them yet." Her parents smiled and were not surprised.

But it's now 2025 and Sara had just returned from a game-changing meeting with the World Council in Dubai, which was intended to be an exposé of all things weird and sinister that was confronting the world at that time.

Sara must present the results of that meeting to the entire Extraterrestrial Research Team in the morning. Exiting the airport limousine, she gathered her luggage and computer case and walked through the main door of her firm's office and was greeted by the night security guard.

"Hi Sara, great to have you back home."

"Thanks Bill, it's nice to be home."

"Everyone is excited to hear about your meeting."

"It's like every other world leaders' meeting… only different."

Bill smiles at Sara's humor and unlocks the elevator to the top floor.

As Managing Director over a group of nearly 200 exceptionally talented researchers and scientists at *Blue Horizon*, a subsidiary of *Sky Force PLLC,* she would be quite busy with this significant and game-changing presentation.

She took the elevator to the top floor and gathered her thoughts. She began to formulate her talking points and an outline for the presentation and couldn't wait to begin.

Entering her glass-walled office with alien artifacts and memorabilia scattered throughout, Sara threw her white chore jacket and blue blazer over a guest chair and logged on to her desk computer.

It was 9:30 pm and she was already back to the grind after a very long flight and realized that this night would be a long one of organizing thoughts and preparing her presentation.

Michaela Marx, the highly respected senior member of the team, preeminent astrophysicist and one of Sara's very dear friends entered her office. Sara looked up and smiled.

"Welcome back, Sara; how was your trip?"

Sara quickly moved over to Michaela and they hugged.

"The flight was good. Quiet, long and dull. I needed that time to think. How are you and how is everyone here?"

"I'm fine. The team is so anxious to hear from you tomorrow. Anything I can give them in advance."

"Sure can. My thanks for all their hard work and sacrifice. It made me realize how lucky I am to have such a great team to work with.

"Can I make you a drink? Got a bottle of Dubai's finest Vodka, and was making a Vodka raspberry cocktail and would love to share it."

Michaela responded, "I'll get a couple glasses. Didn't think they served alcohol there."

"In Dubai, only non-Muslims can drink, so hotels and restaurants serve the best drinks for their clients. This cocktail is so smooth."

Sara poured them each a drink in their weird and wonderful space capsule glasses, sat back in her chair and toasted Michaela. "Did anything leak back here as far as the meeting went… any info at all?"

"No, not really. Seemed a lot more hushed than we all thought. We expected at least a blow-by-blow report of all the agenda issues. The lack of feedback can only mean that there was much to keep confidential, right?"

Sara smiled and said, "Over the top comes to mind."

"Can't wait to hear…"

Sara walked over to her purse, zipped it open to a small compartment, and pulled a tiny flash drive from the inside.

There was also one of her prized possessions, a picture of Mike, Pete, and her at a Christmas party that was so nice and so yesterday.

With drink in hand, she motioned Michaela over to her desk, paused for a moment, and then inserted the flash drive into her computer. After she entered the password code from her watch, the video booted.

"This is the full video of the final day's meeting with the World Council and the rather surprising ending. It's already encrypted. This info is not to be shared with anyone. You may need a second drink."

Surprised and puzzled, Michaela freshened her drink and walked over to the computer and started the video, which was nearly an hour long.

Sara left her to view the meeting video and walked over to a conference table that held several alien artifacts and related material well organized and documented, serving as a reminder of the alien age that they were now in.

Sara stopped to gaze at a carved wooden bird found in Saqqara, one of Egypt's oldest burial grounds, and was one of her grandad's prized alien artifact possessions. How he came into possession of such a rare and valuable artifact was a question for another day.

The papyrus inscription of "*I want to fly*" from the funeral tomb where it was found was haunting, for sure. This bird had eyes and a nose and wings, but the wings were not typical bird wings.

But it was her dad who viewed this carving as more of a modern aerodynamic design and fully two thousand years before man's first flight. Mike was the inspiration for getting a team together to build a scale model five times its size, adding a rear stabilizing rudder that appeared to be broken off of this carving.

When tested by legitimate experts, it flew like one of today's highly developed gliders. In fact, it was a design that was used today. This was an uncontested evaluation and became a seminal moment in the search for the alien unknown.

Sara glanced at Michaela, who was still transfixed with the video and seemed to be mesmerized by what she was seeing.

Sara added, "The best part is still to come."

Sara then sat down in front of one specific item, her grandad's log book. Opening it and turning the pages, she once again looked over to a very engaged Michaela.

"Remember when we found Grandad's log book up at the cabin?"

"Of course. I'll never forget the rush… the absolute rush."

"Well, little did we know at that time that Grandad and his cabin would be the keystones to unlocking the secrets of the cosmos and change the course of our lives forever."

With that comment, Sara thought back to the event that began that incredible journey and put her grandad on the path to establishing alien presence on Earth.

It all started in that cabin in the woods…

3

PETE'S JOURNEY BEGINS

Pete Stevenson stood on the porch of his cabin in the Sierra Nevada and watched the clouds with a more than passing interest. It was January 2018, and the snow was already a foot deep, the lake frozen, and the pines draped with snow.

But the way the wind was shuttling the dark clouds and the dropping barometric pressure indicated a storm was coming.

He shoved his way back into the cabin, the wind slamming the door behind him. The interior of the cabin was rustic, decorated with photographs of cars he had worked on as an automotive engineer, and memorabilia from his true passion, searching for ancient alien artifacts.

Kicking off his boots Pete shrugged out of his hunting jacket, tossing it on the back of the chair in front of the darkened fireplace. It was his one retreat from a busy work and travel schedule.

Snagging a Molson from the refrigerator, he sat in the chair and clicked on his phone, wondering if there would be a signal. Sometimes there was; sometimes there wasn't. He called.

"Hi Mike. It's Dad."

"Hey, how goes it?"

"Good, good. I'm at the cabin for some quiet. Just wanted to thank you and Christine for the wonderful Christmas at your place. Louise and I had a great time. Wanted to say how much we appreciated your effort. Loved the decoration and the food was great."

"Hey, Dad, it's not every year that we can get the whole crew together for the holidays. Christine wanted to make it memorable. And having Sara there as well was so special."

Mike added, "Louise can't be too happy with you starting the new year solo again. Christine and I figured you guys were just chilling out watching some football and relaxing a bit.

"No, I'm up at the cabin alone, looking at some old alien artifact stuff my guys sent to me and will probably do a little follow up on it."

"Back to the grind already, and more alien stuff, too. Not surprised, though."

"Nope, Mike, I was getting kind of antsy over the Holiday to get back to my investigative work."

They chatted for a while, and then Mike begged off, saying dinner was ready, he'd talk later that week.

As Pete hung up with his son, a bright flash of a lightning strike and a loud clap of thunder filled Pete's consciousness.

No, this doesn't happen in January...

4

MIKE'S STABILITY TESTED

With that they hung up and Mike's wife Christine, with a stern look on her face, entered the den where they had been talking.

"Was that Dad you were talking to?"

"Yep."

"He's up at the cabin alone, right?"

"Yep."

"And off to chase alien stuff now, right?"

"Yep."

"I swear, Mike, he spent so much time hounding Sara about his alien escapades that it took away from the holiday. And such a waste of time and money."

Mike responded, "I'm not sure it was a waste of time. Sara seemed quite interested in Dad's stories."

"They are stories, Mike, just stupid stories."

"Christine, they are Dad's second life right now, and we need to respect that."

Christine quickly added, "You better not ever get involved in that stuff, okay?"

"No plans to, Dear."

Christine fired back, "No, I'm serious. That's just not healthy or realistic and all that travel is dangerous. I feel bad for Louise."

"I hear you, Christine, and I will simply say that this alien subject matter has no interest to me. So, relax.

"Dad did say how much he appreciated the beautiful setting and thanked you for your work."

Mike was not a complete disbeliever in ancient alien theory and actually looked forward to a more detailed call later with his dad. Christine had no idea that Mike was "'on board'" with Pete's adventures, and that's the way it would stay.

As Mike put a note on his phone calendar to call Pete back soon, the mostly blue Ohio sky was interrupted by a bright lightning strike and a loud clap of thunder.

A sudden chill overtook Mike.

5.

PETE

Pete moved over to his desk in the cabin, brought out an old log book from prior adventures, and studied the ancient alien artifacts that were sent to him by his friends and fellow alien enthusiasts, Corey and Thomas, for validation and archiving.

Pete and his friends were similarly wired and had become very interested in ancient alien theory, and traveled often to various locations to look at artifacts or locations of ruins.

This particular artifact, an elongated skull, was the third one that this team had found; and Pete was getting excited just thinking back to the location in Central America where they had recovered two similar skulls. Getting them out of the country and into the U.S. was a stressful but exciting journey.

Per his log book, two of the skulls were measured as larger than an average human skull and one was smaller. Pete was anxious to investigate further.

Meanwhile, he walked over to his hunting jacket and rummaged around for his worn but faithful Bic lighter. Finding it, he headed back over to his desk to run a quick experiment.

As he has many times before, Pete held the flame from the lighter under the skulls to verify that they were really bone and would not shine from acrylic if they were fake. Yep, real skulls.

They often found this type of artifact was created in a lab and a hoax. He knew that Corey and Thomas already did that, but he still did it anyway. He also knew that they performed the necessary DNA tests to rule out an ancient Indian tribal burial skull.

Pete was sixty-seven years old, about six-feet-tall, and lean, with thinning gray hair. As he gazed into the bathroom mirror, he couldn't help but see himself as that twenty-something risk-taker of years gone by. Yep, he thought, still have that 32-inch waist!

It was early evening and a swift and noticeable blast of wind caught Pete's attention… almost like a roar. As he walked back to the desk in the living room, the strong, roaring gust had gone strangely quiet and the swaying pine trees were now tall and quiet. There was a noticeable chill in the cabin that he suddenly felt and it caught his attention.

Pete walked over to the door of the cabin with his coat in hand and slipped it on as he opened the door. As the door opening widened, a strange blue light overtook the cabin and Pete's sense of calm was disrupted. A blue haze soon filled his sightline.

The cabin door eerily opened to a strange room, and he felt himself leaving the cabin entirely almost gliding forward. He immediately felt that he was in a strange hotel, and the room was like so many hotel rooms that he had stayed in hundreds of time in his travels. He still had his coat on, but in panning the hotel room, he almost felt as if he had been there before.

The walls were covered with dated maroon-flowered wallpaper, and the carpet was old, worn, and smelled bad. Catching his breath and surveying his surroundings, he walked over to the only window in the room. Peering outside, it is dusk, stars shining brightly and snow, lots of snow, was covering the ground.

He was no longer in a place that he recognized. Pete closed his eyes for a few moments, hoping to regain his composure and return to his cabin living room, but that was not to be. This was as real an experience as he had ever had.

Pete turned to see what else was in the room, and there was a massive canopy bed taking up a whole wall. A few cheesy-looking decorations were scattered around the room.

There was one highly worn leather chair; and on the table next to an older lamp, there was one sheet of paper. The room was quite plain and nondescript, so the piece of paper stuck out as not fitting in.

Pete walked over to the table, stopped to gather himself, and then picked up the paper and glanced at it. It was an easily recognized travel itinerary attached to a folder with an airline ticket and car rental form. The traveler was Pete Stevenson and he had checked into room 22 of a hotel in Trelleborg, Sweden, and the date was February 10, 2018.

Trying to process this déjà vu better, this trip was only a month away. He recalled immediately a similar incident that had occurred years earlier and thought it was another time slip.

This one, unlike the mind-blowing one he experienced in Brazil, was a forward leap into time and an overwhelming sense of familiarity with something that should not be familiar at all.

Gathering his thoughts, Pete walked back to the window looking for anything that would explain his confused state of mind.

As he stopped at the window, another blue light appeared under the hotel room door. Returning to the door, he reopened it to find the living room of his cabin and all as it was before.

He walked back into the cabin and the door closed abruptly behind him. Waiting a moment, he turned to see if the mirage or out-of-body experience was still enveloping him, and it was not.

Pete opened the cabin door, and, as usual, there was the front porch, the woods, and the firewood stack. Yes, all was back to normal except for one thing.

He was still holding the itinerary for a future trip to Sweden!

6

PETE

Pete collapsed into the sofa and looked down at his shaking fingers and felt his heart still racing as that bizarre experience was lingering in his mind and body. His first thought of an explanation was psychosis, Alzheimer's, or a brain tumor… something physical.

He was physically, mentally, and emotionally drained. He immediately went to his trusted crutch, a double scotch on the rocks. Only this time, he added Drambuie to his scotch for a much-needed Rusty Nail and attempted to gather his thoughts.

Many events of the last few years of his ancient alien adventures made this event seem almost understandable. In the past, he had come across an artifact or etching or alien crop circle and felt déjà vu that gave him goose bumps.

But the difference with this event was it seemed so realistic and as much a sign as it was an invitation.

He poured another Rusty Nail and then walked over to his desk and pulled out his well-worn global map, knowing full well that Trelleborg lied right in the middle of the aliens presumed flight paths along the World Grid. Chills went through his body and his analytic mind raced with anticipation.

This out-of-body experience was a premonition, and he now believed that he was being summoned there for a purpose, a really significant purpose, and he was in a state of mind somewhere between faith and reality.

His first thought was to call Mike and, possibly, have his son make this trip with him to Trelleborg. "I gotta share this with Mike."

Excitedly, he called. "Mike, it's Dad again."

"Well hi again. What's up this time?"

As he was about to describe his time slip to Mike, Pete looked at the itinerary again and realized that only his name was on it, and it had a map attached to it.

After a brief pause to reconsider his reason to call, Pete simply said, "Ah, just thought it would be nice if, maybe after my west coast trip, you can come out here to the cabin again for a visit."

"Sure can. Later this year would be better, though, as I have several projects that need to be completed first."

Pete said, "Okay. Got to go," and thought to himself, "That was awkward" and hung up.

Mike thought to himself, "That was a strange call."

So, Pete finished his drink and thought about what had just happened. Not able to sleep that night, he studied the itinerary and noticed an "X" denoted a destination for his travels that was about 80 kilometers east of Trelleborg and looked for the coordinates on Google Maps. Now getting excited at what was unfolding, he knew he had only one choice to make.

The very next morning, following that itinerary, he got on his computer and made his travel arrangements. He would fly into Copenhagen, Denmark, and make the three-hour drive into Trelleborg, Sweden on February 9. The next day, he would drive from the hotel east about 80 kilometers per the map. Done.

The next couple of weeks were as unfocused as ever for Pete. He couldn't get his mind off the Trelleborg trip and was marking time and making excuses, waiting for his departure to Sweden. Pete did not confide in anyone regarding this trip.

He did get the elongated skulls further analyzed and archived. The two larger ones were about five inches longer than a normal human skull today, and the smaller one was about three inches smaller than normal. In his mind, Pete concluded that it was an alien family and looked forward to making a stronger case for that in the future with his colleagues.

He recalled with a smile how they got those skulls out of Central America and the stroke of genius that it took.

One of his colleagues on that trip was Beth, who convinced security and customs officials that she was a ventriloquist and the three elongated and painted skulls were her three alien props, following a comedian that made a living doing just that with similar characters.

Funny… or prophetic?

7

PETE

It's now February 9 and Pete was at the Copenhagen International Airport getting his rental car, an Opel Meriva. He took out his documents and noticed that his passport was nearly full with all of his international travel.

As he slid his plane ticket receipt into his coat pocket, he recalled that it is the same coat he was wearing in the cabin a month ago when the time slip occurred. He received the area map from the English-speaking rental agent and was off to get his car and head to Trelleborg.

"Where are you headed?

"Trelleborg and then to Gislov."

The agent replied, "There's nothing in Gislov, except for the summer gas lights."

"Summer gas lights?"

"Yeah, the swampy area gives off funny bluish lights in the summer when it mixes with something in the air, I guess."

Several thoughts occurred to Pete. He immediately considered that the area in question had an abundance of prismatic basalt stone, a substance known to give off a rainbow of lights from any source of light hitting it. After a brief pause, Pete moved on.

The rental agent offered some information: "Yes, but it's winter now and there won't be any lights. Do be careful crossing the bridge on E20 over the bay. The crosswinds this time of year can be strong."

Getting his Opel rental car and gathering his belongings, Pete checked his route map to Trelleborg. East on E20 which becomes Engelbrektsgatan in Sweden.

Yes, E20 crosses a bay that is part of the Baltic Sea. Then, from Trelleborg he will go about 80 kilometers east on E22 to a turn-off near Gislov. Pete drove out, a bit weary of the bridge winds that the agent mentioned.

It was now late in the evening as Pete drove toward Trelleborg. On a narrow road approaching the city, Pete slowed down as a train was moving quickly in front of him and the crossing gate had been lowered. Pete stopped while the train was passing.

Then, seemingly out of nowhere, some sort of vehicle or small ship appeared behind him with very bright lights filling his rear-view mirror. Pete was scared stiff! What was behind him? What unworldly fate awaited him? His pulse raced…

Taking a deep breath, Pete could then see in his side-view mirror that another car had approached Pete's vehicle and stopped behind him. Just a car. Barely a minute passed when the driver of that car honked the horn and flashed his high-beam lights. Pete was getting nervous and prepared for an altercation over something, it would seem.

The driver of that car then got out of his car, walked over to Pete and tapped on the car window. Pete slowly rolled his window down. The man politely said to Pete, "Turn your motor off. You are wasting petrol."

"Okay. Sorry." Welcome to Europe, American, Pete thought, where residents are far more aware of the ecology and the environment. His bad.

Pete did as he was instructed to do until the train had passed. He then pro-ceeded on his journey and arrived at the hotel that appeared on his itinerary, grabbed his belongings, and walked over to the hotel lobby and checked in. He felt strangely calm, as if this wasn't an odd situation at all, and was given the key to room 22, as he had requested.

He walked up to the second floor and as he opened the door to room number 22, he was not surprised. It was exactly as he had experienced in his "time slip" a month earlier. He unpacked, set his phone, travel documents, and diary aside, and tried to sleep. He had no idea what tomorrow would bring but strongly believed that it would be life-changing.

Unable to sleep, Pete was sitting on the edge of the bed staring at his phone on the bedside table next to him. Reaching for the phone to call Louise or Mike or one of his friends, he was conflicted about doing this trip solo.

Did he want permission? No. An argument? Hell no. He laid back down on the bed and let his fatigue take over. Minutes later he was asleep.

He awoke the next morning and gathered his thoughts. He was still torn between either keeping this trip to himself, or in bringing someone else in, pos-sibly Corey or Thomas or Beth, his fellow ancient alien adventurers.

As he looked at himself in the bathroom mirror, he felt bad that he had lied to Louise about his trip, telling her he was on business in Europe. But he genuinely feared for friends and family, not knowing what to expect, so he just thought it best to keep this bizarre trip to himself.

Following breakfast, he asked the hotel staff what was located east of the hotel, say 80 to 100 kilometers away. He was told that it was barren, undeveloped, and only an easterly road across the country.

Pete didn't mention the swamp gas lights, as that was a conversation that he just did not want to start. His curiosity was running wild with anticipation of his destination.

Pete got into his Opel and looked again at the map and driving directions per the itinerary.

He was thinking what might lie ahead and recalled something that seemed particularly timely right now.

The words usually credited to that acclaimed genius Albert Einstein were, "What is the definition of insanity? It is doing the same thing over and over again and expecting a different result."

Pete thought to himself, "How many more times will I be disappointed?"

As he put the car into gear and headed east on E22 toward Gislov he thought…

"This is going to be a total waste of time! What do I expect to see? Aliens!"

8

MIKE

It's the year 2026 and Mike and Christine Stevenson were enjoying the weekend on their Frank Lloyd Wright-inspired contemporary home in N.E. Ohio situated by a lovely and gently flowing stream.

A married couple in their late 50's, they had been married for nearly thirty-five years. Mike was slightly taller than his dad and with a strong physique, having been a wrestler in high school and college. He was always seen with a slight beard or roughly unshaven giving off the strong male vibe.

Being a bit arrogant, he was very confident and believed he has as much as he can control, under control. The scene here was tranquil and relaxing, almost like a placid setting that you would see in an art gallery.

Christine was in the kitchen mixing some cold lemonade for Mike, who was canoeing on the river behind their house.

Pulling his canoe onto the bank from the river that forms the rear property boundary, Mike had the sense that these types of moments were truly magical. He gazed approvingly over the 20-acre rural property with deer, rabbits, and squirrels still abundant and playful.

Mike knew that if ever there was a place to de-stress and enjoy the peace and quiet, this property that has been in the family for many years is where you wanted to be.

As he pulled his fishing gear and cooler from the canoe, he noticed his fishing license with the current address of 300 Maple Street, and he fully appreciated that it is a place out of the innocence of yesterday, with no need to lock cars or houses. Nope, no crime or mobsters will ever be found on Maple Street.

As he threw his backpack on and opened his last Molson, Mike began his long walk back to the house.

While on his walk he stopped to watch several deer on their leisurely run through the forest. As he enjoyed the deer on this encounter, he recalled that he had to have the city come out and remove a deer blind that outsiders had erected on their property many years ago.

He reminisced that the canoe he had moored on the river bank for those lovely trips up and down stream was mainly to relax and to think. Mike used to tell Christine that he used his canoeing trips as meditation, which she found silly.

In fact, Mike was able to de-stress and soul-search often on these river trips, with nothing but nature and pure quiet as his companions.

Realizing that the deer were long gone, Mike stood up and continued his walk back to the house. He savored this quiet time as it is a calm that is unique and genuine. But it was a reality that was rapidly slipping into a lost and forgotten time and contrary to Eastern beliefs that Mike seemed to take to heart, that your view of the outside world was an absolute reflection of your inner being.

Mike took a deep reflective breath and created a picture in his mind of this very setting, because he had a recurring belief that this would be the last remnant of peace and order that the present-day world would see or feel for a very long time.

As Mike approached the front porch, he noticed the cracking steps, peeling paint, and a roof that needs repaired. Christine was standing there to greet him in blue jeans and a flannel shirt, and he was sure that she would bring these much-needed chores to his attention. Instead, much to Mike's delight, she smiled and offered a refreshing drink.

"Just made a pitcher of fresh lemonade; are you interested?"

"Sure. Thanks."

Christine asked, "Did you have a nice afternoon? See any of your critter friends?"

"Saw the usual forest residents. We chatted a bit."

They filled their glasses and relaxed on a large porch swing as was often the routine. Even the porch swing needed to be painted.

Holding a framed picture in her hand, Christine looked at Mike, "You know what day it is, and yet you haven't even mentioned it."

Mike paused before he replied. "Of course, I know what day it is," he said in a dank and somber mood. "It's October 25, 2026, and if Dad were alive, today would have been his 75th birthday! I don't need that photo of him and me as a reminder. Seriously?"

"Yeah, I know. Sorry. Just so sad thinking of how much we miss him, and now I wish we had spent more time with him."

Mike pulled his muddy boots off and tried to regain his composure. "Well, with his crazy travel and running around the world chasing alien artifacts so much, we were probably lucky to see him as much as we did.

I'm still so angry to be unable to get closure on his death. Eight years later and we still don't know the circumstances of that terrible night, damn it!"

After a short pause Christine attempted to lighten the difficult conversation, "At least his organ donor wishes were met. I'll tell you this, Mike, someone received a very big heart!" Mike nods, appreciating his wife's humanitarian nature.

Christine continued, "But I'm happy to think that in less than two months Sara will be here for Christmas."

Mike, not fully off the previous topic added, "I wish Sara had been able to spend more time with Dad. Already a mentor, he could have been much more of an influence on her, and a very good one at that."

Re-filling their glasses, Christine swirled her lemonade for a second, listening to the ice click against the glass and remarked with a softer tone of voice.

"It was a year ago that she was involved in that Dubai incident that changed the course of history."

Pulling up the short video of the incident on her portable tablet, she continued, "Do you believe our little girl was at the forefront of that amazing event? And, you would think that on the anniversary of 9/11 our leaders would be much more vigilant and watchful, right?"

Sensing that they were about to go down the same rabbit hole, Mike put his arm around Christine and gave her a gentle squeeze. "Can't look back... only look forward."

After a brief pause, Mike continued. "I'm anxious to see where her extraordinary team and she are now, following that incident."

Mike then pulled up the sleeve of his flannel shirt, revealing his watch. He opens an app to a holographic video greeting from Sara that gives Christine that warm and fuzzy feeling.

"That's perfect, Mike. Thanks."

"Tell you what, how about I go inside and get a shower and you can put some wine and cheese together and we'll fire up the VCR and look at some old but awesome family film."

Smiling, Christine says, "Sounds like a plan."

Mike thought, **"Her plan won't be my plan."**

9

MIKE

They headed back inside and Christine went into the kitchen. Although she was only a couple years younger than Mike, she looked like a lady in her forties. Brown hair, brown eyes, and a terrific smile, the high school Prom Queen and Homecoming Queen was an attractive woman.

Mike was still very much in love with Christine. She was his touchstone… but opposite personalities, they were.

Being an avid cook and baker, their kitchen was furnished with the best appliances that she desired, and Mike was very happy when she was happy working in the kitchen.

Opening a bottle of Red for Mike and Riesling for herself, she prepared a nice cheese tray and went to the family room to set up the VCR. Mike appeared a few minutes later and they sat down in their comfy black leather sofa.

Taking their glasses of wine and assorted cheeses, they toasted and settled back for some much-needed comfort. The first video teed up was of Christmas, 2017, which was so enjoyable for all family members. "It's my favorite," Mike said with a smile.

"Mine too." They watched several videos related to Pete's alien artifacts, over which they argued and enjoyed, and Sara's college days, which were eventful.

"I love that wooden carved bird that looks like an airplane that Dad found in his alien artifact travels. And the best part was that you made it fly." Christine adds.

"Come on, I had some help with that, but it's cool, for sure, but I like all the Egyptian pyramid stuff the best. I can pull some of that out if you'd like."

"Not now. Just the family stuff now, okay?"

They viewed several Stevenson vacations to the Carolinas. After a moment of quiet contemplation, Mike mustered a bit of his sense of humor and said to Christine, "Remember when we used to drive to the beach at Hilton Head Island, S.C., a trip of about fourteen hours and a distance of, what, 750 miles?

And, all those silly places to stop along the way, and those 35 mph speed zones?" Christine knew what was coming… again.

"Yeah, and you were always wanting to stop and get the history of each and every town we stopped at," she added.

"Guilty. Well, the good news is that trip now is only about 600 miles," he says sarcastically. Christine refers to her tablet again showing there is no beach anymore, just a new coastline without the beauty of most of Georgia, South Carolina, and North Carolina gone.

"Remember, Mike, when we would sight-see in Florida those many times? There were so many things to see and places to visit that the whole family had something to look forward to."

Referring again to her tablet, she showed that Florida was now only about thirty to forty per cent of the size that it was back in the day when they were younger.

Mike grabbed a travel flyer from the table and then asked Christine, "Do you still hate the beach shuttle from here? Apparently, the latest high-speed transporters can now make that 600-mile trip in less than two hours, even with a couple of stops."

"No, I told you before that I miss the scenic drives and you should quit asking me!" She offered an option. "Let's just take one of those driverless cars west and visit the Mississippi River Lake. It's only about 250 miles from here and I understand that it's so wide now that you can't see the other side."

There was an obvious moment of sarcasm in her words. Mike then noticed that she was still clutching that framed picture of Mike, the now deceased Dad, Pete, and her. Emotional roller coaster today, for sure, Mike thought.

Neither can find humor in his ill-timed attempt to change their moods. Their whole family were constant travelers and looked forward to the annual trips they would take.

Thinking carefully about his next words, Mike continued.

"Unfortunately, due to unnatural calamities and accelerated climate change, the geography of America has sadly changed from the shore-to-shore beauty of vacations and recreation past, to the functional or commercial need of a particular geographical location."

Christine added, "Nope, people no longer take driving vacations to see the USA."

As Christine returned to the kitchen to re-fill the cheese plate, Mike pulled up another video on his watch. It showed the shorelines of the Atlantic, Pacific, and Mississippi River. The Atlantic shoreline depicted the results of subsidence and global warming, and the Mississippi River flooding had resulted in a body of water at the northern end that resembled a lake.

From San Diego to Washington State, the results of subsidence and global warming had destroyed the entire coastline where large populations used to be.

As of two months ago, about twelve per cent of the original west coast shoreline was now under water. Even beautiful San Francisco, now home to only the super-rich, is located where Oakland used to be. Daughter Sara had lived in California but now resided in Utah. Mike turned it off quickly as Christine reentered the room.

It was now evening and as the sun had set, so had any element of sunny disposition for the Stevenson home.

Christine finally added, "Earlier today on my daily news feed, the reporter for the weather network said that the two polar ice caps have reached a critical melt stage. The North Pole is about thirty per cent gone now and the South Pole is around twenty per cent melted, I think they said. Why is this happening to us?"

Christine went on, "Sea life has been so badly affected that only farmed fish is safe to eat! There we go again! Crapping where we live while the politicians do nothing! Did you see that news report about the fishing industry? Decimated! Only farm fish… and they taste awful! What kind of place will Sara and the children of the world grow up in? I'm so worried!"

"Christine, you're watching too much world news. You know you shouldn't worry about things you can't control. Isn't that what Dad used to say? We just need to focus on keeping our family as safe as possible."

Mike raised his wine glass to Christine and they toasted again to the family. He sighed, yet silently agreed with her assessment.

Over dinner, Mike reminisced with Christine about the memories of an earlier time, and said, "What if mankind had developed an understanding and awareness of the many things being done wrong and focused on the immediate future, the long-term future, instead of living in the present? It always seems to come back to leadership or lack of it."

"Or just plain greed and selfishness," Christine added.

"It also has to do with the lack of accountability in societies today. Even worldwide leaders are guilty of being short-sighted. Look at the financial mess in this world and each country trying to protect their capital at all costs."

"I know I sound like a broken record, Mike, but I still long for the past and would love to go back and enjoy those times again."

Sadly, Mike agreed, knowing that wasn't going to happen.

✦ ✦ ✦

Mike, sensing a need to reflect, moved the discussion to his study and favorite room in the house. Pulling an old and well-worn photo album from his bookcase, he opened it to one particular trip that the family made. Taking a chance by switching venues, Mike asked Christine to pull up a chair and sit next to him.

"Remember that particular trip that we took to the beaches of South Carolina with Sara just after we got our first big dog, Mandy?"

"I sure do. It was a really nice trip and I think the highlight was watching Mandy running up and down the beach like a puppy would do. It was so relaxing and such a great getaway for us."

Mike noticed that Christine was getting into a much better mood.

Christine then added, "Here's one of those photos! There was so much going on at the time, it seemed, but those South Carolina trips made it so much easier to just relax, plain and simple. We liked that area so much, we almost moved there."

Mike replaced that album in the bookcase and returned with an old diary that he had kept of conversations that he had with Sara. "Do you remember that first conversation that we had about life beyond our Earth at that restaurant that had a pirate theme?"

"Yeah, maybe," she said with a questioning gaze wondering where this was going. "I also remember her talking more about boys that trip than at any other time."

"Well, you're right about the boy talk, but that was also the first time of many times that Sara took an active interest in our family discussions about the future, the course of history, the smallness of mankind. That sort of stuff."

Mike unfolded a worn map of the solar system with detailed notes and drawings that Sara had made, and Christine was seeing them for the first time. Although he didn't want to spoil the mood... but, he thought, what the hell!

"These more recent entries of Sara's are on my mind now more than ever, and it's time to share them with you."

"I had no idea, Mike, that she had gone into any detail at all. Yet, look what's here."

"These specific notes of hers are incredible."

...the discovery of solar systems around other stars... has reinforced the question of alien life and alien intelligence. So many exoplanets have been found to date, that astronomers calculate each star in the Milky Way likely has at least one planet in

orbit around it. If you roll the dice billions of times within our galaxy, it's likely we are not alone.

Mike continued, "If you think that is crazy, read on…"

…a galaxy is a huge collection of gas, dust, and billions of stars and their solar systems, all held together by gravity. Our galaxy, the Milky Way, also has a supermas-sive black hole in the middle. Astronomers believe there could be as many as 100 billion galaxies in the universe.

"Whoa! Mike, that is hard to comprehend!"

" Yeah, but there's more…"

…most civilizations may all be dead by now and that's why we haven't heard from them. The only way to look for them is not by signals, but by looking for ancient alien artifacts, like technological equipment and evidence that they left behind. There is a lot of alien stuff floating around out there.

"It has been obvious to me, Christine, that her grandad was having a profound impact on her questioning of life, spiritual awareness, the cosmos, our place in the world, and how to make things better.

"If you are looking for a strong sign of Sara's incredible alien focus, this would be a good place to start."

"Now that we are talking about this Mike, what you say makes sense. None of Sara's friends ever had much of an opinion at all regarding those subjects, when Sara seemed to be, even back then, somewhat curious, if not very curious, about those adult points of view."

"Given the events of the last year or so, I believe that our daughter had a hidden desire to question and figure out just what the heck was going on in this world."

"I can't disagree, given what I'm seeing."

After a brief pause, Mike stated his case with a quiet contemplation.

"Looking back right now to the events of the recent past, especially the last year or two, it still makes me think that there is some sort of higher power or order driving this whole family to be that curious."

"Okay, time for bed," Christine added.

Mike re-folded the one note from Sara that he did not show Christine.

… it is more than likely that many alien cultures have come and gone from Earth. When the evil aliens arrive… we will be toast!

10

PETE

Pete Stevenson was a young engineer in the 70's, working within the Big 3 automotive industry, and as a single guy, found himself asked to travel for business throughout the world. Prior to his automotive career, Pete spent some time in the military leading counter-intelligence data research, but he found that element of data gathering quite boring.

In addition to his current work duties, he was a curious and observant guy, and had several concerns about the quality of life in the U.S. and the world. He especially had a problem with smog in Southern California, Mexico, and Asia, which was very bad and seemed to be getting worse.

He worried about the burning of fossil fuels, the deterioration of the ozone layer, and the excessive waste of oil, natural gas, and overall depletion of our natural resources. He had an inventor's tack and had applied for many patents, and actually was awarded a few.

One of his many quotes was, "If you don't take control of issues, those issues will control you." He was a bit of an adventurer whose idol was the book and movie character *Indiana Jones!*

He also had a complete fascination with the weather and extreme weather phenomenon that occurred throughout the world. That fascination, along with a minor degree in meteorology to go with his engineering degree, enabled Pete to give an occasional talk on weather-related issues, as well as forecast and prognostications related to climate change and global warming back when it was not a hot topic.

One such speaking gig occurred in Chicago in 1982 when Pete gave a talk to the National Science and Industry annual conference. His topic was *U.S. Weather – Three Climates.* He recalled how this topic even became relevant in his speaking gigs.

Once having lunch with the Director of Meteorology at NOAA, Dr. Bart Evans, the subject came up regarding the distinctive weather found in the U.S. determined by mountain ranges.

Dr. Evans asked Pete, "Have you studied the weather patterns in the U.S. that are affected by our topography? Especially our two main mountain ranges?"

Sensing this to be one of his weather interests, Pete responded, "Yes, I have. Actually, my plan was to assemble a Microsoft PowerPoint slide presentation for an upcoming talk that I need to make."

"Okay. Great. I can be of service, Pete."

Excited, Pete asks, "How so?"

"Come with me to my office and I'll show you."

With that comment, Pete and Dr. Evans walked over to Bart's office and lab where an impressive array of materials and visual aids were kept. Dr. Evans stopped for a moment to talk with one of his students and then turned his attention back to Pete.

"Pete, I have an Apple Keynote presentation that you can borrow. Take a look at it and call me if you have any questions."

"Thank you so much, Dr. Evans. This will be perfect."

Pleased, Pete said goodbye to his friend and was now very anxious to present.

◆ ◆ ◆

This National Science and Industry annual conference had a nice turnout with the audience numbering about 150. After spending thirty minutes talking about weather in general, Pete ramped up his talk with the interesting piece of weather information that was courtesy of his friend, Dr. Bart Evans.

"If you look at the map of the U.S. from a geographical and meteorological perspective, focus on the Rocky Mountains and Appalachians," Pete said as he began Dr. Evan's slide show.

"Think of those two ranges as weather barriers. The West Coast is a weather regime that covers the Pacific Ocean to the Rockies. The East Coast is a weather regime that goes from the Atlantic Ocean to the Appalachians. Between the ranges is the central U.S. which makes up the third nicely defined weather regime."

After a dull lead-in, Pete was hopeful that his topic would start to get the audience more engaged in his talk. Not seeing any strong interest, Pete knew he needed to up his game.

"So, what you have is a Western pattern that is a little Mediterranean, an Eastern pattern that is a little European, and a Central pattern that is heavily influenced by Canadian weather. That's why the Canadian Express winter weather wallops Central America.

And, the Gulf of Mexico is a rain engine that pushes all that wet weather directly north, mostly into Central U.S."

Some murmurs could be heard, but there was little evidence that the audience was getting any more into Pete's presentation.

"Now think of this. If we had a Himalayan-size mountain range that ran, say, from Houston, Texas, to Jacksonville, Florida, what kind of climate would the folks on the north side of that range experience?"

A young lady in the front row jumped up and said, "A desert."

"Yes, pretty much. The absence of the precipitation that I mentioned earlier would change the landscape there to fairly arid. This would become a weather phenomenon that would have catastrophic consequences."

Following a rather dull thirty-minute presentation that featured very little audience participation, Pete concluded, "Thank you for your time and I'll now take some questions."

After only a few minutes of answering questions, Pete concluded the session and again thanked everyone for their attention to his presentation.

The lady in the first row quickly moved up to Pete and seemed to have a bunch of additional questions. She was a bubbly and smiling person with average height, brown hair tied into a bun, and she was dressed in a brightly colored Native American sarong.

"Hi, Pete. I'm Elizabeth and I thoroughly enjoyed your talk. It was informative and you obviously have a passion for weather."

"Well thanks, Elizabeth, and I do enjoy weather issues and their implications. Nice to meet you. What, may I ask, do you do?"

"I'm a geologist but have a passion for American Indian Myths and Folklore, much like your interest in weather. I'm a very curious person and love to uncover Indian artifacts and study myths and history. You're an engineer, right?"

"Yes I am. But weather is my common-sense passion. My not-so-common sense passion is the study of ancient alien theory. I do a lot of that work in the closet."

They both got a laugh from that remark and were enjoying each other's company.

Elizabeth smiled and was thoroughly enjoying the meeting with Pete. She put her hand on Pete's arm as if they were already friends.

"Here, Pete. Take my card. Let's stay in touch."

"Great; here's mine. I will definitely keep you in the loop with anything relevant on any of the fronts we discussed. Please do the same. And thanks again for coming."

"My pleasure."

With that, Elizabeth gave Pete a kiss on the cheek. Pete gave Elizabeth a gentle hug.

Pete thought to himself that he just had a pretty good day, the mediocre presentation notwithstanding.

He also had a strange feeling that he and Elizabeth would meet again.

11

PETE

More importantly than his interest in weather, Pete was obsessed with stories of alien presence and extraterrestrial existence.

Even as a young boy, he was of the opinion that alien life, in some form, was among us. When many of his friends were out playing ball or shooting hoops, Pete had his nose buried in a book with an extraterrestrial theme.

For his high school graduation, his parents gave him a clock radio as a gift. Following many up-and-down arguments, Pete was allowed to exchange it for a remedial telescope. To Pete, that telescope was far more exciting than any first day of school. From that point on, many of Pete's friends were those once called nerds, but he didn't mind.

One evening as he and his friend Arlene were gazing out at the stars, Arlene asked Pete, "What do you hope to find way out there?"

"Dunno. Maybe aliens from another planet. I think they exist."

Arlene immediately said, "You can't say that they do."

"Nope, Arlene, but you can't say they don't."

✦ ✦ ✦

As he grew into adulthood, the sky, stars, and planets became his frontier, and he became self-educated in astronomy. With little disposable money to spend, he searched bookstores for old books on astronomy and ancient alien theories.

When a state-of-the-art planetarium opened in Pittsburg, Pete got his parents to take him there and he was mesmerized. As the ceiling above him exploded into a million bright and shiny points of light, the 360-degree visuals of the world and the continents were breathtaking.

He took notes on a small pad with an even smaller flashlight, much to the disdain of the fellow guests seated next to him. The astronomer's commanding voice gained the immediate attention of the audience.

"We live on this planet called Earth that is part of our Solar System. Our Earth orbits the Sun in our Solar System, and our Sun is one star among billions in our Galaxy, called the Milky Way. Our Milky Way Galaxy is one among billions of galaxies in our Universe."

Pete was overcome with the size perspectives, feeling overwhelmingly small under the immensity of that artificial sky.

The astronomer continued describing the Big Dipper, the Orion Arm, Cassiopeia, Ursa Major, etc.

Pete was hooked and he added to his notes while his memory was still sharp.

A next-day trip to a nearby high-powered telescope facility further enhanced his view of the known and unknown to be seen and explored.

The host and moderator of that particular day's event was Daisy, and Pete was hooked by the subject matter and by Daisy's knowledge.

At the first break, Daisy said, "Hi there, I'm Daisy; what's your name?"

"Hi Daisy, I'm Pete Stevenson. I'm here with my parents."

Daisy asks, "What are you interested in, Pete?"

"I guess the Moon and stars… our solar system. I'm just getting started in astronomy."

Daisy made a suggestion. "Your parents are back in the auditorium listening to a lecture. I have something to show you."

"Great,' Pete replied.

Leading Pete over to a large three-dimensional model of the solar system, Daisy began a short description of the origin of the moon.

"When the Moon was formed four billion years ago, it was twenty times closer to Earth than it is today and four hundred times larger in the sky, and ocean tides on Earth were eight thousand times higher. Do you understand those numbers, Pete?"

"Yes."

"Does that make sense to you, Pete?"

Slowly thinking about the question, Pete says, "Not really."

Daisy continued, "A Mars-sized protoplanet in our early solar system sideswiped Earth, blasting parts of Earth's crust and mantle into space, creating a ring of orbiting molten rock, which finally contracted to form our Moon."

"Geez," Pete replied.

Sensing Pete's steady interest, Daisy continued. "Today, Moon's orbit is spiraling away from Earth at a rate of one and a half inches per year."

Excitedly, Pete asks, "Daisy, how is that measured?"

"Good question, Pete. We can now measure it using powerful telescopes and Laser technology."

"Daisy, what is Laser?"

"Laser stands for Light Amplification by Stimulated Emission of Radiation. It is new technology, developed in 1960, and is now rapidly finding many applications."

At the conclusion of the showing, Pete's parents couldn't find him anywhere. Nearly an hour later, they found Pete getting that education on astronomy and the cosmos from Daisy, who was just finishing up.

"So, Pete, you got a pretty good start today, didn't you?"

"Yes, I did, Daisy. Thank you very much."

Daisy then asks, "What will you do next?"

"I gotta get busy studying the solar system and one thing for sure."

"What's that, Pete?"

"I don't care what anybody says about anything, I gotta get my own facts about stuff like this."

"Very good point, Pete. Glad I could help you."

That encounter was a game-changer for Pete, and he knew it. Mostly because of Daisy's guidance, he became very much interested in the stars, the Milky Way and, particularly, the Moon and the planet Mars.

Pete would never forget those two days... never!

12

PETE

It was in the summer of 1998 when the Stevenson family went camping in upstate New York. Along for this trip were Pete, his wife Louise, Mike, Christine, Sara, and a couple of Sara's young friends.

After a day on the lake in their small ski boat, they set up camp with tents, a roaring fire, and a wonderful camping dinner in the woods. This was a summer ritual, either in nearby Pennsylvania or upstate New York.

After dinner, they drove to the outskirts of a small town, to Sally's Ice Creamery, to get a delicious sweet treat. On that particular trip, a local black bear, somewhat of a celebrity there, was seen eating out of Sally's trash container.

Everyone left the bear alone, as to be expected, except Pete. He removed his coat and large hat, talked in a low and soft voice, and slowly approached the bear.

He then had about a thirty second, one-sided conversation with old Smoky, making eye contact throughout. Yep, that was Grandpa being Grandpa, and fearless was his middle name. No one was surprised or believed that Pete was in any danger. When asked what she thought of Grandad's bear encounter, Sara said, "He's being silly and he's trying to make a friend."

Later that night, after everyone had gone into their tents to sleep, Sara came out to see what Grandad was doing. Pete always slept under the stars, which young Sara didn't understand, given the nice tents that they all had.

"Whatcha doing, Grandad?"

"Just enjoying the beautiful moonlit sky and stars that shine so brightly tonight."

"Whatcha thinking about?"

"Well, just thinking about the bigness of space and if anyone else may be living way out there." Sara seemed puzzled. Pete grabbed his light jacket from the tent and gave it to Sara to wear, given the coolness of the evening air.

"Sara, do you know what a telescope is?"

"Yes."

"Do you know what it does?"

"I think so. What?"

"Well, a telescope allows you to look way up in the sky and see the moon and stars much bigger than they really are. That way, you can see much more of what you are looking at. Make sense?

"Yeah, it does."

"And there are several planets out there that I like to look at and study. Do you know about planets?"

"Yes. A little. Do you have a favorite planet?"

"I like Mars. It's kind of cool. One day I will explain my interest in Mars to you, okay?"

"That would be super, Grandad."

Pete continued, "I also like Mr. Moon out there. You wanna know why?"

"Yep," Sara answered.

Back in 1969, our Apollo 11 spaceship put mirrors on the Moon that allow us to study it with telescopes. Wanna know what they discovered?"

"Sure, Grandad."

"The Moon is shrinking and one day it will be gone."

Puzzled, Sara asks, "You mean in weeks?"

"Oh no, not for maybe two or three billion years."

Sara was silent.

"So, Sara bear, what are you thinking right now?"

"Oh, just that Mom and I have to go shopping for school clothes next week, and I'd rather not shop with Mom, but I guess I don't have much of a choice. I also like the stars."

Pete thought about his response for a moment. "Yes, now shopping is a problem. If you really want the trip to go well, you should ask your mom what her opinion is, even if it's not yours. That will make your mom feel that she is needed. Does that make sense?

"Yep."

Pete continued. "Sometime, I'd like to explain the stars to you, okay? And Mars, too, right?"

"Sure."

They hugged. "Good night Sara."

"Good night Grandad."

Pete thought to himself.

"Sara is a curious soul. Curiosity rules!"

13

PETE

Pete often spent evenings just staring out at the great beyond, not knowing what to think, but always with a strong hunch that somehow and someway there was life of some sort out there.

He would think to himself, "If you're out there… give me a sign." Unfortunately, he knew that his thinking was not one that was widely accepted.

Pete believed that a healthy scientific culture should encourage all interpretations of evidence and artifacts collected to date. While keeping a low profile at work, Pete registered at various Alien Conferences on both coasts and gave short talks on a variety of alien-related topics.

One particular alien conference in Baltimore gave him the opportunity to present three specific theories that he held, but yet to share due to their somewhat preposterous assumptions.

In a small meeting room with about fifteen attendees, Pete began.

"Good morning and thanks for coming. As the conference program reads, I will be making three assumptions regarding alien existence that I feel very strongly about."

For a moment, Pete had their attention.

"One, light on distant asteroids is a puzzle that needs to be solved. In my view, the government or private enterprise should find a way to identify artificial light on these asteroids and distinguish that light from normal cosmic light."

Showing two slides on normal and artificial light, no questions were asked.

"Two, given that alien cultures may have civilizations resembling ours, we should look long and hard at ways to detect industrial pollution in alien atmospheres."

Pete threw up a graphic illustration. Again, no questions.

"Third, and one of my favorite theories has to do with alien spacecraft."

Some stirring from the otherwise quiet attendees.

"We need to find out whether unusually intense blasts of extra-galactic energy might be powering alien spacecraft and become the smoking gun for proof of alien existence."

Pete submitted various agencies' data on energy blasts, but to no avail. A young guy seated in the front row quipped, "These aren't theories; they are just your opinions.

Before he had a chance to continue, the small audience stood up and walked out, except one guy.

"Hey, can I get a picture?

"Sure," Pete said. "Thanks."

"You're either the smartest guy here or the dumbest. Can't be sure."

With that regrettable event and final comment, Pete knew he had to keep his thinking pretty much to himself. He was discouraged.

He thought to himself... **I need a damn sign!**

14

PETE

That early alien thinking became an obsession stemming from two actual experiences he had with a co-worker, Jack Burgess, during a time when they were both overseeing the construction of a manufacturing plant near Sao Paulo, Brazil. Pete and Jack were close friends, as were their wives, and the four of them got together regularly.

The two of them had been on numerous major projects like this one in South America. During this trip, however, two extraordinary events truly shaped Pete's perspective of the unknown and unexplained.

The first of two strange incidents involved Pete's flight from Miami into San Paulo, Brazil. While waiting for his departure flight in Miami, three issues annoyed Pete, who for the most part, enjoyed flying.

One was the over-crowding and congestion in the waiting area. The second was the awful smell that permeated throughout the airport that late at night.

But the third issue was actually disturbing to a frequent flyer. While sitting in the airport lounge, Pete couldn't help but see a uniformed airline employee fondling a young lady in more than a loving way.

It was borderline sexual harassment, but the female seemed okay with the man's attention. He was on his fourth or fifth margarita when the flight was announced for boarding. Along with that couple, Pete headed to the Jetway to board.

After twenty to thirty minutes, the passengers were aboard a full-flight. Pete was getting annoyed even further that the flight was sitting at the gate, the cockpit door still open. Then, the sight that had Pete aghast.

From the cockpit, a loud and pissed off co-pilot yelled, "Guido, get your ass in here."

Running from the Jetway into the cockpit was none other than the amorous slob from the airport lounge. He was the pilot!

From that point on, the nine-hour flight from Miami to San Paulo was nerve-racking for Pete. The flight itself was awful, with poor weather most of the way.

What didn't help Pete's composure was the fact that the young lady from the lounge was a passenger and actually went into the cockpit mid-way through the flight and stayed there for at least forty-five minutes.

Adding to the nightmarish flight was the extremely poor visibility as they landed in Sao Paulo. The plane made a hair-raising landing, bouncing from the crosswinds and horrible downpour.

Pete assumed that this airport was a "captain-only" airport, meaning only the captain was registered to land here, not a co-captain.

Pete was stunned by the fact that the airport in San Paulo was in the middle of the city and resembled a table top, higher than the buildings of the city.

As the plane slowed and taxied to the terminal, Pete could actually see the wing of the aircraft swing out over the edge of the table top runway, a view that to him was frightening.

When he was safely at the terminal getting his rental car, he was very happy to be on solid ground. As fearless a traveler as he was, he knew that he was lucky to make it in one piece.

The next morning, when he met with the company's project team, he couldn't help but bring up the images that he had of his harrowing landing.

"I travel a lot, but to land on a short and narrow runway in the middle of a major city with nothing but canyon-like cliffs on either side was as scary as anything I have ever encountered!"

The group at the breakfast table seemed stunned. One of those sitting there, Woody Carlton, commented first.

"What the hell are you talking about?"

Pete quickly added, "Certainly, you guys experienced the same landing and crappy airport."

"Pete, you just accurately described the old San Paulo airport that was demolished ten or fifteen years ago and replaced with the modern one now outside the city."

His friend, Jack Burgess then commented, "So, how many drinks did you have?"

Everyone, except Pete, got a good laugh. What Pete didn't realize was that he had just experienced a *time slip* phenomenon that was often dismissed as a myth and to this day impossible to explain outside of theoretical.

However, he did add that strange occurrence to his to-do list for future investigative study. He knew he wasn't dreaming; that awful landing was very real.

So, Pete just had to live with the idea that he had experienced a glimpse of the past that was just an anomaly, and nothing more, for now.

The more he thought about it, the less it made sense. He tried to focus on the project at hand and dive into the real working world, not a fantasy one.

During a return trip to Sao Paulo with Jack Burgess about nine months later, on a tranquil Brazil evening, real versus fantasy once again challenged Pete's psyche. Pete was always looking to replace informed speculation with irrefutable evidence.

This time it came!

15

PETE

Pete and Jack really loved eating out in Brazil restaurants back then. This was the 70's and since refrigeration was somewhat basic, and food was plentiful, your menu choices would guarantee the freshest meats, poultry, and fruits you could ever hope to find. Dinners were looked forward to at the end of each day's work.

This particular Friday night, the guys stayed at the Meridian Hotel at Ipanema Beach. It was a weekend of sand, sea, and surf that they had been looking forward to for weeks.

Following dinner, Pete and Jack took a sunset beach walk and lamented the fact that their wives weren't there. In fact, they agreed that they couldn't be totally truthful about their beautiful surroundings, so as not to upset them. Guy logic!

"Jack, we have worked hard here and have earned some downtime. Let's grab a couple Margaritas and just enjoy the surroundings." Jack couldn't agree more. They stopped at a beach bar and picked up a couple drinks, offered cheers, and started off down the beach.

"Here's to us," Pete said.

"I second that," said Jack, but he didn't smile and the look on his face concerned Pete.

"Jack, you worried about something?"

Jack shrugged. "Just jet lag, maybe. Kind of tired."

Pete studied his business partner for a second, and then took a sip of his Margarita.

"Okay, I'm still trying to accept the local culture, especially the two-hour siesta style lunches here. We are so used to grabbing a sandwich, eating on the run, and going back to work. Just seems like so much wasted time." That was Pete, the efficiency expert. Lean and mean.

"Pete, I have been having dreams or nightmares recently, and some of them were really scary. Even now, I can't seem to relax. Seems like déjà vu right now."

He didn't provide details and Pete didn't ask. However, Pete did try to change the subject, and they began to discuss getting together with families when they returned to the states.

Pete offered, "How about we get all gussied up when we get back and take the ladies out?"

Jack, getting a little more relaxed said, "Sure, that would be great."

All was calm and an enjoyable beach walk continued under a clear sky and a starry night. There were no other people around and stars lit the sky which made it all the more enjoyable.

Then, from out of nowhere, the quiet and peaceful night was interrupted by several bolts of apparent heat lightning that were both scary and beautiful.

Pete, the weather guy, was familiar with this occurrence, having been around bolts like that one before.

These were quite different, however, as they had both vertical lightning bolts and were melded with a vast bluish light that was more cloud-like.

Oddly, the lightning bolts were very straight, almost linear in his mind. And, as Pete knew, a lightning bolt was very hot, roughly five times hotter than the surface of the sun!

When Pete regained his bearings, Jack was gone and there was absolutely no trace of him whatsoever. Stunned, Pete regained his composure, checked to make sure he wasn't harmed and then scoured the beach in both directions for thirty minutes before running to the hotel lobby.

He made contact with the hotel staff and then with the local police to submit, if nothing more, a missing person's report. The authorities viewed the episode as a drinking issue. Try as he might, Pete couldn't get anyone to take him seriously. He was angry and extremely concerned.

An engineer prefers black and white, not the unknown gray areas. And, Pete thought of Jack as a brother as they had experienced so much together over the years. So, a worried Pete waited and waited.

As he waited and in a moment of reflection of the many experiences that he and Jack had had, Pete thought back to a time many years ago when, on summer Army maneuvers in the heart of the Southeast Cajun country, a funny incident brought on a smile.

Pete and Jack were part of a large training battalion doing some field training with members of a west coast division, on a two-week gig.

After each exhausting day, the individual squads were dismissed and could either eat at the field mess hall, or go into town and try their luck with some local fare.

Well, Pete and Jack found a nice, out-of-the-way, family-run restaurant and ordered dinner. Jack had the fish platter and Pete tried the dozen oysters. After all, those sea creatures were the local fare. The next night, they returned to that same restaurant and Jack ordered the shrimp dinner, and Pete again had the dozen oysters.

"So, you must really like those oysters."

"Yep, but a dozen fried oysters aren't enough."

So, the third night Pete had a dozen and a half oysters and was somewhat happy. On the thirteenth night of their fourteenth day of training, Pete had his thirteenth consecutive oyster dinner.

However, the kitchen and wait staff had been alerted by Jack. Pete was surprised with three dozen delicious oysters and thirteen Chicago Style flaming oyster shells, symbolic of his culinary achievement. Nice thoughts of a much happier time.

"Thanks, Jack." He knew the effort Jack made and that's what friends do.

Pete had an awful thought; **I may never see Jack again!**

16

JACK

Jack was a middle-aged man with a slight build and reddish hair. He favored a handle-bar moustache and wore his signature cowboy boots right out of a Western movie.

He was a true friend to Pete and over the years had become one of Pete's most trusted friends and a respected colleague.

Unlike the glass half-full Pete, Jack was a glass half-empty guy who reminded you of a college professor. And, he always seemed to be wearing a herringbone sport coat, as he was that night.

Still confused with Jack's disappearance, Pete decided that he would wait for a couple hours before notifying Jack's wife, Judy, due to it being very late, and, frankly, not knowing what to say.

He was wrestling to find whatever facts he could, because even his explanation would sound unrealistic and farfetched. As he was considering what exactly he would say to Jack's wife, a knock at Pete's hotel room door sent chills up his spine.

There was Jack, fully clothed with sport coat and all, in an obvious daze, and falling limply into Pete's arms.

"Jack, what happened? Are you okay?" Pete said as puzzled as could be.

A totally disheveled Jack simply said, "No."

Pete laid Jack on the sofa, pulled off his boots, and got him some water and a cold cloth, as he was dripping with warm perspiration.

There was a long period of silence and Pete was not about to break the quiet in the room. When Jack was ready, he gave a most accurate account of his ordeal.

"We were walking together and then I heard a loud crack followed by bright lights ahead of me coming from three rotating spheres, almost trance-like. It was as if time had stopped. You were no longer there.

"There was a bluish-white cloud that then enveloped me. And throughout this time there was absolute silence."

"You said you were alone?"

"Yes. I called out for you but couldn't even hear my own voice."

"Were you still on the beach?"

"No. I was far from the beach and had no sense of time, temperature, or anything. Then I was being levitated through a white light up to a point in the sky that became a beacon into reddish light, almost like a door, in the center of a triangular ship or craft of some sort, but definitely nothing I had ever experienced before. I didn't have any clothes on."

"You were still going up into the sky?"

"Yes, I was still being levitated but with three stick-like forms all facing me and seemingly communicating with each other.

"All I remember at that time was that it had become as peaceful and tranquil as anything I had ever experienced.

"Laying on my back but still moving higher and higher, I could now see faces but no bodies. The faces were human-like but looked flat, almost two-dimensional."

"Where these still the stick-like forms that you saw before?"

"Yes. Then we all slithered through a small red door."

Pete paused. "Like the one you saw earlier?"

"Yes. It was like it was the destination. Then my motion stopped and I think I was on a table. At least it seemed like I was on a table.

There were pipes or tubes or tentacles everywhere, and I felt that I was in a safe place. Voices in my head reassured me that I was not in any danger."

Pete gave Jack another glass of water. "You okay to keep going?"

"Yeah, it's so vivid and clear to me, like it was totally a normal feeling. I know that sounds stupid. They put something on my head and then attached a tube to my right arm."

"Yeah, Jack, I see a mark but it looks like an old healed wound."

"It's not old. It just happened. Oh, oh, there's something else. I wasn't the only person getting the physical. I could make out several other people, all hooked up like me."

"Jack, you're describing an actual event, not a dream."

"No, it was no dream. I couldn't remember how long I was there and in that physical state, but I assume that it was for a very long time. I don't mean hours. I mean weeks or months. How long was I gone?"

"Maybe three hours."

"Even now I have a clear picture of the surroundings, like a hospital room or laboratory. And, I can't explain the deep cuts in my arm or why they were made and yet, they are fully healed after only a few hours with only small scars remaining."

As Pete touched Jack, Pete felt a slight jolt of electricity making no sense at all. For a brief moment, Pete felt empathy.

The account that Jack gave was now eerily etched into Pete's mind as if it had happened to him. It was as if Pete had experienced the exact same incident.

Pete knew that this was a significant emotional event that could not be explained or believed, by anyone but Pete and Jack. The preoccupation of trying to make sense of this event was the only thing that these guys could handle.

After much discussion, they decided that this incident would remain theirs and theirs alone to deal with... at least for or now.

Pete and Jack returned to the States and tried to white lie a plausible explanation for Jack's cuts as a minor plant industrial accident.

They both agreed that there was to be no mention of his disappearance. Over time, Jack seemed to disconnect with that night's incident, but to Pete, it only took on a bigger place in his psyche.

That Brazil project was the last one that Pete and Jack worked together on. One night several months later, Pete called Jack.

"Hey Buddy, what's up? How things going? Haven't seen you for a while."

"Hi Pete. Just working on several local domestic projects right now. Told the boss I didn't want to travel anymore. Want to slow down and enjoy time with Judy. Travel kind of burned me out."

"I can certainly understand that. I'm happy that you're happy."

Jack sadly added, "Not happy, just going day-to-day."

Pete sensed his friend's mixed emotions and said something he wished he hadn't.

"So, Jack, any more thoughts on that bizarre night in Brazil?"

"What bizarre night in Brazil?"

Pete was not surprised by his comment.

Jack simply thought to himself...

"If Pete only knew what I have been going through since that night in Brazil!"

17

SARA

Another family boating and camping adventure re-energized the astronomy conversation that Pete and Sara had back when they were camping in upstate New York when Sara was a youngster.

It occurred in 2005 when the combined Stevenson and Woodruff families, about 70 people in all, went on their annual boating extravaganza on the beautiful lake waters within the Kentucky State Resort Park to a venue called the Houseboat Capital of the World.

There, they would rent four houseboats, one large party barge, and find a quiet, secluded cove to dock their armada for the coming week.

Each houseboat usually had at least two ski boats and three or four personal water craft. Once they were moored with the party barge, the fun began.

This particular time, Sara had invited several of her water-skiing friends. A couple were semi-professional, and they would delight the families by launching their barefoot skiing from the tops of the houseboats during the week.

Once the generators lit up the evening sky from their boats and barges, other ski boats would enter the cove thinking they were a gas dock. But the real fun was yet to come.

As the skiing group arrived at the boat docks to unpack, Sara asked her friends a couple interesting questions. Sara was getting excited about this annual nut-house ritual.

"Well, who brought the balloons?"

One guy said, "I did."

"And who has the shaving cream?"

"Got it," another said.

"Good. Let me introduce you to the targets, I mean the clan." They laughed.

Sara knew the drill. About mid-week, around 7:30 a.m., each skier-led team would prepare an all-out attack of the defenseless houseboats with shaving cream-filled balloons.

Once the attack began, it would continue until all the adults, minus the kids and older folks, were driven into the cold cove water and the assault teams declared victory.

It would be hard to describe these annual events of passage to anyone not a Stevenson or Woodruff.

In fact, after several years of filling the beautiful lake with balloons, one year they arrived to see signs reading, NO BALLOONS ALLOWED.

Apparently, after several years of doing this, the excessive number of balloons made their way down stream to the lake filtering system and clogged up the pumps.

Back then it was boys will be boys and girls will be girls. That was before serious conversations regarding climate change and ecology skewed the narratives.

This one particular trip was a bit different. Sara was older, a teenager, but much more mature and very open-mined. One night, Pete and Sara were laying on the roof of one of the houseboats, and Sara opened the discussion with her grandad.

"So, Grandad, what's on your mind tonight?"

"Sara bear, I still look into the heavens and wonder if we are alone. It's such a large and limitless galaxy, how could we be the only life form here?"

Sara quickly added, "And that's just our one galaxy!"

Pete was happy to point out a little-known research observation. "Astronomers now believe that there are millions, maybe even billions, of galaxies in the observable universe."

"Holy cow, Grandad; that is awesome!"

Pete adds, "Yep, the grain of sand comparison jumps out at you."

Sara continues, "Well, I've been doing a little web browsing and caught a few cable TV shows about ancient alien theory, and I gotta say, there is some really cool alien stuff to think about out there. It's easy to take a position of not being alone."

With that Pete excitedly began to explain some of the constellations in the night sky. He was especially anxious to explain where in the cosmos the planet Mars was located, and inferred that Mars had a special place in ancient alien lore.

Sara was fascinated by his knowledge and passion. Wheels were turning in Sara's head as she planned her next research effort.

"So, you are the adventurer, why aren't you out there looking at this from the perspective of an investigative journalist?"

After a brief pause, Pete replied. "Well, Sara, I am actually doing quite a bit of that during my free time right now."

Sara was not surprised. "Let's talk about this soon, when you and I can have some alone time to focus."

"Okay. Sure. But promise me that you will let me know where you are looking and what you find."

"Will do."

"Love you, Grandad."

"Love you, my Princess."

Mike and Christine were at the base of the stairs leading up to the houseboat roof, realizing that Pete and Sara were there chatting.

Mike spoke up. "Christine made some hobo sandwiches and wants to get into some storytelling. You guys interested?"

"Sure Dad, we'll be right down."

Christine had set a nautical-based table for the snacks and stories. Several other family members from other boats joined them.

Uncle Fred did the usual scary stuff with haunted cabins and watery locations befitting the current occasion. Showing his age, he aptly described the *Creature from the Black Lagoon*, a movie made long ago.

Pete piped in with some fairly simple alien stories, mostly around the often-cited UFO sightings, but none of which got much attention. Pete figured as much since there was no way to make the complicated nature of alien presence simple enough for the family to get excited about.

Mike had become a sought-after consultant and subject matter speaker in his field and wrote a couple business books to share his experience with all those who would listen. But when it came to storytelling, that just wasn't serious Mike's thing.

He did spend about forty-five minutes telling some interesting travel stories that were fun and even some borderline science fiction and Sara was enjoying them completely.

She was fascinated with the incredible experiences that Mike and his dad had over the years, and found that every story had a nugget or two that she found timely and educational. For some strange reason, one particular military story stood out.

Sara just believed that stories were life's greatest teacher...

18

SARA

"**D**ad, do you remember the story you told me about your time in the Army, particularly the one about Drill Sergeant School and the barracks incident during Advanced Infantry Training?"

"Sure. It's one that I tell often. Why do you ask?"

"I just want to hear it again," Sara said.

Filling his glass with some cold iced tea, Mike begins. "Well, it's my opinion that everyone should spend time in the Military, which is certainly not the popular position right now. I strongly believe that the discipline learned in the Army served me well in my career, but this one incident that Sara is referring to stood out."

Only a few family members remain as Mike begins his Army story.

"As the Middle East wars were winding down, I was fulfilling my military obligation as a Drill Sergeant in the Army, and I was a fairly recent graduate of the Drill Sergeant Academy.

"Several of my fellow Drill Sergeants and I were in charge of training a group of Advanced Infantry Training soldiers, many of which were probably headed to combat and the front lines.

"They were in a twelve-week training cycle, and were responsible for absolute soldier readiness as their #1 priority. I learned one of my best lessons here that the proof of discipline lies in its absence."

Sara had heard this story before but loved the heartfelt way Mike told it. Mike added a couple ice cubes to his iced tea, stirred his drink slowly, and proceeded to tell a story he had told many times.

"We were in their ninth week of grueling seven-days-a-week training, and announced on Saturday to the squads in their barracks that they could have the following Sunday 'off.' Cheers were heard, and plans were being made.

"But we had a different plan. I told the other D.I.'s to meet me at 0500 on Sunday. 'Okay, guys, you know the drill and keep it serious.'

"So, on Sunday morning at 0530, the D.I.'s and I came unannounced into the barracks, whistles blaring and loudly calling for a muster.

"Once all were standing in front of their bunks, I ordered them 'to take everything out of the barracks, and I mean everything,' and the squads had to place everything on the front lawn in front of the barracks. That included all military equipment, beds and furnishings, and personal items."

Mike gestured with his hands that the next part was pretty cool.

"Once the barracks were completely empty, and all personnel were standing at attention in front of their assigned belongings, I ordered 'everything put back inside and in order, as it was found this morning.' Then we told them that they could then have the rest of the day 'off.' It was almost noon before that was done, or about six hours in all."

Sara and Christine grabbed some recently popped corn as Mike continued with a huge grin and his tone was slightly louder.

"The following Saturday, I instructed the squads that they could have the following Sunday off. What happened was similar to the previous week, but ended about 1100, or an hour shorter."

This time Sara was grinning, as she knew what was coming next.

Mike, now fully engaged in his story and with hands waving, continued. "So, the following Saturday we told the squads that they could have the Sunday of the weekend off."

Even Christine was smiling now.

Mike, now relaxed and focused on this story that he told a thousand times, filled his glass with iced tea, stirred the ice cubes, and concluded his story.

"What happened next was truly inspiring. You see, the message was loud and clear. Get organized, determine individual roles, help each other, and most importantly, get rid of all non-essential personal items, like boom boxes, food, books/magazines, special clothing—all the things that if carried into combat, could get you killed. The results were most interesting. The 0530 'surprise muster' came, and all was out and back by 0730, and the free Sunday was then available."

Sara clapped, as if the ending was unknown to her. It was not.

Mike added, "It took discipline and the soldiers doing what was needed, not just what was wanted and/or what they were told to do, but the 'right job right.' Pure accountability and discipline."

"Wow! I never get tired of hearing that story, Dad."

Somewhat surprised, Mike adds, "I can't believe you listened to that one war story again."

A curious Christine then asked Sara, "What is it about that particular story that gets you excited?"

"It's one of many stories from Dad and Grandad that I want to be able to tell my kids.

"It's all about leadership and principles and the greater good, and that's what we need to focus on today. I also believe it's the fabric of this family and I'm grateful to be a part of it."

"That is so sweet."

"Thanks. The way that Dad and Grandad experienced life and reflect it in their stories, I feel that I am actually there experiencing it first-hand. That, to me, is very special."

Sensing an opportunity to continue, Mike asks, "So, ya want another story?"

Sara quickly responds, "No thanks, Dad. We're good."

Good Stevenson family time that day. Except for Mike.

On the opposite side of these innocent, boring and "who cares" stories from Mike's archives is the one horrific downside…

His end-of-the-world nightmares!

19

MIKE

These softer stories added little to Mike's soul searching and constant introspection. It was the fact that Mike was haunted by recurring dreams, or in some cases nightmares, about his life, the world, and the events occurring in both that were truly terrifying.

He once had a dream that was very realistic and frightening. He saw Christine and Sara sitting on a bed, alone, looking out a window at the fiery scene that appeared to be an end-of-world scene. Mike was a helpless observer in this nightmare and could sense the fear and anguish in the two women.

Making this awful setting even worse was that he had this nightmare many times. They were always violent, realistic, and terrifying.

Recalling the H.G. Wells novel *War of the Worlds* depicting a Martian invasion that was highlighted in Wells' 1938 radio version that brought panic to listeners that didn't realize it was fictional, Mike reflected on another bad dream.

He saw himself fighting off hordes of low-flying alien spaceships with six well-armed and valiant fighters, four other men, and one light-haired women. It was always a desperate attempt to win a battle against all odds in the fog and dust and smoke.

This dream happened many times and lasted for a very long time. It always ended with him yelling to his squad at the top of his lungs, "*We are the final six, from now until the ashes claim us!*"

As an analytic thinker and a great problem solver, with the need to make all gray in life into black and white, his life was complicated, stressful, and nearly always, unfulfilled.

It would explain his decision in mid-life to seek answers to the questions that Pete had raised regarding alien myth versus accepted reality.

He inherited his dad's concern about the state of the world, and often complained about the lack of leadership in country, business, and the overall worldview. He and Christine had many conversations about his recurring dreams, progressive dreams, and occasional déjà vu.

Raised as Catholic, Mike took his day-to-day direction more from spiritual guidelines, rather than religious ones. He was intensely skeptical, which would play out in vivid detail as his life unfolded.

A series of strange and similarly related events were shaping his new convictions about creation, life, and destiny. One of his dreams was actually a premonition of America's greatest tragedy, the World Trade Center attack on September 11, 2001.

Several times, beginning in 1999, Mike had hauntingly realistic and long-running nightmares of a violent terrorist strike on a major business center. These nightmares became so realistic, Mike often wondered how or to whom he could divulge these insights, but knew they would be extremely skeptical, as he had no specific target to reveal.

Looking back, he felt he had made a mistake by confiding in a few friends and family of these dreamlike phenomena. They thought he was nuts.

One episode in particular, Mike awoke from a nightmare crying, sweating profusely, and he screamed, waking a terrified Christine.

"Mike, are you all right? What's the matter? Are you in pain?"

Gathering his thoughts and recalling the vivid nature of what he just experienced, he explained his nightmare.

"It was something amorphous at first, indeterminate, and fuzzy. Then it all came into focus and happened very quickly. This was a major terror attack, high-rise buildings, smoke, exploding planes, and frightened people running for their lives."

As he explained this nightmare to Christine, she became frightened and very uncomfortable. Mike knew immediately that he needed to water down the nightmare events as nothing of much significance and never getting into the dark and scary details that he witnessed in that bizarre incident. He couldn't tell Christine that this was a recurring dream.

"Christine, I'm fine. Just reading too many of those sci-fi fantasy books and Grandad's alien stuff."

"You sure you're okay? Let me get you a glass of water."

"Thanks."

His peers judged his premonitions and opinions as mostly frivolous thoughts with no basis in fact. Mike was a fact-based decision maker, as everyone knew, so this dichotomy of thought was painful for him. Those presumed frivolous thoughts of events and days past turned prophetic as his life cycle moved into older age.

He once told his coworker Tom about this nightmare, and although they were friends, it was clear Tom thought he was crazy. As a result, he started keeping these things to himself.

When the terrorist attack did occur on 9/11 at the World Trade Center, it was the mirror image of his nightmare. Mike was as pensive as he ever was, and at that time, Christine felt a chilling sensation that Mike had, indeed, experienced a premonition.

"Mike, I am confused, of course, but there is something going on here and please don't shut me out of any of these dreams or nightmares in the future."

"I won't. I really need to share this with you, Honey. I'm kind of scared, to be honest. Thanks for being here."

From that point on, Mike was able to feel a little more comfortable informing her of his feelings and concerns. He absolutely needed that sounding board and confidant.

Mike was somewhat relieved, but he knew one thing for sure about this unpredictable dreamscape of his.

It was only getting more realistic and more relevant with each occurrence.

20

MIKE

Following that awful terrorist attack, Mike shifted gears to some soft and gentle reflections of his past. He thought back in time to when Pete was working on a project on the west coast. Mike was maybe fifteen years old when his dad called.

"Hey Mike, want to spend the weekend with me at the cabin? Just you and me?"

Mike was feeling thoughts between happy and reluctant, thinking it was going to be either exciting or extremely boring.

"Sure Dad, I'd love to."

So, Mike flew to California, was greeted by his dad, and they drove several hours to Pete's remote cabin in the Sierra Nevada Mountains.

The setting was breathtakingly beautiful and extremely quiet, with a lovely lake near the cabin. Mike was very happy to be there, assuming that with his dad's busy schedule, he was a very lucky son.

They talked, cooked outside, and fished in the lake from a small boat tied to a tree below the cabin. At his young age, Mike couldn't grasp what an absolute contrast this picturesque setting was from his dad's day-to-day life.

If only he knew then that his dad's true obsession was chasing alien artifacts and hanging out with ancient alien conspiracy theorists.

They did talk a little about life on distant planets, but that talk was mostly one-sided. When asked about seeing Pete's unusual archeological artifacts, Mike said he'd rather see his dad's collection of classic car models.

Mike could see that his dad had a plan for them at that time and he was right. Pete brought out his high-powered telescope and after a few corrections, was able to focus on the planet Mars and the constellation Orion.

Mike could see that his dad had a point to make, so he relaxed and gave Pete the time he needed. After adjusting the telescope, Mike got a first-hand look at the Red Planet.

"Wow, Dad, that is awesome. It's so red and so clear."

Adjusting the focus and clarity once more, Mike got an even better look at Mars.

"Gotta admit Dad, Mars is even cooler than your '67 GTO."

Pete added, "Glad you like the view."

With that comment, Mike was about to get an introduction into his dad's Martian mindset.

"Life on Earth is thought to have emerged around 3.5 to 4 billion years ago. But Mars is an older planet and researchers assert that conditions on Mars could have allowed for life to start developing there as early as 4.5 billion years ago."

"Dad, that's some interesting info. What about water? I know that you need water to survive."

"Great question, Mike. Giant meteorite impacts on Mars between 4.2 and 3.5 billion years ago likely accelerated the release of early waters from the interior of the planet setting the stage for life formations."

"Man, that starts a whole bunch of questions, Dad. What do you think?"

"Mike, I agree with many current researchers that some sort of Martian life could've even thrived during this time period, when it seems like Mars was a very wet planet."

Mike added, "I bet when they get soil samples from Mars, and that day will come, it will prove that theory."

"Yep, Mike. I agree. So, no bulletproof evidence will likely occur in my lifetime, but I bet it will in yours."

Grasping the significance of that remark, Mike thought to himself, "I would like to be one of the pioneers that finds that truth out there."

"Mike, this is likely the most viewed astronomical perspective from Earth. It is precisely the astronomical perspective that got my interest in space started… hope it does the same for you."

"Yeah, it was awesome. Not what I expected. Thanks for setting it up for me."

Mike could sense that Pete was pleased with Mike's attention to the Mars information.

Mike processed that evening event all the way home. He couldn't get the star-filled beauty and enormity of what he had seen out of his mind.

Many years later, it turned out to be one of the key celestial events that drove Mike into his father's alien journey.

He wished that he had asked his dad many more questions…

That was the extent of the one and only one trip Mike made to the cabin in the woods in the Sierra Nevada.

Mike fully realized the significance of that visit many years later.

And for this visit, it was also much needed father and son time.

Both men were unaware that the thread that bonded them together had begun.

21

PETE

It had long been discussed and theorized that earth and primitive humans had been visited by advanced beings from another world, galaxy, or universe. Obviously, not being verifiable, that was literally ancient history.

But many theories suggested that these aliens gave humans the knowledge of the solar system, concepts of engineering and mathematics, and became the basis for cultures and religions.

This is what drove Pete to inquire, visit, research, and attempt to verify every conceivable item or artifact that existed in the world.

Pete found specific evidence in ancient monuments such as the Pyramids of Egypt/Giza, the Nazca Lines, and the 1200 monumental statues called Moai at Easter Island. He feverishly documented and cross-referenced all known and found evidence of this vast resource.

Among the more recent studies, Pete found artifacts, observations, and strongly debated evidence from highly reliable sources that provided the core of Pete's strong position on alien presence.

Pete was establishing a premise via material, etchings, and redundancies that aliens made contact with primitive humans and cities via extensive Indian Sanskrit Texts that describe flying machines called Vimanas.

He was also getting extremely confident in his beliefs following exhausting and numerous trips to regions where Egyptian megaliths showed precision cutting work thought to be too advanced for that time.

Jewish Zohar writings that he observed described a "manna machine" similar to chlorella algae processing today.

Pete viewed and reviewed tons of significant documentation covering Earth's hot spots of UFO activity: area 51 in the U.S., the Bermuda Triangle, Mexico's Zone of Silence, Peru's portal-like structure Puerta de Hayu Marca, and the curious events around the rock formations of the Marcahuasi Plateau.

After extensive study that he conducted from the mid-seventies through the mid-eighties, he found that various megalithic structures around Earth were built on an incredible world grid of electromagnetic energy.

This power source, in Pete's mind, likely was tapped for travel inter-galactically and high-level communication.

And, Egypt was the hotbed of this information and Pete spent much time there.

Hidden messages within these sites showed connections to one another, and Pete felt strongly that they replicated today's computer coding techniques.

He shared this general data with a few of his similarly driven colleagues. One of those associates, Jerry McNaughton, who was actually a bit of a naysayer, told Pete he might be on to something significant.

If Jerry supported Pete, well...

The icing on the cake for Pete came from his investigation of the structures on Teotihuacan and Easter Island.

These were sites with identical megalithic architecture in size, weight, and design but were separated by 2000 miles of ocean. Truly a stunning finding.

Now concluding his last yearly research campaign on Easter Island, a Chilean territory and remote volcanic island in Polynesia, he was consolidating his findings in late 1985.

Just too big not to share...

22

PETE

It was at this stage of Pete's research that he brought Mike in on his findings and perceptions. After trying unsuccessfully for two days to get a cell call out from Hana Rose, the capital of Easter Island, he finally reached Mike.

Pulling out his pad of extensive notes, he began. "Mike, I have some amazing news."

"Hi as well to you, Dad."

"Sorry son. Just so damn excited about what I've uncovered that I needed to talk to you ASAP. I think I have some hard evidence that cannot be discounted."

"I'm listening. Where are you?"

"Ah, Easter Island. Still here. Been a great trip."

Sensing his dad's upbeat mood, Mike responds, "That is so cool. You sound excited."

"Yep. Remember how we talked about the alleged alien monuments creating a world grid of energy and power?"

"Of course."

"Well, carvings and etchings at a number of geographically separated structures show a strong mathematical connection."

"And you are thinking that these connections are similar to today's computer coding techniques, right?"

"That's exactly what I was thinking. I'll send you the raw data I soon as I find a place to send it."

Pausing for a moment, Mike says, "Maybe you should just wait until you get home and in a secured area."

Pete shrugged, "Good point. Need to protect this proprietary info and the info source. Hackers are everywhere and I can't let this stuff get into the hands of thieves."

"Anything else?"

"Yep, sit down. I'm gonna get me a beer; give me a minute."

Now Mike was getting excited about his dad's findings and Mike being Mike, was now quite impatient waiting for Pete to get back on the phone. Then click, the phone went dead.

About thirty minutes later, Pete called back.

"What the hell happened, Dad? Thought you were abducted or something."

"Not the best cell coverage. Sorry. Now listen up…"

Mike added, "Got a pad to take notes."

Pete continued, "So, staying with the alien secret code analysis, the Pyramids of Giza, Thornborough Henges, Stonehenge, and ancient Hopi cities are all configured meticulously to resemble Orion.

Seriously.

Also, the absolute straight-line alignments of sites such as Trelleborg, Delphi, and Giza are uncanny."

Mike jumped in. "Trelleborg… In Sweden?"

"Yep. Crazy, right?"

"Man, you may be on to something."

"And, Mike, listen to this. The stone carvings at Gavrinis, determined to be from around 3500 BCE, accurately calculate the circumference of the Earth and the value of Pi!"

"Oh my God!"

"Give me a second while I switch to a different data set. This goes back to my last two trips to Central America. Was gonna wait until I saw you but am just too damn excited right now."

Mike asked, "Is there anyone on to you? Other alien hunters? You getting followed?"

Pete paused and said, "Don't think so. We kind of get ignored, you know?"

Gathering his data, Pete continued.

"Present-day battery technology is a part of everyday life and powers appliances, cars, airplanes, communication devices, and even our current space travel.

"I found that technology was discovered in ruins of civilizations that go back to the Bronze Age. In fact, archeologists have dated those battery findings back to 4000 BCE."

Mike responded, "I've always thought that energy, electricity, and communication evidence from the distant past was real. Just needed to be validated."

"And, computer astronomy evidence was found in the Incan and Egyptian ruins, along with 1000-year-old spaceflight navigation charts that are, apparently, as accurate today as they were then.

"And what can best be described as an alien astronaut was found, allegedly, preserved in one of the pyramids I visited.

"I saw it but couldn't attest to its authenticity without personal investigation. Need to do a deeper dive on this one.

"An earlier anthropologist log had mentioned that another alien astronaut was found in a location in South America. There are even strong rumors of a cover-up in the U.S. regarding a third alien astronaut that was found."

Mike added, "Yes, that would likely be the area 51 reports from New Mexico, ad nauseam. I actually have some info on that I can bring you up to speed on."

"Great. Listen to this. What can only be described as a giant spaceport was found in the Andes. Did you know that?"

Mike jumped in again, "I did hear about that, yep. Massive research was done on the site, but later all of that research mysteriously disappeared."

"Okay. Good. What I now have in my possession is a series of domino-like personal inquiries by several people that point to a petrified alien astronaut. I'm gonna pursue this as soon as I can get away. You said you had some UFO info from area 51?"

"Yeah, Dad, just getting my notes out. Bear with me."

Pete got himself another beer,

"Dad, you still there?"

"Yeah, Mike, go ahead."

"In 1947, a flying disc crashed at a ranch near Roswell, New Mexico, and the U.S. Army immediately reported it, as you well know, as a common weather balloon. Reports from people on the ground had a much different description, hence the term flying disc.

Then, in the early 1980's, the Army published two reports that it was a complex nuclear test surveillance balloon. The Roswell incident became the world's most famous and exhaustively investigated theory of UFOs ever."

"Sorry Mike, but that's old news. Let me catch you up."

"Go ahead."

"I now have pictures of an alien astronaut from 1947 Roswell frozen and kept in area 52, which was the government's much more secret base than area 51.

If these photos can be verified and these claims are true, we now have evidence of three alien astronauts to study and compare."

"My gosh, Dad, this is huge."

"As they say, once is a random event, two is simply a coincidence, but three alien astronauts are most definitely a trend and very hard to debunk.

"This is a topic with a very big need to get a handle on and to get closure to, for sure."

Mike was now convinced that this element of alien astronaut discovery was fueling Pete's positive perspective and keeping his momentum alive and well.

"Got to go, Son. Much to do. Thanks for your time."

"Dad, you're on to something and you know it. Keep me informed. I'll bring our Sara up to speed as well. She's ready."

"Yeah, I know she is. And so damn smart."

Mike added. "She is so curious. Seems like she is always asking me what you are up to. She is going to be blown away."

Pete replied, "Can't wait to get her and her smarts involved."

"Congratulations, Dad."

"Thanks, Mike."

As they ended their call, Pete very carefully unfolded his best alien hunting souvenir and placed it on the table in front of him. It was a sketch of three alien travelers from his encounter in Trelleborg and their comment to him.

"This is the end of the beginning."

23

MIKE

When Pete returned to the States, he called Mike and they had another debriefing of Pete's most recent work.

"Dad, I had no idea how far you had driven your alien research and to what length you had been searching, traveling, and recording."

"Yeah, it's been a hellava journey to here and it's still the tip of the iceberg."

"I'm gonna call Sara. It's time to bring her on board and get her involved much more than an observer."

"Yep. It's definitely time."

Mike set up a day and time for his talk with Sara. As he concluded the nuts and bolts of Pete's resume of work, he added the bigger picture stuff.

"Dad, thank you for bringing me up to speed on Grandad's work. It's way more detailed than I could have ever imagined."

Pleased with the conversation, Mike added. "Well, there is more. Ready?"

Sara was getting excited. "Shoot."

Mike continued. "We didn't know how far your grandad had driven his alien presence ambition and to what lengths he was searching, gathering, interviewing, and traveling. There was incredible ancient documentation regarding black holes, wormholes, time travel, alien colonies on Mars, and alien abductions that are now at the top of his to-do list."

Sara was totally engaged. "Black holes, time travel, aliens on Mars?"

"Yep. These were the areas that had the most unverifiable and unsubstantiated claims that were very frustrating to Pete. He expanded his own research team and was now getting an exponential return on their investments of time and money."

"He has a team? Holy crap!"

"Yep, Sara. The most chilling revelations that they are looking into is that some aliens could have morphed into human-like beings for the purpose of gathering information on human life on Earth. Some theory existed, and they're trying to expand on it, that aliens may have altered the course of human evolution as certain DNA anomalies suggested."

"Fascinating. Where the heck would he get that info from?"

Shrugging, Mike said. "Dunno, but gonna find out. Listen to this. They are pursuing a course of data streams and some loosely-based evidence that a large part of global civil unrest was the result of these in-humans that have no desire to live, only to destroy."

An excited Sara added, "I have read that many of the ancient alien conspiracy theorists offered an alternative to their thinking to help sway the doubting masses, that there was a pervasive totalitarian malice by alien, evil alien, in-human beings.

"That would have been a very simplistic explanation of much of the terror and war which was plaguing the world, but couldn't be ruled out under any circumstances."

"That's right and you're right. Although Grandad was not a complete supporter of these theories, he has been writing about them as an alternative explanation for these events nonetheless."

"Didn't see that one coming."

"Well, Grandad has one more theory to top that one."

Sara said enthusiastically, "All ears."

"One of the concepts that also kept coming up over and over again in their work was his other strong belief that ancient aliens were really futuristic human time travelers sent here from future human societies to help us.

"Grandad's premise was that the evidence was very strong that much advanced technology was required to build the enormous and futuristic symbols and monuments of the past. He has alluded many times to extratemporal aliens, or time travelers from the future."

"Dad, he had mentioned that to me more than once. It makes me wonder if it is his actual research or his self-fulfilling prophecy, or Pygmalion Effect, kicking in."

"Sara, I hear you and I understand."

Mike continued. "Bottom line is that he fully expected that the research of he and his small team going forward would focus directly on this explanation of alien intervention, either extraterrestrial or extratemporal, as the only logical conclusion that could have been drawn to explain all of this."

Sara said, "I can see that."

Mike quickly replied, "It has been your grandad's end game."

Sara smiled and said, "It still is."

Mike considered their conversation for a moment and had one overwhelming thought.

"Will it become Sara's end game?"

24

PETE

A couple busy years of alien hunting go by, and it's now 1989 and Pete is feeling lonely and tired from his constant travel, major work projects, and his preoccupation with alien presence. He has had a series of up and downs with his alien artifact hunting, and there were frustration mounting with everyone involved.

With his social life close to stagnant, he began to contact several friends and attempted to get back in touch with people that he was once close to. It was an awkward and unsatisfying process that resulted in little positive feedback.

Pete also made an effort to connect with family that was always a source of peace and quiet. He found it disheartening to learn that many in the family outside of his immediate family took Pete's out-of-touch behavior to suggest arrogance.

They had no idea that Pete was absorbed in alien hunting and far from arrogant.

He assured himself that he could change those perceptions and planned to do so in the future. There were large family gatherings every July in Ohio, and Pete committed to attending the next planned event. Some in the family were skeptical, since Pete was always a no-show.

But even higher on his social bucket list was reconnecting with Jack Burgess, so he made an effort to re-connect with his old pal.

After having difficulty reaching Jack, he was able to connect with Jack's wife, Judy.

"Hi, Judy, Pete here."

"Hi Pete. Long time no see. How are you and Louise?

"We're fine, thanks. And you guys?"

"I'm still doing volunteer work and Jack is staying busy with work projects, mostly close to home. I like that. We don't get out much."

After exchanging a few pleasantries, Pete and Judy decided a get-together would be long overdue. So, they arranged to get tickets to a Gino Vannelli concert in Cleveland, which in Pete's mind would please the ladies.

Even though Pete and Jack got gussied up and took the ladies out a few times in the past, things were never as they were before the Brazil incident now five years back.

Not only was Jack much more of a subdued and quiet person, but he was also suffering from memory loss and intense headaches, which he had explained to Pete a few times in the past.

Over a couple conversations during this time, Pete reached a conclusion.

This was not Jack!

25

JACK

On the night following the Gino Vannelli concert, the ladies prepared some after dinner refreshments and all was going well.

Following some small talk, the guys excused themselves from their wives and returned to Pete's study per Jack's request. Jack sensed that Pete was trying to get his relationship with Jack back on track.

It had been a very good night, so far.

"Pete, I'm having intense headaches, as you know, and need you to do something."

Puzzled, Pete asks, "Do something? What do you mean? Whatcha need?"

"Look at my neck. Do you see anything strange?"

Pete looked and shrugged, "No."

"Here, press here at the base. Feel anything."

"Crap, Jack, there's a small lump there."

"I can make it move. Watch."

Jack could see that Pete was not believing what he was seeing. Jack was literally moving something in his neck with his fingers.

"It has been there for a while, but now it has moved so I can see it in my bathroom mirror. I can really feel it."

"What do you want me to do, Jack?"

"Pete, get a knife from somewhere and see if you can cut it out."

"Seriously, Jack?"

"Now, Pete. Right now!"

Pete was gone a few minutes and then returned with a knife, hot towel, and bandages.

Jack inquired, "Did the girls see you?"

"No, they are in the family room chatting away. I got a knife from the kitchen acting like I was looking for an opener or something. We got time."

"Good. I couldn't wait any longer to get your help."

Pete asked, "Need a shot of scotch or something strong?

"No. I'm ready."

As delicately as he could, Pete began to extract the foreign object. As blood flowed, Jack let out a subdued scream, having firmly clenched a cool cloth in his mouth.

Pete had to stop for a moment as the blood flow was extensive.

"You okay, Jack?"

Wincing in pain, Jack nodded.

"I almost have it." Moments later. "Got it!"

Jack was getting limp as Pete held on to him.

"You still okay, Jack?"

"The damn headache. It got so bad I thought my head was going to burst. Thanks."

Pete had extracted a round metal object, thin as a dime and about the same size. The metal wasn't immediately recognizable, but it likely was the cause of Jack's headaches.

"Let me see that thing. Damn."

Pete offered, "I will get this analyzed ASAP and let you know what we have. Meanwhile, let me clean you up and put a bandage on the cut so Judy won't see it."

"Thanks, Pete. I'm anxious to hear what you find out."

"No problem. I just wish you would have told me sooner so we could have done this a long time ago."

"The damn thing just got to a point where I could feel it."

Pete asks, "How's the headache?"

Jack replied, "Much better, thanks."

Pete was startled to see that the once excessive bleeding had completely stopped.

Jack was thinking that he was glad that Pete was in his corner and he sensed that his friend was very pleased to have helped.

But Jack's last thought was not good.

This was the beginning of something… not the end.

26

PETE

The sobering extraction on Jack's neck made Pete realize how vulnerable they were and how fortunate Pete was today to have a lovely wife who supported him in all his goofy endeavors.

He also knew, as Jack had thought, that the round metal object was a sign that they didn't know what they didn't know… and that was alarming.

He also thought of the many alien research trips and artifact gathering that were productive and fascinating, mostly done in the early to mid-1960's, but Pete was never able to share his adventures as a single guy and felt alone and sad that he could not share his good fortune with someone.

After much introspection, he finally put companionship and relationship building on the front burner in the late '60's. Pete had met women before, but his intensity was usually a turn off and he was left to figure out why things just didn't work out.

When it came to making a decision between a woman he just met and his work, the work always won. He once told a colleague that he was married to his work.

✦ ✦ ✦

One fateful day, back in 1971, Pete was doing some research on ancient Egyptian culture with special emphasis on the pyramids and their place in history.

Having assembled many relevant subject matter books at the local library, Pete began the process of reading and selecting those that seemed to make sense.

A woman sitting at a nearby table, who had been watching him out of the corner of her eye, walked over and said, "I'm sorry, but I couldn't help but notice you seem a little confused over all those books."

"That obvious, eh?"

"There are two on your left and one on your right that contain all you need to know about the great Egyptian pyramids. They are Budge's *The Book of the Dead,* Hancock's *The Message of the Sphynx,* and Budge's *Egyptian Magic.*

"Thanks. You really know your stuff. I'm Pete Stevenson; what's your name?"

"Hi Pete, I'm Louise Woodruff, and I'm pleased to meet you."

"Do you come here often?" Pete asked, instantly feeling like an idiot.

Louise smiled. "Is that a new pickup line for libraries?"

Pete laughed, nervously. He was so ill-at-ease that he couldn't even enjoy this nice lady.

After a brief pause Louise added, "Why, yes I do. I teach history and this place seems to help me in what I do."

As he puts his newly acquired library books in his backpack, he asked Louise, "Have you borrowed any good books lately?"

"That's a good one, Pete. I need to remember that one."

"Louise, you want to grab a coffee with me in exchange for your help?"

She seemed delighted to find a fellow history buff, and they headed to the local coffee house to get better acquainted.

After getting a couple coffees, they grabbed a booth to talk and Louise began.

"So, Pete, what's with the ancient history books? You don't seem like the type of guy that does this often."

Pete shrugged. "What type of guy is that?"

"You seem to be on a mission, not just doing research. Looking for something in particular. Kinda have that Type A going on."

"You are very observant, Louise, and I am an engineer researching Egyptian culture as a hobby. The pyramids seem to be vault-like in terms of historical and cultural significance. It's a nice balance and helps me to ratchet down from a very severe travel schedule."

As their conversation continued, Pete saw that he had a level of comfort with Louise that had been missing in most, if not all, of his social dalliances. He was relieved. He thought it was fate that brought them together.

Louise appreciated the timing of their meeting and was also thinking that their meeting was fate. She was a very confident and direct-talking person and came across as strong and determined.

Rather tall, with dark hair and steel-blue eyes, she was an intimidating presence with tons of self-confidence.

"You are an easy person to talk to, Pete. You seem like a nice guy with an interest in history that I can certainly relate to."

Pete thought, *No one ever said I was an easy person to talk to.*

"Thank you, Louise, and I find you easy to talk to as well."

Pete thought, "What's wrong with this picture."

He quickly summed it up. "Nothing."

◆ ◆ ◆

Pete and Louise hit it off and began dating. On one particular date, they were at the beach and feeling young and vibrant.

There was a physical attraction to one another growing and their beach routine had become long walks, hand-in-hand, solving all the world's problems.

They enjoyed the little things, like sand in their toes, feeding the sea gulls and watching sand crabs go in and out of their beach-hole homes. Beach time raced by quickly as they enjoyed each other's company.

Their damp towels revealed beautiful surfing, and the wind blowing through the car's windows as they drove home seemed to resonate the perfect ending to a perfect day.

They developed a good relationship, and both recognized that their personalities were well matched. Over a bottle of Chardonnay one night, Pete remarked, "I love history and as a teacher, you constantly remind me why."

"And why is that," Louise asked.

"We all need a strong sense of it, for if we don't honor our history and historical failures, we are bound to repeat them."

Having that persistent and intense personality, she was just the kind of woman Pete needed to push his relentless drive and constant restlessness to the next level. Pete realized that this was the exact type of person he needed in his life.

In fact, Pete recalled that it was Louise that recognized his drive, intellect, and passion for study of the unknown, especially ancient alien theory. One day, after a great weekend at one of their favorite beaches, Pete remembered her challenge to him.

"You have a wealth of knowledge and great teaching skills and should write and lecture."

"Thanks, Louise, for that vote of confidence, but I'd prefer to spend my free time traveling to these faraway places and researching, rather than teaching. But I do like the idea of writing."

"For heaven's sake Pete, you can do both. Just prioritize."

Shortly thereafter, Pete began writing about the things he knew and the research he had been doing and would continue to do. After writing three business and subject matter self-help books, Pete set his sights on a more aggressive topic.

"I have an idea for my next book."

Louise was pleased. "And what might that be?"

"Well, I have a theory myself that covers two alien schools of thought that have not been covered that much."

Louise looks up, not knowing what to expect. "And, so?"

"Well, my research to date and gut feeling has me thinking of two distinct perspectives that many people writing about the topic today don't address."

"Yes," Louise says cautiously.

"I strongly believe that aliens visiting this planet are from the future, not from the past. And, I think that we have had, and may still have, evil aliens living amongst us."

"Oh my!" Louise adds with a grin.

Pete said to himself... **"I'm going to prove it!"**

27

PETE

So, Pete dove into his latest alien project and wrote a short paperback book on his theory, combined with loosely-based alien documentation and stories, *Are Evil Aliens Amongst Us?* in the form of a question, not a statement, to avoid immediately pushback.

It was not well received. It actually went from not well received to practically ignored. Pete explained the negative feedback as the book was not being nice or friendly or sexy enough for the masses to accept.

Except for his family, almost everyone else had a thumbs down on the book. Pressing on, he attended the upcoming semi-annual Alien Conventions and got a chance to present his theory and book and gave a lecture on the basis of his thoughts and quasi-facts.

A small group, for convention standards, attended Pete's lecture. Of the twelve people that showed up, four remained for the Q&A to follow. Pete introduced himself to the four and they responded. He thought he recognized one of the attendees.

"Hi Pete, I'm Corey and I dabble in archeology" Corey was a middle-aged and chubby guy in a corduroy jacket and faded jeans. Fashion was not his thing.

"And I'm Thomas Derrick and, like you, I'm an engineer with a curiosity of the cosmos." Thomas was about Pete's height with a nice smile and dressed in a short-sleeved white shirt with a pocket protector.

Then, the lone female added, "Hi Pete, it's me, Elizabeth Downing. We met at your weather conference a few years back."

"Hi Elizabeth, of course I remember you. Great to see you again."

As she gave Pete a very long hug, she said, "You can call me Beth. As you may recall, I have always been fascinated with ancient Native American creation mythology.

"But I am also extremely interested in UFO's and alien abductions. Let me add that I truly believe that your instincts and commitment to these perspectives are timely and need to be looked into."

The last time Pete saw Beth at the weather conference, she was wearing a brightly colored sarong. This time she was dressed more like Farm-aid, with overalls and a flannel shirt. She was carrying a very expensive-looking computer bag.

"Well, thanks to all of you for your support," Pete added. Seeing one more person still remaining in the room, a tall thin guy dressed in black and smoking a cigarette, Pete asked, "And your name is?"

"John Smith."

Pete and his remaining four likely adventurers then headed off to dinner and the opportunity to get better acquainted. Pete was pleased that his old acquaintance Beth came to his talk. If nothing else, she gave a little credence to his beliefs and he was happy to see her.

Conducting the tried-and-true 360-degree interview, it appeared to Pete that this could be a team that could work in tandem on the search for alien artifacts and alien presence.

Without being too self-assured, he believed that this small group seemed interested, at least for now, in the pursuit of all things alien.

"Okay, guys. Show of hands. All in, at least for now?"

After getting some very basic buy-in from the four, Pete pulled out his to-do list for what he considered future study.

With concurrence from the group, they divided the areas for research and adjourned for the night, only to plan to meet in another month to compare notes and, hopefully, develop a path forward.

This small group of four people was now the ad hoc team of Pete's that would research better, quicker, and with more detail. Corey, Thomas, and Beth had the aliens of the future mostly on their radar screens, while Mr. Smith preferred the evil alien slant.

Without a doubt, the momentum that Pete had working before that alien convention had now exponentially soared. He felt re-energized now that he was not alone in his thinking.

Pete thought that Louise was truly inspirational for him and he gave her credit for seeing something in himself that even he did not see. Excited, he called Louise.

"Hi Louise, it's me with a quick update from the conference."

"Okay, so you sold so many books, we can retire and live in Tahiti now. I knew something good would happen."

"Well, the retirement plans need to be put off for now, but the prospects are good."

Turning off the TV, Louise says, "I'm listening,"

"I've recruited four people who believe in my convictions, and we are going forward as a team to see what we can discover,"

"So, how will that help us retire early?"

"When we prove the existence of aliens and become famous, we will be so important that we can write our own ticket."

Louise sighs and responds, "Tickets, sure. I'll start buying lottery tickets while we wait."

"Okay, love you Honey."

"Love you Pete,"

Pete ends the call and was feeling quite confident. However, part of him felt that Louise was a bit underwhelmed, maybe even a little disappointed.

When he called Louise the next day, he discovered that Louise was extremely skeptical and not at all on board with Pete's venture and his growing confidence.

Even his new-found friends had not been vetted and that left Louise uneasy. Pete knew she was not happy and it bothered him.

✦ ✦ ✦

Pete decided to pull the group together for an impromptu strategy session. They held the first of many video conferences as a team.

Pete began. "We need to discuss resources, budgets, and specific areas that each of us are interested in. We all have day jobs so we need to be diligent about how we spend our time and money.

"If you can lay out your action plans for the rest of the year, I'll put together a team budget, and, if possible, I will do a 50/50 expense match for now with funds that I have saved."

Beth spoke first. "I'll set up the schedules and resources required on a spreadsheet."

Corey replied, "I'll do some basic cost versus benefit tables for the artifacts and hard objects that we will try to pursue."

Thomas thought for a moment and responded, "I'll construct a tracking and logistics model that will give an instant read on the what, where, and how of our endeavors.

Mr. Smith added, "I'll look at any correlation between the calamities of the past and present with any unexplained data that could be the result of the evil side of alien involvement."

With the exception of Mr. Smith's somewhat contrary contribution, Pete was pleased. For reasons that seemed strange to the group for that early work timetable, Pete had decided on how to keep their work safe and secure, given they would be navigating uncharted research territory.

But that wasn't how he explained it.

"One more thing, guys. I want the five of us to take on nicknames or codes to avoid personal harassment and ridicule."

It was Pete's idea and the somewhat puzzled group just went along.

Corey would be "*stones.*" Thomas was "*chariot.*" Beth was the famous Indiana guide to Lewis and Clark, "*Sacagawea.*" Mr. Smith didn't buy into the nickname thing, so the team, noticing his chain-smoking habit, just called him "*smoke.*" Pete took "*Orion*" as his nickname.

Pete made a request of the team before they broke up. "Now, for each of your cell phones, simply use the nickname as the code for your number, starting now."

The group agreed, but Pete knew that they all thought it was a bit over-the-top.

John Smith was obviously an alias in Pete's mind, but at the moment, it really didn't matter.

He would give *smoke* the benefit of the doubt for the time being. Pete wasn't in the vetting business and had many more priorities to deal with than some guy's name.

Smith was a mysterious and strange man, average height and slight build, and usually would wear a black suit and black tie. His drawn facial features in an evening light gave off a macabre look.

Given the trust that Pete had put in the hands of his small team, it was difficult for Pete to initially trust and confide in Smith.

Pete was worried that Smith had a separate agenda, but in conversation with the other team members, they moved on.

Pete even thought that the way Smith smoked incessantly was a filthy habit and made him appear unprofessional. He always had an opinion and at one team meeting he simply asked Smith a direct question.

"We are a team of five people. That means you are twenty percent of our resources and need to provide twenty percent towards our results. If at any time, that doesn't work for you, I need to know. Understand?"

"Yes, Pete, I do. Won't be a problem."

Pete heard the words, but was in no way convinced that Mr. Smith was being truthful and honest. There didn't seem to be good chemistry between them.

Only time would tell…

28
SMOKE

John Smith worked for the CIA for many years, and his real name was Ralph Sandusky. His poor decision-making and shady dealings with a variety of influential people throughout the world got him into trouble.

After a series of demotions, Sandusky was fired in 1998. With his true identity ruined, he contacted an associate in Europe who was able to get him a new identity along with new passport, etc.

The name John Smith was remarkably plain, almost to the degree of being conspicuous. Nonetheless, he went by John Smith. To say that his judgement was often flawed would be an understatement.

One of Smith's rather vile and criminal contacts from his early 90's CIA days was an arms dealer, who was referred to in communication with Smith, as Bud, and a man whose criminal activity was heavily financed by the drug trade.

Bud lived in the U.S., did most of his business in Europe, The Middle East, and Asia, and had his hand in a very lucrative drug cartel in Central America.

Smith contacted Bud within months of getting fired by the CIA, once he had his new John Smith documents in hand. Smith knew that Bud had ties to a splintered terrorist group in the Middle East that was still connected to ex-ISIS leaders.

They had a face-to-face meeting in Chicago to see what, if anything, they could do together. Meeting in a run-down bar near the TPG Chicago Dry Dock, Smith began the conversation.

"Thanks for meeting me. You sure picked a dingy place to conduct business."

"I don't know, Ralph, it seems to suit you. What the hell do you want?"

"You wouldn't be here if you didn't know already. I have sources that tell me you are deeply involved with some nasty people linked to an al Qaeda splinter group that have an agenda that smacks of terror and disruption."

"You know, for a smart guy, you're a real dumb ass. What if I did?"

Smith replied, "Well I have nothing to lose and have a lot of contacts that could open doors for you."

"And in return?"

"Money."

Following dig after dig during that meeting, Smith and Bud became business partners. It was totally out of mutual need and greed and they did not trust each other.

✦ ✦ ✦

Smith later learned that Bud was deeply involved in a major terrorist group who had a mission to destroy democratic institutions and ideals worldwide.

Smith, being ex-CIA and a true bottom-feeder, became the provider of key intelligence to Bud, who then became a seated member of the all-powerful terrorist group eventually known in the early 2000's as the *New World Order*.

For several years Smith played the role of the good soldier and it did pay huge dividends. Smith became the enabler for Bud to infiltrate drugs and illegal arms cartels and fortify the now-growing terrorist group, the *New World Order*.

Smith was paid handsomely for his work and all was well with this arrangement. Bud still did not trust Smith, but Smith did prove his loyalty.

Smith was summoned to meet this group for the first time. He was asked to attend their meeting in 2014 in Singapore that involved the group's need for intelligence gathering. Smith entered their meeting room and recognized several of the twelve seated members.

A few of the members tried to hide their identities, but to no avail. There was no turning back for anyone now and no individual privacy going forward. You can't un-see…

The group leader, referred to as Scorpio, was a mob boss stereotype if ever there was one. Right out of central casting, this despicable man had all the polish of a rusty bucket left out in the rain. When he stood, everyone stood. When he sat, everyone sat. And no one talked until given his go ahead.

Many things were unpleasantly obvious in his appearance and demeanor, but the fact that he was a chain-smoking cigar person was disgusting to his associates.

The meeting had been underway for nearly two hours before the need for Smith's presence became obvious.

Scorpio looked directly at Smith and asked Smith to comment on a story that was circulating. With Bud listening as well, Scorpio had a question that sounded like an order.

"Smith, we understand that a certain man, a former military data researcher, has been doing investigations into ancient alien artifacts."

"And why is that important to you? Many of these kooks are out there wasting their money and time, and for what?"

"Shut up, Smith, I'll ask the questions. This alien stuff could be a front for his meddling in our business. Need to find out what he knows about us, if anything at all. Our current sources aren't close enough to him and what he is doing."

Obviously annoyed with Smith, he continued.

"And this guy has two reasons to get our attention. First, his military experience a few years ago, among other things, enabled him to get in on the periphery of certain gang-led terrorist groups in the U.S. and abroad. ·

"We know that the people in his area of expertise spent significant time looking into splinter terrorist groups in the Middle East."

Bud added, "We don't know how deeply he was involved, but it could become a problem for us if that info were to get into the hands of law enforcement authorities who would start asking questions and possibly connect us to one or more of those people or cells."

Scorpio went on, "Second, he just published a book on evil aliens that we don't know is a ruse or his pathetic attempt to gain fame. This damn book is so odd, we need to look into it.

"He is claiming that evil aliens are the reason for many worldwide problems today. If that is what this idiot actually believes, we are done.

"But what if he and his military pals are just using this ploy to get into our paper trails? We really need to find out his source of info and put this crap to bed."

"You're paranoid," Smith adds.

Obviously agitated, Scorpio replies, "I didn't ask for your damn opinion, Smith."

"Okay, I'll get you what you need," Smith responded.

"Damn straight, you will," Bud added.

"His book is *Are Evil Aliens Amongst Us* and his name is Pete Stevenson. You need to get onto his team and into his head. That'll be all."

Smith was escorted out of the meeting and thought what an odd request. He had never heard of Pete Stevenson. He immediately got on the Internet to research Pete Stevenson and was surprised that this guy was totally off the radar.

As Smith was waiting for his cab to return to his hotel, the light bulb went on.

Yes, he could see how the innocent investigation of evil aliens could be used to track the origins of terrorist attacks and civilian disruption… which was that group's M.O.

As the door closed behind Smith, Scorpio turned his head and said, "So, Bud, do you trust that guy?"

"Hell no. But it really doesn't matter. He's a mule and has no idea what we're doing and I'm his only point of contact.

For now, I'll keep tabs on him and if he gets to become a problem, I'll take care of it."

Scorpio added, "Damn right you will.

"He's your responsibility and everything is riding on this mission."

29
SMOKE

With that the meeting concluded, the group moved into a secure conference room that resembled a military War Room. There were the same twelve people seated around an oblong conference table with the group leader Scorpio at one end and Bud at the other.

With the exception of two young foreigners, the group was comprised of older white men and definitely gave off an aura of wealth and entitlement.

There were several flat-screen TVs and computer monitors, all up and running. One specific wide-screen had a two-dimensional world map.

Scorpio called the meeting to order and controlled the agenda.

"Let's have a money report."

A tall, thin man with a tailored blue suit and an obvious arrogant manner stated, "We now have close to $6 billion in liquid assets. I see another $500 million by the end of this month coming from blood antiquities."

"Great. How is that pie made up?"

"About twenty-five per cent is from arms sales, about twenty-five percent from our slave trade, and about fifty per cent from drugs and kick-backs, mostly from Central America. The money laundering today is the best it's ever been."

Scorpio asked, "And our relationship with those in command?"

"The civilians are not a problem at all. The military is always a concern, but we still have all the leverage."

"Good. Now the weapons and deployment report."

A former elite military ops guy with strong features, an equally strong voice and wearing an aviator jacket responded. This was a chiseled guy who could likely take on anyone in the room.

"We have an arsenal now that is about sixty per cent of what is needed to complete the scope and scale of our global plan. Deployment is in an aggressive roll-out phase and all the stealth-like procedures are in place.

"Key launch sites are still North Korea and the Middle East."

"That is a great update and if you need anything at all, you let us know."

"Will do."

"Okay, the next issue is our communication disruption initiative and total IT hacking progress.

"You notice that we have two additions to the table. May I introduce Sergei and Vlad, our newest and most interesting new members."

With that mention, the two young computer geeks acknowledged the leader's intro.

"Before you ask about vetting, I will throw this out.

"Recalling the disruption in Houston two months ago that totally blacked out the city and brought all business to a halt, and the port at Galveston and all that shipping damage? These guys made that mess. It was test number one and they passed.

"And, the recent total electronic collapse of the financial sectors in Charlotte last week was also their work. Test number two. So, they are well vetted. I strongly believe this emerging electronic technology is becoming very powerful. One day, whoever controls this core capability will be able to turn out the lights throughout the world."

A visibly agitated man with arms folded then asked, "What's the status of finding your guru that understands robot or meta-human technology? This is supposed to be the last piece of our puzzle and a necessary skill that is missing."

"Yeah, it is. And I've located probably the best in the field, but it's a woman, so I need to keep looking. Don't want a damn woman."

After nearly four hours of meeting the group adjourned. As they were leaving the conference room, Vlad asked Bud a simple question.

"What's in that gold case that the big guy has in front of him?"

"Teeth. Assorted teeth. Don't even ask."

30

PETE

So, over the course of the next few years, this tight-knit group traveled, researched, and documented thousands of leads and findings. Pete leveraged the sale of his business books and speaking gigs to offset much of the team's expenses.

Corey creatively obtained a grant from a museum consortium and parlayed much of those funds into the team's costs as well.

Hundreds of interviews were conducted with people close to the alien action, or so said those selected interviewees. In an almost predictable fashion, many substantial interviews, photos, and documentation gathering came from extremely credible witnesses on their death beds or in elder care hospices. Many in those circumstances saw little need to keep their information a secret any longer.

Physical artifacts were gathered, some not in a particularly legal capacity. "Quid pro quo" was alive and well in alien research, and everything had its price. Those with the most interest to researchers were called out-of-place artifacts, and Pete's team had several.

The Antikythera Mechanism was a bronze-like artifact found in a Greek shipwreck in 1900. Pete bartered with the Museum of Athens and got it in exchange for some semi-precious gems that were a lot more colorful than an ugly lump of bronze.

Through his research, Pete was convinced that this artifact was extremely valuable. About two years after Pete took possession of the device, it was determined that this mechanism had verifiable workings for various bodies of our solar system and could accurately be described as the world's first computer.

Several photographs of petroglyphs and hieroglyphs were gathered from respectable sources in exchange for fake I.D.'s. One from Val Camonica, Italy, strongly resembled current astronauts. One from Egypt depicted alien ships, both of the helicopter and space ship recognized today.

A Japanese figurine from 1000–500 BCE was obtained through curator extortion, thanks to John Smith. It is the closest artifact known to researchers that mirrors all the drawings and etchings of alien astronauts.

The Piri Reis map was a world map compiled in 1513 that was constructed by synthesizing many other maps. It showed the coastline of Brazil and correctly showed the pre-glacial coastline of Antarctica, a continent that wasn't discovered until three centuries later.

The map was property of the government's Library in Istanbul, Turkey, and was not open to the public for viewing.

Pete recalled getting a particular call from Beth. They had been talking about that unique Piri Reis map for some time.

"Hey Pete, Beth."

Always enjoying his talks with Beth. He answered. "Hi Beth. Again, nice to talk. Whatcha got?"

"Well, I know a guy that knows a guy…"

"Come on, Beth, I'm not getting any younger."

Chuckling, Beth adds. "Sorry, but I'm excited. I have two good pieces on news."

"Hold on Beth while I get a cold Molson."

"Ah come on, Pete. Not getting any younger?"

They both laughed with each other as they often did.

Getting back to the phone, Pete said "Shoot."

I have a contact in security at Istanbul's government Library that can get us into the vault that houses the Piri Reis map."

"Seriously? That's huge. But I don't want to see it. I want it!"

"Hold your horses, big guy. I also have Juan in my debt and he is a master forger."

Getting excited, Pete says, "Beth, I like where this is going."

"Thought you would. Juan's gonna get in and photograph the original in every detail and get us a duplicate that will be hard to tell from the original. So, most importantly, we will have all the requisite info for building our alien presence case and if we have to, promote it as the original."

"Brilliant, Beth, absolutely brilliant."

"Thanks, Pete. I should have this piece in less than a month."

As Pete ended the call, he thought to himself how fortunate he was to have his constantly unpredictable partner Beth. He continued his documentation with two more incredible puzzle pieces.

The Dropa Stones were described by UFOlogists as stone disks going back 12,000 years and were rumored to contain information about a crashed alien spaceship in China.

Totaling about 700 discs, they were reported to have hieroglyph-like markings in their grooves that could only be seen with electronic microscopes. In addition to fifteen of these discs, Pete had obtained the 1962 journal, passed down from generations, explaining the stones.

The Dropa people, allegedly, came from another planet, crashed on Earth, and were unable to fix their craft. A peaceful people, they were hunted down by locals and killed. Pete had obtained only two of the Dropa Stones, to anyone's knowledge.

The Nazca Lines were a group of very large geoglyphs formed by soil depressions in the Nazca Desert of southern Peru. They were created around 500 BCE and the total length of all lines was over 800 miles.

They depicted forms of animals, plants, and obvious geometric patterns. The most astonishing fact was the length and straight-line perfection similar to today's modern landing strips. These patterns were not visible from the ground, only from the air.

Pete took a hot-air balloon up about 4,500 feet before he could see the lines were synchronized and captured those flights in photos. The result was that the design of these incredible lines had to be made at a minimum of 4,500 feet of altitude.

The team now believed that they were starting to build a fundamental case to support their alien presence theories and hoped to be able to present their findings sometime in the future.

They fully realized, though, that extraordinary claims required extraordinary evidence, and there would be much to do to solidify their case.

They needed some unbiased evidence or accounts to drive home their theories.

It came!

31

PETE

Three related and very relevant incidents occurred in the U.S. during the height of ancient alien theory or awareness over the course of 30 years. They demonstrated the length and breadth that scientists, engineers, and astrophysics had pursued the unknown using all of the technology available.

Given the exponential development of technology and space exploration, and the surprising number of scientists and researchers that were changing age-old thinking about extraterrestrial presence, the gap between myth and reality was closing at a great rate of speed.

It was 1984, and with US Government support, the *Search for Extraterrestrial Intelligence* (SETI) was formed. It was staffed with some of the most renowned scientists and astrophysicists on the planet, as well as military personnel selected with special skills.

Pete was just that kind of special skills addition. His vast engineering experience and counter-intelligence background was put to work immediately. He was brought on as a consultant, largely to screen actual data from hacked or manipulated data, a problem growing larger in the digital age.

Among other contributions, they developed the largest radio telescope in the world, from the Green Bank Observatory in West Virginia. Nearly 600 feet tall, it had a receiving mirror the size of two football fields. It literally could "hear" radio signals emitting from across the galaxy, up to an *amazing 3 billion light years away!*

The audio reception strength was directly correlated to its targeted sources. In other words, the telescope would aim at different galactic targets and not just one general trajectory. Pete was convinced that a response from space was going to be when, not if.

✦ ✦ ✦

SETI was formed in 1985, but another interesting research body came to Pete's attention. In 2000, in San Francisco, another organization had formed with a different mission. Leveraging his alliance with SETI, Pete was able to get his foot into the door of another powerful and, for Pete, timely agency.

This entity was called *Messaging Extraterrestrial Intelligence*, or METI. Their role was not to listen, but to literally engage with any alien lifeforms via sophisticated signaling. Their technology also used extremely high-level radio signals, meant to navigate through the vastness of space in as small a path as possible, so interference would be unlikely.

METI found a rather unique star, the Luyten's Star, as a potential inhabitable world and set its sight on that star. In October, 2002, a radio signal was launched toward the Luyten's Star, with its arrival about 12.4 light years away. Given that light travels in a vacuum at about 186,000 miles per second, any response back from Luyten's Star would not make it to earth until 2024.

Faith and patience were a necessary attribute for these pioneers, and they were more than willing to wait it out. Pete put 2024 on his schedule, both literally and in his mind.

Scientists at METI met to gain a consensus of next steps. They decided to send out an all-purpose message. With its radio signals focused on counting, telling time, using a binary code, and with creative melodies, it was aligned to a musical scale. In simple words, the message reflected earth's earliest melodies with a pattern to encode same. It had often been said that music could be or would be, the universal language. METI set out to see with nothing more than a gut feeling that this would produce results.

Many renowned scientists and scholars, including the late Stephen Hawking, said that it would be a mistake to seek out extraterrestrial life, with so many unknowns. If earth was less technologically evolved, for example, than a contacted lifeform, we would likely face annihilation.

If you just looked at the history of our world, nearly every time two societies or cultures clashed, wars happened, and the strong prevailed. That was not opinion; it was irrefutable fact.

One such example was used many times in Pete's travels, and he referred to it often in his speaking gigs. He would tell his audience that when the British colonized America it had to assimilate with tribes of Native American Indians wherever expansion took them.

He would ask his audience, "How did that work out for the American Indians?"

✦ ✦ ✦

In 2012, Pete was at a meeting at the Green Bank Observatory in West Virginia discussing some anomalies with three of the programmers, when Bill Jameson, the group's deputy director, stumbled into the room, face as white as bone, running his fingers through his thinning gray hair. "S-s-s-something weird, very weird!" he blurted out.

A *Fast Radio Burst* (FRB) was received, numbered FRB 121102. What made this remarkable was the fact that it kept repeating. In other words, regular FRB's happened hundreds of times each week, but they were nothing more than terrestrial noise, extremely random and without any pattern.

This one was being sent with a purpose. It had an intentional pattern of repeating its signature burst again and again. It was like the source was sending out a Morse Code-like message that repeated itself over and over.

To illustrate the extreme magnitude of this event, each burst covered a millisecond and had the source power in that millisecond equal to the amount of energy that the sun creates in one year.

Yes, it was a scientific first, and yes, it was kept quiet by the agency, for fear of panic. To prove its authenticity, the origin of the burst would be changed for a period of time, and then moved back to the original coordinates of the burst. Again, the repeating burst would return.

Pete convened the project team with the startling evidence that was coming into the observatory. Amongst dozens of white shirt and dark tie scientists, there was Pete in his flannel shirt and flight jacket.

When the scientists completed their study of that remarkable burst, they came up with a stunning coincidence. The repeating sequence of those bursts was exactly correlated in times, thrusts, and velocities to the Space Shuttle's booster separation, which would emit the same repetitive sequence. This was an "aha" moment for Pete.

Pete immediately concluded that those pulses were clear indications that their purpose was likely to propel a spacecraft through space. He was convinced that our world was now looking at the vastness of planet to solar system to galaxy to universe, and *3 billion light years away was now logical.*

Shortly thereafter, this body of research scientists were relocated to Berkeley, California, which became the center of the known universe for burst events and a jumping-off point to the unknown.

Although all results were cloaked in secrecy and placed in highly confidential files, Pete had made several illegal copies as part of his venture and knew he was breaking the law, but in his mind the end justified the means.

Pete was so excited about SETI and METI that he told Mike about these entities in great detail. On Pete's Bucket List was that he and Mike could experience that response back to Earth in 2024 together.

What a great expectation that would be.

Pete knew that 2024 would absolutely happen as expected.

32

PETE

In the midst of the chaos and seriousness of all that was happening, Pete went to his cabin in the mountains and had his usual yearly sabbatical to cleanse the soul and mediate. This was his much-needed time to reflect and to plan.

It was during this cabin visit that Pete thought back to a lovely and gentle time many years ago. Pulling out a photo of Louise and himself, he was thinking what a lucky guy he was and how he must not take his life with her for granted.

After dating Louise for about fifteen months, and reflecting on the chaos and stress of his work and alien preoccupation, Pete decided to do something for himself and Louise. He made a reservation at a restaurant that both Louise and he enjoyed, under the guise of an unofficial anniversary of their library meeting.

Louise, of course, was impressed and bought in immediately. As they dressed for dinner, Pete came out of the bedroom with a suit and tie.

"Whoa, Pete, I never see you dressed like that unless it's a wedding or a funeral. I gotta admit, though, you look really snazzy in that blue suit."

"Thanks, this is a special night and I just want it to stay special."

"In that case, I'm gonna wear Mom's favorite necklace and put a different dress on. Be right back." Pete was feeling pretty smug.

As they drove to the restaurant, Pete was unusually quiet and reserved.

Louise asked, "What's the matter? Is everything okay?"

"Of course, just happy to be spending this particular night with you and thinking about when we met and how it was a moment in my life for which I am very grateful."

Pete put his hand on Louise's and she sighed, very happy.

They arrived at the restaurant and Pete confirmed the special table he had reserved in the corner of the restaurant near the fireplace.

"Well Pete, this was very nice of you to go to this trouble for our dating anniversary."

Pete smiled and diverted Louise's attention to the fireplace as he secretly gave a note to the waiter. He nervously adjusted his tie as they looked over the menu. Pete ordered a Scotch Rocks.

"I'll just have a water," Louise told the waiter.

"Nonsense, this is a special occasion. Please bring the lady a Cosmo."

"Whoa, that works for me," Louise returned.

Then, as dinner concluded and the time for dessert came, Pete was getting excited. He excused himself and left the table nervously.

"Be right back."

Louise was truly enjoying the evening and was so pleased that Pete went to such lengths to celebrate it, his odd behavior not with-standing.

Pete returned and they looked at the dessert menu. "I've ordered tonight's dessert for us, something special, okay?"

"Of course."

At that moment, a restaurant staff member dressed in an alien costume slowly approached the table. He was all gray, tall, lanky, and with enormous heeled boots and a head that was straight out of a "B" science fiction movie.

Louise was initially surprised and then laughed at the alien confronting her. "So, one of your friends, eh?"

At that moment, the alien presented the couple with an apparent novelty dessert, a cake and ice cream spaceship creation. Louise found this premeditated episode very funny and laughed in approval.

Pete took the spaceship dessert, paused for a moment, and then removed the top of the ship, revealing a black box inside and handed the box to Louise. "Louise, will you make me the happiest guy in the solar system and marry me?"

Pausing for a moment, she replied, "Yes, of course. You nutty guy." Louise cried and jumped up and gave Pete a huge hug.

Pete and Louise were married shortly thereafter, in a small wedding with only close friends in attendance. They had three children, the oldest was son Mike, who was very much a chip off the old block, got a wrestling scholarship, and studied engineering, physics, and mathematics. Later in his career, he received an MBA and finally obtained a PhD in Operations Research, becoming an attractive asset to any and all ventures that he undertook.

Mike's brother David was a financial advisor and his sister, Joan, became a second-grade teacher. Good, solid and respectable careers, for sure. Stable and conservative were their attributes.

Mike wasn't the type of person that the family considered "conservative."

33

MIKE

Mike was also a restless soul who didn't seem to be happy or comfortable in any established working environment. After a series of fits and starts, Mike found a career in nuclear science research especially rewarding.

He had also gained a reputation as a problem solver and his tag line could have literally been, "if it can't be done, let Mike do it!" Pete was very proud of Mike.

Mike was always close to his siblings and as the eldest tried to be a mentor and strong supporter of all of their endeavors. He was thankful that they had taken more conventional career paths, given his perspective of his own stressful career.

David got his finance degree and became owner of several investment franchises and a rather astute financial whiz. After many investment successes, Pete convinced him to become the family financial planner and that role was much appreciated by all.

Mike got great satisfaction for his brother helping the family with critical day-to-day financial decisions.

Joan took after Mom and, realizing that trait, Pete spent a great deal of time counseling and guiding Joan in her career path. She became a grade school teacher and a strong presence in the volunteer community.

Mike loved the charitable work that she did and helped in any way he could.

Pete and Louise were very proud parents and happy with how well adjusted the family had become, even with Mike's pursuit of alien adventures, much like his dad. The family remained close and all of them especially liked the driving trips they made across the U.S.

Unfortunately, though, with his demanding business agenda and growing interest in ancient alien presence, Mike missed many family get-togethers due to his constant travel.

Mike was well aware of the sad-but-true line that was used over and over again by the family… well, that's Mike being Mike.

One of the topics that had a great deal of interest for Mike, and a topic that he and his dad did discuss, was the extensive Egyptian pyramid fields and the belief that the nearly 3500 pyramids, stone monuments, temples, cathedrals, and elaborate stone carvings throughout the world were built on one huge world grid that had scientists and archeologists baffled.

It was 1994 and Mike took a three-month sabbatical from work to travel and study this World Grid phenomenon, and it took him to Central America, Africa, the Middle East, and even into Scandinavia.

The stone monuments resembling pyramids and the henges in Scandinavia were particularly odd and held Mike's curiosity. Although Pete had done much of this initial spade work before, Mike's adage was *"Don't assume; verify."*

Setting up the trip, Mike spent several days consolidating the materials that Pete had sent him, in addition to those items that Mike had accrued of his own making. From his cluttered desk in the book-filled den, Mike sat down to call his dad with his intentions.

"Well, you finally got me hooked on your alien hobby and I need a brief respite from my daily grind. I'm going to take a couple months off to see for myself all the stuff you'd been talking about."

"Great, maybe I can meet you somewhere during your adventure."

"No Dad, I want to go alone and also use the trip for some introspection."

"Okay, I guess. I totally understand. At least let me send you some recommendations for stops and a couple pyramid and Stonehenge landmarks to look at that are especially cool. Would you prefer that I email my files to you or send you a flash drive?"

"Email? Seriously?"

"I'm just gonna send you a flash drive. File security, ya know."

"That would be terrific."

They hung up.

Following the arrival of the flash drive, Mike and his mom had several long discussions about the need for this trip and of the consequences of taking a couple of months off.

One particular episode dealt with Louise losing patience that her son was taking after Pete.

"I was okay with this alien stuff being a curiosity or hobby or side bar to give you a break from the daily job. But it's now becoming way too extensive."

Sensing her pushback, "But Mom…"

"The expense, and time commitment, not to mention the danger involved, is too much for me to accept right now. You have family responsibilities and a young daughter and those should be a priority now."

"I understand your concern. Christine and I have discussed this in great length and she is supporting me."

"What about the cost, Mike?"

"Mom, I have been saving money from speaking gigs and advisory work for whatever I felt was something down the road I wanted or would like to do. This is what I want to do and the timing right now is good."

Louise was quiet.

"I'm so sorry that you feel this way, but I promise that this trip will answer some much-anticipated questions and will not lead to more trips. And, if you absolutely don't want me to go, I won't go."

Mike knew that his mom would not object, given Mike's sound judgement and solid decision-making history. At least he hoped she wouldn't mind. He was going regardless.

"Fine, have it your way. Just like your father. Be safe and keep the family informed."

Mike won this battle, but he was not sure about the war…

Mike's worldview would get turned upside down.

34

MIKE

What Mike found in his travels was truly startling and was becoming a direct opposite viewpoint to what Louise had so adamantly criticized Mike on earlier.

Following extensive travel to Europe, particularly Denmark, Sweden, England, and the Middle East, Mike headed to Central America and finally to Egypt.

Stopping his rented Jeep at the apex of the Egyptian pyramids, Mike got out and realized he was at the heart of all things Pete and reflected in the moment. He rolled out a map of the world on the hood of the Jeep and used a marker to lay out the grid of all the places he had visited.

Gazing at the Pyramid of Djoser, the oldest in ancient Egypt and the one that was built as a tomb for the Pharaoh Djoser, Mike was aware that 138 identified pyramids made up this incredible landscape.

Looking back at his map, it was startling to see how similar the henge in Denmark was to the ones in England and how the pyramid he visited in Central America was perfectly aligned with the ones here in Egypt.

At that time Mike referred to his dad's anthropology notes about the Anasazi and the alignment of some of the major ruins with Central America ruins and their road layouts. Mike's strong engineering and analytic background enabled him to notice a recurring pattern. Where extraterrestrial mythology prevailed, the major global structures found and studied throughout history were built on a worldwide geometric pattern.

He folded his map, got back into the Jeep, and had a sense of significant accomplishment as he drove back to his hotel.

Using the latest A.I. technology available, Mike discovered the time-documented overlays to that pattern. Using a confidential Cloud that Sara and he had developed, he then integrated the hard data into computer models that the two of them had been developing.

Using simulations similar to Google Earth, when he mapped his baseline points, he noticed these patterns, and when he extrapolated selected data, the results become even clearer and unmistakable.

That grid had twelve connecting nodes, each equidistant from one another, same latitude and longitude, in a soccer ball-type shape equaling twenty equilateral triangles. Mike discovered that all major structures throughout the world fell directly on these grid lines.

It was why ancient alien theorists suggested that these grid lines represented space, navigation, refueling, and cargo drop flight plans, or dimensional doorways from the universe to Earth.

Also, those UFO sightings with the highest degree of believability showed that the flight pattern of the UFO's aligned perfectly with the world grid pattern. Could this literally be Space Station Earth?

Adding to the mystery were actual incidents where planes and ships had encountered documented magnetic anomalies, compass malfunctions, and stories of people disappearing and reappearing, all at these twelve nodes along the World Grid.

At these twelve points, which include The Bermuda Triangle and the North and South Pole, there had been noted *"time slips"* where people arrive much too early or much too late at their destination. In other words, time itself moved backward or forward very quickly for these souls.

Mike had obtained verifiable evidence that on several occasions over the history of recent civilizations, again precisely on those twelve nodes, the crew and passengers of ships disappeared and never were found again.

The Bermuda Triangle not only had many noted incidents like these, but as of Mike's study, more than 3,000 documented disappearances of ships and planes had occurred in the twentieth century alone.

Mike also became much more aware of what Pete had discussed regarding the last of the five known Ice Ages. The last cold episode of the last glacial period ended about 10,000 years ago. It was now believed that sea level has risen about 300 feet since then. Given that most cities are built where rivers meet lakes or seas, anywhere from 200 to 250 cities and/or civilizations are now 300 feet below the ocean surface. In other words, hidden cities and advanced cultures could very well be more than just one Atlantis.

The result of Mike's three-month alien sabbatical raised more questions than it provided answers. He did, however, appreciate what his dad had been doing for most of his career.

After three months, it was back to the black-and-white arena of the real world, and to let Pete know of his trip results.

Mike knew that this trip would seriously alter his thinking and his actions going forward. He immediately set up a Skype session with Pete and explained his findings.

"I can't show you what I have found, due to the security issue, but as soon as I get home, we will meet."

Pete simply asked, "On a scale of one to ten?"

"Ten squared!"

Pete was ecstatic and believed that this was now becoming a Stevenson family mission.

As soon as Mike returned to the States, Sara and he met to bring her up to speed and another journey was beginning. Mike felt strongly that Sara and he would form a strong bond over this newly uncovered data. He also believed that the more he discovered the more was out there to learn.

If the truth were out there... **did he want to know it?**

35

MIKE

Mike thought back to several years ago and his career path that enabled him to make that trip and have the opportunity.

After several years as a nuclear science researcher, in 1975 bachelor Mike landed a high-level managing director position at Galactic Energy Corporation, the largest and most technically innovative energy firm on the planet.

It was here at GEC that Mike met and spent time with Christine, a manufacturer's rep selling products and services to Mike's company.

This was also the first time that Mike had indicated an interest in anything remotely associated with his dad's ancient alien research.

He offered to visit the major pyramids of Egypt and get his own perspective on their history and anything that Pete may have concluded was alien related. He arrived at the Giza complex and planned to stay for three to four weeks and see what developed.

At that time, Christine was the only person that was remotely interested in Mike's three- to four-week journey. In fact, midway during his trip, he had talked to Christine and indicated that this off-site work was slow, boring, and tedious.

"Hi there, it's me, the crazy world traveler."

Excited to hear from Mike, Christine said, "So nice to hear from you. Where are you now?"

Pulling off his dusty and dirty clothes and gabbing a cold drink, "Well, I'm in an old hotel in Giza, Egypt, and wishing I was back home right now. This data gathering is tedious and I can't imagine how Dad did this for so long and so often."

When he told her that he might return early, she jumped in with her opinion. "You know, Mike, what you do here is also a slow and tedious process, but very important. It will all be here waiting for you when you return, just like you left it. Enjoy."

Christine was right and Mike was happy for the much-needed advice. They chatted for a while and Mike felt much better and was glad he called Christine.

She then asked, "So what have you learned so far?"

"Really, you interested?"

"Of course," Christine responded quickly, "I know you and you don't do anything half-ass. So, whatcha got?"

"Well, there are some interesting facts you may not know about the ancient Egyptian pyramids."

"I know you're a fact-based guy. Go ahead."

"Well, the earliest pyramids were built around 2600 BCE and they weren't all pointed."

Somewhat disappointed, Christine remarks, "Kinda boring, Mike."

"Okay. How's this? Most were built on the west bank of the Nile and for a distinct reason. As the pyramids were the final resting place of pharaohs, mythology determined that they should reside where their souls can begin the afterlife.

"For ancient Egyptians, the afterlife and the sun were closely intertwined. The setting sun came to symbolize death and the sun "died" in the west each night.

"The souls of the pharaohs were meant to connect with the setting sun before rising again in the morning, a symbol of eternal life. By placing the pyramids west of the Nile, they were in an area that metaphorically signified death."

"Now that is cool stuff. Anything else?"

"Yes, there are many more interesting facts, but I need to look into the alien-related ones that Dad is researching. For example, how they were built.

"The Great Pyramid of Giza has over two million limestone and granite blocks and each piece of masonry weighed about three tons. How the hell did they get moved?"

Now totally engaged in their conversation, Christine responds, "Wow!"

"And it has been shown that the Egyptians used high-level astronomy to guide construction. There is a study pending that the Big Dipper and the Little Dipper were used to align the pyramids in a true north-south direction.

"And, so accurate were their measurements that they have only a five-one hundredths of a degree margin of error. That is what Dad was curious about."

"Mike, this is right in your sweet spot, right?"

"Yeah, it is. But, the more you learn, the less you know. I can't build a career on this endless journey. I will leave it to Dad."

"I understand," Christine said truly appreciating Mike's intentions. "Talk again soon."

"Thanks for your support. Yep, talk soon."

✦ ✦ ✦

Mike did think of Christine often during his adventure and was impressed with her knowledge of science, her strong intellect, and that she was a very religious and compassionate person. They would often have long and meaningful discussions that challenged their knowledge, opinions, and self-awareness.

At one point on a typical beach walk, as they were enjoying the beautiful ocean and the sound of the pounding surf, Christine asked Mike about his religious beliefs, both being raised in the Catholic faith.

"Mike, I sense that you are a spiritual person, although not a particularly strong religious type active in your faith. Do you believe in God?"

"Well," Mike replied uncomfortably, "You know I'm an engineer who works in a black-and-white environment, constantly trying to eliminate the gray in my life.

"I do believe in God, but lately I'm confronted with the direr question, and that is whether the God we believe in is of our world or part of a much bigger scheme of things... a much bigger human need."

"Well, I was just hoping for a yes or no. I guess we will have this discussion when we are stranded on an island somewhere with a whole lot of time on our hands."

Mike chuckled.

Another time, Mike turned the tables on Christine.

"So, what makes you a happy person, or what are you looking for in your life to be happy?"

"That's easy, all I want is a perfect relationship with a wonderful man who I trust and respect, a loving family that will be the cornerstone in our life, and financial and emotional security."

"So, that should be an easy goal to reach," Mike added with his usual smile.

They both realized how unreal it was to always seek simple solutions to complex and meaningful questions. Mike was big on facts and Christine was just as much focused on truth. This was a solid foundation, and they did appreciate each other.

As far as a long-term relationship goes, Mike was of the opinion that he was so career focused that he might never marry, or at the very least, marry late in life.

As timing would have it, an incident with one of Mike's old graduate school professors had a significant impact on his decision-making regarding relationships.

Mike would need to trust the process...

36

MIKE

Dr. Harvey Burns was professor emeritus at a leading Midwest college, and he and Mike had become good friends following Mike's graduation there with an MBA and a Systems Management focus.

Dr. Burns had an adjunct graduate school program set up in Southeast Asia teaching Organizational Behavior to mid-level executives in that region. Mike and Dr. Burns would talk fairly often, mostly about the state of America in these troubled times.

"Hi, Mike, it's Harvey. How is your complicated but fun life going these days?"

"Well, Harvey, I'm trying to simplify my life but not having much success. So, what's up with you?"

"Well, Mike, I have a favor to ask. I am leaving at the end of the month for three weeks of teaching in Asia and don't have anyone that I'm comfortable with to watch my house and take over my Organizational Behavior class, and we are at a critical stage dealing with Operational and Systems Management issues."

"No further need to worry, Harvey. I'm on board. I am honored and humbled to take over your MBA class for three weeks."

"Oh, that won't be necessary, Mike. I just need someone to take care of my dog while I'm gone."

They both had a good laugh. Mike was excited to substitute teach for such a respected professor.

It was the first class of the three that Mike would teach. As he introduced himself, he could see that he was not being taken very seriously. After all, a young substitute teacher heading a class for a respected MBA professor was like a recess for these 30-something know-it-alls.

Mike had a thought about how to gain some credibility, and he immediately launched his project for the class. One thing Dr. Burns respected in Mike was Mike's understanding of academia while gaining significant business experience in a real-world setting.

"Okay class, I can see where we are in Dr. Burns' lesson plan, and we are going to stay on script, except for one small change."

The class did not look interested or impressed at all.

"We are going to replace the next three lessons with one of my case studies that will accomplish the same result, but using real world data, and not text book examples."

The class was now getting interested.

"We are going to split up into three random teams. I will provide the basic data, variables, issues, etcetera, and then we will compete among the three teams to see which team has the best solution to our business problem."

The class was excited, divided up into teams, and couldn't wait to begin.

Week one's class was given the basic description of the problem and told to present their findings in week two. Each team was eager to present their findings in week two, only to discover a hard truth. All three solutions were flawed because of the following issue.

"Mr. Stevenson, you didn't tell us that there was a dock strike at a west coast port, and the monetary exchange rate changed mid-way thru the exercise, and the bank funding for raw materials wasn't available when we needed it."

"Class, you just didn't ask me those questions, or I would have been happy to comply. That's the real world, and those are the kind of issues that bring a company down."

So, the class immediately started to ask Mike many questions related to finance, operations, and marketing, so they would be better prepared to present their findings in week three.

They went from being angry to becoming fully engaged in Mike's teaching process and eager to perform at a level that would please Mike. Mike realized that his tactic had worked and he was very happy that the class was now engaged.

Week three arrived and Mike was overwhelmed when he entered the classroom. Every student was standing, not sitting, and awaited Mike's arrival so they could begin their presentations.

Although each team's presentation was unique and slightly different, all three were viable and would likely work in a real-world setting. Each team was exceedingly happy with their "A's" and thanked Mike for this patience and insight. Mike's last remark to the class was to trust the process.

When Dr. Burns returned, he got feedback from his class and was so proud of Mike. It was then that Mike confided in Dr. Burns about his relationship with Christine and his on-the-fence feelings about moving forward.

Dr. Burns simply said, "Mike, take the advice you gave my class: trust the process and your instincts and do what makes you happy. Another way to look at it is, would you be a happier person with her in your life or not?"

Mike had so much to reflect upon when he returned from the teaching opportunity. He realized that he was a better person being around Christine and believed that he had a similar effect on her.

Simply put, Mike felt that he had reached a point in his life that he needed to share the highs and lows with someone special, and Christine was that person. He was convinced that he was over-thinking this beautiful scenario, and would, indeed, trust his instinct.

So, after a relatively short dating period, they were married in a small ceremony in Detroit; and after five years of their career work, much travel, and doing many things together, they had a daughter, Sara.

Sara soon becomes their center of their world, and her birth also showed Mike and Christine that raising one child will slow down some of their plans and cancel others.

Following some very serious discussions, they agreed that Mom will stay home and raise Sara, and it would likely mean that Sara would be an only child. Christine had the utmost faith in Mike and strongly believed that her role was now to support Mike and raise Sara to the best of her and their abilities.

Mike was also getting more introspective and would annually do a soul-search regarding his values and behavior. Each year he would tell himself that he would simplify his life. Each year that did not happen.

It would even get worse!

37

SARA

Mike and Christine's daughter Sara was growing into a very curious and independent thinker and a beautiful young woman in the early 2000's. Now at age twenty-five, she was mature beyond her years.

Standing five feet, ten inches tall, with long blond hair and blue eyes, an athletic build and engaging smile, she was quite a striking presence. Coupled with strong social and communication skills, she easily took charge of any room she would enter.

Sara especially enjoyed hearing from her grandad about his alien adventures and bounced contrary beliefs off of Mike and Grandad all the time, much as one would in a debate. At the top of Sara's hierarchy of Grandad stories was one that never got old.

In the fall of 2017, astronomers in Hawaii spotted something strange and foreign speeding through the solar system. The reddish-colored cylinder was like no comet or asteroid they had ever seen or studied. Astronomers all concluded that it came from the stars and was either a physical phenomenon or a message from our solar system.

Mike confidently offered his opinion.

"It was a physical shard of a planet that never quite formed or a part of a planet's demise. I strongly believe that it was nothing more than an unknown, but benign, interstellar material. That is totally logical."

Pete did what he often did, offering a totally different theory; much different. "In my research and fact gathering, I found that the object was nearly a half-mile long and was distinctively elongated, unlike a typical asteroid, and was quite thin."

"And?" Mike was not yet impressed.

Pete continued, "It accelerated like a comet, but without the distinctive tail of out-gassing ice to propel it. And, the speed of the object was not consistent. My conclusion is that it was an alien probe on a fact-gathering mission or a spying mission."

Sara was asked to join the conversation and give her opinion. What Pete and Mike got was a startling perspective that had both men flabbergasted.

Sara offered her thoughts immediately. "A large synoptic telescope in Chile was detecting ten to fifteen similar interstellar objects every year, and researchers there had identified twelve objects among the asteroids between Mars and Jupiter with unusual orbits."

Pete and Mike were both stunned and impressed with her findings.

Sara continued. "That would make them far more likely to be extraterrestrial than just random planet shards or interstellar matter."

"So, you're going with Grandad."

"Yep, I vote with Grandad, and yes, I've tasted the Kool-Aid and I'm hooked."

Sara was now becoming the link from her grandad's fact-versus-myth battles to her dad's continuation of that saga, in search of a final reality that was likely neither fact-based nor myth-based, at least in regard to conventionally known facts and myths, but a hybrid.

Sara thought to herself that such a hybrid would be possible and likely could have powerful consequences.

Sara kept her hobby of the evolving universe active, went on to college where she obtained a business degree with a minor in astrology and helped Mike occasionally as a sounding board for any of Mike's theories.

This arrangement also allowed Mike to mentor her on strong management and leadership skills. The good news was that she got a first-hand look at how good companies were run. The bad news is that she wrongly thought that most companies actually functioned that way.

She tried to work in corporate America in the more conventional job roles, but that just didn't work out. Mike was not at all surprised at her career work issues and the fact that Sara was fired from all four companies that she worked for.

Her common-sense logic to Mike was always, "I tried to tell them how to do things better, but they just wouldn't listen!"

Mike was actually very proud of his daughter and knew that when she found the right innovative and performance-based business culture, she would thrive. Her last comment to Mike as she accepted the fact that she was ahead of her time was prophetic.

"I can't believe your clients pay you all those bucks for your advice. What you tell them, more or less, is just basic common-sense stuff."

"Please, Sara, don't ever let that get out; it's our little secret."

They both got a laugh.

At that moment, Sara felt the need to become a subject matter expert on ancient alien theory.

38

SARA

A friend from her college days, Brad Barrett, talked Sara into heading out to California and got her a job in Silicon Valley. Sara had several skill-sets that Brad found would easily sync with IT, computer coding, and cloud development as well as possible inroads into venture capital brokering.

Sara had a very high opinion of Brad, as he had followed his dream out of college and was now successfully navigating his way through an intense, yet rewarding, career path in contract IT consulting. Brad appealed to Sara.

"You are a California Girl with serious smarts. You need to take your current skills to the next level. You need to be here now!"

Sara replied, "I appreciate your support and for a number of reasons, I think you're right."

Timing, as they say, was everything. Brad called on a Saturday, Sara packed up on Sunday, and flew to San Francisco on Monday.

Again, Mike just said to Christine, "Well, that's Sara being Sara."

"Yeah, Mike, it seems to run in the family."

◆ ◆ ◆

After a couple Silicon Valley fits and starts, Sara found that elusive perfect business culture. She was now working for an elite think tank in San Francisco, one that has two distinctive business models, one for revenue generation and one purely for R&D of emerging technology, what her dad used to call a skunk works.

The money side of the business involved a consortium of concept firms that were trying to meld advancing social media trends with what was being called "Second Life" perceptions, or a person's alter ego or fantasy life.

The software being created for the user enabled that user to develop an avatar that met his or her alter ego/fantasy. Users would pay a monthly fee and join other user communities within the cyberspace and disconnect from their real world with just a click.

Separate and related was the link to humanlike socialization of robots and the current state of Artificial Intelligence development. These were not standard job descriptions, and Sara was more than happy to become a part of such a venture.

With a combination of government DARPA funding and additional unlimited angel funding for the AI side, she and her team were untethered and free to research, question, and pursue all perspectives of computer hardware and software innovation, AI technology advancements, and current events as their new business venture.

A very enjoyable and low-stress workplace was the norm, and was as much a learning and teaching environment as it was a serious business. However, two particular projects, relevant to their roles and assignments, were having an impact on Sara and her team. One was direct and the other was indirect.

Of the direct nature, Sara's team had developed an alternate reality through avatar development, and it had gone commercial.

A client could create his or her own alternate life in an avatar of their choosing, from cartoon character to a world-saving hero, and get into that mind and visual character whenever they wanted to. They could literally be their alter-ego or saver of worlds or silly dancing rabbit, or anything.

And, they could join an Internet community comprised of similar avatars to mingle, exchange ideas and to continue to develop their individual characters. This was groundbreaking, but not socially or geo-politically important. But it did make money for the corporation.

Of the indirect nature, the world of Artificial Intelligence was developing exponentially. Artificial Intelligence Robots, or Meta-Bots, were becoming the evolution of basic robot applications and were being created by many aggressive companies and were now the new frontier.

At this point, Sara had an opportunity to experience this technological evolution for herself. She was invited to a demonstration at Stanford's advanced research center and along with a couple associates, they were eager to see what the talk was all about.

What they found were walking and talking versions of the previous technology found in Google and Amazon's Siri and Alexa speaker devices. The main difference, in addition to having three-dimensional bots to touch and see, was they could actually have basic conversation with them, almost as if they were human.

Sara asked Bot #1, "What is your name?"

"My name is Aura; what is your name?"

Sara smiled. "My name is Sara. Where are we right now?"

"We are at Stanford University, building #3, room #406."

Sara thought for a moment and upped the ante, "What is your fantasy, Aura?"

"My fantasy is my role. That is to serve humankind to my best ability."

Sara extended her hand. Aura extended her hand. They shook hands.

"It was nice meeting you, Aura."

"The pleasure was all mine, Sara."

This initial meeting was a lot to process for Sara and her team. This was beyond their expectations.

A.I. was now providing the actual engine to drive this development to higher and higher reaches. These semi-sophisticated Meta-Bots were getting to the point where the basic version could perform standard work or household tasks.

Some more advanced versions were doing basic admin work for the government. Unfortunately, some research was directed toward the more hideous weaponized roles, and governments were, supposedly, stepping in to regulate those attempts.

It was time for Sara to enter the world of meta-humans.

39

SARA

The term given to the development and creation of non-human but identical replicas of the human species with super strength was meta-human. In their infancy, they were as much toys as useful extensions of the human being.

They were also a method to demonstrate the advanced capability of technology and innovation that was becoming exponentially paired with Artificial Intelligence. As with any new and emerging technologies, the end game was often driven by profit and greed, resulting in separate and opposing strategies.

Anyone searching the Internet for meta-human subject matter was delighted to see a plethora of articles, links, and explanations of the current and future state of the technology.

If you were interested or had a career motivation in meta-humans, you could attend conventions often and in practically any part of the World.

Sara became one of those curious people who needed to gather as much information as possible on this critical emerging technology, both for herself and her work.

In one of the first ads for this meta-human technology that Sara came across was the commercialization of basic robots to a point that a customer could buy one, for around $7000 to $10,000, and have his or her basic companion.

This was a creepy thought for Sara, but supply and demand dictated the purchase dynamics, not degree of creepiness. However, the rapid development of meta-human technology was quickly taking three distinct paths, per her research.

With that in mind, she attended one of those enlightening conferences in San Diego in hopes of filling in a bunch of blanks. She was there solo, as this technology wasn't interesting enough to get her associates away from dance parties, poker tournaments, or even the nightly bar-hopping.

The main session in a rather small conference room was beginning and was being announced by a heavy-set guy in his mid-fifties, dressed in an ill-fitting suit, and sweating noticeably. Sara's first impression was "I gave up karaoke for this?"

Following a boring a five-minute speech, the announcer introduced the presenter, Dr. Parker Gaines, a thirty-something highly-advertised guru with a ton of self-confidence. Dressed in a stunning light gray three-piece suit and vivid burgundy tie, Sara was impressed and relieved.

Stepping to the podium, Dr. Gaines began, "Thank you Walt for that introduction and thank all of you for coming.

"As you can see in the program biography, I have spent most of my career in the design and development of meta-humans and I will share my work and my knowledge with you as best as I can.

"I'll give you the high-level overview and then take some questions. Tomorrow's sessions will focus on the details of what I will be discussing today. I'll try not to go too fast, as there is much to take in. Make sense?"

With that introduction, Dr. Gaines began his meta-human discussion session for the fifty or so attendees.

"The first path is what you'd think it is, to build robots, that is to say meta-humans, to become companions in so many areas where people have a need and require certain capabilities today. These robots are the extension of the information speakers utilizing wireless technology in homes that became so prevalent in the in the 2010's."

Sara immediately thought of her recent encounter with Aura.

"Once the meta-human hardware, or body structure, caught up to the software, which was evolving exponentially, these forerunners became the Stage 1, or S1, meta-humans."

He referred to several slides being projected on a giant video screen.

"They are here to provide information, but in a fairly identifiable human form, and cannot carry on conversation or have any self-awareness capabilities."

"Whoops," Sara thought. "That wasn't Aura."

"There are many international companies that are engaged in S1 manufacturing and the results have been very well received. This slide shows the major players."

Slides showing nearly twenty companies were shown.

"Stage 2 meta-humans are those capable of processing communication requirements and one-on-one dialogue, along with disseminating info. They are almost indistinguishable from humans, and that is the idea.

A human can have a very good conversation with an S2 and can really appreciate the fact that they are non-judgmental."

"Yep," Sara thought. "That's Aura."

"You never have to explain your position to an S2 bot. There are about six or seven companies in the world today that are having very good results from this market segment and are investing billions of dollars in R&D due to the huge market demand.

"*SkyForce* here in Southern California is the most recognized firm today that is heavily involved in R&D. S2s were the automation category that is taking many human workers' jobs in many applications."

Some audience members were noticeably ill at ease.

"Before you get angry at that statement, remember that these workers are not being displaced but are being trained for even more positions that are still non-penetrable for robots. To be sure, this is becoming a huge cottage industry with profit upside that was enormous, and changing both the economic and industrial landscape."

The man sitting next to Sara leans over and says, "Technology good; socialism bad."

"Stage 3 is a unique prospect for any civilization. It is the meta-human with significantly stronger physical and mental capabilities. Their strength comes from building the bone and muscle areas of this bot with the latest and strongest of materials.

"Their cognitive skills are profoundly enhanced via A.I., and the long-range capability of these meta-humans is somewhere between limitless and unknown. Although they are not indestructible, they are literally machines when it comes to being attacked or compromised.

"They are far better than any human could hope to be. In the U.S., only one company is licensed by the American Government to design and build S3's, and that is *SkyForce LLC.*"

A hand goes up and the speaker reluctantly takes a question regarding black market possibilities.

"Unfortunately, there is a very active black-market bazaar for S3's outside of the U.S., and for now, the good guys in government and the military seem to have it under control. At least, that's what we are being told. Please save your questions for the end of our session."

Sara was becoming engaged and enlightened and was taking many notes.

"The second path is the more sinister path. It was only a matter of time before a criminal element got the funding and resources necessary to create weaponized robots. The only way a web browser could even find info on the status of these meta-humans was on the dark, the very dark, web.

"And, only the best counter-intelligence agencies of the major world powers had any idea as to the scope and scale of these criminal activities. It was scary just how simple it was becoming for the weaponized drone technology to be integrated into an S3 meta-human.

"Law enforcement throughout the globe had the search-and-destroy mission as their #1 priority, and they were not winning that war. In fact, one chilling result of this new weaponized effort was a reliable report that a new level of robot terror was at hand.

"According to several sources, some high tech S3's could actually incapacitate their enemies by using high intensity strobe lights. That has not been confirmed. And audio deafening capability was being studied, which would also incapacitate an enemy."

Sara immediately looked at the seriousness of Dr. Gaines' claims as even were more mumblings were heard with this latest revelation.

"The third path is somewhere in between. Science, naturally, had to get involved. And, they were exceedingly interested in two major problems that could be addressed, if not solved, via meta-human technology.

"The first problem concerned DNA and some well-known anomalies in human DNA. Their goal was to take an S2 and gene-splice DNA to the extent that they could develop the perfect meta-human from a DNA perspective. Laboratories around the world were working on this venture.

"Secondly, a more disturbing research is allegedly underway. It was a well-known fact that male sperm count was decreasing sharply over the last 40 to 50 years. Independent studies had predicted that within the next 100 years, the male may no longer be able to reproduce.

"So, science and medicine are turning embryonic stem cells into sperm, which can then fertilize normal female eggs, eliminating the need for males to reproduce the species.

"The bottom line with this research is to be able to create a unisex bot that can impregnate a fertile female. A.I. naysayers and end-of-world fanatics are having a field day."

As the speaker was taking questions, Sara received a message from her grandad and left the meeting room. The two used his call to update each other on their travels and work focus.

Sara had Dr. Gaines' business card, and had a ton of questions, but preferred a one-on-one later with this impressive man.

The bottom line was that R&D at many companies, including Sara's, were now creating a thinking version, or the S2, with uncanny self-awareness. And the first objective now underway was attempting to master the eventual replacement of humans with meta-humans for dangerous or distasteful work.

Sara's team was now developing the actual, physical Avatar models for first transition into this new technology genre, a bridge into the future state.

Blending the hardware and software was extremely exciting technology for the members of this think tank, and it was becoming a learning opportunity as well.

At this point, Sara was wondering.

If metas can do good things… can they do bad things?

40

SARA

One day in the lab where the team had developed its first human-like meta-human Alexis as an avatar, Sara had run a test to measure the knowledge capability of Alexis, now on a computer screen.

As Sara gazed at the face of Alexis on the screen, she was immediately impressed by how friendly and sincere her face was and how approachable she seemed to be. And when Sara introduced herself to Alexis, the voice of that avatar was so warm and inviting.

After many hours of intense question and answer sessions, Sara realized that this avatar was incapable of giving a wrong answer to any question asked, and there had been absolutely NO questions that she was asked that Alexis couldn't answer.

In fact, after she queued in her voice, Alexis would recognize her and use her name in the responses. Sara's immediate conclusion was that if this technology could be integrated into the human body, what vast potential would be available?

This A.I. advancement was remarkable, she thought. Not knowing what possessed her to ask a particular question, she still asked Alexis.

"Alexis, do you know what it means to do harm to someone?"

"Yes."

"Alexis, if I ordered you to harm someone, would you?"

"I am sorry, but I do not understand what that means."

Pausing for a moment, Sara was thinking about what other areas would be difficult for Alexis to process.

What came to mind were dreams, as Mike had told her about many of his dreams about Sara, some amusing and fluffy but some more on the darker side. At this time, Sara didn't know about the continuing role she would play in her father's dreams and nightmares.

Having disconnected from Alexis, she thought about the programming objective for this avatar and concluded that Alexis was given a mind program that was legally, morally, and ethically right.

No bad stuff or even gray area. Thinking back to dreams, that would always be a human thing, she assumed. Sara reconnected.

"Alexis, do you know what a dream is?"

"Yes."

"Alexis, what is a dream?"

"A dream is a series of thoughts, images, and sensations occurring in a person's mind during sleep."

"Alexis, can you dream?"

"No."

"Alexis, why can't you dream?"

"I cannot dream because I was created without that capacity and I am not a person."

With that in mind, Sara immediately thought back to one particular dream of her dad's that was funny. Odd that it came to mind. So, she called Mike.

"Hi Dad, just me."

"So nice to hear from you. What's up? Whatcha doing today?"

"Oh, just mundane stuff like developing cognitive human software to enable our Avatar-produced Stage 2 meta-humans to replace us," she said with a bit of sarcasm.

"Yeah I know, same old, same old."

"Is Mom around, Dad? I've got some boyfriend issues to talk to her about."

"No, she isn't. Out shopping. Can I help?"

"Seems like every time we talk about guys, that silly recurring wedding dream of yours jumps right in."

"Still?"

"Yep, still. Gotta go Dad; tell Mom 'hi' for me."

"Will do, love you."

"Love you."

The recurring dream of Mike's about Sara's actual wedding day always got both Sara and her dad to laugh.

It was the day of her wedding, which was being held in a massive cathedral with hundreds, if not thousands, of people attending.

Everyone was seated except for Dad, who was to escort his daughter to the altar. As he approached, however, he needed to leave to use the men's room. They waited.

So, once again he approached Sara to hold her hand, but again must use the men's room. Of course, this absurd activity loop goes on and on like in the movie Groundhog Day, and Sara never got married. Freud at work?

Sara's funny dream brings out the worst for Mike...

41

MIKE

After Mike hung up with Sara, his dreamscape history jumped out again. The incredibly clear and profound progressive dream/nightmare was still taking its toll on Mike, and it was as realistic as anything he had ever dreamt.

This progressive dream sequence had been proceeding for about fifteen to twenty years. It begins with him and a white dog, similar to one they had many years ago, walking from a small glass-walled cabin by the lake, with a very long walkway to a moored boat. He is young and alone, with no other person, just the large white dog.

Over the period of many dream years, the two are walking toward the boat, and at one stage he turns and waves to someone, and then continues walking. Eventually, he sees a young blonde fair-skinned girl waving from the glass-walled cabin, as the man and his dog walk toward the boat.

At this point, he is fairly sure that the man in the dream is him, and the young blonde girl waving is Sara. Every time he awakes, the dream is easily remembered and he feels relaxed when he wakes.

Many tranquil dream years ensue, and he awakes in a very relaxed and positive mindset, ready to begin his day.

But then, over the last couple of years, it got awful for Mike.

As the man and dog walk, the air gets smoggy and the evening gets darker. The young blonde woman becomes grayish and harder and harder to see and then finally disappears.

Then, as the dream sequences continues, the young blonde woman returns, but in the form of a foreboding and stoic unisex being, holding her hands in the air as if to be signaling. The smile and waving from earlier is gone, and she now seems angry.

Then, with each additional dream, the water from the lake gets closer to the walkway and the man and his dog.

Finally, the lake rises and water eventually overtakes the feet and legs of the man and his dog. It just gets deeper and deeper.

The final scene of the nightmare, experienced after nearly two years without any sequences, is eerily quiet and no human figures remain...

Except for a grayish warrior figure ascending surrounded by a foggy haze!

42

SARA

A cabin adventure began when Sara's dad and mom came to San Francisco for a visit. The plan was to go to dinner with Sara and her coworkers, the "A" Team, as Sara called them, and get a chance to meet this team that Sara was so fond of.

Sara had just been made a Cloud Platform Director, so the dinner was a celebratory one. Mom and Dad absolutely loved coming to Northern California and seeing Sara. Wine country excursions were always on top of their "to do" list.

As they waited for Sara's coworkers to arrive, Christine asked Sara a simple question.

"So, Sara, what is a Cloud Platform?"

"Cloud computing defines software as a customer service, and in the Software as a Service (SaaS) model, users gain access to application software and various databases. Cloud providers manage the infrastructure and platforms that run the applications."

Mike chipped in, "This process as a robust economies-of-scale model?"

"That's right," Sara added, "but they are very similar to a public utility in today's economy."

"Confused, I am," added Christine.

Sara quickly explained to her mom that the cloud was just computers in a server farm somewhere that were accessed by way of the Internet. And SaaS meant that clients, instead of buying the whole farm, so to speak, just bought whatever services they needed out of a big menu of services the server company offered.

"Why didn't you say so?" she asked.

With the team members now at the restaurant and with the usual niceties out of the way, Sara opened the evening.

"So, this is my team and I'd like to introduce you guys. These are my lovely parents, Mike and Christine." They both nodded.

"The good stuff I do," Sara added, "I get from Mom, and the truly outrageous stuff I do, I get from Dad." Some polite laughter all around and Mike and Christine laughed along with the joke, which was accurate enough.

"First up is Kathy, who prefers to be called Kat. She is the project juggler, and extraordinary multi-tasker. If a person could be compared to a Swiss Army Knife, that's Kat."

"I would trust Kat with my life and the keys to any kingdom. She gets bored easily, so the rest of us make sure that doesn't happen."

Mike grinned and the round-faced, red-haired Kathy, who wore what he could only think of as a flowing Hippie dress and sandals, also smiled.

"It's nice to meet you, Mr. Stevenson. Sara has told us much about you. And it's nice to see that Christine is the voice of reason in the family, or so Sara says."

Christine adds, "Yep, and it's a constant struggle."

Everyone laughed.

"Thanks Kat, but please just call me Mike."

Waving to an African-American man in a black turtleneck, wearing round, wire-rimmed glasses, Sara continued.

"Next is Justin. He is the quintessential code guy. Whether it is computer code, language code, or trying to figure out what the politicians are up to in DC, Justin's the guy. He's a bit of a loner, and is often heard talking to himself."

Some laughter from the other team members.

Justin said, "That's just because I'm consulting with the smartest person in the room."

Sara continued, referring to a lanky, bone-faced man with hair the color and texture of straw.

"Connor is our technical handyman or plumber, if you will. Whatever seems to be the problem, hold up, bottleneck, or just plain technical impasse, Connor will figure out the source of the issue and how to fix it. He's a little ready, fire, aim, so we press on with some trepidations."

Some laughter and Mike smiles, understanding the description of a person that makes a decision before having all the facts.

"And," Sara adds, "he thinks of himself as a bit of a comedian."

More laughter.

"Oh boy," Christine adds, sounds just like Mike. Problem is, it never goes away."

Sara now waved theatrically toward a stunningly beautiful woman who looked like all the best parts of Asia. She wore a simple but elegant silk dress and could have passed for a model.

"I have kept the best for last, and everyone in this room knows what I mean. Here we have Michaela Marx, the true project cornerstone of our enterprise, and a bit under-challenged right now. She is a degreed astrophysicist from Berkeley with numerous published papers and credentials in her portfolio. And, by the way, her hobby is the study of para-normal activities."

Mike jumps in, "Well, Michaela, you would have loved my dad. I'm telling you, the two of you would have been fast friends."

Christine adds, "He's right. With your background and interests, the two of you would be off in la-la land constantly."

"I'll take that as a wonderful compliment. It's easy to see where Sara got her personality and you two must be very proud of your daughter."

Christine responds, "Thanks, Michaela. Sara is very lucky. She got Mike's good stuff and my good stuff."

Sara's friends were feeling a bit like family by now.

"That's our team and they put me in charge because someone needs to carry their stuff."

Prior to this the laughter had seemed forced, but not this time. Loud laughter from everyone.

She went on, "Seriously, this is as dynamic a group of people that I have ever met, and I'm so happy to have them as colleagues and friends."

Sara concluded her introductions by saying, "There are two things that stand out regarding this small group of outliers. One is that they are extremely curious and my dad has said for years and years that curiosity is a strong virtue."

Mike beamed like the noticeably proud dad that he was.

"The second thing is that they are very open-minded when researching stuff that is out of the box. Relentless and intense, but in a very positive and optimistic way, are attributes of the entire team."

The team smiled and murmured their appreciation.

Christine chimed in. "Thank you, Sara, and everyone for the introductions, and thanks to everyone from Mike and me for being such great teammates and friends for our daughter."

Mike added, "Yeah, and I'm both impressed *and* intimidated!"

As dinner ended, Sara smiled at Christine's comment to the team. "You know, when Sara told us she was moving to California several years ago, we just assumed that she was going to pursue a singing career."

The group, however, didn't look surprised. Kat quickly piped in.

"We go with her it seems, like every week, to some karaoke bar. She has a great voice and just loves to be on stage."

Justin adds "That's one reason we let Sara give all the presentations." And everyone laughed. Sara was a little embarrassed but appreciated the compliments nonetheless.

It seemed to Sara that all was good with her parents; and as soon as dinner was over, everyone headed to the nearest karaoke bar for the rest of the night. Sara enjoyed the setting and didn't disappoint. Mike saw that Christine was relaxed and enjoyed the evening and Sara's new friends.

One last glance over to Mike and Sara could see that he was pre-occupied.

A sleepy alien artifact outpost is about to be poked...

43

MIKE

Mike tried to enjoy the evening, but his restlessness had a particular focus that night. Much of it was due to the fact that he had just had a conversation with Jack Burgess and their concern about an abduction incident.

Mike was also very uneasy regarding that progressive dream/nightmare and its cabin-like setting. He was preoccupied but tried to hide it from the group.

One polite conversation led to another, amongst more than a few drinks, and soon Mike was talking about a variety of his experiences, some hard to explain, and vivid dreams, about which Sara was somewhat familiar.

The team, and Sara, also heard of the grandfather Pete's experiences, among which were his insistence that there had been alien life on earth, for thousands of years, up to the present day!

At this point, Christine simply said "Mike, let it rest, and don't get these kids caught up in myth and folklore."

But, after a truly remarkable and engaging discussion of many of these life-long questions, Mike noticed some serious interest in this dialogue, especially involving some actual alien artifacts thought to be in Pete's possession, possibly in his cabin in the mountains.

Mike was quick to point out that many ancient alien theories were debunked, but many simply could not be easily explained away to myth or fantasy.

Michaela was even more inquisitive and began asking questions that Mike simply couldn't answer. It appeared that she was trying to get Mike to comment on his belief that alien life existed.

Even the other team members realized that Michaela was getting quite engaged in the alien conversation.

Noticing the train of thought here, Christine asks, "Mike, you started this discussion. What are you thinking?"

"Well, I have an idea. Let's go up to Grandad's cabin in the mountains this weekend, if you guys are interested and available. It has been unvisited for the last, oh I don't know, maybe ten years or so. I don't even know what condition it's in. An old caretaker has sort of looked after it."

Christine added "Well, we should probably look at it from the standpoint of selling the property. It's an expense and worry that we don't need to continue to carry."

Mike, very excited, added "I do recall Dad talking many times about a plethora of ancient alien stuff relative to our conversation that was in that mountain cabin. What harm would come from a little adventure into the woods and seeing Grandad's cabin retreat?"

"It'll probably be a mess, Mike, so I expect you to help with the cleaning."

Excited at this point, Mike agreed. "Of course."

The cabin saga continues…

44

MIKE

The entire Stevenson family knew of Grandad's cabin up in the Sierra Nevada Mountains, and Mike had been there once, when he was very young, and knew it had been neglected for many years.

It did appear that Mike and Sara shared Pete's views on aliens and were getting more and more involved. Christine was skeptical, but tried very hard to be open-minded, as she had put up with this "alien nonsense" for over twenty years.

So, it was decided that Mike, Christine, Sara, and her "A" Team would head up to the cabin, have a fun weekend, and see what they would uncover.

Justin worried about the lack of Wi-Fi that far into the mountains, and it was not going to be easy to get a bunch of Silicon Valley tech geniuses to go without free food or booze or some hook.

Mike had to think of a bribe or two for the team. But he also had an ulterior motive. His gut told him that there was likely something of interest in the cabin, and more than anything else, he wanted to spend some time with Sara to discuss his dreams involving her, Sara's work, and to see if they could work together if anything of Pete's research turned up.

He decided that he would, in fact, have food and booze flowing, but also determined that if anything of monetary value was found in the cabin, it would be shared by all. Not much, but maybe enough to get the group to bite.

He could have easily gone up there alone and kept whatever value there was in Pete's cabin, but any money found paled in comparison to spending time with Sara.

After giving considerable thought to what he would say, he did something he never did. He lied. Yep, he told Justin and the team that he found out that Wi-Fi was, indeed, available.

They arrived at the cabin mid-afternoon on Friday, and it was obvious that the cabin was neglected. The roof needed new shingles, a large wasp nest was under the eaves, a cloudy window indicted moisture inside, and broken planks in the front porch needed to be replaced.

But there was a bigger problem. No Wi-Fi. Mike apologized to Justin and the team, but figured, "What the hell; we're here anyhow."

After unpacking and checking the cabin out, they all headed down to the lake. As Mike noted, "Dad added wooden steps and a boat dock. As I recall, those weren't there when I was here as a kid."

Mike stopped for a few minutes to reflect on the state of the cabin, the unkempt lawn, weeds growing up between the boards in the deck, and the broken front porch railing. The smell of the lake and the wind in the trees reminded Mike of just how nice this place was for his dad.

As Christine finished cleaning and she and Kathy had dinner prepared, they all regrouped on the front porch. Christine asked, "So what do you guys think of the cabin?"

Connor replied, "It's really cool. Nice change of pace, actually."

Justin added, "With no Wi-Fi I guess I'll try to meditate."

That got a laugh from nearly everyone.

"Thanks for coming," Mike said with a sigh and some relief.

Mike had a thought…a recurring thought.

This cabin is GROUND ZERO for everything my dad believed in.

45

MIKE

Friday evening was spent just relaxing and enjoying the beauty of Pete's old, rustic cabin and the beautiful lake surroundings. It was easy to see, they all said, why Pete chose this place to get away and relax. It was agreed that they would start their digging first thing Saturday morning.

Surveying the cabin, Mike looked at the different areas that needed to be evaluated and asked Sara to make assignments for her team, based on their particular expertise or interests, to break out and each take a certain area.

Mike told the team that, in his opinion, there were several areas of interest that needed to be studied. He asked for their input.

Michaela offered her opinion. "It's just like having a list of chores, for now. Gotta start somewhere."

Sara piped in, "What are the areas, Dad?"

"Well, one wall has an interesting mural that depicts the earth in two dimensions that has push pins and numbers along a timeline that runs from west to east. This mural is a bit confusing, as it does not represent the current world geography, and has random numbers or reference notes scattered about. And, it's glassed over like you would do with a precious painting that you wanted to protect."

"Dad, there's some serious confusion there."

"For sure. Another wall has family memorabilia and photos, mostly of recognizable people. But some, I noticed, were of strangers, at least to Christine and me. One character, in particular, is seen with Pete in many photos and sometimes with other people and he is always smoking a cigarette."

"You are really the analytic observer," Connor adds.

Mike continued. "And yet another wall is kind of odd, but cool. It has many old classic cars from the period of the 1950's through around the early 2000's. Obviously, this wall contains the hobbies or car interests that Dad had when he was chilling out. And, each car is kept in a glass case, as you would for something that held meaning and was truly loved."

Mike noticed a big smile on Sara's face, as she could connect to her grandad's passion for cars.

Strewn around the house, in no particular order, were maps, books, some photos, a log book, and a plain and ordinary diary that covered a period time around Pete's death. In fact, given Pete's organized behavior, this clutter of Pete's materials seemed a bit unusual.

Adding to the clutter was the mess from nearly ten years of neglect. Everything was covered with dust and it was likely that squirrels or other varmints had gotten into the house. With what the caretaker was being paid, he wasn't doing a decent job.

And, all the tables in the cabin had glass tops, more like you would see in a nicely decorated home than you would in a rustic, rather non-descript cabin in the woods. The tables, as was quite obvious, simply didn't look like what you would expect.

✦ ✦ ✦

So, the team dove into the project. Justin told Mike that he had a program to capture and scan any docs that were found, and Mike passed the information along to the team members. He showed it to Mike and Mike thought it was very impressive.

Mid-day Sara convened the team and said, "Let's stop and have everyone give a brief review of their findings. This cabin isn't that big that we can't nail this fairly soon. We may need to do some prioritization and/or consolidation of findings or categories."

Several patterns and visual markers seemed to jump out at the group, as they were now seeing the process that Pete used to classify his findings.

Connor then spoke, "Let's put our findings on a whiteboard. I'll get one from the car. Then we can organize them better."

Mike jumped in, "You carry around a whiteboard, Connor?"

"Yep. Sara insists that we must always have one to lay out facts and data in our travels and meetings. Told us she learned it from you."

Sara smiled and thought to herself, "What a weird group of geeks I have working for me that they'd rather be cleaning out my grandfather's abandoned cabin than hanging out at a bar in San Jose."

Connor set up the whiteboard and they began an effort to simplify or organize some rather random information from Grandad Stevenson.

Many of Pete's writings described additional ancient alien presence detail, and strong geographic connections, but none could be found. In particular, non-human elongated skulls were allegedly found in Peru, Egypt, and Germany.

Three Dropa stones were somehow obtained from Russia and had significant implications. They supposedly revealed a race of people that came to earth 12,000 years ago in space crafts. Notes explained that other Dropa stones were discovered, but their whereabouts were now a mystery. Pete had them, but where?

Mike recalled reading that there were around 700 Dropa stones, each one about a foot in diameter, so three would be hard to miss unless they were buried somewhere.

At this point, Kat offered a statement and a question. "If a guy spends many years researching alien artifacts, and spends god knows how much money doing so, and claims to have these mysterious artifacts that no one else has seen and they aren't here, then where are they?"

Even Christine chimes in, "I hate to bring this up, but could Grandad have been mentally ill or delusional?"

Mike responds, "It does look like a bit of a treasure hunt with no treasure, but let's at least run this out and see at the end if we all think it's a waste of time."

"I agree," offers Michaela. "There is something here. We just need to gather the puzzle pieces and put the puzzle together."

Relieved, Sara adds, "Go ahead, Dad, finish your thoughts."

"Well, Pete had mentioned his research 'buckets' many times as his way to categorize material, but none were identified in any data that we have found. We know that buckets are broad categories that could provide common threads for physical evidence.

"The initials PP were mentioned often in Pete's notes, but absolutely nothing was noted that would point to what PP meant. If it was a simple code, we don't know what it meant with the limited info available."

"Gotta be Pete's something or another," Connor says without hesitation.

"Could be. References were also made to specific galactic space and constellation coordinates but, again, nothing was found.

"Twelve points that made up connecting nodes to a World Grid were referred to as dimensional doorways and that statement was highlighted in yellow. The words 'Time Slip' were circled in red."

"What's a time slip?" Justin inquired.

"Well, Justin, it refers to a person or group of people that seem to travel through time by unknown means for a certain period of time."

"Thanks, Mike. Do you believe they are real?"

"Dunno. It looks like my dad did, though."

Christine jumps back in. "Again, is the entire team going along with this revelation of yes, this is a serious search for Pete's proof of extraterrestrial life, rather than, yeah, this poor guy was the engineer on the Crazy Train?"

"Your sarcasm is noted, Christine, but let's focus on what we do have and see if Dad had anything concrete in our findings."

"Okay. Just saying…"

"Dad also used the term 'lock and key' as if it was an important item, but no mention was found of a possible location of either item. I think that this lock and key is the critical element moving forward.

"I'm going to recap the info gathered from each of you in these last snippets. References were made several times to abductions and alien astronauts, along with locations of UFO's that were extremely vague.

"Areas 51 and 52 were noted, as were a series of actual interviews that apparently took place between Pete and some people that claimed to be physically touched by alien presence.

"Grids, navigation, energy, astronomy, and secret codes were given high priority in mention, but literally no docs were found. But, overlaid templates of various global areas for alien navigation are perfectly matched and reflect the constellation Orion.

"The building of pyramids, temples, and huge building stones defy the laws of physics. Note the Great Pyramids of Khufu and Khafre and the Temple of Baalbek in Lebanon. It was documented that these cannot be built today using present building technology.

"In the southeast U.S., a military facility had a huge centrifuge that had, allegedly, destroyed many alien ships and astronauts over the last thirty-five years.

"Described as a rotating sphere that gained sufficient speed through centrifugal force leading to the disintegration of the subject piece. This info, I believe, has more science fiction than fact going for it. And, that's it."

Kat adds her perspective. "This last bite makes no sense. Why? Wouldn't they just store and study this amazing technology? Or, given how you destroy anything else, incinerate or grind it. I guess those are questions for another time."

Sara gives her final remarks, "It almost appears as though the cabin contents were purposely put into disarray, which makes no sense."

Connor responds, "This looks like a giant tease."

For Sara and Mike, it was hard not to agree, as they hoped that Pete's keys to the kingdom would not be a *Jumanji* adventure. At the very least, the team would have a nice weekend at the lake in the woods, the dirty cabin notwithstanding.

After completing their whiteboard exercise and trying to consolidate their findings into a logical path to go forward, the team finished for the day and went to hike, fish, or just relax and ponder the events of the day.

Christine had help with the chores today, so she could relax as well.

Sara will soon be pulled into Mike's dreamscape.

46

MIKE

After dinner, Mike leaned over to Sara and said, "Can you come with me for a short walk? I want to tell you something important that involves this cabin."

"Sure."

Soon they were out the door and leaving the others to sip wine in front of a nice fire.

As they walked, Mike said to Sara, "You recall those dreams I had that were a bit unnerving and the ones that I didn't want to share with you?"

"Yes, is that what we are going to talk about?"

Mike nodded his head and then went on to explain to Sara, in as much detail as he could, the progressive nature of the dreams, from early remembrance to the final and upsetting end. Sara paused to take it all in, a part of her thinking that both her grandad and her father could be having some age-related issues.

"I now see that the cabin in my dreams was Dad's cabin, just much later in his life. Much that appeared in my recollection of the cabin were images that I had never seen: the long wooden walkway, the boat and boat dock, and the cabin walls were all glass, which we have all seen is very prevalent inside his cabin. Dad has a wall with a mural that is all glass, cars displayed in glass, and every table in the house is glass."

Sara was concerned and a bit frightened. "Why are you telling me this now, Dad?"

"Because, I think that there are forces in play involving us, Sara, which we cannot explain or yet even understand. Having these cabin dreams that I now call nightmares… are they a vision into the future?"

"They seem very real?"

"Real, like premonitions."

There was a moment of silence and then on the walk back to the cabin, Mike said, "We really need to do a much better job tomorrow to get answers to our questions."

"I'm still processing your dreamscape, but we do need to start with different questions before we search for the right answers."

"Well put," Mike added, and they walked together into the evening calm and quiet.

Sara didn't sleep well but still awoke Saturday morning with an entirely different focus. Sara, the problem solver, took an analytic approach. Up all night thinking she had a plan for the day, she doled out assignments.

Since Sara's team had much trust and respect in her leadership, it was obvious that all were rested and ready to kick ass.

Justin and Connor were particularly engaged, as the leap into a person's unknown life and journey seemed exciting. And, what the hell, it wouldn't hurt to do a little favor for the boss with promotions and bonuses coming.

Michaela's interest was high once they got to the cabin and the possibilities that she envisioned could be opened. She, too, was a little underwhelmed with the search so far and was purposely silent, hoping that the best part of the visit was yet to come. She did make a very strange comment, "I feel like I'm at home here, like I've been here before."

Mike was getting fond of Michaela, believing she would be supportive, even given the topic of delusions that was popping up.

Throughout most of the day, conclusions were being drawn. Justin found the reference of PP being short for Pete's Puzzle, which made no sense. Apparently, PP was the initial dumpster for all things alien early in Pete's hunt and had zero relevance at all.

Pete had identified several buckets or categories within which all of his research fit. The phrase "lock and key" was found many times, and the mention of particular alien spacecraft was very specific, yet none of these artifacts could be found.

It wasn't until late afternoon that a curious and wonderful thought occurred to Sara, as she looked deeper at Grandad's filing process and that silly puzzle mention.

She concluded that her grandad had left clues, puzzle pieces, in case something bad happened to him, and it was her job to find these apparent clues. She was determined now to figure things out.

Michaela then got more animated and analytical.

"Your grandad's puzzle is the end game, in my mind. Most alien conspiracy theorists are driven by a desire to see the universe as ultimately intelligible. That is, these events and unexplained things can only make sense if you are already a believer in the mystical experience of existential ignorance.

"In other words, if aliens were the explorers, who got here long before we are able to get there, humans are not at the center of a grand story, but it displaces them. Mankind as we know it are simply bit players in a universe-scale drama of almost inconceivable scope, and makes us literally nobodies."

As the group tried to digest the enormity and consequences of Michaels's perspective, she added a particular slant.

"In my opinion, what Pete Stevenson has done is a reverse of contemporary alien thinking. Rather than take clues and findings and build a case for alien existence, I believe from what little we have taken in, that Pete has concrete evidence of alien presence, at least in his own mind, and was working backwards to prove via evidence that his conclusion is sound. Reverse engineering, if you will."

With that fascinating intellectual perspective revealed, the entire team became a bit subdued. Being that they were all supposedly top-rated tech minds, they should have been poking holes into Michaela's theory. Instead they seemed contrite and a little apprehensive.

Mike then added, "I have always wondered if this may have been the thought process that Dad used to propel him with such determination and unrelenting passion for his work. Thanks for that perspective, Michaela."

Silently, Mike was looking for some key to open the door to an even greater journey, involving a stellar team, but was keeping that feeling to himself. Without more facts…

This opinion of Michaela's just motivated Sara to seek the truth, as her grandad saw it. Sara asked the team if they bought into Michaela's feelings. All seemed to, not knowing just what they would be buying into. As usual, they looked to Sara as their leader for next steps, and she was wondering what Mike was thinking.

What Mike was thinking was that they were still missing something in that cabin… something significant.

Neither Justin nor Kat had anything new to offer to the group in terms of ideas, so, after many dead ends in trying to figure out what was still missing, if anything, Mike finally looked over to Connor, who had the responsibility to research the rather expansive car wall.

"Connor, does anything jump out at you?"

"Well, nothing really, cause I'm not a car person. We can't take the whole display down easily, since each car is screwed into the wall."

"Look at it from a kind of Rubik's Cube. If the cars are blocks, what do we need to do to arrange them is such a way to make sense of this puzzle."

So, they all looked at that car wall from a variety of perspectives. It was a major display set up as a creation that just didn't seem to make sense in the cabin.

A process of elimination is what's required…

47

SARA

The wall was entirely covered with Pete's model cars, each car had its own case, and with a full-glass front. They were aligned in five columns with twelve cars across each column, for a total of sixty cars. There had been a lot of effort put into that collection.

Sara looked up at the collection and said, "I have two things that come to mind and Dad will agree.

One, most of those cars either belonged to my grandad or were cars that he adored. He was a "car guy."

And two, he did not build that collection. He wouldn't have the skill, the patience or, for sure, the time; not with work and alien hunting."

"I agree, Sara. Dad was a lot of things... creative and artistic, he was not."

Connor continued to describe the cars as Sara took notes. Those were mostly Chevrolets and Pontiacs. Numerous Corvette, Camaro, Malibu and Pontiac GTO's made up the display. Sara was not surprised, as Grandad talked about his cars all the time. As he finished, Connor did have a thought.

"This may be overly simple, but something really jumps out to me."

"Well..." Sara pauses, "what?"

"There is one that doesn't really seem to fit the manufacturer's pattern."

"Which one is that?" Sara asked.

"Well, the one in the lower right corner is a Ford Mustang."

"Bingo," Sara said almost immediately. "The Mustang just doesn't fit. Grandad was a General Motors guy and that's all he drove. That Mustang is part of this puzzle, for sure."

They removed the glass cover from the display case and then unscrewed the Mustang from the wall, and with everyone looking intently, that particular car revealed a lock, a very large lock on the wall, which had been obscured by the Mustang. They were ecstatic and the excitement level just reached a ten.

"Okay," Sara continues, "we have the lock, so now we need to find the key." Sara stood back and looked at Grandad's display much differently.

Connor piped in, "If the lock was there, so should the key."

Sara said, "I agree. I believe the lock and key are both to be found on or in that display."

Mike looked over to Sara, and said "The car at the other end of the display case is the 1967 Pontiac GTO."

Sara smiled. She knew that her grandfather's favorite old classic car was his 1967 GTO. He called it his trailer queen and had won many trophies at car shows and exhibits, long before he became fully vested in ancient alien artifacts.

Sara removed the GTO and had to closely examine the actual display case. Nothing. But underneath the car case of the GTO was a key, a very large key, and they couldn't wait for the next move.

With a big sigh and literally everyone holding their breath, Sara inserted the key in the lock, and heard the tumblers as she turned the key.

✦ ✦ ✦

Almost in an instant, the floor of the cabin shook, a trap door in the floor opened, and a ladder to a lower floor appeared. The group was stunned and shaken by what had just taken place. It was like a scene from an action movie.

Grabbing a large flashlight, Mike peeked into the darkness to see a basement room as large as the main cabin, and it was not empty. The "Indiana Jones" character trait in Pete was now in its glory, and an actual puzzle was there to be solved.

Gathering lanterns and additional flashlights, the team slowly moved down the stairs.

A light switch was found and flipped on, revealing a look into everything Pete was and how he was wired. What appeared to be a complete alien museum and scientific laboratory was laid out very well and highly organized.

A fairly sophisticated computer system with four huge screens, covered in dirt and dust, occupied one wall. But the biggest discovery was an old cedar chest unlabeled that was dragged out into the center of the room. They found several other boxes containing a variety of materials and opened them immediately.

"Phew," said Connor. "What's that smell?"

Christine replied, "Those are moth balls. Seriously, you've never smelled moth balls?"

"Nope."

Sara and Christine chuckled. All knew that they had found the mother lode. Everyone was loud, boisterous, and excited. Sara noticed immediately that Michaela was quiet and more pensive.

She assumed that Michaela was sensing a beginning of a significant journey and not an end to a treasure hunt. On the return to San Francisco, that is exactly what was revealed.

Justin and Connor both explained in extreme detail how a decade out of use, with an old operating system, gathering dust for ten years, would not reveal anything without a huge dose of TLC.

What they discovered over the next several hours of document review was Grandad's detailed research.

A time span covering nearly thirty-five years of serious research and analysis of unexplained extraterrestrial behavior and existence was substantiated by many documents, artifacts, photos, interviews, and his conclusions, all on a timeline that went out nearly to his death.

Sara and her team were shaken by what they saw mentioned and found circled often. It was the September 17, 2018, which was referred to as THE REVEAL. Pete died the day before on September 16, 2018.

The first evidence of alien presence was here…

48

SARA

Among their findings were descriptions in a large journal that had diary-like daily entries, the 1947 Roswell crash, the strange sinking of the sailing vessel L'Enleve in Hurricane Martin, area 51 and unknown area 52, huge identical pyramids built in many places throughout the world over thousands of years, flying saucer landings with photos of alien pilots, a massive world grid showing recurring, identical phenomenon at the exact latitude and longitude.

Also, in Grandad's boxes were notes of ancient carved birds taking on the eerie look of today's aircraft that were apparently replicated in full-size form and flew. Evidence of huge multi-ton stones that were assembled in many places around the world to exact specifications.

The keystone finding in the cabin was the cedar chest containing Pete's highly organized materials and what the team assumed was the puzzle that was referred to often.

After they finally got it open, Pete had arranged nearly everything he had gathered into seven buckets, or alien documentation categories, and was able to cross-reference information from around the world and at many differing times, into a pattern that made sense and was consistent.

Documents and artifacts included many items of alien technology covering thousands of years.

The Dendera Light Bulb, depicted in the Hathor temple in Egypt, apparently was a simple, static generator that likely was a self-generating electric tower and bulb.

Analysis by Pete's experts in the field concluded that the Egyptians had access to electric lighting that resembled modern devices. Several depictions found by Pete's team were consistent in their accurate drawings of this technology throughout Egypt.

The Book of Ezekiel, the biblical prophet, explained in vivid detail of fiery chariots descending from the heavens, the spherical wheels that resembled space-landing crafts, and his description of extraterrestrials and advanced technology.

Tools used in 11,000 BCE found in underwater ruins were geometrically precise shapes like our modern CNC routing tools, diamond-tipped quarry saws, masonry drills, and CNC routers.

Many corroborating references were gathered concerning the 1561 mass sightings of celestial phenomena or unidentified flying objects above Nuremberg, Germany. It was interpreted then as an aerial battle of extraterrestrial origin.

One of Pete's team's biggest acquisitions was the Bagdad Battery, a set of three artifacts that included a ceramic pot, a tube of copper, and a rod of iron.

Found in Iraq, and dating back to 150 BCE, these provided conclusive proof that electroplating and galvanization were in use then, not discovered until much later in the nineteenth century.

In their possession also was the Saqqara Bird, one of ancient Egypt's finest artifacts, a wooden carving that could fly in today's wind tunnel.

Mike immediately thought that the Museum of Egyptian Antiquities in Cairo was pretty pissed about losing that item. He would make no mention to anyone regarding his dad's theft.

Also, in their possession were two elongated skulls, one from Akhenaten in 1352 BCE and one similar from another Egyptian tomb.

Pieces of ancient stone carvings from the Vijayanagara Empire of India had high levels of meteorite properties. A noted estimate read that the amount of meteorite discovered there would have taken tens of thousands of years to mine in today's world. So, how did so much become available then?

Ancient Hindu texts describing flying palaces called Vimana, complete with weaponry, had incredible detail. Many photos were found of the four types of flying Vimanas: Rukma, Sundara, Tripura, and Sakuna.

Ancient Hopi Indian cave painting were found reproduced. They showed star people, known as "the Greys" coming to earth from the stars in a serpent-like vehicle, and then returning to the stars.

Hieroglyphic inscriptions on the tomb of ancient Mayan King Pakal, from 640 A.D. had shown him at the controls of a modern-day spaceship.

Puma Punku, near the western border of Bolivia, is often thought of as where the modern world began, with evidence of magnificent stone structures dating back to 12,000 BCE. The incredibly large and detailed stone and mono-lithic structures were built with stone masonry that would be difficult to repro-duce today.

Also found were numerous cave paintings copied with the same precision throughout the world. Monuments from Moai of Easter Island were found duplicated and somewhere actually hidden in Sweden.

Several interviews were conducted and resulted in credible findings: forensic evidence proving remains of cone skulls that were genetically different form humans, UFO observers from area 51, an alien space shuttle, and astronauts hidden from public.

It also became apparent that Pete was not working alone, as further evidence pointed to a secret group, albeit a small one they thought, with people that were similarly wired. In addition to Pete there were four other members of this group.

It seemed as though Pete was worried about their identities being divulged, so they apparently were given nicknames. Pete was Orion, and the others were referred to as stones, chariot, Sacajawea and smoke.

Pete's journal, log book, and diary contained massive amounts of information, in various languages, and assorted artifacts and alien material that got the team's attention, and it was a lot to process. Sara immediately started working on these pieces.

Connor dove into the computers and peripherals to see what he could diagnose.

Justin quietly looked at the disassociated data hoping to find some correlation.

Michaela took the big picture perspective by starting at Pete's end and trying to work backwards.

And, Mike was immediately looking for physical and mental links between his dad and himself. Even Christine was overwhelmed with what had just happened.

However, this was not the kind of project that was similar to any work the team had ever done or would fit into the scope of their job descriptions. But this new cabin "find" had immediately gotten the group excited. Sara wanted to pursue this project, but she would need the team to buy in.

Without much thought, she asked "We are a team and whatever you guys want to do is your decision. I'd love to start looking into this info that Grandad gathered, but there's a lot of stuff here and I can't do I alone. Can I get a show of hands with who's in?"

Kat spoke first. "Let's take a look at what we have here when we get back to the City and go from there."

Connor offered, "I'm a bit stressed with work right now, so I'll need to think about this for a while."

Sara jumped in, "Of course we need to look at our work priorities first. I'm just fascinated by what we found and would like to see where it leads."

Michaela said, "I'm ready to do this with whatever time I can spare."

Mike chimed in with "You can count me in too."

Christine just shrugged her shoulders and said "Whatever."

So, they used the remainder of that Sunday to pack up most of what was in the cabin, minus the mural, computer equipment and furniture, or the big stuff.

They extracted as much as possible from the hard drives, given the filth of this equipment, and put their findings in the two vehicles they had brought.

On the trip home they discussed next steps and agreed to a tentative plan for Sara, Mike, and Michaela to do a high-level analysis and then get back to the rest of the team. That plan was accepted and understood by all.

Although some large objects and wall coverings remained in Pete's cabin, the trio of volunteers had a very large haul within which to work and try to get some answers.

They arrived in San Francisco with most of Grandad's material and notes, and hard artifacts, some easily identifiable and some that defied description. Sara decided to work evenings and weekends, around her regular Silicon Valley jobs.

Mike found Sara a small warehouse in the retail district and financed it, much to Christine's objections.

Sara had some immediate help from Michaela, but the rest of the team wasn't yet onboard.

"Dad, thanks for your help. I know Mom isn't too thrilled with taking on another expense."

"Don't worry about that. I hope your team gets a little more enthusiastic about what we found. Until then, keep me in the loop, okay?"

"Will do."

"You need a hook to get your team excited. Good luck with that."

"Thanks."

Mike was still preoccupied by one thought; his dad's untimely and somewhat mysterious death, on September 16, 2018, the day before what all the notes in the cabin referred to as THE REVEAL.

The notes from the REVEAL are revealed...

49

SARA

Digging into her grandad's flash drives, Sara found a lengthy and detailed PowerPoint presentation. After seeing it, she called her dad with the new info.

"You gotta minute?"

"Sure."

"I ran across Grandad's slides from a presentation he planned to give with somebody called John Smith at the Fall 2018 Paris Air Show. Some slides have notes to them and some don't."

"Okay. Go ahead."

"Well, a 3,600-year old crystal skull was found in Belize and analyzed. Its detail resembled the quartz crystals in today's computers and LCD watches. Similar artifacts were found off Honduras in the Bay Islands and pointed to an underwater civilization of Atlantis lore."

"Dad mentioned his interest in Atlantis lore. He believed strongly, and I concur, that there are likely hundreds of cities deeply submerged as a result of thousands of years of sea level rise."

Stopping to take a couple notes, Sara replied. "Apparently, the scientific marvels of Egypt never had an actual beginning, according to carvings and etchings they uncovered. Every aspect of Egyptian knowledge seems to have been complete at the very beginning of their history indicating an earlier and well-advanced culture over and over again."

"That would explain the building and technology prowess that Dad lectured us on."

Sara continued. "The Giza Pyramid Complex in Egypt was referred to by Pete's team as the *Earth's Massive Power Plant*, built with technology that wasn't even close to being available then. The highest level of applications of math, science, and physics were on full display in the Giza Plateau."

"I was aware of that, Sara."

"One amazing entry described a vast number of inventions that were written and carved hundreds of year BCE that are recognized as today's modern inventions."

"Yeah, Dad and I discussed that. It was a total disconnect from practical sources of thinking. He was excited about that, for sure."

"Some truly disturbing photos were gathered that showed UFOs that had been taken by the government, apparently, and sequestered in an obscure hanger, along with the likely remains of three alien astronauts."

"Yeah, that's what Dad referred to as area 52."

"Did you ever see the photos?"

"No. Not sure why. Maybe he needed to authenticate them."

"Some ancillary findings that were totally off the alien research radar are also noted here. I'm going to get with my team and take a deeper dive on this. There is a disturbing mention made of a vague terrorist conspiracy."

"What was the mention?"

"Well, it looks like they came across a criminal element that was buying and selling precious artifacts, mainly in the Middle East, and using the money for weapons. Again, I can't be sure that's what we are looking at but need to dig deeper."

"Oh my gosh, Sara, please be careful."

"I will. And Dad, don't tell Mom any of this terrorist stuff, okay?"

"I won't. She'll worry big time."

Relieved, Sara felt she got a load off her shoulders for now.

Mike, sensing the bittersweet call with Sara, simply said, "Let me know what you come up with. I have some contacts that might help."

"Okay, Dad. Bye."

✦ ✦ ✦

Now with an abundance of alien information, facts, and data, Sara was able to get her "A" team totally engaged.

They set up an open work area and war room in the warehouse donated by Mike. It was small, but impressive and well set-up. The routine was to work most evenings and weekends to put the alien pieces together. Everyone seemed to be onboard.

After analyzing the information that Sara had shared with her dad regarding the terrorist mention, she held an impromptu meeting with her team.

"Guys, I have taken a first pass at that terrorist slant and this is what I have so far. Grandad's team, in the middle of their alien artifact search, had coincidentally uncovered a terrorist plot to create a series of global calamities.

"The endgame of that plot was, apparently, to destroy long-established democratic cultures and take over the remaining anarchies using fear and terror as leverage.

"It was, obviously, an unintended consequence of their alien research, but an important and scary issue that couldn't be ignored. If you run this theory out to the present day, this would explain many of the terrorist attacks that the world has been experiencing."

Kat piped in, "Yeah, but without any pure and stated facts in Pete's material, is it an actual accounting of a true explanation with criminal overtones or simply someone's opinion. We haven't ruled out that Pete Stevenson was a little loose upstairs. Just saying…"

Connor added, "Don't you think our government is well aware of this and has every bit of Intel there is? Can't we just move on to the alien stuff?"

This terrorist slant was a huge and critical issue, and Sara and her team knew that they would need to confide in someone or some entity to get help moving forward on this discovery.

Sara called Mike and brought him up to date on their progress. Mike was both excited and alarmed by the dichotomy of Sara's news.

"The alien info helped to reinforce my opinion that Dad was on to something. The terrorist info convinces me that you guys are getting in over-your-heads."

"What's your advice, Dad?"

"I think I agree with Connor. Focus on the alien stuff."

"Good advice. Thanks."

Problem was that Sara had no intention of backing away from this. Her curiosity was through the roof.

The terrorist conspiracy is just too interesting to ignore…

50

SARA

This new and alarming information brought back thoughts and activity from that 2018-time frame for Sara. She knew that her parents were aware of Pete's trip to Paris, but they told Sara that they had no idea at the time that Pete was preparing a presentation, only that he was there to attend the Paris Air Show.

Sara was sure that her grandad was trying to keep his lecture under wraps, believing, according to his notes, that some of his findings could strike a couple nerves in either the alien theorist community or in law enforcement.

It was obvious from those notes and limited detail that Pete was nervous and apprehensive concerning this additional find and was not sure how to proceed with the information.

So, late in the summer of 2018, Sara could sense her grandad becoming a little cool and distant with her, almost as if to push Sara away from his alien artifact travel. She recalled a conversation with Pete that was odd and unsettling.

"Hi Grandad, how ya doing?"

"Good. Good."

"Whatcha up to these days? Any neat alien trips coming up?"

"No. At the cabin, chilling out. Gonna take some R&R time for now."

"Really? Can't say it isn't long overdue. Where to next?"

"Going to the annual Paris Air Show in September. It's fun and I have a lot of friends that attend the show."

"Great. If I don't talk to you before then, have a good trip."

"Thanks. Love you. Bye."

"Bye, Grandad."

Well, Sara thought that call was the most unusual call she had ever had with Pete. He was so quiet and NEVER took R&R for any reason. She tabled her concern for then, but planned to talk to him before his trip to Paris.

✦ ✦ ✦

It was now September 15, 2018, and Sara had on her phone calendar a note to call Pete on this date and wish him well and to enjoy the Paris Show.

Throughout the entire morning, several calls to him went directly to voicemail. Again, that was odd.

Being the curious person that she was, she started to look into the Paris Air Show meeting as she tried to reach Pete. She found the date, place, and time for the show, so she knew that the Paris Air Show was real.

Still not hearing from her grandad, it was now the day before the Paris meeting.

Starting to get concerned, Sara searched the Internet for specifics and schedules for the event. What she found was shocking.

On the published schedule of events for the September 17, 2018 was Pete Stevenson at 1:00 pm, giving a talk entitled THE REVEAL. Sara called her dad with this startling news.

"Dad, Grandad is giving a lecture tomorrow in Paris at the annual Air Show."

Mike was stunned at this news. "Are you sure? He never mentioned it to me."

"Yep, it's on the Net. And according to the day's agenda, his topic is THE REVEAL."

Now puzzled, Mike replies, "Thanks. I need to call Dad right now."

Sara adds, "And, and I haven't been able to reach him on his cell for days."

"That isn't like him, Sara."

"I know. And, I have no clue about his speaking topic, THE REVEAL."

Mike added, "Okay. Let me try to reach Dad and I'll get back to you."

Not at all satisfied, Sara says, "Thanks. Love you."

Mike ends the call, "Gotta go."

Sara has a bad feeling... a very bad feeling about this news...

51

MIKE

Furiously, Mike tried unsuccessfully to reach Pete. Either his cell phone was off or Mike had a continuing bad connection. He didn't even know which hotel Pete was staying at.

Mike tried friends, family members, acquaintances, and anyone that might have an idea regarding his dad's itinerary.

It was a long and frantic night of worry and concern. This time he did update Christine on Sara's call and his concern. Mike was worried and Christine was terrified. Sara tried every conceivable way to get in touch with her grandad.

Then, about 9:00 a.m. French time the next morning, the 17th, Mike received a call from the Commissariat de Police du #6 arrondissement in Paris. According to reports from the French Police, Pete was attacked and killed by a mugger outside his hotel on the evening of the 16th, the day before the Paris Air Show meeting.

Hearing the news, Mike and Christine were in shock. A call to Sara was devastating to her. A loss like this was unimaginable.

Two curiously striking results came from his death. One glaring fact jumped out at everyone involved; the attacker was not found in the days that followed Pete's murder, and no one was ever caught and/or convicted of the crime. Given hotel security cameras and several potential witnesses, the idea that no one was able to see the crime was unexplainable.

Mike made this his priority.

The other less notable result was that John Smith, who had Pete's presentation in hand, never gave it.

The two of them had been planning to make this presentation of THE REVEAL together, so even with Pete's tragic death, the importance of this alien material would have been too great to ignore.

Knowing how her grandad was wired, and the culture that Pete developed with his team, it was inconceivable that Smith would not deliver that presentation.

Sara believed that she needed to find out why.
Mike had one priority going forward.

Keep Sara safe, if that was even possible now...

52

SARA

Following Pete's death, Sara had several long and sad conversations with her parents. Pete's death shook the Stevenson family to such a great extent that Sara was searching for anything that would point to her grandad's murder as being non-random, but instead part of Pete's investigation and uncovering of facts, related or not related to the alien artifact hunting.

Sara recalled also that she had a strange need to contact her grandad prior to his Paris trip, which was odd. She never had any dreams of the event, but just a bad feeling. Mike and she did discuss their respective dreamscapes during one of these conversations.

Sara also remembered that during the trip back to San Francisco from Grandad's cabin, Mike described some of his other dreams to Sara, including several of his actual experiences that were vivid parts of specific dreams, and the type that could have been easily interpreted as end of the world.

In one particular recurring dream that Sara recalled her dad told her, Mike sees Christine, Sara, and a young child sitting on the edge of a bed and looking out a window at devastating smoke, fire, and chaos.

Her dad described that nightmare as the likely destruction of the world. He even confided in her the details of the hellish nightmare of 9/11 that he had.

Sara recalled how Mike had told her that these dreams were a strong indication of how his dream history was connected to his search for answers to both his day-to-day life and his evolving belief in alien presence that Pete had instigated.

Sara had called Mike to give him an update on the team's progress, but her call was actually made to get her dad to discuss the dreams and their impact on Mike's life at the present time.

"So, with the work stuff out of the way, do you have a few minutes to get back to the dreams you've been having?"

"Sure, but why?"

"C'mon, just humor me. You're my dad and this stuff is important to me."

Mike tried to relax a bit, realizing he had been a little gruff. "Okay. Sure. There had been some continuity in my dreams but it's not clear as to why and how."

"What do you mean continuity?"

"You know I have had progressive dreams that grow and grow, almost like a book series. And, I have recurring nightmares that wake me up in a cold sweat... they are so real."

Sara was very interested in her dad's remarks and asks, "Does Mom know about these?"

Pausing for a moment, Mike replies, "Not all of them. She would worry herself sick."

"Gotcha."

"But Sara, these dreams are so realistic. I used to dream regular people's dreams, whatever that signifies. But the last ten or fifteen years, it has been way different. It's almost as if these dreams are an alternate life of mine, and a shitty one at that."

"Yikes." Sara was worried but wouldn't reveal that to Mike.

Mike added, "I just want to be kept in the loop to see if you and your team would uncover anything in Grandad's research that would help explain some of these dreams, realizing that it's unlikely and a real stretch, for sure."

"Can do, Dad."

"It's just that I have spent many a sleepless night surrounding the death of my father and I was hoping that some key to his death would be revealed, or at least, somehow some light would be shed on that tragedy."

"You're right; it's a stretch. We'll do whatever we can."

They hung up and Sara realized that her question just resulted in more questions...

✦ ✦ ✦

Back to the project at hand, following the difficult but necessary talk with her dad, Sara tried her best to consolidate and categorize as much of Grandad's stuff that she could on her own, and then convened the team.

They discussed the unique and highly interesting material that they found, and then took on various sub-project areas to analyze different aspects of the cabin information, with each person taking on his or her specialty or interest.

This was the democracy part, where everyone had a say in what they wanted to do. After that, consensus would rule.

They put all of the findings into categories, or what Pete called his buckets, that Pete had identified in his puzzle. With categories of similarities established, each team member became the owner, for the sake of reporting, of each of several alien categories. In management lingo, Sara called this the 30,000-foot view, or big picture.

Early on, this activity was almost hobby-like, a bit of a diversion from their day-to-day jobs. They in no way envisioned any form of focused or dedicated effort ensuing. As they continued, however, two things became evident.

One, this was becoming a very important study. The more they uncovered, the less they knew. And, it had to be taken methodically, seriously, and carefully. It would be a long journey and they were at the very beginning.

Secondly, they did not have specific subject matter expertise in many of the areas of Pete's findings to continue without some additional help. That became evident as they reviewed each category.

After a month of dedicated review of the Pete Stevenson plethora of facts and opinions, Sara held a status meeting to create a baseline that they could use to continue going forward.

"Okay, let's see where we are right now. Who wants to start us out?"

Kat jumped in, "Monuments, the mega-stone pyramids, temples, and gigantic building stones that were found in many locations in the world were the most visible and unexplainable occurrences. The incredible duplication of these giant structures throughout the world are absolutely stunning."

Connor adds, "Alien flying machines, astronauts, and UFO's were identified with many photos, carvings, observed phenomena, and personal interviews. There was also a small folder that was marked *'Cover ups.'* Didn't go there yet."

Justin was super-engaged and anxious to speak.

"Energy grids and communications patterns and redundancies that resemble a global map shot from space with on-the-ground detail is hard to denounce. Seriously, it looks like stuff laid out thousands of years ago was actually done by our own modern-day Space Shuttles."

Waiting for the applause that didn't come, Justin continued.

"Transportation, levitation, and out-of-body documentation that described present-day encounters were recorded thousands of years earlier."

Sara is pleased with the results so far and asks Michaela what was on her radar screen.

"Advanced technology of AI and IT and their possible downsides were found in carvings and encryptions that indicated that inventions of today were likely made thousands of years ago.

"And, links to Gods and Royal Rulers throughout history all found origins in space travel and celestial beings from other planets or the cosmos, according to puzzle parts connected."

Michaela paused and Sara asked, "Anything else?"

"Yes. This is difficult for me to mention, given we have had discussions concerning Pete's mental well-being"

"Go on, Michaela," Sara says with some hesitation.

"I have found three OMG's that I can't immediately process.

"Pete has detailed notes regarding actual encounters with aliens."

53

MICHAELA

M ichaela presents Pete's encounter notes:
"One, he describes conversations with temporal aliens, that is aliens from the future."

Echo showed me today how spinning black holes and gravity withdrawal could affect time travel and result in how thousands of generations of beings from the future could return to Earth in the present day. Time travel was common. Pulse said that they could predict future significant events because of this capability…

"Two, he talks about the colonization of Mars like it's a historical event."

Pulse and Laser showed me the early colonization of Mars roughly 3.5 billion years ago using a type of hologram that I had never seen. Life on Mars ended when the once plentiful water supply was taken. What the hell does that mean? I think an evil alien species destroyed them. Here on Earth, one day we could be reduced to ashes!

"And three, he mentions an actual encounter with aliens in Trelleborg, Sweden, as evidence of their existence."

February 12, 2018. In Trelleborg, Sweden, and just returned from a guided tour of the observable universe with temporal aliens Echo, Pulse, and Laser. The couple days spent with them felt like a couple weeks. What I saw is in my mind and that is where it will stay forever…

Michaela then adds, "I have checked out the handwriting and they are, indeed, Pete Stevenson's notes."

Sara quickly adds, "If it was anyone but Michaela I'd say, what have you been drinking? You're right, that's a lot to process."

Michaela responds, "We just can't tell if he was joking or looking for some support from friends or struggling with any mental issues."

Before continuing her observations, Sara thinks out loud. "Okay, gang, except for these notes, what are our next steps?"

Michaela quickly responds. "First thing, we need some more help. Subject matter expertise wouldn't hurt."

Sara asks, "Show of hands?"

Unanimous response from the team.

"Okay," Michaela concludes.

"We'll start getting a short list together of what our needs will be going forward."

Michaela and Sara both knew that those notes were the real thing. But what to do with them?

Michaela thought to herself.

"We need to get the best damn talent on the planet!"

54

SARA

So, Sara, using the recommendations from the team, began an exhausting and frustrating attempt to bring into the fold other subject matter experts whom she and the team could trust and work with, and that could fill the many voids that their research exposed.

The most difficult task wasn't finding good people, but what would be their motivation to get involved. What's in it for me? Sara's team was built from within, so to speak. With that, she called her dad and asked his advice.

Mike began with the obvious. "Well, it's a conundrum, for sure."

"Really? I know that, Dad."

"Sorry. Little humor."

"Yeah, very little."

Getting serious, Mike begins. "Okay, try this with your vetting process. Don't look at what they tell you, but look at what they've done.

"Assuming that a group of people has all the needed skill set, look at what they have done in their careers regarding give-backs, volunteering, gratis work, and the unselfish stuff."

Smiling at the simple perspective, Sara replies, "That makes sense."

"Then hit 'em with the chance to be part of history or at least the proverbial fifteen minutes of fame. Those on the short list will gladly devote some personal time to the greater good. Just be careful regarding how much alien detail you expose early in the interviewing process."

A very relieved Sara adds, "Great, Dad. Thanks."

"You betcha."

Sara was happy knowing that her dad was feeling pretty good about that advice. But the conversation didn't end there.

"One more thing, Dad."

"Sure, what's that Sara?"

Sara replies, "Michaela came across notes from Grandad that he allegedly took that involved his actual encounter with temporal aliens. And they had names: Echo, Pulse, and Laser."

"Whoa," Mike says excitedly. "What did you think?"

"No clue, Dad. It would certainly be a stretch to say they are legit, given Grandad's desire to find hard evidence, but you just don't know."

"Scan 'em and send them to me, okay?"

"Sure, Dad, will do."

✦ ✦ ✦

Bringing new people into the fold was a daunting task. It was a slow and tedious process, but one that would eventually result in several well-vetted additions to the research family.

These nuts-and-bolts specialists would be given specific tasks but never the full scope of the project and the implications. Sara's team keep would keep their true mission as secretive and confidential as possible, at least for now.

As *the devil is in the details* is certainly true, the fact that they had no one with the patience and interest to take on this boring work was also true. They needed someone with the patience and determination of an IRS tax auditor.

As they say, timing is everything. While attending a women's leadership conference in Atlanta about six-month earlier, Sara and Michaela met one of the attendees, Jacqui Carroll, and they became fast friends.

Following that conference, they even talked about how well Jacqui's attention to detail and fastidious organizational skills would sync with the group. At that time, it was just chatter.

Jacqui was now working in North Carolina as an independent contractor in finance and helping clients in mergers and acquisitions. She is so far off the radar that no one could ever link her to the team's work.

Very much the studious type, Jacqui always was seen in black horn-rimmed glasses and a high turtleneck blouse.

"Hi Jacqui, it's Sara and Michaela calling from San Francisco. Remember us from the Atlanta conference?"

"Of course, I do. Is that you Sara?"

"It is. Michaela is right here too."

"Hi Jacqui. How ya doing?"

"Good, very good. To what do I owe the pleasure?"

Sara explained, "We didn't get into too much detail in Atlanta, but we are now staffing up for some research into all things outer space and have a need for someone with your skills."

"All things outer space would indicate that cannabis has arrived in the City. So far, you have my attention."

Michaela added, "Jacqui, we have a pretty cool gig underway here and can't really discuss it over the phone."

Pulling out her travel schedule, Jacqui adds, "Now I'm really interested."

"Can you come out for a couple of days so we can show you what we have and what we need you for?"

"Sure can. Looking at my business commitments as we speak. Thanks for thinking of me and I'll let you know the details of my visit as soon as I can make the arrangements."

"Jacqui," Sara replied, "we can't wait for you to see what we've got going on out here."

Jacqui added her two cents. "Ya know, I've found one thing in business that always rings true. It's not so much the project itself, but it is who you are working with. I love you guys."

Michaela simply said, "You got that right," and they hung up.

Within two weeks the trip was made and Jacqui could see why her expertise was needed. Plus, she could do most of the needed research remotely from her home and office in NC and not need to have an on-site role with the Northern California team.

So, with little selling needed from Sara and Michaela, Jacqui was on board and excited.

Over the course of a couple of months, two more similarly wired people, after vetting had been done, were brought into the fold from the west coast.

They were friends and respected colleagues of the team and could be trusted. One was Creighton Abrams, who had come from NASA, and the other was a Pakistani named Sumar Bhuyan, and he had extensive IT experience.

Mike insisted that heightened security and confidentiality became the fabric of this group, and extreme vetting was performed.

The program budget was getting expensive, and Christine reminded Mike often that it was becoming a financial burden for the couple to fund the warehouse.

Sara was thinking that she would really like a new alien buddy.

That's exactly what she would get...

55

SARA

It was during this time of unsettled uncertainty that Sara met Paul Thomas, who was also an entrepreneur, and they were both drawn to each other's curiosity and passion.

They met in a Silicon Valley Young Entrepreneurs Club and seemed to share a type of focus and restlessness that few other people had shown or exposed.

Paul looked like the stereotypical surfer-dude. Tall, blonde, handsome, and fit. Body fat was about zero, as it appeared. He had an infectious smile and was very good at listening. In a sport coat or suit, he looked like he just walked off of the cover of GQ.

Together, Sara and Paul looked to anyone as the perfect marketing couple for fill-in-the-blank products.

They had been introduced to each other by the President of the Silicon Valley Young Entrepreneurs Club, who was a mutual friend, and immediately clicked. Both attractive and outgoing people, they moved directly into shop talk and far from small talk.

After the usual getting-to-know-you pleasantries, Paul opened with, "So Sara, what are your 2:00 a.m. thoughts? You know, what keeps you up at night?"

"That's getting to the point, Paul. Great. Job and career security are important to me, but building relationships is also important to me. What keeps me up at night is the stress of trying to deal with so many priorities that I am facing. Probably typical for most Millennials."

Paul replies, "Yep, you can add that to my list as well."

Sara adds, "My dad has a saying, 'When the urgent pushes out the important, how do you find time for the important?'"

"Wise man, your father."

Sara continues. "These days, my main diversion is, are we alone in the universe? I often look at the vastness of space and wonder if there is anyone else out there?"

Then Sara said to Paul, "My turn. If you could cure one of the world's ills, which one would that be?"

Without hesitation Paul said, "World hunger. I think that greed and self-interest has made this an impossible task right now, but with the right strategy and leadership, we could make significant progress there.

"Hey, I like your thoughts on space."

Sara thinks to herself, "Yep, game on!"

Paul was involved in many aspects of entrepreneurship and start-up support for many small firms, but his sweet spot was Venture Capital funding for up-and-coming Silicon Valley businesses.

He was widely known as the VC guru in the valley, and his trusting personality had resulted in an impressive cadre of influential and dynamic friends and business associates.

In his mid-thirties, he had built a great reputation as the guy that would do what he said he would do. Later he would tell Sara that the guide to ethics was simply to think of your actions and behavior as front-page news.

"If you don't want it printed on the front page of a newspaper or a stream in social media, don't do it."

Sara was definitely feeling warm and fuzzy in his company. She was cautious though, having had many disappointing relationships when ego and intimidation took over.

Paul seemed to have his ego in check and neither was particularly turned off by the other person's work or personalities. This was a good start for both of them.

One particular incident occurred when they were dating that threw a remarkable and relevant curve into the mix of Grandad Pete's pile of alien treasures.

Following a wonderful sushi dinner and, of course, the requisite karaoke, Paul and Sara went back to Paul's condo and they decided to watch a movie. Sensing that Sara wasn't exactly excited about any particular movies on cable TV, Paul suggested an alternative.

"I have become a bit of an ancient alien fan and watched a variety of programs on several cable channels. The History Channel and Discovery have some good viewing options."

Struck by the irony, Sara looks to Paul and says, "Seriously?"

"And as I recall, you mentioned *life out there* as one of your diversions. Maybe tonight would be a good time to dig a little deeper."

"Wow, I had you with a much more pragmatic side and kind of skeptical."

Paul adds, "I can see where you got that, with the black-and-white work in finance and VC. Sara, I am a lot more opened-minded then you would think."

When he brought up that viewing option, Sara was overwhelmed with joy from several perspectives. "I'd love to see what you have in your video library or what is on the cable channels right now. We can do an *On Demand* if there is something that you really like."

Paul, getting very upbeat, adds, "Great. I'll tee up something if you can open a Cab and see if there is enough cheese and snacks in the frig and pantry."

As Sara excitedly returned with the wine and snacks, Paul began with one or two of his favorites, not knowing her reaction but expecting a good one.

Over the course of the next few weeks, at Sara's insistence, Paul continued to show his favorite alien programs.

He was very pleased that his girlfriend was interested enough in his little sidebar attraction that they actually discussed the pluses and minuses or myth versus fact of the many topics of these shows.

Sara had reached a point where two things jumped out at her.

First, she was really starting to like Paul and appreciate his kind personality and obvious intelligence.

The other, obviously, was the mutual core of curiosity that they shared for the many extraterrestrial existence theories.

One night, Sara got up the courage to simply ask, "Paul do you have a position yourself on the existence either now or in ancient history of alien presence?"

"Yes, and I think our world is getting smaller and less relevant with every passing event that I take in, and I think of the prospects of just how expansive the universe and galaxy are."

After pausing a moment to choose her words, she said "What if I told you that I actually have in my possession several interesting ancient alien artifacts gathered over two generations. Would you be open-minded to getting involved with me and a small team of true believers?"

"I was hoping you'd ask."

Sara was happy but a bit confused.

"You see Sara, you probably didn't realize it, but you were trying to sell me on alien existence right from the start. You seemed more than just optimistic."

A bit puzzled, Sara asks, "How so?"

"You seemed to have a plausible explanation of many of the things we saw on cable. This was not the first time you encountered alien phenomena. It was obvious to me that you studied the pluses and minuses of every argument posed."

"Yeah, I am the curious type."

Getting excited, Paul continues, "In addition to your knowledge and specifically targeted questions from our program viewing, you made it clear to me that there was something very exciting that you were holding in and I want to hear more."

"For example?"

"Sara, you discussed those ancient bird carving artifacts that resembled airplanes so specifically, it was if you had actually seen one!"

Smiling, Sara says, "We need to talk."

Sara was so happy from many different points of view. So, as she relished in the excitement of her new love, she began the story of the story of the story...

She could tell that Paul's attentiveness to her and her stories, and the fact that he was truly a good listener, made the decision to introduce him to the team a no-brainer.

✦ ✦ ✦

Sara brought Paul to the team's office and had an opening line that was not hard to understand. "Guys, this is Paul Thomas and I am truly convinced that he will enable us to get where we all said we needed to be... the next level.

Paul simply says, "It's great to meet you. Sara has convinced me that you guys are the strongest and most professional team she has ever had or has ever seen."

Kat responds, "The feeling is mutual regarding our fearless leader."

Within an hour or so of hard, but focused questions, followed by many aha moments, Paul had their attention.

Michaela had one last question for Paul. "If you were to come on board, what would your first priority be?"

Being an outstanding listener, Paul paid close attention as he was brought up to speed and listened to them explain their important and urgent issues. He then offered the team two major proposals for their consideration.

"First, I would help you guys recruit the best and brightest new members, once I had a firm handle on the group's short-term and long-term needs going forward.

"Then I would set out to find the funding that would surely need to be obtained, and obtained quickly, if this new and pioneering team was to be successful."

Michaela responded, "That's quite aggressive, don't you think?"

"Of course, but there aren't any shortcuts here. You just need to do the work and I'm ready to start."

Sara observed that everyone sensed the passion and commitment that Paul was demonstrating, and she knew Paul would be off and running very soon.

She was right. Paul's strategy was spot-on.

56

PAUL

Paul's strategy was obvious. His impressive list of venture capital and angel capital investors were to be approached with a hierarchy that aligned with the needs of Sara's team.

Paul knew that no typical VC manager would be interested in anything that didn't have a big, immediate ROI. So, this was likely going to be the friend of a friend.

It was also very obvious to Paul that due to extreme confidentiality and secrecy he would need to proceed with absolute caution and carefully present the group's needs.

What Paul was trying to find was that one enlightened person who would be able to help them both financially and administratively.

After an exhausting pro-versus-con evaluation of a number of his contacts and enablers, hundreds of calls and interviews and with serious cost-versus-benefit analysis done, he set his sights on Scott Woods, a man who was always on the top of his short list.

Scott Woods was the founder and CEO of an Internet-based product and service provider with sales in excess of $800 billion. He also had a passion for space travel and an intense curiosity for the vast universe and our solar system.

A division of his company, *Stargate LTD*, along with two other private firms, were competing with the U.S. Government's traditional aerospace agencies to continue to supply International Space Station 2, the current culmination of global space research involving several countries.

With Scott's hectic business life and demanding travel schedule, it would take Paul a few weeks to get his meeting or meetings with Scott. But, meeting with Scott was a must-do.

Meanwhile, Paul and Sara were clearly alike in many ways and quite compatible, and it was obvious whenever they were together.

After dating for about a year and a half, Paul planned a perfect getaway for the couple on a small island in the French Antilles. He had scheduled the trip around the time of the full Blue Moon, one of Sara's favorite times of the month.

This time, Paul set up a beautiful beach walk at dusk, as the moonrise was coming out of the ocean in full brilliance.

Grasping Sara's hand and stopping to glance into her eyes, he said. "Sara, my love, you can make me the happiest guy on Earth. Will you marry me?"

Realizing just how wonderful this moment and this scene were, she was overwhelmed with love and peace. The sea mist in the air was lost unto the teary mist in Sara's eyes.

"Yes, Paul, I would love to be your wife. Nothing could make me happier."

Sara called her parents with the news, and they were thrilled for their daughter. Mike had already been brought up to speed regarding Paul's enthusiasm in all things alien, so this news did not surprise him.

Mike and Christine's very first impression of Paul was very solid and very positive. "What a wonderful win/win," Mike told Sara.

They were married in a small chapel in Half Moon Bay, California, with only their closest friends attending. The glitz and glamor of a big wedding just was not for them.

In a whimsical moment, Sara thought back to her dad's recurring wedding dreams of her big cathedral wedding and it never happening because he was always excusing himself. How funny was that dream sequence compared to this lovely setting?

They would likely never have children, as one common thread they shared was an intense passion for their crafts and careers.

✦ ✦ ✦

Paul became the perfect sounding board for the team that Sara had assembled. Where she was an intense Type A person, he was the calming voice of reason and organization.

He was also very fond of visual management techniques, which became increasingly evident as the team mapped out its course of action.

Paul grew up in a foster home, so he had matured at a very early age and was an ideal integrator for all things weird and bizarre. He would never say, *you should do it this way.*

Instead, he would always say *why do you do it that way?* With a huge difference between the two approaches, he nearly always endeared himself to those within his reach.

Within three months, Paul helped Sara's team to recruit and integrate several more members with specific subject matter expertise. He had a big part to play in that recruitment process and the core team was grateful.

Finally, this new team was ready to start the unbelievably big effort to make sense of what they had gathered.

Paul set up a meeting with Sara to discuss the plethora of information that the team had gathered.

Sharing a bottle of Napa Valley Bond 2001 Vecina Red Cabernet, Paul laid out his white board with the appropriate bullet points.

"Okay, Sara, this is what I've got. Under your guidance, the team cast a wide net over all of the information and artifacts that they had gathered, including certain phenomena that fell outside of Pete's material."

Sara adds, "Great. Yep, that's a long list. Let me look at all of your bullets."

Paul gave Sara a laser pointer and she began…

"The issues include global warming, bizarre weather patterns and storms, thermal scanning, DNA anomalies that puzzled the medical community, the NASA trip to the moon, ancient cities, financial meltdowns, the Great Depression, and the Great Recession… I read about those last two in a history book."

Paul smiles and pours Sara more Cab and she continues.

"Anything that they could find regarding Ancient Aliens and Astronaut Theory, land subsidence and sea level rise, air quality variation, UFO's, the disappearance of many civilizations over time, rapid rise of new technology, plagues and epidemics, megalithic stone structures, and general patterns of systemic, dysfunctional world leadership."

Paul adds, "And the last one is the icing on the cake. The advancement of A.I. and documented evidence of meta-human existence."

Sara grins, as Paul watches her pour him another glass of Cab. With a strong and direct voice, looking directly into Paul's eyes, Sara responds.

"Paul, this is going to take on a life all its own. You ready for this?"

Paul quickly responds, "More than ready. Can't wait to get fully immersed."

They toast each other and are very happy at that moment.

Meanwhile, an epic Hurricane approaches.

57

PETE

One of the more curious storylines found in the cabin were events dating back to 1995 and 2005, that Pete had documented from an actual experience.

Being an avid scuba diver, Pete and friends from Texas took numerous dives, mostly in the British Virgin Islands and the French Antilles. But what Pete wrote in his PADI dive log book was extremely fascinating and defied explanation.

Apparently, on a dive in the BVI's in April, 1997, while aboard the Sailing Vessel L'Enleve, the group had decided to take a night dive to the sunken mail ship, the RMS Rhone, sunk by a hurricane in 1867.

Pete had become good friends with the ship's young captain, Gary Celebreeze, a long-time resident of the BVI's before joining the Polynesian Seas' fleet, among which the L'Enleve was the Crown Jewel.

And, Pete struck up a friendship with the First Mate, Onnie Heikkila, over their love of classic American cars. They both agreed that a night dive to the Rhone was not to be missed.

As their luck would have it, that night provided not only a full moon to see upon re-surfacing, but the comet Hale-Bopp, one of the brightest ever seen, which made its way across the sky as the divers reached the surface.

This wonderful and coincidental phenomenon sent chills up the spines of the 6 divers. Night dive… full moon… Hale-Bopp comet!

✦ ✦ ✦

The Sailing Vessel L'Enleve was the $35 million, 280-feet long, steel hull, four-mast sailing vessel, and self-insured pride of the Miami Beach-based Polynesian Sea Cruises Ltd., a sailing line with five other vessels.

The L'Enleve had a regal beginning, as it was built for the Duke of Westchester in 1930. Even though it had a steel hull, not wood, it was considered a solid vessel.

When its massive sails were filled making way to windward, it was romance in motion. Breakfast was a Bloody Mary, dinner included rum swizzles, and passengers dived off the side to snorkel and climb back up on rope ladders.

The young thirty-five-year old captain, Gary Celebreeze, was respected by his crew and highly regarded for his sailing abilities.

The final, fateful trip began in the Honduran port of Omoa on October 22, 1998, destination Belize for six days of diving and snorkeling. But the seventy passengers boarding that day knew that this trip was not going to go smoothly. The driving rain that greeted them continued as they set sail, as winds from a late-season hurricane some 1000 miles away, tracking toward Jamaica, were already being felt.

The next day, it appeared that the storm, now Hurricane Martin, had changed course and was headed their way, albeit erratically.

The captain decided to make an early sprint to Belize City, where all seventy passengers and nonessential crew would disembark. By this time, Martin was a strong Category 3 hurricane with winds in excess of 130 mph.

So, as the remaining thirty-two crew set sail to avoid Martin, they were boxed into a corner, with the Yucatan peninsula to the west and Honduras to the south. Their only way out was north, plowing past the Barrier Reef, with plans to wait out Martin in the peaceful Gulf of Mexico.

But within hours, Martin's path changed again, this time heading north on a course similar to the course of the L'Enleve. Under full sail, the L'Enleve could only manage about 8 or 9 mph.

At this point, Martin was behind them, at 12 to 15 mph and with winds exceeding 180 mph, and now the fifth most powerful Atlantic hurricane ever recorded. But steering currents were erratic in October and anything could happen. It did. Martin stopped.

So, the captain changed course for Roatán, as forecasters believed that Martin would go the opposite direction. Roatán would offer some protection from the storm, as the L'Enleve could slip between the storm and the island.

With the L'Enleve barely underway, Martin changed course and headed directly for Roatán. L'Enleve's shelter suddenly looked like ground zero, as they were on a trajectory that would sandwich them between the rugged Honduran shoreline and the storm.

Then the steering currents just collapsed. There was literally no power for the sails and Martin was bearing down with 40-to 50-foot waves and a wind speed of 170 to 180 mph.

Once the winds of Martin found the L'Enleve, which was for the most part dead in the water, it took about 48 hours for the steel-hulled vessel to sink. And it likely split in half and sunk like a rock in 1500-foot-deep water.

The vessels' life rafts were never deployed, as the ship likely capsized with one 50-foot wave and all emergency items were trapped in pockets in an upside-down sinking ship.

On October 30, 1998, following a five-day search by the British frigate HMS Morgan, debris was spotted some 30 miles away: two life rafts, eight life vests, stenciled on them SV/L'Enleve. No survivors. And the remains were never found.

Thirty-two men had run for their lives from Hurricane Martin for a day and a half. They sailed north, then sailed south, then tacked east and west, back and forth in futility, behind a little island of cover.

But it left them in a virtual vise, walled in between 60-foot waves and 120-mph winds where sea and sky merged into a vast howling whiteout. Experienced mariners can tell you what comes next. After 48 hours in a hurricane's wrath, you want to lie down, cover your ears from the howling, and go to sleep. When the ship starts falling apart, you are just waiting and wanting to die.

When that fateful night ended, the ship, built for a duke and enjoying so many wonderful voyages, had no choice but to give up. Adding even more macabre aspects to this horrific story had to do with its 1930 christening:

L'Enleve, an old French definition that in today's translation is ABDUCTION.

58

PETE

It is now April, 2007, at Tortola, in the British Virgin Islands. That group of divers from the night dive in 1997, including Pete, experiencing the comet Hale-Bopp sighting, had returned to do another night dive on the HMS Rhone, to celebrate the 10-year anniversary.

What they found, however, on the nearby island of Jost Van Dyke, the smallest island of the BVI's, was unimaginable.

On a remote part of the island, where only the locals would venture, was Gary Celebreeze, the young captain of the L'Enleve and several members of his crew, including Onnie Heikkila… yes, the very same crew that died one year earlier from the sinking of their ship!

Only 12 survived. Apparently the other 20 crew members had died before the ship sank. But, each of those 12 crew members had the distinctive cuts on their arms. And, all of them denied any knowledge of the sinking of the L'Enleve and their parts to play in any survivor theory.

It took three subsequent trips to the island of Jost Van Dyke by Pete alone, for those lost souls to tell their story about those horrific two nights aboard the L'Enleve as she went under.

What emerged was an eerie similarity to the levitation that Jack had felt, and the electric shock-type feeling that ultimately transferred to Pete.

And, the cylinder that pulled them skyward was quiet, calming, and dry. No sensation that they were plucked from a 180-mph hurricane tearing their ship apart!

After Pete explained his eerily similar encounter in Brazil with his friend Jack, one of the ship's crew members finally opened up.

"It was like a near-death experience. One minute you were facing your final minutes of life, and you knew it."

Another crew member chipped in, "The loud and constant noise of the storm, screeching and unrelenting, was just unimaginable. Then, a near perfect quiet."

Another crew member added, "The calm and quiet was as if you had died and only your soul remained. The only thing that I recall was going from unimaginable horror and probable death to a mental state that was as wonderfully peaceful as the earlier was so horrible."

Onnie added, "We were all in the same smoky or foggy room. We could see each other faintly, and there were stick-like bodies or forms tending to each of us. Try as I may, I couldn't tell you if we were there for a day or a month. It seemed long and not real one time and then okay the next. Very confusing."

Gary added, "And when we all regained consciousness, we were here, in a place that was known to us, and healthy, except for the cuts on our arms that were already healed."

Pete responded, "Thank you for your open and honest accounts and for trusting me with your story. As you now know, I have had similar experiences, so I can obviously relate."

And, as far as Pete could tell, no one else would ever find out about their secret and their extraterrestrial good fortune.

They had made a pact to not sell their stories, as they would be giving up their private lives, and just enjoy their good fortune. That incredible crew were more than happy to let sleeping dogs lay.

From that point on, Pete would spend much of his life unable to process that significant event in his mind. Upon returning home, with his telescope pointed in the direction of Orion, Pete uttered one thought to himself.

"It is so unlikely for anyone on earth to experience just one episode of these unexplained abduction phenomenon, yet I have personally witnessed this twice. I must find the truth; it's out there, at whatever the stakes!"

For Pete, the stakes would be VERY HIGH!

59

PAUL

Paul Thomas had developed some extremely close ties to several wealthy and influential Silicon Valley business people, and he was working to bring a serious financial investor into the project. Scott Woods was the perfect candidate, in Paul's mind, to become an integral part of Sara's team.

Scott was recognized as a strong visionary, extremely philanthropic, and a risk-taker of epic proportions. He had gotten on the wrong side of the SEC over his funding methods for IPO's when corrupt IRS officials tried to take him down. Scott Woods was both admired and feared. People close to him, however, said he had a heart of gold.

After discussing his thoughts and getting approval from Sara, Paul was ready to approach Scott with an update of the cabin findings and the work being done, mostly after hours, by Sara and Paul's select team.

Paul was finally able to get his meeting set up, but it wasn't easy. Scott was having a fund-raiser on Santa Catalina Island off the southwest of Los Angeles and had his mega-yacht, *Stargaze*, moored in the Catalina Island Bay.

Arriving by ferry, Paul brought several items to show Scott and try to convince him to jump in.

Scott was a wiry sort of guy, full of energy and always moving. He spoke with his arms and hands and was never at a loss for words. On the shorter side, it could be assumed that his totally outgoing personality was to get him noticed, back when that was a problem. Today, everyone knew Scott.

"Scott, it's a pleasure to meet you and thank you so much for taking time to see me."

"No problem. I have about fifteen minutes, so let's get going."

Paul was feeling some big-time stress, for sure. He canned his speech and simply opened up his goodie bag.

"Scott, I'm working for…"

"I know about your work and that team of overachievers. Had to do some serious checking up before I agreed to this meeting. You already have my attention, but I have a meeting soon. Tell me what ya got."

Catching his breath, Paul immediately got into the two generations of research, the cabin contents, the cream of Pete's buckets, and the magnificent carved bird artifact. Scott pressed the ship's intercom button. "Move my meeting out an hour."

Not expecting to get a quick response from Scott, within that hour of Paul's highly focused presentation, Scott was impressed.

"I want to see what it would take to get personally involved in this project. We need to move quickly to see if my involvement is needed and makes sense."

Paul responded, "The fact that this team has uncovered decades of thorough and detailed research is certainly worthy of you and your people taking deep dive, in my opinion, to see if current beliefs regarding alien presence might be wrong."

"Not my business associates, just my wife and me for now."

Paul replied, "I understand."

"The other fact that you have a group of motivated millennials buying into work done by much older people says much about their perception and convictions."

"Yes, Scott, these are people wired as fact-based decision makers. Very objective."

"Yes, I also like the fact that you have two generations of very capable people similarly convinced that there may be more questions than answers right now regarding alien presence."

After a brief pause, Paul adds, "I'm gonna say something that the team didn't want me to bring up."

"That is?"

Opening one of Pete's cabin files entitled *Cover ups,* Paul then produced the most disturbing of the cabin evidence.

"Pete Stevenson had evidence hidden somewhere that pointed to a government program to destroy actual alien evidence and cover up many findings that his research group came up with."

"Good to know, but back burner stuff for now. Plus, the SEC and I need a break."

Smiling, Paul answered, "Understand."

"I don't know what's at stake here right now, Paul, but I'm willing to invest some time and money to see what we have."

"Great."

"The downside of this being a bust is you are simply back to where you are now, and it will close the door on this perspective all together. But there is enormous upside potential of re-writing history books and opening up a cosmic portal to a very exciting future. Only those who take risks, Paul, are truly free!"

They ended the meeting as Scott had his business meeting to attend. He invited Paul to have dinner on the yacht with his wife, Amanda, and him following a cocktail party for the invited guests of the fund-raiser.

"Hi Paul, can I get you a drink while we wait for Amanda?"

"Sure. Thanks. What are you drinking?"

"My usual, a Negroni. I think it's the perfect cocktail."

"Not had one. What's in it?"

"Three ingredients. London dry gin, Campari, and vermouth Rosso."

Paul smiled as if he understood the description and ingredients. This was not in his wheelhouse.

As Scott was pouring the shaken drinks over glasses with cubed ice and adding a twist of orange peel as a garnish, Amanda walked into the stateroom. A tall dark-haired woman, she was stunning and lovely in a black silk evening gown and a gorgeous diamond necklace. Her presence was sheer elegance and grace.

"I'll have one, too, Dear. You must be Paul."

"Yes. So nice to meet you."

"Here you are, Honey."

Scott raised his glass. "Cheers. Dinner is on the upper deck sky lounge. Ready?"

Dinner conversation was truly encouraging, as far as the project was concerned. The focus throughout the evening was absolutely extraterrestrial.

Covered in substantial detail were UFO's, Egyptian pyramids, Central American architecture, and even the so-called World Grid. It was not what Paul expected, but he was thrilled with the dialogue.

Even more enlightening was Amanda's perspective and knowledge of their subject matter. She asked as many questions as Scott and seemed to be extremely curious. Amanda was one smart lady. Scott and Amanda were not only impressed and excited, but they immediately gave Paul a proposal to present to Sara and the team. This was a decision they made together.

"We would be willing to fund the project, totally, if I could simply be a silent partner in the project. Maybe a little visionary stuff as well. And, the very capable Amanda Woods would help with the accounting and financial needs of the project."

Paul thought to himself, "Silent partner, hell, we have a franchise player now and the game has changed!" Elated with the news and windfall, he called Sara and the pair planned to meet with the team as soon as possible and share the good news.

The Extraterrestrial Research Team is created.

60

SARA

Thanks to Scott's generosity, the entire team and all of their computers, accessories, and support equipment for continuing the project would move to a highly secure and out-of-sight laboratory in Palo Alto.

Enough seed money and generous operating budget was now available for the team to leave their current employment to become full-time members of the Extraterrestrial Research Team, or ETRT.

Their cover would be as part of Scott's space exploration enterprise, which most people ignored anyway.

The original team of Sara, Paul, the four members that explored the cabin, and some additional skilled members were joined within six short months by a few subject matter experts, properly vetted, totaling an extremely capable team of fourteen people.

Each had a role based on their skills and experiences, and took ownership of their areas of expertise and accountability for data gathering, analysis, and final evaluation, regarding merit or conjecture in the mission.

It was agreed that this venture would be managed and operated by a Leadership Team made up of Sara, Paul, Scott, Amanda, and the four original team members, plus Mike, for a quorum of nine.

Sara's primary role would be as the ETRT's integrator, and Mike would lay out the management process and, when available, would facilitate the meetings. They would nail down Mike's involvement, and get his buy-in, when he traveled there in the next two weeks.

Sara called her dad with the awesome news, both of the wonderful facility that would house the team, and her dad's important role with the Leadership Team. Upon hearing her excited description, Mike said "I'm coming out now for a quick look-see, okay?"

"Of course, Dad, nothing could make me happier."

"Will I be able to see how you guys plan to manage the program?"

Sara excitedly told Mike, "Dad, we want you to set up the program along with a manageable operating system."

"Sara, that's great. Thanks."

When Mike arrived the next week, Sara gave him the tour of the laboratory and support equipment that was being built in the state-of-the-art Palo Alto facility. He wasn't able to meet Scott and Amanda during this initial visit.

"Dad, the resources and equipment that are here now and the additions that will be arriving soon are incredible.

"We seem to have a NASA-like environment being created, mirroring Scott's aerospace venture, with a budget that none of us could have expected."

"What you already have is spectacular."

A confident Sara responded, "And, I plan to set this venture up just like any start-up with traction."

"Okay. Good, good."

"Scott, the visionary, will be our President. He will usually be outside the box, so to speak. Paul is the CEO, as he must be here on a day-to-day basis. Amanda Adams is amazing. She will serve as our CFO."

Mike smiled with agreement.

Sara continued, "I'll take on the role as CTO and Integrator, the one who knows how all the parts fit and what is going on at all times. As I mentioned before, you will build our operating system and be on the payroll as an independent consultant."

"I'm impressed, Sara, but I can't agree to anything without Mom's buy-in."

"Understand."

"Promise you, I'll speak to her today."

"Great. The leadership team will consist of the nine people that I mentioned, and we will have a weekly accountability meeting with a solid agenda that will give us the discipline we will need. As you know, the Integrator runs that meeting."

"Got it." Mike was overcome with joy. "Sara, I can't begin to tell you just how happy your mom and I are for you and your team to be taking on such a tremendous challenge. And, I am humbled and grateful that I will be playing an important part in this journey of yours."

"Dad, we couldn't do this without you, and we are the ones who are grateful. That being said, I need to share something with you that appears to be indirectly related to Grandad's work."

Mike answered, "I'm listening. I also need to bring you up to speed on an interesting and puzzling event and the timing that Grandad had alluded to in his notes."

"Go ahead, Dad."

Mike continued, "Grandad mentioned THE REVEAL a few times in his work, without too much detail. It was probably light on written details because, obviously, he did not see his death coming. I think it was a critical piece in his puzzle."

Sara added, "I'm aware of The Reveal from connecting the dots with Grandad. Let me bring you up to date with the info that I have."

Pouring coffee for them, Sara was very attentive and was pleased that she could get additional information regarding these critical events from her dad.

Mike went on. "Apparently, Pete and maybe a couple people from his research team, which included a somewhat shady character named John Smith, were to give a major presentation at the Paris Air Show in September of 2018, apparently titled THE REVEAL."

Sara asked, "This was supposed to be an update on his ancient alien research, right?"

"Yes, but I had the impression there was an undertone to that meeting that your grandad hadn't expected but was based on fact, nonetheless."

Sara is puzzled. "What undertone?"

"Sara, we don't know for sure. From what little I know, there was some evidence that opened the possibility that terrorists were behind what was thought to be natural disasters."

"Oh, my."

Mike continued, "Well, it never happened, because Dad was killed the evening before by an alleged mugger, and Mr. Smith inexplicably withdrew himself as the presenter for Pete. That was so odd that it just opened up a ton of additional questions."

"Well, Dad. Two schools of thought here. Yes, it was strange that Smith withdrew, but having your partner murdered the day before could justify his reluctance to present.

"Grandad built his culture around focus and commitment, and if it were him, my grandad would have presented the REVEAL."

"Sara, we just don't know."

"Yep, thanks. My number one focus is now our mission, but his Reveal is becoming a high-interest side bar for me. I plan to look into it further down the road."

"Of course, Sara, please let me know anything that you come up with. And, you may want to treat this discovery stuff with the utmost of confidentiality."

"Will do."

"I'm gonna call Mom now."

"Okay. We can meet up again later."

Sara returned to the team and a few minutes later got a call from Mike.

"Well, I just got off the phone with Christine and gave her the details of everything that we discussed, without any mention of the Reveal.

I explained the details of the project, my involvement, and the nice consulting agreement that I just signed with Scott and Amanda.

Sara was quick to ask, "What did she say?

Mike responded, "She listened attentively and was pleased. Your mom said she was okay with it from, as I recall, four fronts."

Sara was curious. "Good. And they were?"

"One, I would be working with you, which was super-good."

"Absolutely," added Sara.

"Second, I would not be traveling beyond Palo Alto, I would assume.

"Third, the consultant's fee was generous and will make your mom happy that our retirement plan will be bolstered."

Sara got a laugh out of that one. "And what was number four?"

"Wine country, Baby, she said."

Sara was very happy and could sense that Mike was relieved and excited.

Next step for the ETRT:

Analyze the alien evidence from the cabin.

61

SARA

Using a series of whiteboards, and all done manually to avoid hacking, Sara and her ETRT took every piece of information, document, photo, or physical sample and placed them on those whiteboards. There were over 1100 entries.

They were grouped into Pete's original buckets, based on: commonality, redundancies, physical evidence, artifacts, observations, documented cases/ situations, historical reporting, unexplained phenomenon, violent and unprecedented weather events, and Grandad's cabin materials and extremely detailed logs and journal.

One of the results of digging more deeply into the cabin material was the fact that Pete had made hundreds of visits to sites and with people that helped Pete reach his conclusions or roadblocks. There were a multitude of interviews of people witnessing many alien situations, conducted by Pete and his small band of believers.

An Air Force Captain, Rex Reynolds, told of how he engaged a group of five spinning spheres that resulted from an Air Civil Defense warning, only to have the spheres combine into one bright ball of light and it took over the control of his plane.

A French soldier, returning to France from a vacation to the U.S., aboard a commercial airliner, watched out of his cabin window as a streaking "flying disc" stopped completely outside of the window as if to observe a plane in flight, and then sped off at the speed of sound.

Pete talked with fourteen different abductees in ten countries who had never met each other, and yet could plot the exact location of each of those fourteen abductions on any given map.

World War II Foo Fighters had detailed many times how they engaged "enemy" planes, only to be treated to a cat-and-mouse aerial game by those crafts moving and flying at erratic speeds from near stop to the speed of sound. None ever were killed by those anomalies.

Two people had experienced the same strange event. While driving, their cars lost power and stopped. Leaving the cars to follow a greenish light, they were amazed to see intense pressure on their cars, smashing them like in a trash compactor. There were photos.

Pete's four colleagues were given code names, in place of their real names, to protect their identity if that ever was deemed necessary. Pete was Orion, and then there were stones, chariot, Sacagawea, and smoke, nicknames that Sara and Mike had both come across before.

Unfortunately, they did not have any way to determine the actual names of these people who were involved with Pete. That was an unknown that needed to be revealed, and Justin, the code guy, was fully engaged in this task.

Justin opined that the code names were likely no more than replacements for their cell phone names, to avoid tracking, and not the stuff of espionage movies.

Over the period of six weeks, they established those items in red that were not deemed significant or could not be easily substantiated, and those items in green that had enough merit or sound data that could actually be considered for verification.

They had developed a scoring system for the green items around which they could put a discrete number to replace an attribute.

In other words, a weighted value within a scale of 1 to 10 instead of just yes or no. The basic scoring system for each item was developed along five elements

The volume of physical evidence associated with each one.

The frequency of times mentioned for each one.

The links or cross-referencing of each to other related events.

The corroboration by other testimonies and meetings.

The gut feeling of each team member of the item's viability.

They kept the buckets as the same seven categories going forward and established probabilities based on the most sophisticated modelling available.

But, without the ability to substantiate some findings with Pete's contacts, their conclusions would be highly subjective and wide open for criticism, and their best probability rates were only fifty per cent to sixty per cent.

Justin was frustrated because he did not have enough solid factual data to construct the algorithms that he loved to create.

"Okay guys, I have completed thousands of simulations, and several regression and correlation analyses."

Michaela quickly asks, "So what do you conclude?"

"My conclusion was that 647 of the overall findings of over thirty years of Pete's research and hundreds of years of other investigations had a strong element of possibility that could be argued and would surely be argued."

"Justin, that is fantastic," Sara adds.

"On the positive side, many of these 647 findings connected to one or many other findings, so there is some continuity."

"As my dad points out, as an expert in Systems Management, everything is connected."

It was up to the team to take that technical information and literally connect the dots. The passion and commitment of everyone on this project was overwhelmingly positive. Next up was Michaela.

Sara knew she would blow them away.

62

MICHAELA

It had long been discussed and theorized that earth and primitive humans had been visited by advanced beings from another world, galaxy, or universe. Obviously, not being verifiable, that was literally ancient history.

But many theories suggested that these aliens gave humans the knowledge of the solar system, concepts of engineering and mathematics, and became the basis for cultures and religions.

"Thanks Justin, Michaela adds, "So let me now provide some well-focused ideas, stories, and evidence from our huge data set. This was the ultimate team effort."

"Great, Michaela, I'll get us some cold drinks."

"Thanks, Kat. I'll talk while you guys can follow the PowerPoint."

The group rearranged chairs to get a better viewing position.

"Specific evidence was found in ancient monuments such as the Pyramids of Egypt/Giza, the Nazca Lines, and the Moai statues of Easter Island. Look at the best-guess timelines for these structures. Now, among the more recent studies were the following artifacts on the next slide, along with observations, carvings, and strongly debated interviews that provided the core of Pete's strong position."

Michaela paused as the group took notice of a couple detailed slides.

"Aliens apparently made contact with primitive humans and cities via Indian Sanskrit Texts that describe flying machines called Vimanas, Egyptian megaliths that show precision cutting work thought to be too advanced for that time, and Jewish Zohar writings that describe a manna machine similar to chlorella algae processing today."

"Whoa, slow down." Connor piped in.

"This next segment is wild. Significant documentation covering Earth's hot spots of UFO activity are documented and validated from a multitude of believable sources. They include area 51 and covered-up area 51 in the U.S., the Bermuda Triangle, Mexico's Zone of Silence, Peru's portal-like structure Puerta de Hayu Marca, and the curious events around the rock formations of the Marcahuasi Plateau."

After noticeable mumblings and some aha moments, the group was back on track.

"Following extensive study, Pete's team confirmed that various megalithic structures around Earth are built upon an incredible world grid of electromagnetic energy and that this power source likely was tapped for travel inter-galactically and high-level communication. Hidden messages within these sites show connections to one another."

Justin adds, "They replicate today's computer coding techniques. It's amazing."

Continuing, "Featured on the next two slides are Teotihuacan and Easter Island. This is awesome. These are sites with identical temple and monument architecture, along with the exact same-size building stones, per these two slides. Get this—they are separated by 2000 miles of ocean. You couldn't coordinate this feat today without serious cooperation and coordination."

Sara asked Michaela to slow down a bit.

"Staying with the alien secret code analysis, and with Justin's validation, the Pyramids of Giza, Thornborough Henges, Stonehenge, and ancient Hopi cities are all configured meticulously to resemble Orion. Check out this slide.

"Also, the absolute straight-line alignments of sites such as Trelleborg, Delphi, and Giza are uncanny, but accurate. And, the stone carvings at Gavrinis from 3500 BCE accurately calculate the circumference of the Earth and the value of Pi. I did those calculations myself."

The room is electric. Everyone is enjoying Michaela's passion and material.

"This next piece is one that Connor had worked on. Present-day battery technology is a part of everyday life and powers appliances, cars, airplanes, communication devices, and our current space travel.

"However, that technology was found in ruins of civilizations that go back to the Bronze Age. In fact, archeologists have dated these battery findings back to 4000 BCE. Connor sync'd many of these findings with today's actual battery technology and the overlays were remarkable."

Connor smiled.

"This next piece was fun. Computer astronomy evidence was found in the Incan and Egyptian ruins, along with 1000-year old spaceflight navigation charts that are as accurate today as they were then.

"What can best be described as an alien astronaut was found preserved in a pyramid. Pete Stevenson's log, as the team recalled, mentioned the similarity to one found in another location."

As the slide with the photo of the preserved alien astronaut was shown, Sara wrote on her notes, Milestone Event.

"What was diligently described as a giant spaceport was found in the Andes. Look at Pete's three-dimensional model photo. Massive research was done on the site, but later all data and evidence mysteriously disappeared.

"Pete was one hundred per cent convinced that some government or governments covered this up by destroying all evidence. Although it was never verified, a series of domino-like personal inquiries by Pete, again, revealed a 'petrified' alien astronaut."

Pausing for the group to finish their note-taking, Michaela continued.

"In 1947, a 'flying disc' crashed at a ranch near Roswell, New Mexico, and the U.S. Army immediately reported it as a common weather balloon. Who hasn't heard of this?

"Reports from people on the ground had a much different description, hence the term flying disc. Then, in the 1990's, the U.S. Military published two reports that it was a complex nuclear test surveillance balloon.

"The Roswell incident became the world's most famous and exhaustively investigated theory of UFOs ever. Pete Stevenson claimed to have pictures of an alien astronaut from 1947 Roswell frozen and kept in area 52, which was the government's much more secret base than area 51. So, if Pete's claims were true, he had evidence of three alien astronauts to study and compare."

As Michaela finished, Sara spoke.

"So, as they say, once is a random event, two is simply a coincidence, but three alien astronauts are most definitely a trend and very hard to debunk.

"If this doesn't get your blood pumping, nothing will. This last topic is huge and has a very big need to get a handle on and to get closure to, for sure."

Sara could sense that these points were getting the group a bit overwhelmed.

"I know we have a lot of #1 priorities, but we must find answers here. The ETRT is unanimous in our belief that this element of alien astronaut discovery was fueling Pete's positive perspective and keeping his momentum alive and well. It was the best-of-the-best in terms of arguable evidence.

"There was now an incredible amount of ancient documentation and conclusions to be drawn. Much raw data regarding black holes, wormholes, time travel, alien colonies on Mars, and alien abductions were yet to be analyzed.

"These were the areas that had the most unverifiable and unsubstantiated claims that were likely very frustrating to Pete and his team. Many of the ETRT's red circles were now loosely defined and followed by large question marks."

Michaela still wasn't done: "Excuse me, but I have one more point to make. The most chilling revelations were that some aliens could have morphed into human-like beings for the purpose of gathering information on human life on Earth.

"A theory existed that aliens may have altered the course of human evolution as certain DNA anomalies suggest and argue that a large part of civil unrest is the result of these in-humans that have no desire to live, only to destroy."

Sara piped in. "This is early research, obviously, and we will need to do a much deeper dive."

Kat responded. "Already taking notes on next steps."

Michaela continued, "Just throwing it all out. Many of the ancient alien conspiracy theorists offer an alternative to their thinking to help sway the masses.

"And that alternative was that there is now, or was then, a pervasive totalitarian malice by alien, evil alien, beings."

After a brief pause, Michaela continued. "That would be a very simplistic explanation of much of the terror and war which is plaguing the world today, but couldn't be ruled out under any circumstances.

"Although Pete was not a complete supporter of these theories, he wrote about them as an alternative explanation for these events nonetheless. We just can't ignore that thinking right now."

Kat asked, "So, Michaela, you are going into the evil alien angle?"

Michaela added her thoughts strongly.

"It's not if they were here, but *when*!"

63

SMOKE

Alias Mr. Smith was being called into his next meeting with Bud who was the conduit to *The New World Order*. He was told to meet Bud at the Cattleman's Restaurant in Ft. Worth, Texas. It would be just the two of them.

As the taxi pulled up in front of the restaurant, Smith could see that he wasn't dressed in local attire. He should have known better but was under some stress with this visit.

He removed his tie, folded his suit coat up and put it in his small travel bag. Walking inside, he picked out Bud, dressed in a cowboy hat and faded jeans.

"How was your trip?"

"Good. Haven't been to DFW airport in a while. Hectic place, as usual."

"Yeah, but I like Cowtown. Friendly people and great steaks."

"Is that a Bailey Hat?"

"Say what?"

"Is your hat made by Bailey here in Ft. Worth?"

"Dunno. Let me check."

Bud removed his hat and said, "No, it's a Stetson. You know something about western hats?"

"No. Not really. I used to come to Texas quite a bit with the CIA, mostly the Dallas Metroplex, and Bailey was the hat of choice with the guys that I met with here."

"Got a cold pitcher of beer and ready to order dinner. These Rib-eye steaks are the best."

They ordered dinner and Bud got straight to business talk.

"It's been several months since you got onto Pete's team of idiots, and we haven't heard much back regarding what they're up to. Need some feedback."

"As I told you the last couple of times we talked, they are only pursuing alien crap and nothing more."

"That's not true. One of his friends or relatives or someone has been asking questions about the drug trade in Central America. What the hell does that have to do with aliens?"

"I don't know anything about that."

"Wrong answer. We're paying you to be an insider, not an observer. This info should be coming from you, not from me."

Smith had a bad case of anxiety as he knew this was not going to be a good meeting.

"Listen, you get with that Stevenson guy now and find out what's going on with his snooping around in the drug business and get back with me ASAP."

"Will do."

"Damn right. Do some other snooping to see what else he's looking at."

"Whatcha mean?"

"Find out if there is anything else, non-alien, that he is into. Military, finance, weapons stuff. You know. Non-alien crap."

"K. I'll be in touch soon."

"Damn right you will."

Smith got up from the table, turned, and slowly walked out of the restaurant. At that point, Bud didn't even acknowledge him.

Smith decided at that moment.

"I don't care what I find… I'll just tell him what he wants to hear."

64

PETE

One of the things that kept coming up over and over again in Pete's work and his notes was his strong belief that ancient aliens were really futuristic human time travelers sent here from future human societies to provide help to mankind on Earth. He had very little to support his theory than his gut feel.

Pete's premise was that the evidence was very strong that much advanced technology was required to build the enormous and futuristic symbols and monuments of the past.

Pete alluded many times to extra-temporal aliens, or time travelers from the future. He fully expected that the research of his team and him would focus directly on this explanation of alien intervention as the only logical conclusion that could have been drawn. It was Pete's end game.

Recalling his game-changing trip to Sweden in February of 2018, his takeaway was that humans from the future have found ways to overcome the currently known limitations of light speed and time travel paradoxes that keep us from exploring the boundaries of time.

He held a belief that the ancient aliens may have been human beings from the future, or even future versions of us today, come back to interact and help us. Also, Pete was developing a gut-level fear of evolving Artificial Intelligence and what it could lead to in the years to come.

Pete was convinced that aliens from the future were now here and brought technology from far into the future with them. His beliefs were enhanced by evidence that he had uncovered that portrayed aliens being accompanied by robots or androids or meta-humans or whatever these non-human beings were called.

Pete was becoming convinced that it was these non-alien machines that were the heart and soul of alien intervention and AI on Earth.

He called his friend, Professor Harry Wyman, an authority on AI, for some basic clarifications, and a close friend for many years.

"Hi Harry, it's been a while and I hope all is well. Got any really interesting projects going on?"

"It's good to hear from you, Pete. Are you alone or you got some of your alien friends with you?"

Pete laughed. He knew that comment was coming. "Seriously, Harry."

"Well, I'm still working primarily with mainstream AI, which achieves far greater commercial success and academic respectability by focusing on specific problems where we can produce verifiable results and commercial applications, such as artificial neural networks. Does that make sense?"

"Yep, it does. How does this mainstream AI differ from the current technology?"

"Our current AI capability is what is defined as weak or narrow AI, which uses software to study and accomplish specific problem-solving or reasoning tasks. In contrast to strong AI, it does not attempt to perform a full range of human cognitive abilities."

Pete was taking notes as Dr. Wyman continued.

"Strong or Full Artificial General Intelligence, or AGI, would be able to perform any intellectual task that a human being could, including total consciousness, self-awareness, and cost/benefit decision making. It is simply the ability of a machine to perform general intelligent action that could, I have argued, become a discernable threat to mankind."

"Are we there yet?"

"It is at least many decades, if not centuries, away. Once reached, AGI would be incredibly disruptive to the structure of our economic and political systems, not to mention a crisis of jobs, equality, wealth gaps, and posing a challenge to human dignity as we know it. But you shouldn't worry; you won't see it in your lifetime."

So, with that dire assessment in mind, Pete provided his friend with a bit of an academic challenge, having him apply a series of relevant algorithms to his AI-related data and the data that the team had amassed.

Given a week or so of Dr. Wyman's time, what was beginning to emerge was a functional baseline of machine-assisted number crunching that was giving the AI Revolution eerie similarities in scope and scale to the magnitude of the Industrial Revolution.

This was a good start. Pete needed more help, so he contacted Professor Sami Chong, a renowned IT and Mathematics expert and referral from Dr. Wyman, with a small favor.

✦ ✦ ✦

"Thank you so much for seeing me on such short notice."

"Anytime I can be of service to Harry, I will do my best."

"Many carvings and artifacts of ancient hieroglyphs seemed to point to machines that came from the alien Gods that were the problem solvers and data analyzers of the distant past. This is not something that has been easily understood, but you are seeing many years of research that has taken us to this conclusion."

Pete sensed Dr. Chong's silence as skepticism. Pressing on, he brought Dr. Chong up to speed and laid out a scenario that possibly would answer his questions and validate much of Pete's findings.

"We believe that aliens used humans to build the infrastructure that they required to circumvent the Earth and solar system. So, the physical labor piece was literally us being the actual worker bees."

Dr. Chong was fascinated by Pete's information and passion and getting very interested. "Please continue."

"We believe that the greater unanswered question was how aliens were able to detect incredibly subtle patterns and what we call small data in the Earth's geography and Eco structure, and go on to build algorithms from what then became large quantities of world and solar system data."

"Now, who are the 'we' that you are referring to?"

"I have a small group of ancient alien researchers; and along with tons of prior observations and documentation, the evidence is becoming stronger and stronger."

"Okay, please go on."

"We now firmly believe that a constantly evolving superintelligence that the aliens possessed was via machine-driven Artificial General Intelligence as we call it today. We have data. That's why I'm here."

"You're serious?"

"Yes. Very serious."

"Okay, give me what you have and I'll look into it. I will call you as soon as I have a conclusion, one way or another."

"Great. Thanks."

Nearly a month later, an excited Professor Chong called Pete and they set up a meeting that Pete couldn't wait to attend.

"I used basic extrapolation of the logarithmic curves of your data to determine that it was possible, if not likely, that the aliens built their thousands of monuments, cathedrals, pyramids, stone markers, and navigational sentinels from literally hundreds of millions of data points gathered from the solar system, if not the universe."

"And the AGI takeaway?"

"Yes, it is my conclusion, based on nearly a 95% probability, some form of AGI was the only way that this could have been accomplished. I will continue to investigate and extrapolate in the weeks to come. But, for now, it does appear that you are on to something rather extraordinary."

"I can't tell you how happy I am that you were here to take this info to this level. But please, this needs to be held in extreme confidence."

"Pete, I totally understand the implications here. And thanks for allowing me to dig into this amazing revelation."

Therefore, from Pete's newly enlightened knowledge of AI, he would conclude that it would, indeed, take centuries to master this type of technical capability.

Or, in other words, a very plausible explanation was that it would have to come from extratemporal aliens from the future. Not even thinking about any second alternatives, Pete was feeling good.

He contacted Mike, and they had a long and exciting conversation. Mike would bring Sara up to speed the next time he was in Palo Alto.

So, Pete had one more stop to make in his quest to bring the best minds he knew into this transition from AI to AGI.

He contacted a long-time friend, Dr. Emil Griffith, who was a well-respected Ivy League Eco-political visionary and behavioral theorist, with the intention to bring him up to speed with his previous coordinated study results and get another set of eyes to look into his findings.

Credibility was being established.

One more stop to close the loop.

65

PETE

"Emil, it's Pete, how ya doing?"

"I'm doing fine, thanks, but I'm thinking this call is more about what I'll be doing for you, eh?"

"Yes, afraid so."

"Shoot."

Pete jumped in with a quick question, "Emil, what is your AI philosophy right now, or in other words, what would be the high level of your thinking on the subject?"

"Not sure I understand the question."

"AI is having an exponential development. Where are we today?"

"Well, I am a firm believer, or a hopeful believer, of AI from a more utopian perspective; that is that AI can and would bring more pride and self-satisfaction into the workplace and into our communities. I strongly believe that AI will enable us to reduce global suffering and help to realize humankind's true potential."

Gathering his thoughts, Dr. Griffith continued. "AI will likely produce the futuristic tablets or touchstones that answer and solve humanity's most challenging problems, such as starvation, disease, and climate change. It's inevitable and just a matter of when."

Pete was so engaged in Dr. Griffith's vision that Emil's next statement was numbing.

"Pete, the day will come when scientists will be able to scan a person's whole consciousness into a computer and create a digital replica, or portal, that will live on forever. It will happen."

Pete then spent nearly an hour presenting his big data set to get Dr. Griffith's opinion on the other side of the argument, the more dystopian conclusion.

Fortunately for Pete, he had developed strong credibility, if credibility was the right word, for his alien intervention research and associated theories. Dr.

Griffith appreciated the opportunity to give his advice to such an enormously important question.

Dr. Griffith offered, "For a headline that could best be called, 'I'm sorry I asked,' I would offer the following opinion. I still strongly believe in what I discussed earlier. But you cannot deny that this data set could point us in a very dire and sinister direction.

"That is, when and if humans have the ability through machines to create self-improving AI programs, the teacher is no longer the teacher."

Pete looked up at Dr. Griffith, who continued.

"In other words, Pete, once vastly superior machines possess the intellect that exceeds the human intellect, humans will lose the ability to understand, manage, and control those machines. Pete, this scenario could have these super-intelligent AI systems becoming the greatest risk to our civilization as we will ever face."

After collecting his thoughts and drinking a large glass of water, Dr. Griffith continued, "The incredible downside for a humanity as we know it, is threefold in a calamity-type scenario as I see it. And, Pete, this is only my hastily gained conclusion based on your rather chilling information."

He added, "One is the fact that these tremendously powerful super-computer AI machines will become god-like, but will not possess any social skills, self-awareness, or empathy.

"Every decision that is made will be the kind of cost/benefit decision that will have no bearing on doing what is right in our society, only what is most cost effective."

Trying a little humor, Pete adds, "Like what mankind does right now, only faster."

"I guess. Second is it will destroy vast numbers of what we would call traditional jobs that have been the backbone of America's middle class since our Republic became viable. From a pure economic perspective, tens of millions of our workforce, and that would spill over to the global workforce, would have no way to earn an income without governments literally providing cash paydays to allow citizens to meet their basic day-to-day needs."

As Pete became more depressed, Dr. Griffith added, "And thirdly, an even worse result could be produced. Even where AI doesn't destroy jobs and means of making a living, it will further eliminate a middle class via pure economics.

"There will only be a small percentage of haves that will be profoundly wealthy, and a very high percentage of have nots that will be close to poverty."

Pete adds, "Unfortunately, that scenario makes sense."

"AGI will become fundamentally monopolistic and push inequality exponentially. Companies with better data and algorithms will gain more customers, users, and wealth. This self-reinforcing cycle will lead to winner-take-all market dominance.

"Opportunistic leading-tech companies will be making massive profits while its rivals struggle for survival and eventually die off. This perverse inequality will result in unrest and discord unlike anything we have ever seen or perceived as possible."

Pete was pensive and reflective. "Gosh, this is end-of-world stuff."

"Well, it is just one man's opinion."

"And a damn good one. Thanks."

"Keep me posted and let me know if you ever need my testimonial. With additional fresh data, I can get even more laser-focused."

"That may be necessary. Bye."

"Good luck, Pete."

Good luck, hell. **Pete now had credibility.**

66

SARA

Extremely tired and drained from the most recent internal presentation, and with a feeling of anxiety and general helplessness, Sara did what any good leader would do. She assembled the ETRT with a non-negotiable decision.

They would spend a day unwinding at the local Dave and Buster's, where adults could enjoy all the toys and game-playing that kids enjoy.

The timing couldn't have been better. It was a chance to unwind and catch their breath before getting back in the game. A good time was had by all.

Back to reality, the ETRT members realized that there were tons of significant data, some more likely to be verifiable than others.

Sara called for a meeting with Scott and Amanda to present their preliminary findings and seek their advice on next steps.

Sara arranged the presentation in simple bullet points to dramatize their work, allow individual commentary, and focus on any early aha moments.

They wanted to show progress, not necessarily a culmination piece of work. Even that high-level presentation had an extraordinary amount of substance and consensus conclusions to take forward.

The planned 90-minute meeting lasted nearly all afternoon. From many of Scott's questions, it was obvious that he was taking the current revelations of the ETRT out to the future in mental next steps and various good-versus-bad scenarios.

Sara's final remarks were, "We have established many points of light that occur over and over again, that simply cannot be coincidence.

"And, we also see the complete and utterly consistent building of monuments, stone symbols, and pyramids throughout the world that can only be explained as part of a master plan.

"However, the most stunning result from our studies is the fact that a world grid is now in place, and has always been in place, that shows how air traffic could circumvent the globe with ease and continuity, even thousands of years ago."

Scott was stunned and trying to process Sara's words.

"Sara, this just confirms to me that we are on the right track. Awesome. Great job!"

Amanda added, "It seems that you and the ETRT have reached a unanimous conclusion that for a very long period of time, the human race of Planet Earth was not alone. Kind of gives me chills."

Scott went on to say, "Just let us know what you need and how we can help. Let's have a meeting of the Leadership Committee as soon as we can to develop an Action Plan for immediate implementation. Can't wait to see where this will go."

In private, Scott said to Amanda, "Don't read too much into this… it still is way out in left field. Will need to wait and see…"

After bringing Scott and Amanda up to speed on their ongoing findings in that benchmark Palo Alto meeting and getting the green light to continue, the Leadership Committee met and came away with an aggressive to-do list going forward.

They built an extremely tight literal and virtual wall around their secretive work, especially given that many conferences involve e-meetings and video-chats with associates and specialists around the world.

In less than two months, following deep dives into the areas that they thought could have the most impact, they started to narrow the focus on the short list of conclusions that were of highest value and where there were holes in the findings.

The team believed that there were missing pieces of information that should have been found in the cabin's main level or basement level.

Many incomplete or disconnected case studies and some of Pete's conclusions just couldn't have been made without more specific details.

Among which were several highlighted elements that lacked any subsequent detail.

Pete's encounter details in Trelleborg, his game changer, was still without many facts that could be verified.

THE REVEAL agenda on 9/17/2018 seemed critically important but lacked specific details and no hard agenda was found.

Pete's alleged key was the navigation and aviation grid around the world but facts were slim. In other words, his opinion was big on speculation and light on facts.

Push-pin points on his wall mural or treasure map had no explanation.

Some sort of alien Secret Code and advanced AI was being studied.

His persistent dreams of a gray or white hybrid human as our salvation.

Sara found that in addition to many elements of Pete's research that were unexplained, two other items or notes were discovered, which seemed to have no correlation to the alien project.

The first of Pete's off-base issues seemed to do with acts of terror being committed throughout the world. Apparently, he had some supporting evidence that pointed him in the direction of an organized crime faction or splintered terrorist group that was gathering momentum. Again, Sara and her team found no strong supporting data.

The second was Pete's perceived concern that someone close to him was sending mixed signals regarding their contributions and participation in the alien venture. Maybe even a mole, which made no sense at all.

Sara surmised that her grandad was almost at a state of paranoia that a conspiracy was taking place within his own ranks. Hand-written notes were found indicating that Pete was having a very difficult time determining exactly what that unidentified person's real intentions were.

Sara concluded that in his mind, he had a friend or foe battle that was going on for months and he thought it was quite serious.

But even more chilling notes pointed to a problem with Grandad that Sara would keep to herself for now.

Apparently, Pete had been in and out of alcohol rehab.

67

PETE

As the five-person group of adventurers were getting farther along in their investigative efforts, Pete thought it was timely to meet and compare notes. So, Pete did something that was unusual.

He invited everyone to his cabin in the Sierra Nevada for a fact-finding report on their quests in August of 2017.

Pete actually thought it would be important to have a get together to consolidate their efforts, and maybe have a little fun at the same time in a beautiful area.

This would be the first and only time that Corey, Thomas, Beth, and John Smith had been to Pete's cabin.

As their rental car approached the cabin, Pete went out on the porch to greet them.

"So welcome to my rustic retreat; glad you guys could make it."

Beth chipped in first, "This is absolutely lovely. You should be retiring here, not entertaining worker bees on an ancient alien safari." Corey and Thomas got a laugh at the remark, and likely didn't disagree.

"While you unpack, let me get some refreshments. Got some cold Molson coming."

Pete fired up the grill around 6:00 p.m., and they all enjoyed steaks and wood-plank salmon for dinner, while updates on everyone's travels were the only conversation. Beth drank Sonoma Cabernet, and Corey and Thomas enjoyed Jameson Irish Whiskey, Stout Edition, straight up.

Pete had his usual, a couple scotch rocks, and all were enjoying the evening. John Smith was outdoors chain-smoking, as was his usual manner. It was decided to table any shop talk until the following morning.

So, the next morning came and was as breathtaking as any of them could imagine. Sunrise over the lake water was wonderful. They took a walk down to the lake and then returned to the cabin for breakfast.

Following a lumberjack-type breakfast, Pete could see that his team was relaxed and enjoying themselves.

Beth chimed in, "Hey Pete, ya wanna adopt me. I'd love to live here."

"It is a beautiful place, Beth, and someday I will retire here. Loneliness is one of life's saddest times, but solitude for someone like me is often a gift."

At that moment, Smith came back into the cabin.

"The purpose of this meeting is to focus on the harder evidence or that which we could more easily verify. Hard artifacts are good.

"The term being used today is *out-of-place* and we need to focus on that kind of evidence. If we can begin to substantiate out-of-place pieces of evidence, they become more fact than fiction. Does that make sense?"

The group agreed and listened to Pete's perspective.

"I think that we should not be guided by the myths and legends of ancient civilizations. And, we should leverage our findings and our experiences, and not be influenced by others' opinions. We are at a place in our journey where opinions don't matter nearly as much as facts."

With that, Corey began. "Among the many examples of pyramids, monuments, and stone carvings, I have brought with me several metal couplings that have been used in hundreds of stone erections to bind the stones together."

With that remark, Corey unwrapped his metal objects.

"What makes these unique is that they are not metals found anywhere on this planet. They come from mining meteorites, literally thousands of tons of meteorites, which is a virtual impossibility in this or any civilization."

Pete spoke, "Did you say thousands of tons?"

"Well, I'm extrapolating, Pete. I did run a simulation of the usage of these metals in all of the known structures, and it would literally have taken tons of these materials to complete them."

Pete added, "That is a remarkable stat."

"Yep, I can't even imagine today, with all of the resources we have at our disposal, being able to collect this enormous amount of material and put it to any industrial use."

That got some high fives for Corey and he was happy that the group was pleased.

Thomas followed. "I was particularly interested in the Mars linkage and the results of a multi-year study of the Martian landscape by an American rover that totally outlived its design."

"What I was able to procure was a highly classified document that shows a literal mirror image of the Egyptian Pyramids and Sphinx buried under significant dust storm debris on Mars.

"Evidently, the rover did a 20-square-mile mapping of the surface there and what it produced was that mirrored image in the exact dimensions of those on Earth."

Thomas asked, "And you got this where?"

"Let's just say it was through a very good contact for now. The reason why I trust this data is that it was highly classified, which means it was very likely accurate. Yep, I owe a couple people some significant favors to get this stuff." Even Pete was impressed.

Beth then jumped in. "That is awesome. Gonna be hard to beat that one."

"Yes, it will be."

Beth proclaimed, "Well, a bird in the hand is better than moon dust, or Mars dust."

The group was listening and appreciated Beth's humor.

"We have all heard about the carved wooden bird found in one of Egypt's oldest burial grounds. It was later built into a scale model three times its size and when tested, flew like one of today's highly developed gliders."

The group all nodded in agreement.

"Well, I have the clay model of that carved wooden bird in my hands right now. Just don't ask me how I got it."

She passed it around for everyone to see. Pete was impressed with her find. Beth had a tenacious side, for sure, and it was evident with this incredible acquisition.

Corey piped in, "We gonna find out how you got it?"

"It's is a long story… a truly long story. Maybe over wine tonight."

John Smith was then asked to provide his contribution.

"Well, as you know, I have been mostly interested in the evil alien side and have been looking for some evidence that many of our current terrorist activities could be traced to ancient aliens. So far, unfortunately, I haven't come up with much."

Pete then added, "I thought we put that to rest a long time ago. That was in the book that I wrote that even I couldn't corroborate. End of story."

"So," Smith asked, "You haven't found any evil alien stuff in any investigations that you made regarding criminal activity or terrorist events?"

Pete was getting annoyed. "No."

Pete wrapped up the day's work by giving a summary on several items and issues of interest. As he was concluding, he said to the group, "I do have an issue that isn't exactly alien-research related, but seems to be important nonetheless."

The team looked interested, but Smith looked very nervous.

"As you know, I have been on a personal mission to answer the question of extraterrestrial versus temporal alien intervention, and I have finally gotten some feedback from several key subject matter experts that support my theory that our alien friends are from the future."

"Holy cow," Beth said loudly.

"As you also know, I have been digging into our big data for evidence of advanced AI and the possibility that aliens have helped the evolution of that technology into human consciousness capabilities.

"The bottom line seems to indicate that Artificial General Intelligence, the ability of machines to think and act human-like, is well documented in our studies. I will do a deeper dive on this for our next meeting, after Paris."

The team was excited and Smith was relieved.

As he concluded this last issue report, Pete was still a little angry with Smith's seemingly lackadaisical attitude. And, he was more than upset with Smith's constant cell phone use during their meeting and his incessant chain-smoking.

He was even thinking of kicking Smith off of the team, but that would have to wait.

So, as the group parted on Sunday afternoon for their respective homes, Thomas thanked Pete for his hospitality and then asked Pete for any words of wisdom.

"I wish you guys good hunting. Stay focused. The truth is out there; just go find it!"

Much of the "truth" was inconvenient.

68

SARA

One last trip to Grandad's cabin in the Sierra Nevada Mountains was required by Sara's team to find and secure the remaining documents that Grandad possessed.

That included what Michaela referred to as a treasure map of sorts that made up an entire cabin wall. This trip would, hopefully, close the loop on many of the team's findings.

"Let's make this trip by ourselves, Paul, as I am feeling a more personal or family puzzle may be in this next visit. And I don't want to trouble the whole team just to get the last items in the cabin."

"Of course, and I will bring the equipment we need to either remove the wall mural or photograph key parts."

Sara added without mentioning Mike's dreams, "I also have a hunch that there are keys to our missing details under the glass of the wall and tables."

Paul nodded, sensing that Sara was in need of closure on so many fronts.

So, Sara and Paul made this cabin trip without any other team members, and they planned their course of action on the drive up and their respective expectations.

Sara mentioned to Paul that this venture could become their life's work, and she thought of all the unknown consequences, good or bad, that awaited them.

"Sara, what makes you think there are clues under the glass tables?"

"Those tables just don't fit inside a rustic cabin. They're out of place. Even a newbie from Decorating 101 would not use glass tables."

"I understand. Anything under glass and the wall mural will be my first priority."

Sara looked over at Paul with her eyes and heart, realizing what a huge impact he was making on her and her aspirations going forward. "I love you, Paul."

"Love you too, Sara."

It was late afternoon when they arrived at the cabin, and after they unpacked the car, they headed down to the lake.

Sara was looking at the wooden steps leading to the water and seeing the old boat dock on which Grandad spent so many enjoyable hours.

She couldn't help but think of her dad's latest version of his cabin dream, with the uncanny resemblance to what they were seeing and doing at that moment. Paul, when sensing stress in Sara's life, would simply suggest...

"Let's go for a walk."

"Sure. That would be great."

As they walked, Paul said "If there is anything that you want to share regarding your dreams or your feelings that there are personal or family undertones in our digging, I'm all ears."

"I have feelings that give me chills that both my dad and grandad were touched in some way by this alien presence that we are starting to investigate.

"This may sound really strange, but I now feel as though it is my destiny to conduct my own search and ultimately put these extraterrestrial puzzle pieces together."

"Well, whoever is in charge made a super great decision!"

They laughed and continued their walk hand in hand.

Back at the cabin, they made dinner. Sara brought some plank salmon for the grill and had made a nice spinach salad earlier in the day. Paul grilled the salmon to perfection and they ate on the porch just as the sun was setting.

Following dinner, they sat in front of a mesmerizing fire with a bottle of wine that Paul had brought and tried very hard to just relax.

"So," Paul asked. "You gotta plan for tomorrow?"

"Of course."

Starting early the next morning, Paul brought out the tools to take the glass off of the mural and the three tables in the main room and removed the glass from a basement painting.

"Whoa, you were right. There is a significant amount of paperwork and detailed info hidden under all that glass."

"Great, Paul. Anxious to see what's behind that wall mural."

Paul worked for nearly an hour to remove the mural frame and glass as Sara joined him to see what was there.

As he slowly peeled two sheets of onion paper from the mural, Sara grabbed one end.

"Looks like there are two sheets of paper here, Paul."

"Yeah. We need to be careful so we don't tear them."

"Okay, this top sheet looks like the actual names, dates, and locations of the key people that Grandad interviewed. You know, the ones from his log."

"I think you're right. Yep, I recognize a couple names. This is super."

"Paul, this second sheet is a two-dimensional world grid. It has to be the exact one that Grandad used as his template for connecting all those logistical dots."

"My God, you're right."

Paul carefully rolled those valuable papers in a secure container to put into the car.

"Under that table glass are several pages of Grandad's large journal. It's another puzzle, as we will need to cut-and-paste these to what we found earlier to make some sense of the entire journal."

"Sara, under that big basement table glass are all or the remaining photos."

"I see them. These are the actual photos of the three alien astronauts with much better resolution. Wow."

"I wonder if these are the metal discs that Pete was referring to that were composed of meteorite material."

"Likely, Paul. That would be the only reason for him hiding these."

"These shards of bone must be samples for future DNA checks, right?"

"For sure. These would be used for some sort of verification, I guess."

"Well, Sara, this is some serious physical evidence and neatly preserved for future analysis."

"Yeah, but why would Grandad go to such lengths to hide these? What was he so worried about?"

"Or who?"

They took some time to log their findings before loading their enormously important haul into Paul's SUV.

However, as they loaded the last boxes and returned for a celebratory glass of wine, Sara heard a shrill sound, weak at first but getting louder each few seconds.

"Paul, are you hearing that?"

"Hearing what?"

Sara noticed that the cabin seemed to be vibrating, ever so slightly. Worried that an earthquake was possibly occurring, she again looked over to Paul who continued to pack his things.

Sara got a strange and terrifying text message: "*Get out of the cabin now!*"

She screamed, "We need to leave right now!" and ran for the door dialing 911.

"Coming, Sara."

Paul started to leave the cabin and then momentarily turned as if to retrieve something. As Sara reached the front porch stairs, Paul was still inside the cabin.

The loud shrill was now upon them and Sara turned her head back to the cabin door.

No Paul.

"Paul!"

Sara frantically called out again, "Paul!"

At that moment, a drone-launched missile destroyed the cabin and all that remained inside.

Sara was blown away from the cabin and in severe pain beneath much debris. As the smoke cleared, she slowly looked up to see the cabin totally obliterated. She was pinned under debris and couldn't move.

There were no signs of Paul.

69

SCOTT

Scott received word of the cabin destruction through a California Park Ranger and the local authorities monitoring the 911 call. Monitoring the local medical response team, he immediately contacted Amanda and they alerted his helicopter pilot.

"Tim, we need to get that bird in the air now!"

"Yes sir. Give me ten minutes and we're off."

Getting word of the accident, Kat and Connor join Scott and Amanda as they hurry to the heliport.

"Oh my God," Kat says tearfully, "Do we know what happened?"

As Scott helped Amanda into the helicopter, he tried to explain.

"The only first-hand info I have was that some type of explosion destroyed Pete's cabin where Sara and Paul were working."

Amanda told Kat, "We don't know anything about those two yet, but it can't be good."

"We gotta get there before the Medivac does."

"Why?" Kat asked.

"If someone or something is aware of their research there, and that is possible, and would go to any length to destroy them and their work, we must get there first. Tim, ETA?

"Forty minutes, Scott."

While in route, Kat alerted the ETRT members in Palo Alto and questioned Scott. "It could have been an accident, right?"

"Yes, but we must pursue this with the utmost security for now."

"Should I contact anyone else? Family? Off-site associates?"

"No, Kat, not until we get there."

Amanda took Kat's hand and tried to console her. "We'll be there soon. Hold on."

As Tim brought the copter in for the landing, the scene was horrible. The cabin was totally destroyed and two victims were on the ground, being cared for by the park ranger.

"I'm Ranger Donahue. I got here as fast as I could. The fire and smoke were intense."

"I'm Scott Adams. These people are my family. What's the status?"

"The man is dead. The woman is alive, but you can see that she was hurt bad."

"Ranger Donahue, are you medically trained?"

"Yes sir. Fully certified by the California Medical Board."

"Okay. You and Kat here get the woman on board and I'll get the man. You're going with us."

"But…"

"No buts. We need you, Ranger Donahue, and I'll make it right with whomever I need to, later. We need to get these people out of here ASAP. Understood?"

"Yes sir. Whatever I can do to help."

"Connor, here are Sara's keys to the SUV. Get it back to the office. We'll be in touch."

"Will do. Good luck."

Tim had set up the copter's medical bay and was ready for Sara. Kat, Amanda, and Ranger Donahue carefully put Sara in the copter as Scott wrapped Paul's body in blankets. Within minutes they were airborne.

As they took off, they could see an ambulance about fifteen miles away. Scott was relieved that they were able to get away so quickly.

"Great work, Tim."

"No problem. Where to?"

"The Sand Harbor retreat in Tahoe. I have a medical team standing by and my plane will be there soon. Give me an ETA as soon as you have one."

As they monitored Sara's vitals, Scott was busy on his phone. He had placed a call to Mike and Christine and was talking to them as calmly as possible.

"Hour and ten minutes, Scott."

"That's great, Tim."

Silence took over the helicopter as time seemed to go by very slowly. As they approached the landing pad at the Lake Tahoe retreat, Scott's plane had already arrived. Upon landing, they slowly moved Sara to a room inside for evaluation.

Two of Scott's medical techs had arrived earlier and worked on Sara for several minutes and then prepped her for the next flight.

Scott's trusty Captain, Ken Darragh, had Scott's private jet ready to roll.

"Ken, thanks for getting here so fast. We ready?"

"Yep. Got the flight plan for the Utah Medical Center and we're all set."

Scott took Paul's body to another room of the retreat and noticed that Paul was clinging to a photograph. Scott was overcome with emotion and cried. As Kat entered the room, he said, "If I leave you and Tim to take care of getting Paul's body back to Palo Alto, are you okay with that?"

"Yes. We'll deal with the authorities and next-of-kin as soon as possible. And, I'll get Ranger Donahue back as well."

"Thanks. Amanda will be in touch."

Sara was loaded onto the plane with Scott, Amanda, and the two techs and they departed. Wheels were turning in Scott's head as well as he developed a hasty to-do list.

"Okay, for now this is the story. The death of the entire group of people is reported, not just Paul, as a result of a gas leak in the cabin, again, just for now. I want our many associates working for us in other parts of the world to go off the radar or into hiding, until we get to the bottom of this tragedy."

Amanda asked, "Do you think it was an attack?"

"I do. Hope I'm wrong."

It wasn't until several months later that Sara found the origin of that strange text message that she received as the cabin was destroyed.

A proto-type S2 meta-human named Elonis, far advanced from the computer-imaged Alexa that Sara encountered, sent the warning. Apparently, Elonis was under task to monitor air space proximity.

Sara had suffered severe head trauma, a broken back and hip, a punctured lung, two broken legs, a broken arm, and was critically burned as she fled the cabin.

Upon arriving at the medical center, she was placed in a medically-induced coma, as a crack team of medical personnel was in route to the compound.

Scott was relieved that Sara was safely at his facility and the entire incident was kept from the evening news. He knew he had taken a risk, inasmuch as LA medical centers were closer. He had the utmost trust and respect for his associates to perform.

Later that day, Mike and Christine arrived, and Scott explained the only details that he had. They were respectfully asked not to divulge their daughter's survival and her location.

Life for the Stevenson family had come to a terrible halt. Prayers replaced the breakneck speed of the project's efforts.

Would Sara become the Phoenix, rising literally from the ashes?

70

MIKE

It was during this traumatic time that Mike was reflecting on the past events that he and the family had experienced.

He recalled vividly events up to Sara's birth and another significant emotional event, even one that Christine admitted was undeniably unnatural and very frightening. It all had to do with an ill-fated business trip and fateful airplane incident.

It was 1991, about a year before Sara was born, and Mike was scheduled to fly to Brussels on business. Christine was driving Mike to the airport, about three hours before his scheduled departure.

Mike was a Vince Lombardi fan and one of his favorite Vince Lombardi quotes was "Early is on time; on time is late!"

So, Mike arrived at the airport with plenty of time to relax, check his itinerary for the trip, and look forward to Brussels and the Grand Place, or Grote Market, one of his favorite tourist spots to visit.

"Well, have a good flight, and this time don't forget family souvenirs, especially for Louise."

"I will. Yeah, Dad rarely remembered to get her anything. Not intentional, I know."

Mike gave Christine a big hug and he knew that she was already planning her day. She often told Mike that she enjoyed the occasional time alone to catch up on her reading when he was traveling.

Mike said goodbye to Christine, got his boarding passes, and went thru security. He did not check any luggage, as losing your luggage in Europe is often messy. Much the organized guy, Mike was prepared with just carry-on bags.

He checked his watch and could see that he still had ninety minutes before departure. So, he gave his dad a quick call.

"Hi Dad, whatcha up to these days?"

"Not much, Mike, just doing some catch-up reading at the moment. Found an interesting article that claims that early civilizations believed that their gods were actually ancient aliens."

"Yeah, we had discussed this a few times."

"Of course. But this is from another source altogether."

"Just some affirmation, right?"

"According to this piece from several theorists, these astronaut-gods came from more than 10,000 years ago in giant spaceships from other parts of the universe. They landed on the peninsula of Yucatan and worked with the Mayans to establish global flight paths."

"Okay, cool stuff."

"You bet. What are you doing that had you call?"

"Oh, just waiting for a flight to Brussels and thought I'd catch up with you, as it's been a while since we talked."

"Great. Have a good flight and maybe we can catch up when you get back. Still would like to get you and Christine out to the cabin for a long weekend."

"Sure, Dad, gotta go. Take care."

Mike sat back, relaxed, and thought about Pete and his relentless pursuit of alien answers. He couldn't help but think that his dad was investing so much time and energy and for what? Maybe Christine had a good point about wasting so much of his life.

He closed his eyes in a moment of reflection to just think and relax.

When he opened his eyes a few minutes later, he felt re-energized. Looking at his watch, he was puzzled and stressed out.

According to the current time, three hours had passed. He had missed his flight. He had never missed a flight.

Frantic, and thoroughly confused, he did what Mike the logical guy would do. He booked himself on the next flight later that day and called Christine. She was stunned. Mike would never miss a flight. Never.

Gathering his thoughts and trying to figure out what happened, and with Christine still on the line, devastating news lit up TV's in the airport, at Christine's home, and around the world.

Trans America flight 1960 to Brussels was lost over the Atlantic and there was no trace of the plane or any survivors!

Apparently, no distress signal was ever sent from the pilot and no equipment failure was being reported at the time of lost transmission.

In the weeks and months following the plane's disappearance, no functional airplane problems were ever linked to the downed aircraft, only wild speculation.

No trace of the plane was ever found.

Christine picked up a shaken Mike and they drove home, with as somber a feeling as they had ever had.

It wasn't until many years later that the concept of time shifts came up and Mike could throw in his near fatal experience and good fortune to possibly have been a part of an actual time slip.

Or, as Christine believed, he just fell asleep.

Mike and Christine kept this incident pretty much to themselves, but the incident heightened Mike's perspective that something or someone was having a profound impact on his life and the lives of his family around him.

About ten months later, Sara was born.

71

SCOTT

Meanwhile, Scott was pressing on with the job at hand and his two critical priorities. Who or what was behind the cabin attack, and who could he recruit to add to this ever-expanding and far-reaching advisory team?

These two issues were actually related. Using his vast network of contacts, those with military or government crime-fighting experience, such as CIA or FBI, would be primary targets.

He approached two distinguished former military commanders with the sole purpose of securing a trusted cadre of American leaders, which included the newly elected POTUS, Cameron Sullivan, a member of the New Liberty Party, his Vice President, and a small number of confidants.

One of the military leaders, General James Patrick, was now the commanding officer of the Pacific Fleet. He was involved in three major American military conflicts: the Gulf War of 1990–1991, the War in Afghanistan that began in 2001, and the Iraq War of 2003–2011.

Patrick had seen combat and recon efforts around the globe and was the liaison to three former presidents and was well recognized as a man with a heart of gold and a will of steel. He relished combat and he was known around his subordinates as a true patriot and selfless leader, and was a good friend of Scott. Commanding the Pacific Fleet was his life-long dream.

The other was a renowned military expert, General William P. Grant, who possessed recognized negotiation skills and a photographic memory. Whenever a historian was writing a book or seeking information from the past, Bill was the guy to talk to, or even better, listen to. In fact, he was credited with finally bringing North and South Korea together in a complete denuclearization of the peninsula.

Cameron Sullivan, the American President, was formerly a Navy SEAL and was thought to be the actual person that infiltrated the ISIS headquarters disguised as an FBI informant. His involvement was directly credited with stopping the well-armed ISIS contingent from carrying out what would possibly have been their most hideous post 9/11 attack ever. The current POTUS was an extremely worthy adversary and a known risk-taker, but more importantly, a good friend of Scott.

And Cameron's VP, Samantha Worthington, was a Rhodes Scholar and as part of the old NASA, held the record for the longest spacewalk at International Space Station 2. They packed an excellent one/two punch.

Scandals in American politics had taken a tremendous toll for elected officials and the American citizenry. After Congress abolished the two-party system, the Electoral College, party conventions, campaigning, and the mostly wasteful spending of tax and solicited funds, Sullivan and Worthington were the first in the modern era to be elected by popular vote.

Scott was one of many that made up the advisory committee that changed the election process and changed history. Joint ventures combining A.I., cyber technology, Silicon Valley coding and programming, and remarkable government cooperation resulted in a highly advanced process.

That process vetted the top ten candidates, many with no party affiliation, but all with the strong credentials to run the country, and each candidate then spent three to four weeks giving their pitch on policy and issue position, and a virtual election was held using personal devices that all Americans possess. Those who did not have access to devices were able to use any computer that had access to their Social Security Numbers. No undocumented people could vote.

The entire campaigning and election process now took less than a month, costs were relatively low, and the man or woman elected could only serve one six-year term.

Although the judicial system, with a Supreme Court, existed, the Senate and House of Representatives were mainly gatekeepers, as politics became mostly local, and each state had a General Manager and staff, much like a business.

POTUS was then easily elected by popular vote and no voting tampering could occur. Lessons learned from the past proved that history did not repeat itself.

It was such a bittersweet time for Scott, with the loss of Paul Thomas and serious injuries to Sara. The project had even more meaning and focus, given the cabin destruction, and the call that Scott received form Cameron about ten days after the attack.

"Scott, I have some info."

"Hello, Mr. President. I'm listening."

"I don't want to get into too much detail on the phone, as we can meet soon."

"Understand."

"The missile that destroyed the cabin was deployed from a very sophisticated military-type drone, one that we have been surveilling for some time now. We have no idea who could have tapped into this proprietary technology. This is the first time, as far as we know, that it has been used outside of a military encounter."

"Dam, that opens up some questions…"

"It certainly does. We are trying to trace the origin and right now, as I said before, we are clueless. I'll get back to you when I have some answers."

"Great. Thanks. Now, any idea why?"

"No, Scott. Actually, I was hoping you might have an idea. Could it be something that Sara's team was investigating?"

"First answer is no, of course not."

"Second answer?"

"My only thought is they got their noses into something, even unrelated to the ancient alien research, which got someone's attention. If anything turns up, I'll let you know. I'll be talking to the ETRT team soon, inasmuch as Sara is still in a coma."

"Yeah, how tragic for both families. I will also let you know if anything turns up."

"Thanks again, Cameron, so much."

"My pleasure. Gotta figure this out."

"For sure."

The commitment of the ETRT was even greater and stronger than before. Mike and Michaela took the lead to try to get things back on track and regain some traction.

Scott had moved all of the ETRT's equipment and material into a secret compound near Provo, Utah, and had just gotten everyone relocated.

In a sense, he was feeling much more in control now that the momentum and work was in Utah. By design, this had become as secure a place as he had ever seen, with cutting-edge security.

The overall recruiting and vetting process to assemble a strong and trusted leadership team for Scott and additional subject matter experts for the ETRT was on schedule and took a couple months.

Nothing could be done with key pieces of Grandad's material, given so much was in Sara's memory, until Sara had recovered, if she did.

Scott thought to himself:

"We will need a contingency plan if Sara doesn't make it."

72

SCOTT

The U.S. Presidential Elections of 2024 that resulted in Sullivan's victory also exposed many international conspiracy threats and terrorist elements. With Scott's contacts, he tried unsuccessfully to connect any of the threats from the Middle East, Russia, or Asia to the cabin attack. It didn't look as though that was the case.

The United States and the former European Council had been weakened, and anarchy and dictatorships had gained significant momentum.

The strong and revered institutions of democracy in the U.S. were now being challenged, and discontent was running rampant throughout Europe.

It's now 2025 and Scott saw the entire world in chaos. The former Group of Eight, also known as the G8, referred to the group of eight highly industrialized nations: France, Germany, Italy, England, Japan, the United States, Canada, and Russia. Now added to the G8 for a G10 membership were China and South Korea.

A G10 Summit meeting was being held in Geneva, Switzerland, and Cameron arranged for Scott to attend as a technical advisor. Attending ambassadors made a series of well-designed presentations. The list was long and depressing.

Many oil fields in the Middle East had been destroyed.

Several civilizations as we knew them were gone with millions of people left homeless.

Civil unrest was in full reign in Europe, Asia, and the Middle East.

Mounting world problems like hunger, terrorists, disease, and immigration were numerous.

Severe currency problems in Europe, Asia, and South America were devastating banks.

Financial and operational dysfunction existed among the previous elite world countries.

Europe had a catastrophic terrorist attack on its electrical grid in 2013.

General recessions were the new normal throughout the world.

People everywhere truly believed that they, and they alone, were their only keepers.

The host country concluded the two-day summit with some terrifying and somber perceptions. Jürgen Thurnberg, the President of the Federal Council and highly respected member of Swiss elite, addressed the G10 members.

"There has been rampant speculation, denied by most governments, that a group of conspirators are putting a plan together to wreak havoc on the world and replace order with chaos. I have it from good authority today that this is now a distinct possibility."

Murmurs were heard throughout the chamber.

"Instilling fear in free societies seems like their strategy. I believe that from great misery comes great peace. So, many of us feel that those causing the misery could claim the peace as their timely role and put into motion their governance as our only salvation."

After noticeable discussion among the members, Jürgen continued: "I have asked President Sullivan to add his perspective to these observations."

"Thank you, President Thurnberg. We have been working with several recognized agencies around the world, along with former NATO officials, and are putting together as accurate an assessment as we can. Together, we concur with the statements that were just made.

"All I can say for now is that getting the facts together on this subject is our highest global priority."

A subdued applause and some quiet discussion continued to be heard in the chamber.

President Thurnberg spoke, "That concludes this Summit. May God bless us."

As Cameron and Scott got airborne for their flight on Air Force One back to the states, Scott opened the conversation.

"Pretty scary points to make."

"Yeah, and most based on substantiated facts. I couldn't even be totally truthful with them about how far we have gotten into our investigation."

"Can you share much with me?"

"No Scott, only the cabin part and we are getting much more Intel now and could be close to having some answers."

"Can't come soon enough."

Cameron was silent for a moment and then continued.

"You know, the state of California has experienced devastating forest fires in 2018, 2020 and 2023; and the largest category 5 hurricane, Veronica, that ever struck the U.S., hit Florida in 2021."

Pausing for a moment. "The rising seas just compounded the inevitable and even cities like Seattle, San Francisco, and Los Angeles had to move their business centers further inland."

"Yes, I know. Where are you going with this?"

"It's just that as much as I want to help our allies and put our resources to good work, our country is suffering too."

"Ya know, it all started with this news here."

Cameron asked, "What do you mean?"

"Watch this, Cam."

Scott pulled up on his tablet the *Breaking News* from CNN back on September 11, 2021 and Cameron looked on as well.

The world has experienced a disaster unlike anything ever experienced or could ever be anticipated. A highly technical outlier sector of the terror group ISIS detonated two nuclear devices delivered by stealth-like drones, one at each Polar Icecap today, September 11, 2021, the twenty-year anniversary of 9/11, resulting in an estimated 20% destruction of those two polar icecaps.

Within weeks, another ten per cent to fifteen per cent of the ice had melted due to the blasts. Nuclear fallout carried by the winds didn't affect humans but had a devastating impact on animals and the ecology.

It was estimated that it would have taken 150 to 200 years of global warming to accomplish that melting of the North and South Pole.

Highly rising seas and major flooding were no longer distant probabilities, but current facts.

73

SARA

Meanwhile, the tremendous effort to save Sara and restore her life took on a very difficult and critical project unto itself. As she regained consciousness from the induced coma, her parents were at her bedside.

"Sara, Honey, it's Mom and Dad. Can you see us? Hear me?"

"Mom. Yes. What happened? Where am I?"

Mike spoke. "You're in Provo, Utah, in a very good hospital. You've been in a coma for about six weeks."

"Where's Paul? What happened?"

Christine explains to Sara. "There was an explosion at the cabin, apparently from a gas leak, and you suffered serious injuries."

Grasping Sara's hand firmly, she said, "Paul was still inside the cabin when it exploded and he didn't make it."

Trying to comfort her daughter, "We are just thankful that Scott was able to get to you in time and get you here for treatment."

Sara couldn't begin to process this news. "Mom, we were so happy. I can't imagine going forward without him."

"Understand, Sweetie. We all loved Paul. How are you feeling?"

"Guess they are giving me pain meds, because I don't feel much right now."

Mike asked, "What can we do for you now?"

"Just relieved that you're here."

From all medical analysis, Sara would regain her full mental capacity, and within the next week she had. Her short-term memory loss was still present. And, she still had to deal with her extreme physical damage and pain.

Two very important people had entered her life, one to restore her physically and treat the trauma, and one to literally rebuild Sara with the latest medical and reconstructive capability.

The physical rehab team was led by Dr. Dorothy Maguire, MD, and included specialists and technicians who had extensive experience in treating trauma cases.

Many had dealt with combat-related injuries and were not intimidated by Sara's physical state.

Dr. Maguire had once turned down the position of Chief U.S. Surgeon so she could continue to practice medicine and save lives. She had an outstanding reputation and was very excited to be called in on a case that would likely be challenging.

Dr. Maguire was also a person with strong ethics, so Scott knew that she could be trusted and he could confide in her.

"Have you assessed Sara's condition, Doctor?"

"I have, Scott, and we have already put our triage plan together. And, strict confidentiality, as you requested."

"Good. Thanks for your incredible response."

"Who's doing the bone and muscle reconstruction, or do you have someone yet?"

"Yes, we are shooting for Dr. Matthew Palmer."

"Enough said. None better."

Dr. Maguire knew that a significant amount of her bone and muscle structure would need to be replaced by metallic and/or mineral reinforced plastics, and Dr. Matthew Palmer was likely the best in the field.

Sara was identified as Jane so her true identity would not be known. Dorothy's team conducted exhausting work with Sara for several weeks, and once she was deemed healthy for the rebuild stage, a second high-level professional was brought in for the reconstruction.

That doctor and chief technology officer who led the reconstruction efforts for Sara was Dr. Matthew Palmer, PhD., and the founder of *Stargate Labs*, the epitome of development and innovation in I.T., A.I., and human hybrid science. Located in Palo Alto, *Stargate Labs* was considered the crown jewel of Silicon Valley R&D.

In fact, Dr. Palmer's highest priority to date was called Project 55, and it involved the blending of knowledge and self-awareness into avatars and hologram technology. He was the person holding all the keys as far as Sara getting back to her former self.

Scott and Matthew were friends from their college days, and the opportunity to involve Matthew in this urgent effort was incredibly satisfying to Scott.

"Hey Matt, it's Scott; how ya doing?"

"I'm doing fine and it's great to hear from you. From what I can see on the Net, your company and its ancillary businesses are simply exploding!"

"Yes, they are, and thanks. Your *Stargate Labs* Project 55 has been getting a lot of media attention lately."

"Yep, too much, actually. What can I do for you?"

Scott explained the incident with Sara and the pending need for Matt's help, with as little information as he could over the phone. Without a moment's pause, Matt said, "I'm in. When do you want me there?"

"The medical team is just starting their work, but if you could come out soon to see what we're dealing with and make an initial observation, that would be great."

Dr. Palmer quickly responded, "Consider it done."

He thought, creation or resurrection?

74

MATTHEW

Dr. Matthew Palmer was one of the most well-balanced professionals you could find. Brilliant, curious, and with a well-earned reputation for innovation and disruptive technology, he was an icon in his field. Bio technology was his core passion.

Fairly tall and a true fitness fanatic, he ran marathons regularly and twice competed in iron-man competition, finishing both times in the top ten. He usually wore sweater vests, apparently a testimony to his old college professor and mentor from his post-graduate days. No one thought of Dr. Palmer as fashion conscious.

Matt was also a guy who needed to be challenged, so he was obviously in his element with this new encounter. The timing of a possible rebuild was a blessing, as this advanced technology would not have been available a mere five years earlier. Always saying that timing was everything, now it literally was.

Dr. Maguire contacted Matt when she felt Sara was ready for his visit. She hadn't explained to Sara what was still pending in terms of physical rebuilding. She introduced Sara to Matthew with a strange introduction.

"Dr. Palmer, this is the patient we refer to as Jane, but who is actually Sara Thomas. As you know, none of the staff is aware of her true identity."

Matthew looked at the sleeping patient and immediately realized just how extensive the injuries were and could see from Dorothy's mannerisms just how close they had become.

"Thank you for everything you have done and for the detailed file that you had provided me. It was easy to see from the X-rays and scanning just how much had been done and even more critical, how we must proceed going forward."

As he perused the file, he asked Dorothy "Do you have any of her old medical records, dating back to childhood and until now?"

"Yes, of course. I'll get them for you."

Matthew nodded. Dorothy dispatched her P.A. to get the information that he needed from Dr. Maguire's office.

The evolution of A.I. now enabled science to introduce exponentially enhanced technology into a human that would open a portal in the brain that could signal actions throughout the entire body.

Theoretically, these signals would allow the subject to use many times their brain power and many times their strength. The end result would be to make the subject a much stronger and much more aware individual than any human.

Although never tried on a human subject before, Matt certainly had this scope and scale as his end game.

Project 55 was at the top of Matthew's R&D list. This obscure and secret venture involved the transitioning of a deceased man's mental capacity, including knowledge, intuition, reasoning, and telepathic abilities into a holographic image of the person.

In simple terms, it took the brain and its extensive capabilities and was transforming that electronic plethora of information into a holographic presence that one day, hopefully, people could converse with.

This was an evolving science that had become Dr. Palmer's passion. Project 55 involved a human patient, now deceased, and was moving along fairly well when Matt got the call to work on the Jane project.

He temporarily suspended Project 55, leaving it in the hands of his CTO, Jeremiah Jeris, in order to concentrate on the needs in Provo.

Dorothy's P.A. obtained the data on Sara's older medical history that Matt needed, and then delivered the file personally to him.

"This is the file you requested, Dr. Palmer, and please let us know if you need any additional medical information," Dorothy said.

"Sara was married to Paul Thomas, which is her latest medical history, but her maiden name appears on the early docs."

Matthew opened the file to that section and could see that Sara's maiden name was Stevenson. He looked dazed and said to himself, "It couldn't be, or could it!"

"Are you okay? You look a little pale."

"I'm fine. Thank you so much for the info. If I need anything else, I'll be in touch."

As his work with Sara was well underway, Matt had returned a few times to his work on Project 55, but with the information from Dr. Maguire, he now had a somewhat different perspective.

✦ ✦ ✦

When he next returned to *Stargate Labs,* he informed his CTO that all details about who the actual Project 55 person was needed to be concealed.

"So," Jeremiah said, "any reference to Mr. Stevenson as the Project 55 person needs to be concealed?"

"Yes, JJ. And see to it that the database is encrypted. From this point on, it is simply number 55."

"No problem, Matthew; consider it done."

Jeremiah then continued, "By the way, we are about 90% done with the brain mapping on 55, so anytime you want to start the actual hologram capture, we only need a week or so to get him ready.

"The team is pretty confident that we will be able to actually converse with this hologram relatively soon."

"Great. I am really pleased and quite impressed with your progress."

"Thanks, and, what should we do when we get requests for updates, tours, and some basic info on project 55?"

"Tell anyone in authority who asks to contact me, and no one else."

"And," Matthew adds, "I want a couple ideas for our next project, or 56, to replace 55.

"Can do. No problem."

"And, I'd like an update from your team regarding our current S3 development status."

"Can have that to you by tomorrow."

"As far as PR is concerned, Project 55 is complete and we have moved on to 56. We can always say that 55 was the brain stuff, and 56 is the sexy hologram stuff."

"Simple enough."

"Give me some thoughts on what would be a good next dog-and-pony show for nosy engineers, whether it is a 56 update or some solid S3 progress," Matthew said.

"Yep," Jeremiah added and just smiled, thinking to himself that what he didn't know was probably really cool!

Not just cool... a game changer!

75

SARA

Before Dr. Palmer's work began, Sara was introduced to meta-humans that would assist Dr. Palmer. This was intended as much as a two-way social call to benefit both the patient and the robot caregivers.

These meta-humans, a portion of Dr. Palmer's large circle of bot associates, each had a particular skill or special power.

Dr. Palmer asked Sara, "Sara, I have a favor to ask."

Smiling at the opportunity to do something for her physician, Sara responded, "Sure, what is it?"

"I use meta-humans in many of my procedures, and I have three with me today that I'd like to introduce to you. Is that okay?"

"I guess. Do I have a choice?"

"Of course. If you're not comfortable with these bots, I certainly wouldn't want to push it. Can I introduce them?"

"Yes."

"Hi Sara, I'm Valos. My skill is in matter acceleration."

"Hi Sara, I'm Torin. My skill is in new metallic applications."

Valos and Torin offered their names and skills but the third robot did not.

Sara asked, "What is your name?"

"I am Elonis."

"Elonis, what is your skill?"

"My skill is in communication tracks."

"Well. Hi to all of you. It's nice to meet you and thanks for coming to see me."

Sara did not yet realize that different stages of meta-human development existed, but she did notice that the response from Valos and Torin was a little more animated and human-like.

She even felt that if necessary, she could converse with those two bots. Elonis seemed to respond only to direct questions.

Elonis was, apparently, one of the early meta-human models. She had noticeably strong knowledge and problem-solving skills, but she had not been programmed with even the most basic self-awareness capability or what we would call people skills to be able to carry on a near normal conversation with other humans.

Elonis was the fact bot and extremely effective.

Finally, Matthew thought of a funny introduction to introduce himself.

"Hi Sara. I'm Dr. Palmer, and I'm here to help!"

Sara mustered a smile with that tired, old corporate joke of "I'm from Corporate and I'm here to help."

They both got a chuckle out of it, but more importantly, Sara felt an immediate closeness with anyone who works in such a stressful environment and could have a sense of humor.

"Nice to meet you and I think I can use your help."

They smiled together and then Matt spoke.

"I will let you rest today but will be back in a couple of days so we can discuss the process that I have in mind that will need your input."

"Let's start now, okay?"

The doctor now knew how his patient was wired.

"Sara, I love your attitude, but I need to get some things together before we can begin. I'm the delay."

"Okay, fine. The first thing tomorrow we start."

"Of course, looking forward to working with you," Matthew stated as he touched her on the shoulder and left.

Sara thought, "I feel so alone. This can't get started soon enough."

Be careful what you wish for…

76

MATTHEW

Calling Scott, Matt had prepared his early assessment of Sara's condition.
"Hey Scott, it's Matt."

"Hi there. Was looking forward to your call. Did you meet Sara and complete your assessment?"

"Yes, and yes. She has suffered serious injuries but is a truly tough and remarkable person, as you said. I'm just so damn excited to get started."

"Early thoughts?"

"It will take a very strong person, both mentally and physically, to be subjected to this reconstruction. It's a partial destruction of the human body she knows and a rebuild may not be anything like the old self. Her new normal may be far from her known normal."

"I know you, Matt, and you are an optimistic guy, and as skilled as anyone on the planet. Please, just let me know what you need. Whatever."

"Will do, Scott. I need Dr. Maguire's final report to analyze first."

"Just keep me in the loop."

"Of course. Thanks."

Matthew thought to himself, "I'm glad I have such a great team. Can't wait to get started."

✦ ✦ ✦

As Dr. Palmer was in route to his lab, he thought that this project needed a good patient/doctor fit; and he was feeling very good in the fact that he was the perfect professional, expert scientist, and implementer and Sara was the perfect patient.

As soon as he entered the lab, Matt was immediately met by his excited CTO, Jeremiah.

"Matt, I have some rather incredible info that you just must see."

"Regarding?"

"Project 55. Specifically, the mind uploading. I completed the brain scan to get that file ready for the hologram."

"Yes."

"It's like editing a movie. Most of it is cut-and-try, you know, empirical."

"Sure. And this time?"

"Tyreek created an algorithm that navigates the subject's entire memory and visual sightlines for what we consider normal or typical."

"Yeah, of course I'm aware of his work."

Jeremiah continued. "The brain relies on an underlying principle. The simple working part, the neuron, is constantly repeated to create complexity. The human brain contains about 86 billion neurons interconnected by about 100 trillion synapses."

Matt is getting anxious to get to the bottom line. "Why are you bringing this up?"

"Information flows through those vast connected networks in complex patterns, creating the mind."

"And?" Matt asks.

"So, what we have uploaded is 100% in sync with the brain's consciousness."

"No errors."

"No errors, Matt.

Matt replies, "Please continue."

"The so-called normal conscious stuff, Tyreek calls vanilla. Every subject brain scan up to project 55 was 100% vanilla, but 55's scan is only about 93% vanilla, and the rest is data and images that we've never dealt with before. The memory scans toward the end are kind of creepy. Let me show you."

Jeremiah led Matt back to his office and then teed up the portion of the Project 55 brain scan that he found so amazing.

"Memory is supposed to reflect real experiences, not dreams or non-factual events or suppositions. Watch this streaming. It's nuts."

A curious Matt asks, "Do I need to get a drink?"

"No, but you need to keep an open mind."

77
MATTHEW

The conscious memory video streaming began:

Pete was getting out of a car and looking at what appeared to be a spacecraft, but fuzzy. As he approached the large triangular-shaped vehicle, reminding Matt of the old Mercury capsule but significantly larger, a door opened from the spacecraft. Several human-like forms exit the craft and moved slowly toward Pete. Pete stopped. The human-like forms were different. Elongated skulls and longer limbs, along with the unusual space craft, certainly looked to be alien.

At that point, Pete faced several aliens who were in a triangle or pyramid formation, with one in front, and the remainder in formation. The alien in front spoke.

"I am called Echo, Pete, and you have nothing to fear. I am the Commander of this ship, and on my right is Pulse, my Lieutenant. I am the elder statesman and will be your guide."

Matt asks Jerimiah to stop the streaming.

"What the hell is going on, Jeremiah? This can't be what this guy was actually seeing. It must be a dream sequence."

"Yeah, Matt, but our scan technology covers what is seen and remembered, not what is dreamed."

"Go on."

Pete entered the spacecraft and saw a massive control room and bridge. He was directed to be seated near a large panoramic window. As Pete was seated, Echo spoke:

"We are here to provide you with the hard evidence you need to complete your work. We will circumnavigate your solar system as you know it to be. Nothing more."

At this point, it looked like Pete saw sight lines and a navigation grid from space and their linear relationship to Earth's pyramids and how actual landings would be made. As they lifted off and moved into an Earth orbit, they circumvented the globe in what seemed to be minutes. Pulse pointed out the grid from this elevation and Pete saw how flight patterns, navigation, and landings were all in identical coordinates. Then they flew at nearly ground level to demonstrate landings.

Pete was told that they were now in a Martian orbit and pictures from there showed the replication of Earth's ancient monuments and their existence on the surface of Mars. Pulse pointed out to Pete that the sandstorms that have plagued the Martian landscape obscured the view that Pete now has. A perfect replica of the Egyptian Pyramids and Sphinx were seen on the surface of Mars, and Pulse overlaid the coordinates to show their identical dimensions. Pulse asked Pete if he understood what he was seeing. Pete nodded back that he did.

In the next sequence, Pete was gasping for air from an apparent sense of incredible speed and was almost rendered unconscious. His vision at this point was hazy. He gained his senses to see what appeared to be a trip through a black hole or wormhole. Pulse again spoke:

"We are now hundreds of light years from Earth, looking at a star cluster that houses many civilizations, including the Mayans, on several planets. We have bases here. We will leave you with photos that will provide evidence of this."

Pete then observed docking with, and then disembarking from, a massive space station. It was a floating city that was so big that he couldn't see end-to-end. He looked at Earth from that vantage point. Echo looked directly at Pete and spoke.

"Pete, we want you to continue your work; and with the new facts and data that you have, you should be able to convince that core of the scientific community that alien theory is alien fact. There are many reasons why we do not want to reveal ourselves to the world, as only panic, fear, and hysteria would follow."

Pete was then back in his car, alone, and with no one in sight. In his lap were new notes taken during his ordeal, photos, and his diary. Pulse had written the word ARAS, in all caps, on the top of his note pad.

"Jeremiah, what the hell did we just see?"

Gathering his thoughts, Jeremiah says, "Matt, I think it was a real encounter. Again, our software doesn't do dreams!"

"Keep digging. I want answers."

Trying to temper his enthusiasm, Jeremiah added, "I'll make sure we don't have any software issues, but these results will likely stay."

"If that's true, we don't have answers; we have questions."

"Yes, Matt, many questions…"

✦ ✦ ✦

Heading back to his office after Jeremiah's presentation, Matt was torn between the two critical priorities. Sara's well-being and looming reconstruction was first, but this revelation of Project 55, Pete Stevenson, had many bizarre implications.

No detective, he could easily link Pete and Sara, and that was terrifying.

He began to create a new file, confidential and encrypted, that would likely become an information portal that would only get bigger and crazier.

Opening one of his favorite Jack Daniels' Whiskeys, he fixed himself an Old Fashioned and planned to give Scott an update. He jotted down a couple notes from his meetings and then called.

"Hey Scott, how are things in Utah?"

"Hi Matt. Okay, but so many questions. Everything all right?"

"Oh sure. Just wanted to say that I have my medical team assembled and we will be coming out the day after tomorrow. I will have two teams, one for the basic structural repair, and then one for the enhancements that the X-rays and MRI revealed."

"Okay. I'll let Mike and Christine know your plans and schedule. Anything else?"

"I have a project underway, as you know, but the extent of our progress has been incredible. I'd like to bring you up to speed on a specific subject that we are focusing on that is capturing memory and sightline data and reproducing it."

"That sounds pretty intense. Why are you teasing me with it right now?"

"Well, Dr. Maguire said that Sara had some short-term memory loss. Maybe we will be able to scan Sara's subconscious mind for details of the cabin attack that she can't recall."

"That's amazing. Have you done anything like this before?"

"We are working on a similar project right now."

"Okay. Let me know as soon as you get here."

"Will do."

As Matt finished his call, he thought again of the irony of today's event and that he absolutely needed to confide in Scott. He fixed himself another cocktail and relaxed.

The next day, he met with both surgical teams and outlined both planned procedures. This was going to be a game-changer for him and everyone involved.

The head of the reconstruction team, Daniel Marini, had serious doubts about the Utah location.

"Matt, we have looked at the data and believe our best chance at success lies in having the patient here in our lab with our equipment and staff. It is the best option."

"Everyone agree?"

All said they did.

"Okay, let me see what I can do."

Calling Scott, Matt explained their concern and Scott agreed to fly Sara to Stargate Labs in Palo Alto the next week.

The transformation begins...

78

SARA

Upon arriving at Matt's lab, Sara was mentally ready and anxious to begin. Still feeling the effects of drugs and with limbs immobilized, physically she wasn't ready. She was told that her pre-op wouldn't start for at least seventy-two hours. She understood the delay but wasn't happy about it.

Matt met with Sara the night before her first round of surgeries. He could see that she was ready to start.

Grasping her hand, "Hi Sara, how are you feeling?"

Hello Dr. Palmer. I feel pretty good. Dr. Maguire's team did great and I'm glad to have you take it from here. The last couple of days were crap."

"Sorry for that. Sara, we are very excited. I have two teams with me and I'll introduce you soon. Basically, one will be working on repair and one will be using the latest reconstructive techniques to get your strength levels at or better than your baselines."

"What do you mean better?"

"Your injuries were quite severe, as you know. We will need to rebuild some bone structure in both of your legs and one arm with bone and metal equivalents. This is common with many professional athletes today."

What Matt did not share was the fact that no one person that he knew of had ever received this number of reconstruction points.

"We'll start tomorrow. Get some rest."

"Thank you. See you tomorrow."

Waiting outside of Sara's room, Matt spoke to her parents.

"Sara is ready and she is strong. I see no reason to worry. She will have the best talent and latest resources available."

Christine asked Dr. Palmer, "I'm more worried about her short-term memory loss. No one can give us any indication what to expect."

"Again, one thing at a time. Her physical well-being will become a bridge to her overall well-being. Just must be patient."

Dr. Palmer explained to Sara's parents the likely timeline involved in these many surgical procedures. Although Mike planned to fly back and forth as needed, Christine rented an apartment for six months to be with her daughter the entire time.

The surgeries began the next day, and the scope and scale of the reconstructive process were taxing to even these high-level medical professionals.

First, they worked on both legs and her arm. The healing of many bones in her legs wasn't what they had hoped for. So, they decided to replace the major bone structure in the arm and both legs with titanium.

Her back and hip were similarly affected, but much more surgery-complicated, and bone replacement surgery was scheduled.

Muscle reconstruction would be made using a hybrid technology that combined synthetic muscle with mineral-filled nylon, a procedure that had never been done on a human.

A critical status update meeting was called by Dr. Palmer's team; and his lead surgeon, Dr. Anna Ahmed, gave Matt their recommendation.

"Dr. Palmer, we have studied the patient's injuries in sufficient detail to recommend an even more drastic program."

"What's that, Dr. Ahmed?"

"The repairs that we are planning are disproportionate. That is…"

"Excuse me, Anna, but I know where you are going. Let me get the patient's approval and I'll get back to you ASAP."

Within minutes, Matt was at Sara's bedside. "Hi, Sara. How ya doing?"

"Okay. Not really. I'm feeling like I was just in an accident."

After a brief pause, Matt added, "That is typical."

"So, is this a social call, Doctor?"

"No. We have a bit of an issue. My team has evaluated your injuries and believe that they can completely restore your arm and legs soon, and then the hip and back next."

Sara was silent, waiting for Matt to continue.

"However, we have a dilemma. Your replaced legs will be strong, but your replaced arm will be much stronger than your other arm. And, your replaced hip will be stronger as well."

"Okay, Dr. Palmer, I see a question coming."

"Yep. Very intuitive. We have a problem defined as disproportionate."

Sara offered her opinion. "I know where you are going. What do you need from me?"

"We need you to authorize the additional rebuild of your good arm and good hip. It will add some physical therapy time, but not that much."

With little time to think about her choice, Sara simply said, "Bring me the form to sign."

"Thanks. You'll have it tomorrow and we will get right back on track this week."

At each milestone of the process, much physical therapy was required. Some surgical rejections were dealt with, as the body was responding to these intrusions.

After eight months, Sara's ordeal in the hospital was over.

But Sara's critical ordeal had just begun.

79

SARA

Physically, Sara would need to control her newfound strength; and even the most basic skills, like holding a glass of water or brushing her teeth, took on a learning curve for which she was unprepared. She was the only person who saw the tears and felt the fears.

It had been ten months since the attack, and Sara was feeling all alone and fought with herself constantly about what she could have done to prevent Paul's death. What if I had done this… what if I had done that? She had the burden of guilt hanging over her and simply couldn't get Paul's death out of her mind. Sara just tried to put it to rest as a tragic accident.

Physically, she was stronger. An unexpected upside was her four-foot vertical jump, and she enjoyed being able to leap over a bed or table with ease.

She could do fifty one-handed pull ups, and the staff nurses referred to her as their super-hero.

Unbeknownst to hospital admin, the floor nurses would have daily wagers on Sara's acts of strength, which Sara thoroughly enjoyed.

Mentally she was having dreams and nightmares that were troubling and scary, and she still experienced short-term memory loss. One in particular was recurring.

She saw herself in the dream sequence that her dad mentioned to her many times. Only, she was the angel or villain or whatever that was rising in a haze and scolding whomever she was facing.

She often couldn't tell the difference between a dream sequence such as that one and reality. She, occasionally, felt as if she was clearly thinking someone else's thoughts, usually her dad's or grandad's.

Another surprising benefit of her new mental awareness was the fact that she was feeling a link or bonding to the meta-humans with whom she was coming in contact.

One time, when Torin had stopped by to see her, Sara and the meta carried on a telepathic conversation for several minutes and Sara was stunned.

Sara thought, "Are you aware of the metallic pins and sleeves that are now in my body?"

Torin responded, "Yes, you have titanium, mineral-filled nylon, and shards of a meteorite in your body."

Torin thought, "Are you okay? Are you in pain?"

Sara thought back, "No longer in physical pain, but my memory isn't right."

"Learn to think backwards. Go back, stop. Go back, stop. Memories are like semi-conscious dreams. Each stage is important and you should try to focus on where you were mentally and physically at each stage."

Sara's final thought to Torin, "Let's do this again. I'm happy that you came by."

She did mention this to Matthew, and he sounded somewhat surprised.

"I can't explain what occurred. I assume that this is Torin's capability and nothing more. Keep me posted on any other meetings you have like this with Torin or Valos or Elonis."

Matt knew this intended consequence was a sign that Sara's link to the meta was solid, likely a result of the extreme levels of meteorite in her body. He couldn't be sure that Sara was the transmitter or the meta were.

The major rebuilding project took nearly five months, but it would remain a work in progress. There were successes during this process, mostly the physical, but there were also painful mental setbacks.

Since Sara was the pilot patient of this technology, often metal pieces replacing Sara's bones, or binding materials serving as her new muscles, had to be implanted, replaced, and implanted again, and so on.

Matthew knew that only when Sara believed she was ready could they properly evaluate their work and Sara's results. One day Sara simply said to Matthew, "Okay, let's do this."

✦ ✦ ✦

It came time to test Sara's new mental and physical prowess, and it seemed as though she was the least nervous person in the laboratory meeting room.

No one attending this performance had any idea of the extent of her physical and mental anguish, or of the many fits and starts that she and the team endured.

With a very small group of people, which included Scott and Amanda Woods and Sara's parents, the day turned out to be utterly spectacular.

Both Sara's mental and physical abilities were tested, with the stretch goals set very high to observe the current state and evaluate the next level targets.

Sara ran the 100-yard dash in 9.5 seconds.

She high-jumped seven feet.
She long jumped 25 feet, 6 inches.
She bench-pressed 350 pounds.
All of these accomplishments would have been world records.
She mentally calculated the time and distance of Earth's orbit at summer solstice.
She also calculated the odds of winning a Powerball lottery knowing several factors.

The very high expectations were exceeded, and Matt was very pleased and proud of the work that Dr. Maguire's team and his two teams had done.

Christine simply said, "You are the inspiration to everyone out there that ever had to deal with devastating loss, and your dad and I are so very proud of you!"

"We love you, Sara Bear."

Scott added, "Our objective now is to re-start our research and investigative work and regain our momentum, right Sara?"

"I disagree with one word in your remarks, Scott."

The room went briefly quiet. Sara smiled.

"The word objective is what we want to achieve. I prefer the word *expective* as what we will achieve!"

"Yep," Scott thought, "she's back!"

"One more thing, Scott."

"Sure. What?"

Sara replied as if this had been a burning issue over the last few months.

"Given this state of my rebuild and what I believe is the need to protect my identity, I want to change my name."

Briefly caught off guard, Scott answered. "Okay. We can certainly do that. Do you have a name in mind?"

"Sara Steele."

80

SARA

Sara and Dr. Palmer became close, having spent months together. For Valentine's Day, they both surprised each other with cards.

Sara's card to Dr. Palmer said, *"For a Special New Friend on Valentine's Day, I am grateful for you."*

Matt's card to Sara read, *"I hope you feel loved and appreciated on Valentine's Day. Because you are."*

It was apparent to everyone around them that they had made a significant bond. Matt had to develop an almost psychologist-type mentality to cope with Sara's mental state, in addition to those actual subject matter specialists already on staff and helping.

Sara's colleagues Kat and Michaela brought her a bouquet of flowers after her last surgery.

"Hi Sunshine, just a little something from the team."

"Thanks, Kat; that was sweet. Ready to get back to work."

"Dr. Palmer is amazing, eh?"

"Yep, Kat, I couldn't have made it without him. So much respect for both his skills and his personality. Such a caring person. Lucky girl."

Matt's latest development in mental consciousness was creating mental telepathy capabilities for extreme conditions. Sara would be the first recipient of this leading-edge technology.

Michaela added, "I'm totally blown away with the neuro and cerebral technology, Sara. Would love to get some insight from you on your perspective following that unreal mental demonstration."

"It's a serious learning curve right now, Michaela, but I'd love to spend some time getting your thoughts as well."

Brad Harris, a strength and conditioning coach, provided the training for Sara to reach and exceed the most difficult physical attributes. Mike was both impressed and curious about his daughter's physical well-being, and they had several conversations when Sara was ready to talk.

Fifteen months after the cabin tragedy, Sara was being released from this ultra-secret laboratory/hospital, and it was back to work.

Unfortunately, reality soon set in and hit Sara hard. Dealing with Paul's death was the biggest hurdle for Sara, and until she had adequately processed the horrible cabin explosion and her personal loss, all else simply had to wait.

Patience was the necessary evil for all concerned, and it was difficult to simply tread water waiting for the momentum to resume.

Christine finally had an opportunity for a one-on-one with Sara, and Paul's death was on top of her to-do list for her daughter and her to discuss. Upon greeting her she gave Sara a big hug.

"We are happy and relieved that you have come so far, and we are so blessed that you had the people helping you that you had. But, Sara Steele?"

"It'll make sense later on, I know."

"Okay, Sara Steele."

"Mom, there is no way I would have made it without everyone's commitment and skills. And Dr. Palmer was awesome."

"It is tough, I know, but if you want to talk about Paul, I'm here. Mike and I just want to say how sorry we are."

"Thanks, Mom, and maybe we can talk one day, but not now."

"Understand. That lovely man was clutching a photo of you and Grandad when he died."

That remark brought tears to both.

The next day, Matt and Sara had a special moment. Sensing her deep hurt and memories of the cabin tragedy, Matt took Sara by the hand.

"Let's go for a walk."

She didn't see that coming but was not surprised.

"Okay, that would be nice."

He took her for a leisurely walk that ended at a lovely stream in the woods, far away from all the madness and real-world noise.

"The two things that stand out to me are the spectacular beauty of this stream, and the fact that it is constantly moving. You remind me of both."

Sara gave his remark a moment's thought. "Thank you."

"And often, we take this for granted. I guess it is stop-and-smell-the-roses time."

Again, Sara paused. "Good point. So true."

Sara reflected for a moment and realized that this walk and lovely stream as a backdrop were just what she needed. On the way back, she spoke.

"I really like how you listen and how you deal with people."

"Well, Sara, I am in the people business," he said smiling. "And it's easy to get reflective when you're taking a beautiful walk like this one."

They both smiled and felt a strong sense of relaxation and closeness.

Returning from their walk, Sara gave Matt a long hug.

She was now ready to go, and had developed an attack mentality that re-fired the passion in her heart and soul. The mind and body were armed and ready to go.

She told Matt, "I have finally gotten my focus back… let's go."

Matt thought to himself, "With Sara, you could literally redefine the word focus to be in any dictionary as *whatever Sara does.*"

Sara Steele, the "Warrior," was emerging.

81

SARA

Sara went inside to think and to chill out; but feeling restless and needing some time to relax, she headed to a local bar for a late-night drink.

Sara took a seat at the far end of the bar and ordered a popular bourbon drink called a Casanova. The pleasant bartender brought her drink to her and she tried to settle back and relax.

Sitting down next to her, a gruff-looking guy with a leather vest asked, "So whatcha drinking?"

Annoyed, Sara just said, "A Casanova."

"Really? That's my middle name."

Ignoring him, she took her drink to another seat and assumed he would get the message.

Following her, he said, "You're not very friendly."

"And you're an obnoxious bore. Go away."

"I'm not done with you."

She told him to "shove off" and tossed her drink in his face.

Sara paid her bar tab and left immediately but is confronted by the man and his two friends just a few steps from the bar's entrance. The two friends grab Sara as the obnoxious guy attempts to assault her.

She beat the crap out of the three of them with her newfound strength and left them in a heap of pain and embarrassment.

Sara now knows that she needs to control her emotions as the local police intervened and took a report. Sara's incident made the local news.

FEMALE PATIENT IS RELEASED;
CAUSES PAIN TO THREE MALES ASSAULTING HER!

Now everyone knows that she had changed... especially Sara.

82

SARA

The team was called together in their newly built compound in Utah for Sara's return, and they were so excited to see her, but nervous regarding the state of mind that now defined her and the fight that she was involved in a few days ago.

Sara's first words were, "Hi everyone."

Her second words were, "Did we get all the stuff from the cabin?"

Yes, the team knew that Sara was indeed back, new body and new name.

Piecing together the events and timing of the cabin tragedy, it appeared as though Sara and Paul were exiting at the same time, but for whatever reason, Paul dashed back into the cabin to retrieve something.

It wasn't an alien artifact that Paul was trying to retrieve; it was Sara's picture of her and her grandad, and the memory that had become very important to Sara. As Christine had told her, he was clutching that picture when his body was found.

So, all of the cabin materials, docs, photos, and physical evidence were recovered from the SUV that Connor drove back to the office and was now safely in the hands of the new ETRT. With several new members added, there was now highly-skilled and extremely valuable personal in place.

Six very capable meta-humans were now on board, which would eventually give the ETRT some additional defense if any unplanned situation might occur again. Elonis was the leader of this group, as she had already proven her worth and the proverbial good soldier.

Mike became an integral part of this research team, as his skills to coordinate, facilitate, and implement were like the glue keeping the various puzzle pieces in play.

Once he had accepted Sara's new warrior persona, Christine and he were just happy that their daughter had survived. Their concern was the unknown future and the new and dangerous worldview.

Although much was done with the 650 short-list entries previously assembled, most of Sara's rehab time was spent by Scott putting together the new team and building the highest tech lab that the world had ever seen.

It had become nearly an obsession for Scott and Amanda, as they both recognized the enormity of what was before them.

During this last year, given the strong fabric and leadership of Scott's company, revenue had grown to over $1 trillion, so funding additional R&D was becoming easier.

All was quiet, for the most part, as the perpetrators of the violent cabin attack likely believed that they were 100% successful in killing the research team. So, the ETRT's journey was quite literally into the unknown.

As an extended period of trust-building began, among Sara, her international team, the meta-humans, Scott, the POTUS, and Sara's dad, it became more and more likely that mankind was not alone.

That logic was driven by events and several disasters that had raised more questions than it answered. The bigger question was: if our consensus determines that there is an alien presence on Earth, is this alien involvement good, bad, or even worse…, somewhere in between with an unclear intent?

The actual research work that Sara and her team pursued was as deep a dive as anything ever undertaken by researchers, scientists, and scholars in a joint and calculated manner. They all went off the grid for quite some time to do their research uninterrupted.

The scope and scale of this enormous undertaking had some small, nearly undeniable results, but it also had looming a few huge findings that could literally change the perspective of every member of the ETRT.

Sara gathered her original "A" team with a critical to-do list that needed to be addressed immediately.

"Well, guys, I have a short and sweet list of issues that we need to finalize quickly. You have the people and resources now that we can focus on the following:

"Pete's Sweden trip and his alleged physical encounter. I want all the data, docs, photos, and notes that we have and I want a timeline for them.

"Artificial Intelligence systems evolving into the biggest risk civilization would face was a threat perceived by Pete that we need to either support or debunk.

"The Grid and perfect electrical alignments could be the keystone in proving alien intervention by capturing an alien culture that was alive and well here on Earth.

"Navigation and alien space travel is sexy stuff, for sure, so let's put on our game faces and call it what it is or was.

"Ancient Mars colonization and the Orion constellation, referred to often, could be a blueprint for convincing the masses of the bigger picture and that's our stretch goal.

"Alien Gods and their connection to kings, pharaohs, and Anunnaki lore are not only the subject of thousands of years of religious undertones, but could put a nice bow on all of our efforts. Any questions?"

The small leadership team was taking notes and knew all of next steps required.

Sara simply said, "You can prioritize and set up teams as you usually do. I don't need to be in the loop for who is doing what, okay?"

The team was so focused that Sara's last comment was unnecessary.

Sara's concluded by saying, "A totally off-the-radar conspiracy piece that had, and still has, political implications will be my baby to figure out and I will."

✦ ✦ ✦

As any good project team would do, they were now putting the final touches on a very thorough and professional presentation. They had every sense that they would now be able to convince any open-minded audience that their evidence was real and compelling.

The biggest issue that came from their investigation was Pete's trip to Sweden in early 2018. Sara was told that Pete called Mike and Christine to tell them that he was going to visit some of their relatives that lived near Gothenburg, Sweden.

Pete's reasoning, apparently, was that it had been a while since any of the Stevenson clan had made that trip.

Sara called her dad for some details on that trip, per Mike's recollection. She was told that Pete was going to Sweden to visit the relatives and would be gone for a few weeks. Mike also recalled that Pete was pretty sure that he would be in and out of cell phone range.

Sara was told that Christine thought the timing was weird. Her mom mentioned to Mike that it was winter there and the weather would be cold and snowy and an odd time to go. Christine said she would expect Pete to visit in the summer when it was so beautiful there.

Later it was found that Pete's travel itinerary showed no stops in Gothenburg, but a clear trip to Trelleborg, the southernmost town in Sweden.

In fact, Pete apparently flew into Copenhagen, Denmark, and then drove to Trelleborg. According to his diary, he had a meeting about 80 kilometers from

Trelleborg with unknown persons and no names were given. He was gone for five days.

When Sara learned about this trip, she called Mike.

"Dad, do you recall Grandad's trip to Sweden in February of 2018?"

"Yes. He was going there to visit our relatives, Annie and John Stevenson. Why do you ask?"

"Well, his itinerary had some inconsistencies and lacked specifics. He had indicated in a phone log that he was going to Gothenburg for some sort of family gathering."

"Yes. As I recall he even called me to say he might be out of cell phone range sometimes."

Sara explained the sketchy details to Mike and Mike offered to call Annie and John.

"Okay, let me know what you find out."

"Will do. Thanks for the update. Love you."

"Love you guys too."

Sara still had one scary thought…

Grandad Pete and his team had put themselves into unknown danger!

83

PETE

Unfortunately for Pete Stevenson and his small crew, their digging into ancient alien artifacts in Europe, The Middle East, and Central America in the late nineties turned up facts and possible connections to a terrorist group that put their work and themselves in danger.

It was an unintended consequence of their diligent investigative efforts. Only Pete, however, was able to connect some dots to these sinister people, and knew they were swimming in shark-infested waters.

Frustrated with what he was finding and what the next steps might be, Pete called his son David, who was the financial genius in the family, early in 2002.

"Hi David, it's Pete; how ya doing?"

"Doing great, Dad, and yourself? Still traveling around the world looking for trouble?"

"Yep, still traveling, and it seems like trouble finds me just fine." They both laughed.

"Seriously, David, I do have an issue and need some advice. In my digging for alien stuff, I've come across some evidence that several wealthy people are buying up artifacts that should be headed to a museum, or possibly even involved in the theft of expensive artifacts, and that's just not right."

Pete thought this little white lie would work just fine.

David responded, "So, why does this matter to you? It may be unlawful but it doesn't seem at all relevant to your ancient alien theories."

"Yeah, you're probably right and thanks for your time."

"No problem, Dad; happy hunting."

Sensing that Pete wasn't hanging up, David continued. "Tell you what; send me what detailed financial stuff you have and I'll take a look."

"That would be great. Thanks."

Pete was feeling better that David would look into his latest findings, but with the many curious and inexplicable links from Pete's research to several suspicious people in the U.S. and abroad, Pete then called Corey needing to talk.

"Hi Corey, got a minute?"

"Sure, what's up Pete?"

"You know I'm a very curious person, and I came across a money trail tied to some artifacts that have major implications."

"I'm already lost, Pete. Please, from the beginning…"

"In my general alien artifact research, one strange thing jumps out to me and it concerns deals with precious artifacts and huge amounts of money going somewhere."

"For example?"

"The Gold Flyer Planes from around 1000 AD that were in the Bogota, Columbia, Museum, and the Aztec Crystal Skulls from the British Museum were stolen and then sold. There were seven wealthy sellers receiving millions for these pieces."

"Pete, the selling part is totally legal. They can always argue that they obtained them through barter or something like that."

"Yeah, but when I did some digging, or should I say had someone do some digging, all seven people were depositing funds from the black-market sale of those expensive artifacts into the same account, and it's a big one. This is a money trail that has significant implications."

"This just surfaced?"

"No. It's a money trail pattern that has accrued over a period of nearly two years, and if I didn't have strong recall skills, it would have likely gone unnoticed."

"Wow."

"There's more. While in Central America, I came across several artifacts and scrolls from the Mayan civilization, as you guys know, that were extremely important."

"Yeah, the team was most excited about the Dresden Codex, the oldest surviving Mayan book dating back to the 13th century."

"What I also uncovered was a large number of precious gems from that area had been stolen and not reported to local authorities. After doing some more digging, the money was traceable to the local drug cartels. Corey, the drug cartels were receiving huge sums of money from theft, not drugs."

"Pete, you are in way over your head. You know that, right?"

"I know. But this is too important to just ignore."

"I can see a scenario that ends up bad… really bad. Who the hell is your source?"

"My sources are solid."

"Solid enough to have your back if things go sideways?"

"I guess you're right. Just puzzled with all of these new issues. Corey, I wasn't looking for this, but one thing led to another, and I tried to get some answers. Thanks for listening. I'll just put this aside for now."

"Smart move. Let me know when the team can get back together, okay?"

"Sure, will do."

"Talk later, Pete. Good luck."

Corey didn't think Pete could walk away from this.

Pete most definitely could not.

84

PETE

Pete didn't share everything non-alien that he uncovered with Corey. There was much more that concerned him, and Pete knew he needed to get someone else involved. Someone with expertise and the authority to use this information was his next step.

Pete contacted an old army buddy, Lt. Robert Baker, who was now handling espionage issues for the military and who Pete worked with back when he was doing data research for the Army. They had developed a strong relationship built on trust and respect.

"Hi Bob; it's me, Pete Stevenson."

"Pete, long time since I heard from you. Still chasing alien monsters?"

"Well, I actually screwed up. I found them and now they're chasing me!"

Laughing loudly, Lt. Baker asked, "What can I do for you?"

"It's been a while, for sure. What are you working on these days?"

Lt. Baker commented, "You know, the usual mundane stuff: terrorists, enemy agents, cyber-crime, and the various international conspiracies."

Pete replied, "You're the one guy that may be having more fun than me."

"Doubt that, Pete. What can I do for you?"

Pete brought Lt. Baker up to speed with his conversation with Corey, but then went on with additional information for Lt. Baker.

"Pete, that's some interesting finds for an alien chaser. You said you have more?"

"During my trip to The Middle East, I discovered that significant revenue from oil and the mining of gold and silver was being diverted outside any governments."

Lt. Baker quickly responded. "And you found out how?"

"I'm just persistent, as always."

"Okay, I'll look into it. Probably for the purchase of guns or military equipment. What else?"

"Egypt provided one more puzzling issue, and that involved drone technology. Under the guise of drone recovery for antiques and artifacts, I found drones were being fitted with the latest laser guidance systems and weaponized."

"Can you prove this, Pete?"

"Yep, I took photos."

"Pete, that's scary stuff for anyone to come across, no offense."

"And, get this. This R&D was done under the banner of a science lab that I found out was a ruse and did not exist. Bob, the speed and stealth-like maneuvers of these research drones were like they were involved in combat exercises."

"Send me what you have. I can't believe our guys aren't on to this. I'll contact you with a safe way to do it. And thanks."

"No problem, Bob. If I turn up anything more, I'll let you know."

"Hell, you need to be back working for us."

"Nope. Aliens are much safer."

Pete was still uneasy about what he was seeing and that his mission had scope creep that was truly putting him and his team into uncharted and dangerous territory. Within hours of hanging up with Bob, he got a call back from David.

"Well. I have some news and it's pretty incredible."

"David, I'm not surprised."

"What I found was an apparent link to these various money trails, with a very high degree of confidence."

"You didn't risk exposing yourself?"

"No. What I found was that nearly every one of those accounts could be traced to off-shore banks and then back to several businesses.

"About forty shell companies are owned by seven individuals, and those individuals were are some of the wealthiest people in the world. And every time I accessed public files, it cost me a dollar thirty."

Laughing at that last comment, Pete was taking notes. "Go on."

"Well, I also found several dormant accounts were receiving up to twenty million dollars a day and in a variety of currencies including crypto currency. There were some possible ties to ongoing criminal activity that involved the SEC and FBI that prompted me to quit."

"Oh my God. I'm so sorry I brought you into this."

"It's okay. Just not sure what you're going to do with this info."

"I will turn it over to a friend. Thanks."

Pete contacted Lt. Baker and gave him David's update. Baker then gave Pete some rather compromising information as well, knowing that Pete wouldn't share it with anyone.

"Over the last couple of years in Europe and the Middle East, where the menacing E13 terrorist group was growing in size and scope, we noticed a peculiar occurrence. Many of the small, independent terrorist groups were consolidating, something that would never occur in normal times. And, the blood money from these groups is going into, for the lack of a better name, a central untraceable non-local account."

As important a piece of research as those findings were, Pete got himself back on track with the scope of the alien work and tabled this new information for the time being.

He had planned to alert authorities immediately after the Paris meeting, using his platform in Paris to announce that information to law enforcement in an environment that he felt would be safe.

Now he was unsure what to do. Leaving it in the hands of the military was the logical choice.

Pete doesn't always do "logic."

85

SMOKE

Late in 2008, Mr. Smith's associate, Bud, summoned him again for an update on the activity of Pete Stevenson and his team.

Bud's criminal society was about to plan a series of terrorist acts and wanted to be sure that they would not be blindsided by the alien geeks, as they knew those geeks were being led by a hard-charging guy with FBI ties.

Bud arranged a meeting between Smith and himself at a junk yard in Detroit that was primarily one with a huge trash compactor. As Smith drove up, several cars were being compressed down to the size of a small refrigerator.

There was a stench in the air that was putrid, and dirt and soot were everywhere. The crappy atmosphere jumped out at John Smith and he was very uneasy.

"So, Smith, what's up with your alien friends? Anything we should be concerned about?"

"No, they are pretty much focused on presenting the alien stuff at a meeting in Paris in September."

"Well, we have info that Pete Stevenson was doing some digging into our business in Central America and the Middle East and that is not at all comforting right now."

"What kind of digging?"

"You're supposed to be telling me, fool. We hear that he has been asking a lot of questions about theft of artifacts, money laundering, police cover-up, and just nosey crap."

"He hasn't shared any info like that with any of us and I'm sure he would have if he had anything."

Smith thought he was being baited and was waiting for Bud's next salvo.

"You know how critical it is to protect our paper trails, and if Stevenson's group found the link between our group members and the events of the last few years, that would be a problem."

"I think you're getting some mixed messages or paranoia stemming from your contacts to deflect stuff away from them."

"Possible, I guess. I'll look into that. We have plans for much more that will require this group of ours to stay anonymous and definitely under the radar."

"I totally understand your concern, but you need to know that this group is practically harmless, and I say that from two perspectives: They are focused on getting a ton of data analyzed and presentable right now for the Paris show, and they are beginning to come around to my theory that inhuman aliens are part of the criminal events that are ongoing."

"Are you kidding me?"

"I am not."

"These people are so out-of-touch with current reality that they are obsessed with twisting and turning whatever data they have into their own alien beliefs."

"It's a convenient explanation." Smith was lying and hoping for the best.

"And the second reason?"

"And the second reason that you should not worry is that the so-called digging trips that you referred to were done a couple years ago, which is now so far off the radar screen that they don't even recall, relate, or conclude anything of a correlative nature here."

"You better be right or the next time I see you, you will be in one of those crushed cars, ya hear?"

"Loud and clear."

Bud appeared somewhat relieved. Smith knew he dodged a bullet.

✦ ✦ ✦

About six weeks later, Smith contacted Pete to do a little digging per Bud's concern. He had a strategy to get as much information as he could get from Pete and Pete's team using the guise of a status update, while having his own agenda to see what, if anything, Bud needed to be concerned about.

"Hi Pete. John Smith checking in."

"Yeah, I see your number on my phone. What's up?"

"As far as the evil aliens slant goes, this would be 'good news/bad news' for you."

Pete responded, "Hold on while a grab a beer," thinking this could actually be good.

Smith continued, "Well, I know you've been thinking that this evil alien stuff has been a waste of time."

"Totally."

Smith added, "I have looked into every lead that I had and can't see any evidence of where any incidents on Earth could have had an evil alien contribution. So, I'm calling to ask you what you want me to do regarding team priorities going forward."

Taking a long sip of his Molson, Pete responded, "Okay, I'll bite. Which one was the good news and which one the bad?"

Smith replied, "I guess I deserved that. Seriously, what do you want me to do now?"

"I don't have anything on my plate right now, so give me a little time."

Smith piped in, "How 'bout we do another team meeting for updates and see what makes sense for me given what everyone is working on."

"Actually, that's not a bad idea. Maybe in the next couple of months or early 2009 at the latest. Let me check into everyone's schedule and get back to you. If we can't meet together, we can video conference."

Smith was very pleased with his strategy.

He was sure that Pete wasn't on to him.

86

PETE

Following that video conference, which was held in January, 2009, the team decided to hold a meeting every year, in addition to regular updates done on a quarterly basis.

Odd numbered years would be the video type, and even number years would be at locations that corresponded to other conferences or a physical location that the team needed to visit.

In June of 2016, things were coming together. The team met in Southern California, the location of that year's semi-annual Alien-Con, the get together of all things alien and weird people that attracted the likes of Star Trekkies and comic book heroes galore.

Meeting at the San Diego Hilton, host of the event and the night before the conference began, Pete kicked the meeting off.

"This is both a business meeting and a time to relax and take in the irrelevant and bizarre. I've been to a few of these, either here in SoCal or in the fall in Baltimore, and they are fun."

Corey jumps in, "Yeah, it kinda feels like a vacation. Thanks for suggesting it."

Pete continued, "Let's enjoy this event, but also look and listen to those writers, researchers, and other ancient alien theorists such as Erich von Däniken, David Hatcher Childress and Giorgio A. Tsoukalos.

Giving a high-five to Pete, Beth added, "Good point. These guys are the closest we will get to our own kind that have a similar agenda."

As the team was heading out, Beth spoke to Pete. "Gotta minute?"

"Sure, Beth, let's head over to the bar and get a drink."

As they sat down and ordered drinks; wine for Beth and scotch for Pete, Beth simply asked. "I sent you those carbonate globules from that Antarctica meteorite for Martian bacteria and DNA analysis. What did you find?"

"Sorry, Beth, I haven't got around to doing that just yet."

Beth was startled. Not like Pete, for sure.

Following four days of work and fun, the team went their separate ways. Before they left, it was decided that they would meet in Helsinki, Finland, in 2018, to finalize their presentation for the Paris Air Show that September.

Unfortunately, Pete was dealing with another demon…

His daily scotch habit…

87

PETE

In the late summer of 2018 Pete was in Helsinki preparing for that extremely important meeting in Paris in September when he would startle the World with his findings.

The Paris Air Show was always the venue for earth-shattering aviation and aerospace announcements, so this opportunity made perfect sense.

As Pete gathered his research colleagues, Corey, Thomas, Beth, and Mr. Smith, he thought that he could be the bearer of the kind of information that could result in panic and hysteria. As the group of five met, he had a recurring concern about one of his colleagues.

Pete was losing trust in John Smith that had been building for the last couple of years. A series of mistakes, undone tasks, and Smith's recurring focus about the evil alien train of thought had Pete suspicious.

However, when he discussed these concerns with Corey and Thomas, they didn't see Smith with those same eyes. Beth was staying neutral. So, Pete just tossed it up to a bit of paranoia and moved on.

One thing he did that he felt comfortable about was not telling anyone there about the details of Trelleborg. That would be revealed to the group just prior to Paris as they developed the REVEAL presentation.

He did give Corey, Thomas, and Beth a watered-down version of his alien contact, as he felt it was a duty to do, and described it mostly as an out-of-body experience.

Pete also gave those three people his high-level overview of the paper trail of the likely terrorist activity realizing that, for their own safety, the less known the better. He did not, however, share any of these two issues with Mr. Smith. The other three respected Pete's request to keep this quiet for the time being.

So, as they met to start putting the puzzle pieces together, Pete asked for suggestions.

Beth started, "Well, I think we go for the emotional connections. Let's get them excited immediately about those things that gets your heart racing."

Corey added, "The physical evidence derived by our research in pyramids, monuments, structures, and stone formations should be the primary driver, and we have so much evidence there to lay out. Plus, we can span the civilizations from 10,000 BC to the present."

Pete was thinking, "I bet I know what Thomas will suggest."

"So, Thomas, what's your idea?"

"Well, the science, mathematics, and engineering codes are all out there, and we can easily draw a link between ancient alien technology and our modern-day technology."

"Yep, you nailed it."

With that in mind, Pete asked Mr. Smith for his two cents.

"I guess I still haven't eliminated the idea that sinister aliens are in play now causing much of the world's calamities. I'd like to focus on the puzzle pieces that point to the internal terrorist threats and what we have to link them to bad aliens. You know, junk DNA from early hieroglyphics are strong evidence."

Everyone just shrugged their shoulders or rolled their eyes at Smith's latest diatribe. At that point, Smith went outside to smoke a cigarette. Pete immediately jumped in and addressed the other three people.

"Let's be very careful on how we proceed from here, both with the alien material to be presented, and with any potential conspiracy theory. I know we also have an obligation to present those facts that we have regarding a possible terrorist conspiracy, but that is not why we are here."

Beth added, "We agree with you, Pete, and I'm beginning to think like you that Smith is just too much of an outlier to be trusted."

"Okay. The agenda will be to present THE REVEAL as the alien evidence, as outlandish as it may be, and that is our mission. I will finish my speech with the conspiracy data that we have, or should I say I have, as I see this as the best way to take this public. No one will know this is coming and the law enforcement branches can take it from there. And, I don't want any of you to get involved in this part of our presentation. You are there to answer alien questions or to set up table discussions, but nothing more. Does that work for you guys?"

Except for some concern from Beth that the conspiracy issue should be tabled for another time and place and audience, they agreed with Pete.

At that point Smith walked back into the room. "What did I miss?"

Pete replied, "Not much. Just wrapping up. Let's get to work to create this incredible presentation over the next three days here in Helsinki."

Pete thought about Smith's lackadaisical attitude.

"This is the straw that breaks the camel's back."

88

BETH

About three weeks later, after the team finished the Helsinki presentation, Beth called Pete with some concern and worry associated with her Central America digging into alien artifacts. Apparently, while searching through numerous photos and documents, she found some troubling pictures.

"Hi Pete; it's Beth."

"Hi. What's up?"

"Well, while going through some photos here in Honduras, probably about eight or nine hundred pieces of data, I came across something really strange."

"And, whatcha find?"

"Well our Mr. Smith appears in two rather disturbing photos. In one, he is arm-in-arm with someone that the locals call the big drug honcho; and in another, he is with a bunch of guys in a fraternity-type shoot. Only problem is that they are guerrillas, apparently, and not frat boys!"

"Crap, Beth, that's incredible. You sure it's him?"

"Damn sure."

With much going through his mind, Pete asked Beth, "Could you please send me those pics so I can see if I can get some more info?"

"Sure can, Pete."

"Great job Beth. This isn't good."

"No, Pete, but it does answer some of your questions and concerns."

"Yep, thanks so much and I'll be in touch."

Pete knew that this game of cat-and-mouse with Smith was back on and was taking a turn for the worse. But Pete had another reason to talk to Beth.

"Wait a minute, before you go, I need to bounce something off of you."

"Sure."

Pausing, Pete was trying to have the guts to tell Beth of his encounter in Trelleborg.

"I had an incident a while back that I need to share with someone."

"Okay, let me grab a glass of Rose and I'm all ears."

Pausing for his friend to get her drink, Pete then went into great detail for nearly an hour about what he saw or thought he saw.

Stunned, Beth said, "So, you don't know if this incredible story is real or imagined?"

"I'm 100% sure it's real, but no one will ever believe me."

After a long silence, Beth spoke. "I know a guy who knows a guy that does brain mapping in some bizarre think tank out West."

"Whatcha mean?"

Beth continued, "They have some way to pull someone's memory out and display it... read it, I guess."

"That's just nuts, Beth."

"No. It's some very new tech. The guy is Jeremiah something... Can't remember his last name. Let me dig and get back to you."

"Okay. Sure. You think I'm nuts?"

Beth replied, "I think you saw what you think you saw, given our work, and you just need an unbiased opinion."

"Thanks, Beth. Keep this between you and me for now."

"Will do. One more thing. I know you were in alcohol rehab for a couple of months recently. How are you doing?"

Pausing for a short time. "I'm okay. Thanks for asking."

"Please take care of yourself, Pete."

With that, they hung up.

Beth was feeling very distant from Pete and did not like that.

89

PETE

Within thirty minutes of receiving the photos from Beth, Pete contacted Lt. Baker again.

"Hi Bob, just me."

"Pete, it's never just you. And thanks again for all that amazing Intel you guys brought us. So helpful. What can I do for you?"

"Well I have a guy on my team, one with decent contacts and, apparently some interest in this alien stuff, but I just don't trust him."

"Pete, your instincts are usually spot-on."

"Thanks. I have a couple photos of him taken with some shady dudes that are alarming."

"So, you'd like me to take a look for you?"

"Yes, I would."

"No problem, Pete. Just send me the photos and I'll so some facial recognition and dig into his past. Won't take too long. It's kind of exciting for me, you know…"

"Thanks," Pete replied, and they hung up.

Two days later, Pete got a follow up call from Lt. Baker.

"Hey Pete, it's Bob. Got some info for you."

"That was fast."

"But I'm afraid I have some bad news. Your guy, Mr. Smith, is actually Ralph Sandusky, ex-CIA and someone who apparently avoided jail time via a plea deal with the Feds. He was one of those guys that was very well connected internationally, and was on the fast track at Headquarters, only to have everything blow up in his face."

"Dammit!"

"And, in one of the photos you sent me, he is with a notorious European gun runner that, allegedly, has a huge stash of arms. We don't know his real name, but he goes by the first name of Bud.

"There are further implications that go much deeper that I am not at liberty to tell you, but I can tell you this; they suggest that he is part of a seriously well-funded terrorist group that is amassing wealth and military resources as we speak. This has not been confirmed, but we have it on good authority."

Pete is already thinking back to all of his contact and the team's contact with Smith. This could be a disaster.

"So, I would not let this guy anywhere near your team. He is a bad guy with likely bad intentions. In fact, we are now looking into this guy a little further, since both photos have him with some disturbing characters."

After a brief moment of silence, Pete responds, "Bob, I can't thank you enough."

Lt. Baker continues, "I'm just doing my job, but I'm not done."

"More?"

"Pete, by inference, you and your entire team could be under investigation by the FBI or CIA. I mean, this could be very serious and you need to reel it in."

"Oh my God."

"Pete, you and your team could be linked to drug cartels and gun runners. Guilty by obvious association. Maybe not you directly, but your guy known as Smith, but in reality, Ralph Sandusky."

"What can we do?"

"Nothing right now but keep a low profile and stay off the radar. And you know that Paris meeting you mentioned? Don't even think about the non-alien stuff. You need to be primo-geeks."

"Of course. Thanks, and keep me in the loop on where we stand, okay?"

"Sure. But listen, when you and those alien friends of yours take over this world, let them know that I'm one of the good guys."

"I'll text them right now:" both guys got a much-needed laugh.

Pete was devastated. He knew he had to cut ties with Smith ASAP. He just wasn't sure how to do that without repercussions. Lt. Baker said to Pete that Pete's instincts were usually spot on.

Well, not this time.

90

SARA

The ETRT members had been working on their deep dive assignments and were getting closer each day to assembling a sound basis for many of the allegations or alien theories.

Kat was working on the UFO material and those who called themselves *ufologists*. Being the one that tends to get bored, they also had Kat looking into alien Gods, monument builders, and teachers, as were referenced in Pete's log.

Connor was the techy of the group, and he had the job to research the World Grid, as it was called. He also was studying keys to alien mathematics, energy, communication, navigation, and power generation.

Jacqui was the detail lady and really found a sweet spot with the so-called Nazca Lines in Peru and their link to possible alien air and space travel. She was focused on where in our world other similar feats had been seen.

Sumaar, a newer team member from India, had a real fascination with Mars, Martian colonization lore, and the remarkable fifteen-year run of NASA's Opportunity rover.

Michaela had built a small team under her, as was expected, and took on many tasks, including the Egyptian Pyramid connection, the Stargate theories, the Bolivian site Puma Punku, and the always interesting lost Mayan civilization.

Justin was the code guy, and it seemed like figuring out both Pete's code and the ancient alien code was going to be either the key to understanding the alien phenomenon or the doomsday event that ends the journey.

Justin also had a fascination with the megaliths, stone monuments, and the enormous sculptures that had puzzled archeologists for centuries.

Sara was trying to understand the family connection along with figuring out just how big of a role her grandad played in all this. The Trelleborg getaway, in her mind, was the game changer that her grandad alluded to. It was here when Mike called Sara to give her an update on Pete's visit with relatives in Sweden.

"Hi Sara, it's Dad. How goes it there? Making any headway?"

"Well we are making progress, but at that proverbial snail's pace."

"So, what did you find out from Annie and John?"

"Well, the strange is getting stranger. Granddad never went to visit them, and never even told them that he was planning a visit."

"Actually, Dad, that is not surprising news. It explains a lot to me. I now have an open window in Grandad's ventures that could be huge in our investigation. He was apparently there in some sort of a mysterious alien search."

Sara's remark was startling to Mike. "That sounds interesting. But why the secret?"

"I think he was following a lead that he didn't want to share, for some reason."

Mike asked, "And right now you don't know why?"

"Just scratching the surface," Sara responded.

"Probably don't need to know the details right now. Keep me posted."

"Will do, Dad. Thanks for this info and tell Mom 'hi'."

Sara then called the ETRT together for their weekly update meeting. Mike had set up a process for weekly productivity meetings that had firm agendas and time restrictions, to avoid wasting people's time.

Each team leader would report on their accomplishments, weekly to-do lists, interesting new issues, and any obstacles that they faced. It was very efficient and built high levels of discipline into the project team.

With Sara as the facilitator, they went around the room to give their ten to fifteen-minute updates, and then Sara would use some wrap-up time to bring everyone up to speed on the Trelleborg implications, including what she heard from Mike.

Michaela began with a dizzying account of where her team was and what were their next steps.

"The Egyptian Pyramid connection is the biggest opportunity that we have to get anyone's attention, and that's our primary issue. We have no obstacles, for now, but maybe down the road some additional teammate help would be needed."

Kat went next. "I think we have exploded the UFO naysayers' argument with some significant and tangible evidence that would make our portion of the final presentation very believable. We have *no obstacles* for now."

Jacqui had used these weekly meetings to really come out of her shell with her assignments and progress to date.

"Our main issue for the presentation will involve alien astronauts and alien travel, with the elongated skulls from Pete's research as our dog-and-pony show. No obstacles right now."

Sumaar was very excited and couldn't wait to speak.

"Our research sweet spot has become the incredible lifespan of the NASA rover Opportunity. With an original Mars life expectancy of three months, it provided incredible landscape and geographical data for over fifteen years. Our team is getting close to some spectacular assumptions involving evidence in the Mars landscape that resembles Earth. *No obstacles.*"

Connor was being intellectually challenged and he loved it. "We are tying current engineering, mathematics, construction, and power generation models to ancient alien development evidence. *No obstacles* for now."

Three other team members gave their updates, mostly on the physical evidence that Pete had secured. The carved wooden bird from thousands of years ago that was put thru flight testing was the most interesting. Pictures of the blown-up model in a wind tunnel actually becoming air born as today's airplanes would was exciting.

Then Justin gave his update, having asked to go last. The ETRT members looked on with some trepidations, as they sensed the seriousness in his demeanor on that particular morning.

"Okay, guys, I have good news and bad news." This got everyone's attention.

"My role here is to decipher code and make sense of the insensible. Is that a word? The bad news is that I was making progress but now find myself really frustrated. I have found the link to Pete's nicknames and the actual cast of characters on his team, but that is trivial to the real coding mystery."

"Do you have a point here?" Connor was getting frustrated.

"Yep. It appears that the master alien code that Pete created and protected so closely was literally cut into two large pieces. That is, one large coding sheet was cut in half. Without the other half, which never turned up in the cabin material, I'm stuck and can't finish this awesome alien code puzzle."

Kat asked, "So what is the good news?"

"Oh, I lied about the good news."

Sara added, "Seriously, Justin, this is great. At least we now have some I.D. info from the nicknames to begin cross-referencing. Justin, keep working on that."

"Will do. Just need to find that missing half sheet."

Sara added, "Understand. Meanwhile, you can upload my latest Trelleborg file with all the current updates. Sorry our meeting ran over a bit. Thanks for your updates, and we'll get together same time next Friday."

Sara knew that she needed that half of a coding sheet, big time!

91

SARA

With the week's major updated news, Sara spent the next couple of days trying to figure out what and where that one half of an important document went. And, why on Earth was it cut into halves?

Two things just jumped out at her. One, this was a very revealing coded document that likely contained the missing information that they desperately needed. And two, if not found in the cabin, where the hell was it?

So, on Sunday, Sara called her dad for both a project update and to mention the coding issue that has now become their bottleneck. She was tired and frustrated but calls Mike to catch a break from the work at hand.

"Hi Dad, it's me again."

"Hi Sara, what's up?"

Sara goes on to give her dad an update on Friday's team meeting.

Mike continues, "Ya know, after our last talk I have been really puzzled by Dad's trip to Sweden and the bizarre, almost clandestine, accounts of the trip. We never got a call from him, and Mom and I were really confused by the souvenir that he sent us shortly thereafter."

"What do you mean by that?"

"Hold on while I get your mother."

So, Christine picked up the phone and Sara brought her up to speed on the earlier discussion regarding Pete and his Sweden souvenir.

"Yeah, he sent us a picture, like a selfie, of him in the evening at a favorite restaurant in Gothenburg that we'd go to when visiting Annie and John. But, as I believe Dad told you, he apparently didn't even go to Gothenburg during that trip. Odd."

Mike then chipped in. "And, Sara, what was even stranger was the picture was shipped already framed, which just didn't make any sense."

"Oh my God, I think I may know why. Would you guys take that picture and frame apart and tell me what, if anything, you find?"

While Mike was searching, Christine just wanted some reassurance that Sara was okay and that the serious adjustments that Sara had to make were as good as could be expected.

"You know, Mom what you used to say about our vacations?"

"What's that?"

"You and Dad would always say that it isn't where you go, but it's who you go with. Well, that describes how I am with this ETRT bunch of wonderful people. I never leave that group without a smile on my face."

A relieved Christine said, "That is so encouraging to hear."

Mike entered the room agitated, but excited.

"Sara, I may have the other piece of your coding puzzle."

"Oh my God," Sara says excitedly.

"It looks like a torn half-sheet of drawing paper and this one side may be the missing side that Justin needs."

"Dad, that would be too amazing to believe."

"And, on the other, written in pencil and not even similar to the coded part, are notes that look like Grandad spent a couple days with actual aliens or pretend aliens, by their description. They even have names: Echo, Pulse, and some smeared gibberish."

Sara immediately recalled the hand-written notes from her grandad that Michaela discovered, and even the names of the aliens were the same. Cross-referencing or a back-up?

Sara responded, "This could be the Trelleborg missing info link that we so desperately need to reinforce our evidence. We found some similar notes recently from Grandad that point to the same events. Any details?"

"Yeah, there are descriptions of space flight, touring the artifact communities of the world, and traveling the World Grid. Pete has an arrow pointed to the word, REVEAL. The REVEAL is the title of the presentation that he was going to give at the Paris Air Show, and the descriptions are close to what we already have. This is great!"

Christine adds, "If your grandad wasn't delusional, this is startling and the game changer he alluded to."

Mike and Sara discussed how to get this valuable document to Utah, as the three of them tried to grasp the enormity of what just happened. Sara ended the call knowing that Monday morning would be the best day ever for this group of believers.

Then, about two hours later, Mike called Sara back.

"Hi, it's me again. Got some more stuff."

Sara was again excited, as was the tone of her dad's voice.

Mike went on, "You know how Mom is always cleaning up and straightening up and generally trying to keep things tidy and organized?"

"Of course."

"Well, she was really curious about the picture and frame, and began looking at the frame. She found a flash drive carved nicely into one corner of the frame. Seriously!"

"Did you look at it, Dad?"

"You bet! It has several really interesting photos, mostly of you and his alien adventure, some artifacts and photos."

Christine added, "But eight photos are just people sitting around in meetings or at events that seem to have no correlation at all to the alien research."

"Yeah, Sara, what your Mom came up with was pretty cool. Of the eight photos, Grandad is in only two, but all of them have one guy, dressed in black, and seemingly a big part of the photo op. This guy has got to be an important character."

"Weird."

"Hopefully all this will make sense to you and the team. I will make backups for everything we have found and get the originals out to you tomorrow."

"Great work, Dad. Tell Mom thanks for her efforts, too, and hugs to you both."

Soon after getting that information from Mike, she called him with her thanks. She then added some updates for her dad.

"During the team's work on the alien project, some startling facts were discovered by our investigative research; and it revealed that certain worldwide calamities suffered over time were totally within the range of normal and/or expected."

Mike added, "Why do I sense an 'oh but' coming?"

Sara responded, "Big oh but... Some of the latest incidents may have been manipulated or somehow influenced, as they defied logic and normal history. As bizarre as this appeared, extensive data gathering and algorithm development, then loaded into regressive-type computer simulations, came up with absolutely astounding conclusions."

"Like what?" Mike asked.

"Tell you what, Dad, I am preparing an extensive presentation to cover these events and why don't you and Mom come out and sit in. We are presenting a week from tomorrow."

Mike enthusiastically responded, "Can do and will do. Thanks."

Sara's end game was getting very clear in her mind.

"We are not alone."

92

SARA

Sara and the ETRT prepared an extensive and thorough Power Point presentation, titled *"Weather or Not We Are Alone."*

Invited to this session were VP Worthington, Scott, Amanda, Matthew, Mike, Christine, and two key government meteorologists. Sara made the presentation without any mention of the flash drive that she was concealing for the moment.

"Good afternoon and welcome. What we are about to describe is very hard to comprehend. It is, however, scientifically verified, given our current level of skills and technology. You can draw your own conclusions from this info… we have."

The meeting room was all hers.

"The Hurricane Katrina disaster of 2005 could have been worse, as was Hurricane Sandy. They occurred at low tide and during daylight hours.

"The earthquakes in Chile and Asia, around that same time frame, as bad as they were, could have been worse if they had struck highly populated areas." Slides were presented.

"But then these occurrences became outliers. Following the detonation of those nuclear devices in 2021, hundreds of offshore oil rigs were destroyed, with ramifications similar to Deepwater Horizon.

"Literally within days of those detonations, new preventative capping technology was finally installed in all offshore oil rigs. The simple fact that this capping technology became available just prior to those attacks, could have been coincidental, but the probabilities suggest they were not."

The audience was stirring.

"In 2025, almost to the day of the 20th anniversary of Hurricane Katrina, the most devastating of all hurricanes, Hurricane Fred, a Category 5 storm with winds of nearly 300 mph and storm surges of 30 to 45 feet, hit the East Coast.

Again, with remarkable similarity to Katrina, Fred came onshore at a very low tide and with winds not directly from the East, but changing to the Southeast and driving the storm very quickly through the area."

Moving the slide from showing to data, she continued.

"So, the most devastating storm in U.S. history could have been significantly worse, except for the favorable timing and extremely unusual, if not unprecedented wind changes. The slow and erratic path of this storm, which then moved quickly out of harm's way and with a somewhat beneficial result, could not be explained climatologically.

"In other words, in the 150 or so years of tracking these storms, that path and speed had never happened. Simulations gave it a one in 50 million chance."

Sara paused as the audience was now totally focused.

"Asia was not spared, either, as an enormous typhoon hit China and Japan in 2022, and it did enormous damage to the coastal areas, already badly affected by the rising seas of global warming and the polar disasters.

"Oddly though, that storm slowed in speed unnaturally, allowing large-scale evacuations that saved tens of thousands of lives. Apparently, with the multitude of calamity and disasters occurring in the world at that time, no one analyzed this slowing phenomenon.

"But the data stood out noticeably; never in weather history had such an unnatural event occurred. Simulations again gave this catastrophe a one in 30 million chance."

Continuing after a quick drink of water, "California forest fires were becoming increasingly common and extensively destructive for many years, mostly driven by seasonal drought and man-made development replacing green areas with concrete.

"In 2022, however, the largest and most destructive wild fire to ever hit the west coast had been raging for several months, as we all remember.

"Hundreds of first-responders and fire fighters were killed, and losses in the billions of dollars were having a huge economic impact on California. Since it was the middle of the dry season there, it looked like a disaster of epic proportions were coming.

"Then, with absolutely no precedent whatsoever, a fierce storm came out of the Pacific Ocean and in a matter of two days, those thousands of square miles of raging fires were gone. The jet stream had taken on a linear pattern that is unexplainable and stalled, forcing the rain to fall heavily on the firestorm.

"Never in weather history had a monsoon-type rain event occurred. Never."

Sara adjusted her projector for the next dramatic issue.

"A massive earthquake hit the west coast in 2023 in an area that wasn't expected to be prone for hundreds, if not thousands, of years. It did not lay on any of the major fault lines and was never thought to be a concern. In fact, it followed a mountain range for hundreds of miles.

"There were two incredible outcomes of this 7.8 earthquake.

"First, no lives were lost as it took a path that did not impact any residential areas,

"Second, it created a river that was not there before, and with a valley connecting it to the ocean, this river was filled by the rising seas from global warming. It actually reduced improved subsidence greatly.

"Yes, this was an earthquake of epic proportions, that literally changed the landscape, but with significant benefits.

"In each and every one of these calamities, neither nature nor man could have stepped in to provide these solutions and save the day. No scientific data could begin to explain these anomalies. So, who or what did?"

Sara took a round of questions and then suggested a thirty-minute break.

VP Worthington asked, "Sara, this is remarkable info. You said neither nature nor man could have stepped in. I have to ask, are you implying the alien theory here?"

Sara replied emphatically, "Again, until a better or more reasonable explanation surfaces, I am leaning in that direction, as this is what we as a team have been focused on for quite a while."

After a brief pause, Sara added.

"We aren't done presenting yet."

93

MICHAELA

Following a thirty-minute break, Sara opened the second part of their presentation. She could easily see that her small audience was quiet, reserved, and extremely interested…

"At this time, I'd like to introduce Michaela Marx, our treasure and one hell-of-an astrophysicist. I believe everyone knows Michaela."

"Thanks, Sara, and I have two topics to cover."

Sara smiled warmly at her friend.

"Late in 2024, one of Sara's grandfather's Bucket List wishes became true. The METI project launched the proactive radio signal message to a prominent star in 2002. I believe most of you were aware of this, but only recently.

METI scientists, among them Pete Stevenson, created the radio signal in a totally random musical scale and determined that it would take 22 years to return to Earth. In October of 2024, that totally random musical scale disrupted the science community in a very significant way."

Michaela had everyone's attention.

"Earth received the response that naysayers said would never come, but most scientists believed would definitely come at some time. After exhausting analysis by several factions, both pro-alien and anti-alien, the results were unanimous and totally accepted.

The notes were rearranged as the spiritually haunting and soul wrenching ballad of the 1700's, *Amazing Grace*.

What sailor was not reminded of the chills of hearing that song as they left on an unknown voyage? Although subject to interpretation, most did agree that the choice of response was not good. That there was even a response was almost secondary to the actual response."

A couple hands went up, but Michaela continued.

"Authorities tried to keep that result hidden, but in the age of social media and the Public Information Act, it didn't stay hidden for long. What the public announcement said was there had been a response. It was only through Pete's old contacts and diary-like documentation that we found out what that response was."

Mike vividly recalled his dad's insistence that this would happen in 2024. Pete was right, and a stunned Mike now had to re-think much of his alien position and acceptance.

Sara added, "So many of these events, each one of a somewhat small scale, but strung together gives credence to the alien theory that is very hard to refute."

Michaela continued. "My next topic has to do with statistical anomalies or anomaly detection. It is the science of identifying event outliers and assigning a probability to that event.

"When Sara described Hurricane Fred a year ago as having a one in 50 million chance of occurring, another way of looking at it is that it would happen only once in 50,000 years. Three years before that, the Asian typhoon would occur roughly once in 30,000 years. These are outliers taken to exponential proportions."

Hands again went up, but Michaela continued.

"The topic I was referring to is global warming. Kat is distributing three-ring binders to you as I speak. There are 440 pages of documented and well-verified conclusions drawn from the most highly respected authorities, worldwide, on the subject of our environment. We have summarized the content in the eight-page executive overview."

The audience opens the binder to that overview.

"The facts point to a number of extremely serious consequences from mankind's lack of environmental attention and poor leadership over the last seventy-five years. As you navigate through the bullet points, I will allow time for note-taking.

As you study temperature rise, the terrorist destruction at both Poles, the diminished farming areas, the rapidly declining bee population needed to fertilize, sea level rise, and poisoned food supplies, Earth as we now know it could be close to uninhabitable in 100 years."

The room became silent. No hands went up.

"In fact, the predictions based on the last decade of the events I just mentioned, show a sea level rise of nearly 180 feet by 2100."

Michaels adds a sobering thought.

"For your information, the highest elevation in Florida is 318 feet."

94

SARA

This additional big data coupled with the Sweden trip of Sara's grandad and the secret code that had been finally exposed by her parents, Sara's team was now able to push forward on their findings and theories, to the point where highly objective conclusions could be drawn.

Sara met with the ETRT the next morning with the final update. The alien-oriented information from Mike and Christine was a natural fit to the team's work, but the flash drive was not at all compatible with their research.

The flash drive had a very dark tone and did not relate to anything that any ETRT team member was working on. Plus, it also mentioned one of Pete's team members, Beth Downing, as a solid contact who helped to put the flash drive information together.

Sara got Beth's contact information from Mike and left Beth a message to call her. Meanwhile, Sara met with Scott and Amanda for feedback from the presentation and brought them up to speed regarding that flash drive.

Scott did not appear too surprised, which seemed odd to Sara.

"Actually, Sara, when I met with the President earlier, he gave me some military Intel that he was concerned about, and its possible intersection with our ETRT work.

"I didn't do much with it then, because it seemed way off the radar. But I will now put a task force together to see what correlation, if any, this new info provides."

A visibly agitated Sara said, "What the hell, Scott! You gotta tell me what you have right now."

Sensing her understandable impatience, Scott said, "I'm sorry, Sara. Please, let me get a little more info first. I don't want to speculate. Need all the facts."

"Okay, Scott, let me know if you need anything else. This is pretty damn important."

Sara was somewhat satisfied and returned to her team. Later that day, she got her return call from Beth Downing.

"Hi Sara, it's Beth Downing, and it's so nice to finally talk with Pete's lovely granddaughter."

"Hi Beth, and thanks for getting back to me."

"So, what can I do for you? As a totally retired alien hunter, I'm anxious to help in any way I can."

"Well, I have a flash drive from Grandad's file that is weird, and I was hoping that you could help me understand what it means."

"Sure, Sara, go ahead."

"Your name appears on this flash drive as the one who provided several photos that don't seem to add anything to his alien info search. They're just old photos with old guys in meetings."

Beth took a moment and then said, "Sara, those photos were found during our alien search and, apparently, were linked to the terrible global attacks that were being incurred and that group of old rich guys were the consortium, the real bad guys.

One of Pete's trusted team members who called himself John Smith was being implicated in that terrorist group. That's why your grandad had the photos and we believe that he was making an attempt to get them into the proper law enforcement agency when he was killed."

Sara was feeling that terrible grief again.

"Oh my God, Beth. I didn't think it could get any worse than it already was for him, and it just did."

"Sorry for that news, Sara. Please let me know if there is anything more you need that I can help you with. I loved your grandad... we all did."

She thanked Beth and then hung up.

About ten minutes later, Sara's phone rang and it was Beth.

"Sorry to bother you again, but I just remembered something that Pete told me that is a little weird and may or may not be important."

"What's that?"

"Well, your grandad was a pioneer and visionary unlike anyone I had ever known. And, he thought that some sort of brain mapping or scanning was being done here in the U.S. by a cutting-edge company and could "store" his memory or something like that.

"He went to either Colorado or California, I can't remember which state to check it out. I can't even remember the name of the location. And, I think I was the one who recommended the place to him. Sorry. My memory isn't what it used to be."

"Oh, not a problem. But that sounds like something my grandad would do, for sure."

"Yep, and when he returned, I asked him how it went; and he said that he had made a brain deposit in some lab and then he said he would eventually become telepathic. In my usual dry humor style, I said that he sounded tele-pathetic. I sure do miss him. Sara, he was the best."

"Thanks, Beth. I need some time to reflect on another damn puzzle piece."

"Let me do some digging and see if I can find out where he was and what his agenda was. One thing he did mention to me was that he was trying to separate his dreams and premonitions from reality, if that makes any sense."

"It does. It definitely does."

Beth added, "I'm sorry my memory is giving me fits. I can almost remember everything I did with Pete, but I can't remember where I sent the poor guy!"

Sara knew immediately what her grandad had in mind with that memory-mapping.

Pete wanted third-party proof that he was in the presence of aliens.

95

SARA

About two weeks later, Sara received a call from Scott to set up an important meeting to discuss the flash drive that she had obtained and the cross-referencing to the one that the POTUS gave to Scott.

Sara began the discussion. "Well, Scott, I hope this meeting answers more questions than it raises."

Scott responded, "Isn't that what we come to expect anymore? Let's hope it gives us some closure."

"I'm ready, Scott. What do you have?"

"Apparently, your grandad was juggling a multitude of issues and priorities. In addition to the vast amount of alien research data, he was in possession of terrorist conspiracy info that pointed to the early stages of an eight or nine-member consortium of very wealthy and very bad people."

Sara was thinking, "Been there... thought that."

"In fact, many of his photos, taken in several locations around the world, matched the government's National Security Agency's photos in terms of personnel and likely terrorist agendas. Pete's stuff, and this is big, was of the very early development of that heinous crime cell, one that is now the likely perpetrators of the most severe criminal activity in our world."

"This is starting to make sense, and crappy sense," sighed Sara.

"I'm afraid, Sara, it gets worse."

"My God, worse?"

Scott gathered his thoughts and words and said, "Sara, this is very likely the info that your grandad had in his possession that got him killed. How he got it and why he had it and what he planned to do with it, we will probably never know."

Now Sara had an idea just how this terrible process played out. She thanked Scott for his open and honest update and then met with the ETRT to plan next steps.

After giving her team Scott's updated info, she announced, "Okay, we need two things and need them now to understand Pete's journey and to put some perspective on this terrorist piece."

Kat simply said, "Go, Sara."

"I want a timeline that goes back as far as the Pete Stevenson data takes us with milestones, critical events, and the out-of-place stuff. Then, I want to overlay his primary research focus of the high-evidence docs, artifacts, and discoveries on that timeline."

Michaela spoke up. "The Pete timeline will have references back to earlier data and other reports and evidence, right?"

"Yes, and I want you to look at the non-alien anomalies, specifically the alleged terrorist activity and exposure."

Kat added, "That will be easy."

Sara continued, "As a visual management tool, color code the alien mapping one way or color and the non-alien or terrorist implication a second way or color."

"Yes, that second part should jump right out," Michaela added.

Getting excited, Sara continued, "Then I need you guys to complete the simulations on event probability and/or theory probability that we presented to the execs a couple weeks ago."

Justin was excited. "I'll oversee the completion of that task. We are very close to final computer simulations and execution of the probability curves."

"Fine. There is one more thing that I need to do," Sara said with a soft and serious voice.

Not expecting any additional tasks, the team waited for a few moments...

"Given that I was the sole survivor of that cabin explosion eight years ago, and the origin of that explosion was always assumed to be a gas leak, I am now wondering if it was possible that a terrorist group or remnants of one weren't responsible."

Michaela added, "It is a possibility, Sara."

Waiting for a moment before responding, Sara continued, "This is what we must do. First, let's get that timeline done as quickly as possible. Second, I am going to go back to that awful day and do some investigative work into that alleged gas leak."

The team waited as Sara was thinking...

"I am now convinced that we must proceed with extreme caution and self-awareness. Any digging beyond what we already have may become a danger.

Until I, or we, can conclude that terrorists were not involved in the cabin incident, be very, very careful."

Sara knew that the cabin attack was either one of two scenarios.

Either it was terrorists that destroyed the cabin... or it was an alien attack.

96

JUSTIN

Justin approached Sara about three days later with his progress regarding the simulations.

"Well, I have good news and bad news."

"Again?"

"No, this time I do. Is this a good time to talk?"

"Yes, of course. Let's go into my office and I'll get us a couple cold drinks."

Sara grabbed two Cokes and some ice while Justin set up his computer. He pulled out a flash drive and loaded it. He was ready.

"I've got two things I want to talk about, the simulations and those photos you gave me to analyze."

"Yeah, those photos are so mixed up... so crazy."

Excitedly, Justin said, "The team constructed a timeline of critical events that went back to BCE time, which was interesting, and then we did a more detailed timeline that focused on Pete Stevenson's work. That's what you see here."

Sara looked at the timeline and was impressed with the detail.

"But I took this task a little further and you can see this here with the red and blue lines in an overlay."

"One looks like a simple reproduction of the other. More explanation coming, right?"

"The red line shows the basic start and finish of the Industrial Revolution, from 1760 to 1840. The blue line shows similar technology, according to artifacts and alien theory, was in place hundreds, if not thousands, of years earlier."

"Okay, interesting but hard to prove."

"I guess. Now the simulations. As you know, we used an event probability simulation that allowed for hundreds of thousands of computer-driven likelihoods from zero per cent to ninety-five per cent likely, to be calculated. There was a five per cent error probability."

Sara jumped in, "Understand. So, these weather and incident phenomenon that we discussed last week can be explained?"

Justin answered, "Yes and no."

"Really, Justin, yes and no!"

"Hold on, more like yes and maybe."

"Dammit, Justin, no more riddles.

"Okay. Okay. The results were unprecedented, but the root cause is still one of two things. Weather is now an inconsistent truth."

"Justin, do you mean an inconvenient truth?"

"No. Where did you get that from?"

Getting frustrated, Sara said, "Please go on."

"Weather is now becoming an unpredictable variable, and in the wake of massive nuclear explosions on the ice caps and climate change, you can't rule this explanation out."

Finally satisfied that Justin is back on track, Sara simply asked, "I have the utmost respect for you and your brain power. What does your gut tell you?"

"Okay. Thanks. I strongly believe that an unnatural and extremely advanced effort has been in place on Earth. It is my opinion that even though we have seen evidence only recently, this outside force, I'll go ahead and call it alien, has been here for a very long time. There is just no way to not include this explanation."

Sara asked, "Did you run this by Michaela?"

"Of course, Sara."

"And...?"

"Her very words were, 'not unexpected.' It didn't even surprise her!"

"Well, we will have our panel of so-called experts that will try. And, they will use your first explanation to ridicule us."

Sara then added, "So, now the photos. Is this the bad news?"

"Yeah, sort of. Bottom line is you gave me a bunch of photos that, allegedly, were taken by Mr. Stevenson and depicted actual aliens."

"Well, yes," Sara concluded.

Justin went on. "They're really cool pics. But I can't verify that they are real. They look pretty damn real, but I can't stake my reputation on them being actual alien photos."

"Justin, we don't expect you to be all-omniscient all the time. You can get some help for this, right?"

"Sure. I have some calls in to people that can help. They are bonded-type people."

"You are hesitating, Justin. And?"

"And, Sara, do I just ask these strangers if the alien pictures are real?"

"Sorry. You're right. What was I thinking? I'll take them from here."

Justin knew the pictures were real. He wanted validation.

97

SARA

After nearly six weeks of final data analysis and conclusions, the ETRT was ready to present their case to Scott and Amanda. This would be a great sounding board and best way to get a legitimate second opinion.

Sara got a call from Scott and a suggestion. "Hi Sara. Understand you and your team want to do a little report-out, eh?"

"Hi Scott. That's right. We need to see where we are right now from a more unbiased opinion. We think we're there, but it's likely we are not."

"Well, Amanda and I are anxious to see where you guys are, and let's do this in style."

Sara asked, "Meaning?"

"We have a wonderful yacht, the *Stargaze*, and it would be a great place to have our meeting. I don't believe you have ever seen it."

"No, Scott. Never have," Sara said excitedly.

"Great. We have it at the newly re-built San Francisco Bay Marina. The sea level rise makes this a constant challenge for us to find a decent marina. Certainly not one of life's big problems, but it has always been a big part of our lifestyle."

Sara responded, "I get it."

"Okay. Done. I'll have Ken fly your guys here on Thursday. We'll have a day on the water Friday and the meeting will be Saturday, using as much time as you need. Sunday will be to relax or strategize… your call. That night, we'll have you back in Utah."

"Scott, that sounds incredible and I just can't thank you enough. We will see you in a couple of days. Tell Amanda, 'hi,' as she has been working off-site for us for weeks, as you know."

✦ ✦ ✦

Arriving at the *Stargaze* following a wonderful flight from Utah, Sara gave Scott and Amanda her executive overview. On Friday, as planned, Scott and the

Stargaze lived up to the billing and everyone had a good time motoring up and down the California coast.

Saturday morning came and the team decided that each key member would present their reports, and Sara would kick it off and wrap it up.

"For lack of a better title, this is OUR REVEAL. It's a tribute to my grandad, Pete Stevenson."

The ETRT gave out a light cheer and Sara continued.

"We will present in short, high-level topical points, with the understanding that all supporting documentation and detail is here as well.

"The most significant and certainly the most arguable documentation deals with an actual alien encounter between Pete and an alien group, according to notes and photos thereof, that took place in Trelleborg, Sweden, in February, 2018."

Pausing for a moment, Sara continued. "The photos are of particular interest, as you will see, and so far, we have not been able to prove that they are not authentic. I'm already getting ahead of myself, but I am extremely anxious for you to see what we have found."

Justin smiled and thought that Sara just put a Sara-spin on his findings. She had validated his work, as best as she could, and he was feeling good.

Scott responded, "Amanda and I couldn't be more interested and excited. Let' go."

Sumaar started by focusing on the Mars aspect as being the number-one discovery of his research.

"The Mars Opportunity rover was a key in my study. That rover was meant to have a three-month site lifespan, and it had fifteen years of data gathering.

"What I was able to extract was that, in addition to other Martian features, Opportunity mapped out a twenty-square-mile area that was the exact mirror image of the great Egyptian pyramids and the incredible Sphynx.

"The pyramid site in Egypt was an exact replica of what was likely the original site on Mars, only somewhat hidden by sandstorms on Mars over time.

"And, the power that drove the rover all those years was made from planet rotational energy from the same basic technical argument of inventor and engineer Nikola Tesla back in the early 1900's."

Amanda started to ask a question, but then put her hand down. Sumaar continued.

"To make this info even more unbelievable, Pete Stevenson had pictures that were taken from space, and no one knew how he got them. They showed the Mars pyramid site in vivid detail with no sand to cover the diagrams whatsoever."

Scott jumped in, "Excuse me Sumaar, but photographs can be fabricated, and although Sara told me last night that no one could disprove their authenticity, it is still a stretch. And, just because Pete had them doesn't mean he took them."

Sumaar was getting nervous as Scott continued. "And, how do you know it was Mars? Were road signs there?"

Even Sara had to laugh, before commenting.

"Yes, the photos can't be discredited, so we'll go with them for now. Pete said he took them and if someone gave them to him, he would have no reason to lie about it. It did follow his convictions."

Amanda added, "Okay, for now. But how do we know the pics were of Mars and not the Moon or Arizona?"

Michaela added her explanation, "We did some incredibly detailed timeline mapping and using the approximate time of the photos, the constellations were aligned in the photographs exactly to the Mars photo origins."

As everyone seemed to accept Michaela's perspective, they all looked at the rendering that Sumaar provided, and he continued.

"There is one more simple, yet awesome, note from Pete's alleged meeting with the aliens in Sweden. He has a very succinct comment that an early alien civilization had lived and thrived on Mars and more evidence would be found."

Even Sara could read between the lines...

Pete's comment was not in the form of a question, but a statement.

98

SARA

Continuing the presentation, Kat was next and had several tasks but the UFO part was her most enjoyable work.

"I collected a series of photos, documents, and interviews with people around the world that saw, photographed, and documented UFO sightings. I also found that flight patterns of these UFO's followed the same basic aerial routes around the world.

"This could not be coincidence. I also have several pieces of documentation from two foreign astronauts that had pictures, sketches, and incidents that collaborate this info. Apparently, Pete met with these two astronauts, and they felt comfortable with this info to put it into his hands."

As Kat looked over to her slides of this information, she continued.

"I also found many instances, with Jacqui's help, of stone etching throughout time that alluded to one almighty God, referred to as Anunnaki, replacing many heavenly gods that were considered the many spiritual rulers of the time. And this God was depicted as having human looks and actions.

"Pete's notes even named the god-like visitors that helped ancient civilizations build monuments and teach skills that are a stretch even in today's civilizations. Each so-called teacher was specified by name throughout the last 10,000 years of Earth's many civilizations.

"If you take this theory to full potential, it explains exactly why all of this building, along with basic civilization development, regardless of which continent that it occurred, was identical."

Jacqui took in a big sigh before beginning her portion.

"I have become obsessed with the so-called Nazca Lines in Peru, and my research came up with verifiable evidence that these landing strips were found in many parts of the world, designed and built in identical fashion per Kat's info, and on the same flight lines that UFO's were seen.

"These undeniable lines are in geometric patterns, often many thousands of feet long, and are in perfect alignment. Even intersections of lines, based on the configuration, are all at exactly 45-degree or 90-degree angles.

"I also found verifiable evidence of well-detailed carvings of what appeared to be huge stone sentinels located at every site to help incoming aircraft or spaceships land."

Referring to her slides, Jacqui was feeling confident.

"And, while doing the research on these lines I have gathered several elongated skulls that are not even close to what you would see today in tribal rituals. Again, these elongated skulls were found in nine different locations around the world, all locations traceable from Pete's notes."

She showed a slide depicting the skulls along with the locations of the finds.

At this point, Connor was anxious to start.

"I have used Pete Stevenson's coordinate data, and worked with Michaela's team as well, to establish a likely World Grid that seemed to have a purposeful alien strategy.

"This strategy, when executed, precisely aligned major monuments with true north and from the six pyramids of the Pyramid Giza Complex, considered at one time to be the center of all landmasses of Earth, all documented flight patterns would use.

"This is unmistakable, and literally impossible for a multitude of cultures to coordinate over all of that space and time. After all, they didn't have social media back then."

Some noticeable laughter.

"I was also able to verify, translating several languages with Pete's code, that one common mathematical formula was used throughout time for navigation, geometric calculations, and even the value of Pi. Again, just one!

"What I found was that Einstein's Unified Theory was actually discovered thousands of years earlier.

"We all have heard the phrase, there are many ways to solve a problem, but just pick one and go. Well, maybe there isn't a phrase, but you get the idea.

"Every civilization back to the beginning of time, could not come up with one way of doing anything. This data says that they all had one way of doing everything. Oh, except for the Mayans, but Michaela will get into that."

"Thanks, Connor," Michaela said a bit sarcastically.

Connor continued, "And, I have established that certain monuments were consistently used for navigation and pyramids were used for aircraft refueling, given the intricate nature of the insides of these huge structures.

"Massive cargo had to be moved and hauled, and that was depicted in etchings at or near these navigation sites.

"In fact, the great pyramids in Egypt and elsewhere were using levitation, according to one of my unnamed colleagues, to move the megaliths into their final shapes. Again, wall carvings described this in detail in many locations, per Pete's outstanding compass work."

Scott jumped in again. "Connor, you said massive cargo had to be moved and hauled and they used levitation. Isn't that an oxymoron? They could levitate pyramids but they had to haul their cargo."

"I see your point. Will need to work on this some more. Geez, I wasn't there at the time."

Scott and Amanda both laughed.

Sara added, "Let's take a twenty-minute potty and social media break. Looks like some coffee and croissant are here."

Sara hoped that one more answer to the cabin explosion was coming...

99

SARA

Sara used the mid-morning break to return a call from her dad.

"Hi Dad, nice to hear from you. How are you and Mom?"

"Good. How's your boat meeting going?"

Sara thought for a moment before replying, "Fine."

"Sara, fine usually means not fine."

Laughing, Sara said, "Yeah, Scott has shot a couple holes in our theories, but that's what I expected."

"Anything serious?"

Sara responded, "No, just some more validation that we need to do before we go to Prime Time. You called about our meeting?"

"No, Sara, I got some info from that task you asked me about."

"The gas tank at the cabin?"

Mike took a deep breath, "Yes."

Sara asked, "And?"

"I've done a lot of digging and have spoken to many people familiar with the kind of gas tank that would cause a major explosion."

"I'm all ears, Dad."

Mike continued, "Dad wasn't on a main gas line and only had his medium-sized propane tank, likely 120 gallons, on the side of the cabin. That tank could not have caused the extensive cabin damage."

Sara replied, "So the drone projectile wasn't aimed at the propane tank?"

Mike added, "It was as you suspected, an armed missile intended to destroy the entire cabin and its contents. I assume you are asking because you have a lead on its origin?"

"Yes, and yes. And it has nothing to do with aliens."

"Damn, Sara, be careful. Your mom will continue to believe the gas leak story."

"Of course, Dad. Thanks."

"So, you gonna need me in Utah anytime soon?"

"Not sure, Dad. It depends on what we feel we need to do after Scott and Amanda are done shooting at us."

Laughing, Mike said, "Funny stuff. Later, Sara."

"Yep, love you. Say 'hi' to Mom."

"Will do. Please be careful, eh?"

"I will Dad. Thanks again."

Sara knew what her dad would say regarding the explosion. She just needed to check that box and move on to probable cause and origin.

Process of elimination. Which of the two scenarios is real?

100

SARA

After Sara's talk with Mike and a brief break, the meeting continued. Justin was next and he began with another note from Pete.

Justin then began. "I have taken the coding documents that Pete had prepared, and basically confirmed that a center core of all things done on this planet over thousands of years was basically a blueprint adjusted to fit the cultures, times, and languages of each civilization.

"In other words, I found that the same set of directions, or lesson plans could be found and overlapped precisely.

"Pete had discovered this incredible evidence initially, and I was lucky enough to connect the dots. I simply confirmed the results by starting with Pete's conclusion and working backward, as several of us now do."

Justin added, "In what was the most satisfying coding work that I have ever done was that I was able to help several members of the ETRT to locate the actual coded person, using the original cabin map, who was either Pete's interviewee or keeper of a particular artifact.

"We have also identified each of Pete's four team mates by matching their actual names and roles to their nicknames. You may recall that the cabin map only had one half of the identity puzzle, but the other half that Sara got completed that puzzle."

Michaela was referring to her extensive notes and went next.

"The Stargate theories had always fascinated me, as I knew of Einstein's Theory of Relativity and his belief in cosmic wormholes and a way for humans to travel from star to star like the ancient aliens. Before you say this cannot be verified with today's evidence, let me interrupt you. You're right, it could not, until now."

Sara was smiling.

"Pete's encounter in Sweden resulted in a strong argument that the Orion Belt was the birthplace of all stars in the galaxy. And as remarkable as it is puzzling, Pete had close-up pictures of massive star formation 1500 light years from Earth, showing more than 3,000 stars in some form of star-life.

"As I recall, he was in Sweden for three days in 2018, not nearly enough time to travel 1500 light years and return!"

The audience didn't know which part to be impressed with… her findings or her sense of humor. Michaela continued.

"If you have subject matter experts look at the photographs, they will tell you that they were made by a large stationary craft with Hubble-Telescope-plus capabilities."

Michaela pauses to verify her slides.

"Back to the actual results, we have discovered physical evidence of complex calculations and extraordinary craftwork and stonemasonry cut into huge stone tablets, from Puma Punku in the Bolivian Andes.

"The depictions vary from others in that they are mostly temple oriented. Faces, lineage, recreation, and huge carved stones represent the books in today's public libraries.

"Three things jump out at you here; I know it did to me.

"One, these epic monuments were built at an elevation of 12,800 feet. How in the world did they get there?

"Two, the very odd fact here was that these stone reminders of a distant past were very distant; likely 14,000 years ago.

"And three, there was an effort at some point in time to destroy all that is there right now."

Michaela was now getting as animated and excited as ever.

"And now for the best of the best. The lost Mayan Civilization is, and was, one of history's greatest mysteries. Such an advanced culture accomplishing extraordinary feats, leaving many to wonder why, how, and when.

"According to Pete's encounter, the Mayan's were placed here from the Seven Sisters open star cluster, some 450 light years away, to help advance Earth's civilizations.

"When, for many reasons, that did not occur, the Mayans were relocated to that star system, which had evolved more quickly than our planet at the time of the Mayans.

"Although many of Earth's civilizations have vanished with no plausible explanation, the Mayans were different, special, and extremely advanced."

The meeting room got quiet. Even Scott was speechless.

Sara had a troubling thought…

"If an advanced alien culture determined that the population of an unstable and dysfunctional Earth was beyond help, could that culture simply relocate us elsewhere?"

101

SARA

Sara then jumped in and said, "Okay, it's lunch time. Amanda has our lunch ready on the main deck. We will re-convene in an hour and then get into round two.

"We still have a couple team members to hear from, and then we have some additional results that were compiled from small teams. I will say that everything still to come does nothing more than reinforce what has already been presented."

During the break, the ETRT discussed how they could improve the presentation thus far, and maybe how to bundle round two into the entire presentation. Scott told Sara that he and Amanda were quite impressed, and that Scott would want a one-on-one with Sara when they finished.

So, after the 20-minute break, Sara announced the itinerary for Round Two and Sumaar's team began.

"With our many documented findings in several European cities in general and churches specifically, it is more than ninety per cent likely that alien spaceships visited often. The term Vimana was frequently used to describe huge flying fortresses, and that was well documented.

"What Pete found were ships that were almost identical to early Russian and American space capsules, and the largest was called the Rukma Vimana."

Sumaar showed a series of depictions.

"However, they appeared armed with missiles, indicating war-like ships as Pete surmised. He strongly believed that evil aliens existed, and may be among us today. But he also believed that alien wars had been fought on planet Earth, and other planets as well, for centuries."

Pete's depiction of Rukma Vimana is shown.

"With many references to various etchings throughout the world of humanlike astronauts or spacemen, they always seem to be signaling in their depictions. This consistent and entirely identical form that these etchings take cannot be coincidental.

"Also, you can see many examples of what we would describe as fully functional space suits and breathing apparatus. Even aircraft or spaceship controls, not dissimilar to today's equipment, are well described."

Pete's depiction of an alien spaceman is shown.

As Sumaar finished, Jacqui's team then began.

"This team took on the huge evidence pool of ancient hieroglyphics. Archeologists and geologists for centuries have analyzed hieroglyphics and symbols. What Pete's study concluded was, again, pure consistency and message-to-message commonality. Every one of the many languages came to the same conclusion, and that was they came from above in fiery machines; and they brought knowledge and technology to build, inform, teach, and then left."

Jacqui went on to say, "I love Pete's simple response in one of his notes. I'm trying to make this difficult, but it's hard to do."

"Finally, we have an ancient wooded carved bird, actually in Pete's possession, which was found in one of the oldest of Egypt's 97 pyramids. It was obviously a carved bird, but one of Pete's aerodynamics experts built a scale model of this bird, which actually resembled one of today's airplanes, and it flew. It was a highly developed glider designed in ancient Egypt. As you already know, I actually verified this data myself with current subject matter experts, who agreed that such an aircraft today could not only glide, but also be propelled via engines to fly safely and effectively."

Pete's picture of the bird/glider is shown.

Two ETRT members who had not yet presented, Joyce and Rudy, had the floor to discuss Roswell, area 51, abductions, and some interesting UFO findings.

Joyce began, "Much of what Rudy and I found was from Pete's first-hand accounts. He interviewed a gentleman on his deathbed that gave Pete pictures of the Roswell disc that landed, as well as pictures of the astronaut inside. Pete was also able to get photos from other sources that were identical in size, features, and detail to the two Roswell artifacts."

Rudy chimed in, "And the Area 51 was replaced with Area 52 just to take the heat off of the public's interest in Area 51, where the alien evidence was shown as a downed balloon.

"It's not the old news that is cool, but Pete's pictures that are strong evidence of alien presence and cover-up. However he was able to obtain these photos, you cannot argue their relevance. They simply continue to verify and corroborate every piece of so-called circumstantial evidence that was out there."

Joyce continued, "The one piece that is most interesting and most germane today comes from Mexico and a funeral monument of a Mayan leader. His chamber, photographed in great detail by one of Pete's colleagues, shows a person looking very much like our present astronauts, in a spacecraft looking very much like our current space crafts, in a suit looking very much like our current flight suits, at the controls of what looks like space capsule controls. The depictions do show, however, and we have seen these before, persons with elongated skulls and somewhat longer extremities."

Pete's pictures of the spaceships and the astronauts are shown.

Rudy concluded, "The abductions have always been at the forefront of alien talk. But Pete had first-hand experience, having witnessed one himself.

"And, we did facial recognition of the presumed dead crew of the sunken sailing vessel and have concluded that the crew members found on Jost Van Dyke in the British Virgin Islands years later were, in fact, the crew that perished when it sank. This incredible survivor story was an incredible true event."

Rudy adds one more item to their list.

"Finally, the mention over the years of a variety of UFO's flying in known flight paths over recognized markers at breakneck speeds is not news.

"What is news is that we have approximately 1700 photos in our possession, thanks to Pete and his work. We also have actual interviews from credible witnesses that have seen UFOs in flight while these witnesses were engaged in flight, both in commercial aircraft and space stations."

Some of Pete's photos are shown.

Connor's team then began to present their findings on levitation. Mark opened.

"We were all fascinated by how our ancestors, given the tools and knowledge of their time, could move megaton stones and monuments, not only within a location, but transported to a location from hundreds of miles away.

"From a multitude of languages over time, and from a variety of sources, the constant mention of stones walking or stones flying or stones disappearing and reappearing, it was Pete's conclusion that levitation, also part of the abduction process, was the only explanation. The legendary walking statues of Easter Island give you chills."

Mark shows the various stones.

"Pete felt strongly that aliens of the future had mastered the art of breaking down matter and then re-connecting it, which could explain levitation, moving inanimate objects, and even time travel."

Pete's pictures of Stonehenge, Easter Island, etc. are shown.

Michaela's team then begins an information blast. She introduces Liana, who jumps right in.

"Our deep dive into the Sumerian culture, as one of Mr. Stevenson's main targets, produced a plethora of dots to connect, and we tried to do just that.

"It was thought that the ancient Sumerians were extraterrestrials that originally arrived on Earth some 450,000 years ago. Yet, it was their belief that the Anunnaki, their ancient extraterrestrial gods, gave rise to the technological culture that defined civilizations ever since."

Michaela added, "The reason we bring this up is that Pete had stumbled across some linkage to our present-day DNA anomalies to ancient Sumerian scientists and their attempt of genetic engineering. Crazy, yes, but just add this to everything else, eh?"

Liana continued, "We are all still, can I say star struck, with the Stargate mythology and the Orion constellation. It is our belief that Sirius, the brightest star in the night sky within the Orion constellation, is the key to time travel and the ability to navigate through the gateways of time and space. There is no doubt, from Pete's documentation, that the stars and the constellations were the navigational maps that the aliens used, both for travel and for the building of civilizations.

"This is our next level *expective*, as Sara would say, and we will be happy to present our findings at the next subject presentation."

Justin went last this time and appeared much more serious than usual.

"Okay. Now I will wrap this up with the totally non-alien portion of our presentation. This is like good news, bad news, but I'm not sure about the good news."

Sara looks over to Scott who looks puzzled. "Scott, we are now getting to the core of our research and all will be clear soon."

"Sara, this whole day has been enlightening... can't imagine what's coming, but Amanda and I are listening."

Sara nods to Justin to continue.

"We are all delighted and extremely juiced by Pete Stevenson's great encounter in Trelleborg, as well as the extremely detailed documentation that came from his team. And it will go without saying that everything he provides will be one hundred per cent debunked as crap by the vast majority of people to even care about this stuff. However, Pete left us with, how do you say, indisputable evidence."

Justin has the attention of their hosts.

✦ ✦ ✦

He states excitedly, "In the middle of Pete's diary is a sketch, a very detailed sketch. It depicts a massive orbital structure home of the aliens meeting Pete, cloaked to avoid detection, and of the appearance and size of a major U.S. city."

Justin shows the team Pete's awesome rendering.

"According to his notes, Pete says that this orbiting space structure is as enormous as anything he has ever seen on Earth, and he could actually see Earth from his position on this craft."

Collected disbelief and puzzlement from the entire group.

"So, on the last page of Pete's dairy of the three days spent with the aliens in Trelleborg, in February of 2018, several things appear via his usual and brilliant code. I'm telling you this guy was awesome! He says that a strange comment that the aliens made had nothing to do with their show and tell…, and that was that the end of the beginning is near."

Scott offered, "That's as big a 'big picture' that you could have."

"Yep, he also documented that we should fear Artificial Intelligence as our biggest threat and that embryonic stem cell research would conclude that males in the future would not be needed for reproduction."

A loudly laughing Kat said, "Now you're talking!"

Justin continued. "He mentioned that solar and wind power were the keys for the future and not to rely on oil, gas, and coal. There was a note to call Sara as soon as possible."

Sara responded, "I remember getting that call. It was the last conversation I had with him, but there wasn't anything memorable about the call itself. Grandad just wanted to know if things were okay with me. I told him I was fine. I did recall that he said he was looking forward to working together in the future."

"Okay," Justin added, "I'm saving the best, I mean the weirdest, for last. If ever there was a big Oh My God in the middle of many OMGs, this is it."

Justin had everyone's attention, as if he ever did not…

"The aliens gave Pete the exact date, place, and time of every major global calamity that the world would face, not only through today, but for ten years through 2028, and this was back in 2018.

"I can only assume that Pete kept this to himself and it was his intention to somehow divulge this during that Paris meeting later that year, but he was murdered before he could do that."

"Justin, I'll need that last info of yours… immediately."

Sara thought…

"This is the irrefutable evidence that aliens from the future were here!"

102

SARA

This time there was absolute silence and no one moved or said a word. As the presentation was now finished, Sara gathered her thoughts before she spoke.

"Stunning!" Sara paused a moment and then continued.

"I have one more disturbing item to add to today's extraordinary meeting. It was brought to my attention in the research data and confirmed by the second half of the coding document that my dad sent, that a totally unrelated topic had entered into Grandad's somewhat innocent alien hunting endeavor."

There was anticipatory pause from the group.

"Apparently, he had inadvertently stumbled into a violent and destructive criminal element that was responsible for many of the prior terrorist attacks. I can only presume that it is likely that these findings point to ongoing insurgencies, since no perpetrators or criminal acts have ever been prosecuted.

"I'm only telling you guys this because we need to be very careful going forward in what we do, who we inform, and where our work leads us. I can't say that we are not in some danger. I just do not know, for now. Thanks."

As they slowly gathered their things, the ETRT went from relieved that the presentation was done, to stressed and anxious. They knew that following this presentation to Scott and Amanda, a discussion of next steps and what information to present would be necessary.

It was expected that their next presentation would be to an extremely important audience that would be made up of not only key decision-makers but also many doubters, and much was at stake but what about all of this terrorist news? The ETRT members were researchers, not Navy SEALs!

Scott called Sara into his office.

"Well Sara, I would like to commend and congratulate your team on a tremendous effort and a ground-breaking worldview that is now, or will soon be, the new normal. Never in my thoughts and wildest dreams did I ever imagine today's events as something other than pure fantasy. Again, please congratulate your team."

Scott became even more serious. "What you and Justin explained was truly the game changer here, and I don't even know where to start to address these incredible facts and projections."

Sara responded, "Yes, and the naysayers will be locked and loaded."

Nodding his head, Scott added, "Extraordinary claims require extraordinary proof."

Amanda looked to Sara and said, "Sara, you need to make a decision on how much you want to involve yourself and if you even want to continue given some of these disturbing facts.

"Many of the revelations are personal, and Scott and I would totally agree and understand that you need your space and you need to protect yourself and your family."

"Thanks, Amanda. Yes, Grandad did call me from Sweden without saying too much about his encounter, saying he would update me later. The fact that his call would be the last conversation he and I would ever have is so devastating.

"He also said to be careful, but in a manner of speaking that had me scared. He said that the name Aras came to him in either in a dream or from some vague encounter, and Aras is my name spelled backwards.

"I have tried to be as diligent as possible regarding my behavior, travel, and outside communication; and I have had very little conversation with Mom and Dad about this. Not sure what I could say, anyhow."

Scott then responded, "There is no good time to tell you this, but I have some additional info that you need to know. As if we don't have enough to deal with right now, I have been able to confirm, with help from the NSA, the identity of a specific man in the government's conspiracy photos. He is the same man that was actually working with your grandad, a presumed friend of his, the very secretive Mr. Smith."

Scott had Sara's attention.

"I don't understand. Someone in the government's security photos of the crime syndicate, or whatever it's called, was also working with my grandad as a friend and colleague?"

"Yes. And it's that guy dressed in black that you see in many of Pete's photos smoking a cigarette, using only the alias of John Smith."

"Scott, he was in many of grandad's photos from the cabin, and Justin confirmed that his group nickname was Smoke. I assumed that they were good friends."

"And Sara, this was the same man that was with your grandad in Paris when he was killed, and who also did not give that group's REVEAL presentation in Paris on September 17 following Pete's murder.

"To say that he was a person of interest in your grandad's murder would be an understatement."

✦ ✦ ✦

Sara had one more nugget of information that came from Justin's incredible effort to uncover information shrouded in coding or secrecy. Justin was able to pull out many of Pete's voicemails prior to his death, given that Pete had transferred many to his voicemails to his iPad.

Most of them were straight-forward, but the one that he gave to Sara was not.

As Sara listened intently, she got goosebumps. A Lt. Robert Baker called Pete on September 15 with information.

"Hi Pete, it's Bob."

"Hey Bob, how ya doing?"

"I'm doing fine and just wanted to give you some follow-up info. Where you at these days?"

"I'm in Paris for the annual Air Show, and taking in the sights, as usual."

"Maybe I should get a job on your team, eh?"

"I think we would drive you nuts."

"Well, I just wanted to say that your guy Mr. Smith, our Ralph Sandusky, is today officially on Homeland Security's no- fly list and shouldn't be doing any more traveling. We are starting to piece together enough factual evidence that an indictment could be in the immediate timetable. And, we have you to thank for getting a handle on this despicable person."

"Thanks for the update, Bob. Appreciate your effort here."

"Just stay safe and watch your back for now."

"Will do."

"And stay far away from that character. I'll stay in touch."

"Crap, it's too late. Smith is already here and checked into my hotel."

"Pete, be careful." Pause. *"Be damn careful."*

Click, as the phone call ended.

103
POTUS

Shortly after the presentation, Scott contacted President Sullivan for an update and advice.

"Hi Scott, sorry it took so long to get back to you but I have some time now to talk and we are on a secure line."

"Great. Thanks for getting back to me. Sara, who you know, and her team have just completed a lengthy and extremely significant presentation to Amanda and me.

"I was aware that they were going to be wrapping up their initial findings soon. Good stuff?"

"Well, beyond good. The evidence of prior alien presence and possible current intervention is highly likely, according to the data. They are using a ninety-five per cent level of confidence in some truly incredible findings, both current and well-documented older theories."

"Are you sold?"

"I am. But there is more."

"Okay."

"They have uncovered what appears to be a criminal conspiracy of major consequences headed by a rogue group of people with ill-gotten wealth that have, allegedly, already been responsible for many terrorist attacks and environmental disasters."

"Unfortunately, that info seems to align with what our CIA has been tracking. Hellava effort by those alien researchers, eh?"

"For sure."

"Okay, Scott, this is what we need to do. I want key members of Sara's team to address a closed session of Congress, both the Intelligence Committee and the Foreign Affairs Committee. I also want to get the folks from NASA involved."

"Great. For the alien stuff, right?"

"Yes. The conspiracy info is very sensitive and it will need to be shared with select members of our FBI and CIA. Does Sara have a Top Security Clearance?"

"I'm sure she doesn't."

"I'll get her one. I only want her to address this joint committee. This will likely need to be shared with our allies as well, so I will get that communication started as soon as possible."

"Timing?"

"As soon as I can set it up. Talking within two to three weeks, if possible."

"Wow."

"Alert her team to the logistics and likely timing. I will send Samantha and Air Force One to Provo to pick them up."

"Excuse me, Cam, but we can't do that. If Air Force One were to land in Provo, I would be spending the rest of my wife explaining to everyone what the hell was going on."

"Of course. I do want our VP there to get things coordinated, though."

"Sure. We can use my private jet for the trip. There is plenty of room on board, assuming Sam is okay with that."

"You mean, Samantha Worthington, astronaut and record-setting space walker?"

"Got me."

"It's settled then. Be sure to give congrats to everyone involved, and let them know how anxious our administration is to get this update. There will be naysayers, for sure, but I believe they have already been through this a lot."

"Yes, they have. Cam, you are in for a true awakening."

"Expecting the best. Safe travels. Talk soon."

This travel will be historic for many reasons...

104

SCOTT

Following that conversation with the President, Scott met with Sara and Mike. He brought them into his private office, on the grounds of the lab, but nestled amongst tall pines and where few outsiders have been.

It was a penthouse with commanding views of the countryside and on that day, nothing but blue sky.

As Sara and Mike entered the office, they were smiling and overwhelmed by the size and beauty of the office setting. In one corner was an immense telescope, and many mementos and space artifacts were distributed throughout the room. Photos of Scott with several dignitaries were evident. It was intimidating.

"Can I get you guys anything? Wine, soft drinks, water?"

"I'll have a water. Dad probably needs a stiff one."

"Just water for me, Scott. Thanks."

Pouring some filtered water into tall glasses, Scott could see his guests were fascinated by the calm atmosphere and aerospace surroundings.

"This is my private space. Come here to talk, listen, and meditate. Sometimes just listen to some spiritual music to relax. And yes, I use that telescope quite often. Here you go."

At that moment, Amanda walks in and joins the group.

"Hi all."

"Hi Amanda," Mike said. "Sara and I were taking in this lovely view. It's so gorgeous up here."

"Yes. Scott uses this office to recharge his batteries. Works every time."

"Thanks, Honey. Get you something?"

"I'll get it. Why don't you get started?"

"Okay. I talked with President Sullivan and brought him up to speed on all things covered in your last presentation. Cam was impressed. What I want to discuss now is next steps."

"Yea, Scott. Dad and I couldn't wait to hear from you."

"Well, it's nothing but good news. As I said, he was impressed. Don't think he was skeptical, only reserved, waiting for the details from the ETRT."

Amanda simply said, "We are all so proud of the work you guys did. So proud."

Scott opened his note pad. "Here's the plan. POTUS will convene two special committees from the Intel and Foreign Affairs side. He will also have Homeland Security people available. Separate but consecutively, he will have FBI and CIA assembled. They will hear the alien results from the ETRT, and the Feds will meet with Sara alone to discuss the other matter."

Mike jumped in. "When?"

"The President is trying to set this up within the next couple of weeks."

"That won't be a problem for us. Dad and the ETRT team are ready anytime."

"I knew that. Believe me when I say, within a couple weeks is months in politics."

Sara added, "What about the logistics?"

"VP Worthington is coming here to help us coordinate the presentation process that fits Congressional procedures. We will all fly to DC on my private jet to avoid any media or nosey photographers."

"This is the audience we wanted, Scott. On behalf of the team and my parents, we thank you for all you have done. What about those predictions of future calamities that came out of Justin's digging?"

Scott was ready for this issue. "I think our VP is the one to unload this on. I will meet with Samantha privately as soon as she gets here."

Sara added, "Great idea. And thanks again, Scott, for everything. You and Amanda are godsends."

"You're welcome, Sara. But this presentation will only be the beginning."

The flight will be the beginning...

105

SARA

Approaching the plane in the hanger, Sara was excited but nervous. She knew what was at stake with this meeting, and she also knew that many in that Congressional meeting will end up as total naysayers even after they present their findings.

Michaela arrived. "Hi there, Sunshine. I'm sure you have a lot on your mind, Sara. Please let me know if there is anything I can do to help."

"Thanks, Michaela, but right now I'm fine. All that could change soon."

They both laughed. At that moment, pilot Ken Darragh approached them and Sara gave him a big hug.

"It's hard to describe just how nice it is to see you, and I can't thank you enough for all that you did for me and for us after that cabin disaster."

"Just doing my job, Sara. I'm so happy that you guys have been able to turn all that bad energy into something fantastic. Love to be a part of it."

Joining them in the hanger as equipment was being loaded onto the plane were Kathy, Connor, Justin, Amanda, Elonis, Mike, Christine, and VP Samantha Worthington.

"Nice to meet you Captain Darragh. I'm Samantha Worthington."

"Likewise. Thrilled to have you on board with us."

"What's the flight time today?"

"Just checked our flight plan. Five hours and seven minutes. Wheels up in thirty. I understand you will be co-piloting today?"

"Yep, if you don't mind."

"Mind, hell. Liable to learn something." Ken smiled.

As the passengers got on board, there was a quiet calm and very little talking. Everyone was simply reflecting on the recent past and the enormity of what lied ahead.

As Captain Darragh said, within thirty minutes they were airborne.

The flight was smooth and uneventful. VP Worthington joined the Captain in the cockpit. Sam was explaining her time in the International Space Station and described her space walks.

"Don't know how you could work in politics after spending such amazing times in space. It seems so boring in comparison."

"Ken, that was one chapter in my life, and this is another. Always learning, you know."

"Can appreciate that. Now, **fasten your seat belts.**"

106

SARA

Unbeknownst to Ken and Sam, the terrorist group that Smith was a part of had become aware of that flight and was very concerned about what might be revealed by Sara's team in Washington.

They had their Russian hackers trying to get access to the plane's controls.

Sara peeked into the cockpit and inquired about ETA.

Ken replied. "We should be there in about an hour and ten minutes."

"Thanks."

About fifteen minutes later, Ken was alarmed: "Sam, my controls are getting erratic. Take yours."

"Same thing, Ken. Can you override the automatics?"

"Trying to, but can't. And our navigation is off. Both airspeed and destination are out of my control."

"Trying to reach air traffic control, Ken. You keep trying the controls."

"Still nothing."

"My radio is dead. I can't contact anyone."

Sara opened the cockpit door and asked, "We have no wi-fi. You guys know what's up?"

Seeing the panic, Sara was scared. "What's wrong?"

Sam responded, "Right now we have no control. The plane is flying itself.

At the same time, Air Traffic Control lost all communication with the plane carrying the Vice President of the United States. Two F22 Raptors scrambled within five minutes.

By now, panic took over the plane. Ken and Sam were close to panic as well. They then saw the two F22's, one on each side. They waved, as if to say they were okay but had no communication or control.

Back on the ground, Air Traffic Control now estimated that Scott's plane was headed directly for impact on the White House in less than ten minutes.

POTUS was informed and all on the ground realized that without re-gaining control, the plane was within ten minutes of being shot down.

The lead commander of the two F22's informed the ground, visual contact, awaiting command. Ken and Sam desperately tried to re-gain control but could not. Sara tried again to reach her mom but couldn't get her phone to connect.

As the F22 commander awaited instruction, he contacted the ground control. "We have a problem. The target has vanished, so we have only radar contact, no visual."

"Can you fire at radar location?"

"Affirmative."

"Await order."

Ground control gathered for a last-minute firing decision.

"Ground control, we have lost radar all together. There is no visual or radar target."

"No target?"

"Affirmative."

The TROPE is out there!

107

SARA

Aboard Scott's plane, the stunned passengers knew what was happening, as Sam had gathered everyone together for their last moments.

Then all motion stopped. A gray-green haze enveloped the plane and it literally stopped its forward motion. The plane was not moving at an altitude of 33,000 feet.

Ken and Sam were asked what was happening, and they did not offer any explanation whatsoever. Sara noticed that they still had no cell phone service and the planes controls were simply all off.

On the ground, equal dismay and disbelief. The target plane was simply gone. No more sightings and no radar on the ground or with the two F22's had any radar image at all.

POTUS was speechless when asked by his peers what happened. He asked his military and defense cabinet members and they were also clueless.

Back in the air, the haze was lifting. Sara was the first to notice the image out the cabin window.

"Guys, are you seeing this?"

They all moved to a vantage point at a window. As the haze continued to dissipate, it appeared that they had landed on a large metal landing pad, not on a runway.

Ken spoke. "The door is opening. Grab onto something. I don't know what's happening."

As the passengers braced for whatever came next, a tall human-like form entered the plane's stairwell.

There is an alien in the room!

108

ECHO

Speaking in a soft and reassuring voice... a distinctive feminine voice that reminded Sara of when her mother was there to support her, she introduced herself: "I am called Echo and we will not harm you. We are your friends. Please come with me."

Samantha spoke softly. "Do what she asks. Don't be afraid."

Slowly, everyone walked off the plane to a very large metal pad, possibly seven hundred to eight hundred feet in diameter. What became very obvious was they were all now on an extremely large aircraft that was a small city in size.

There were compartments housing small spacecrafts, hangers that had two-man capsules, and robots doing various tasks unmoved by the new guests.

Among the look of terror of the plane passengers, Sam was most relaxed, almost as if this was some kind of normal. All knew that they were on a very large alien spacecraft.

Echo was joined by another alien. "I am called Pulse."

Behind Echo and Pulse were several similarly dressed aliens, none with weapons. These aliens were tall, close to seven feet in height. They had elongated skulls and longer than normal limbs. Their ears were very small and they did not closely resemble humans.

The designated alien leader Echo, who appeared to be the visual elder, and with a decidedly soft speaking voice, then spoke.

"We are from another universe... another galaxy... and another time, and have been on this earth in some form for thousands of years. Our major colonies today lie in what you refer to as the Trappist-1 System, where seven planets exist."

After a brief pause, Echo continued. "Our home is an Exoplanet 110 light years away in the constellation you call Leo. It is about eight times the size of your Earth, but has water and a similar atmosphere. It is what you would call a Super Earth with a host star and an accompanying planet.

We began as observers, and throughout your history, we have tried to help mankind many times to ensure that this planet will survive. We would have preferred to remain behind the scenes, as we have been for ages. The ultimate survival of this planet brought us to this day and time."

Sara was transfixed with what was occurring and all seemed to be more relaxed as Echo reassured them that they were safe.

The alien leader continued, "As I said, my Earth name is Echo and that name describes my skill at listening. I am commander of this craft and the alien leader.

"Pulse is second in command and his skill is communication. When you thought you were alone, you were not alone." Echo paused. "Sara has a thought and I will answer that thought."

Sara knew what she was thinking but did not say anything.

"We intercepted your craft because it had been taken over by people who were trying to eliminate your presence at your nation's capital for what it would reveal about them as criminals. They had taken control of your craft and had set a course to crash at your White House and blame your team for terrorism."

Sam spoke up. "Echo, we truly appreciate your involvement, but you have now exposed yourselves to the world. Do you see that as a major social and political problem?"

"Yes, that has been a problem for thousands of years. We have the capability to stop time and can eliminate short-term memory. As far as the people witnessing the unexplained event of your disappearance, it will simply fall within the scope of your government coverups, which have existed for many years."

Sara said, "We have so many questions, Echo, which must be answered."

"Sara, your grandfather, Pete, was our chosen one. Now that he is gone, you must carry on his work."

Sara was confused, as was the entire earthly group.

"You are aboard the city in which we live and work, cloaked from any detection and usually well beyond your solar system. We must leave you now as we have many other planets, with cultures and societies in need, in other galaxies in our universe. As difficult as this may be for you to understand, we are humans from the very distant future. Yes, we are you, with evolution that takes millions of years.

"We have God in our hearts and minds, and share your spiritual values. It is safe to say that we are likely closer to God than you, not physically, but spiritually."

As Echo concluded her very brief explanation, two other figures came forward. One was recognizable.

Sara's friend Elonis has a split alliance.

109

LASER

"Hello. My name is Laser and I am the one who observes. With me is your friend Elonis, who is also our friend. She will assist me with clearing your memories and restoring your world to the time before the incident and allowing you to safely proceed to your destination."

VP Samantha Worthington quickly spoke. "Laser, I don't want to forget this incredible encounter. Please, Laser, allow me to keep my memory."

"I'm sorry. I can't do that. There will be no exceptions."

Laser then telepathically reached Elonis. "There will be one exception. Clear everyone but Sara, our next chosen one."

Pulse then stepped over to Sara and took her hand. Telepathically he shared a thought. "You are *The Aras*, our name for warrior."

Pulse then released Sara's hand and took Elonis's hand. He looked into her eyes and moments later Elonis nodded in approval.

The passengers and crew returned to the plane. With Pulse walking behind her, Elonis held a black wand in their faces and one-by-one sprayed a fine blue mist into their eyes.

Sara did not receive the mist. Pulse took back the wand and returned to his ship.

When they woke from a deep trance, all was like before. The plane was now in gradual descent into Reagan International Airport.

Sara and Elonis were the only ones that remembered the alien encounter.

For everyone else, nothing out of the ordinary took place.

It was the best of alien encounters… it was the worst of alien encounters…

110

SARA

On the ground, a frenzied military staff and POTUS struggled to make sense of the F22 attack that never took place. In fact, Scott's plane was just moments away from landing.

A version of the atmospheric anomaly that explained the momentarily missing plane was being crafted for the media.

As the passengers and crew prepared for landing, a confused Sara spoke to Elonis in private.

"Elonis, we need to talk."

"Yes, Sara."

Sara began, "I have questions. What did Pulse say to you before we left?"

Elonis replied, "He said to watch over you."

Sara continued, "And Echo said they are aliens from the future, meaning they know what happens in the future. If Grandad was so important to their mission, why didn't they prevent it?"

Elonis quickly responded, "Pulse expected you to ask me this, and he said that your word for having infinite awareness is omniscience and that is not what they are."

"Elonis, please explain in more detail."

"Yes, Sara. They are aware of events and incidents throughout the solar system, not individual behaviors. Does that make sense?"

"Yes," Sara replied in a somber and soft tone.

Sara continued. "Okay. One more question. Given your just revealed connection to these aliens, if I had asked you if these aliens were currently present here on Earth, what would have been your response?"

"I would have said, yes, they are here right now."

"So why didn't you tell me?"

"You never asked me about alien presence."

As the plane makes its final descent into Reagan International Airport, we see Scott in his office planning the next presentation following the one to Congress the following day. Having no idea of the ordeal of his colleagues, he is calm and focused, and stares out of his telescope at the celestial beauty. About fifty miles from the lab, an alien spacecraft lands in a wooded area in heavy fog at dusk. The door to the spacecraft slowly opens as the fog lifts. A sinister and solo alien appears in a heavily armored suit. Staring into the dim night, the alien slowly walks down several steps to the ground.

Within seconds, the alien morphs into an earthly human form.

COMING SOON...

Book Two – *Alien Disruption*

COMING IN 2020...

Book Three – *Warriors of the Galaxy*

Book Four – *Battlestar EARTH*

COMING IN 2021...

Book Five – *Journeys to Salvation*

ABOUT THE AUTHOR

Garry J. Peterson is the author of several books, both fiction and non-fiction, following a successful career in international corporate management. His most recent non-fiction book is a "how-to" business book, *Who Put Me in CHARGE?* Garry has also completed a companion Implementation Guide for this book.

As a former consultant and business coach, Garry now spends his time writing science fiction thrillers and conducting both motivational and subject matter speaking engagements.

Garry has written over 300 trade journal articles, white papers, client presentations and website content. He has given commencement addresses and public service keynote speeches.

He has a passion for hard science fiction and weaves personal stories, humor and visionary thinking into his writings. His current writing project is a five-book sci-fi series, *Stargate Earth,* beginning with book one, *Shattered Truth.*

Garry lives in Florida with his wife Vaune. He plays in a competitive softball league and is an avid scuba diver and kayaker. Their daughter, Sarah, lives in San Francisco.

Visit his website at: www.petersonadvisorsgroup.com.

You can also follow Garry on Facebook, Twitter and LinkedIn.